THE LAKE OF STOLEN BONES

BOOK TWO

THE CHILDREN OF VERUS TRILOGY

PAULA WESTON

PRAISE FOR THE SHADOW OF THE EAGLE

'*The Shadow of the Eagle* will sink its talons in you, and won't let go until well after you've turned the final page!
E.C Glynn (Author of *Heretic Behaviour*)

'The world building in this book is nothing short of breathtaking.
Reading at Isaac's

'*The Shadow of the Eagle* manages to deliver a narrative that's as much a searing critique of religious manipulation as it is a high-stakes adventure.'
Erin Arkin

'I highly recommend this book. It is a well-written, well-edited, engaging and exciting page turner.'
Annemarie Book Adventures

'Great characters, a compelling world, and a slow-burn romance that kept me turning the pages.'
Sar Reads

'What a book! I was hooked from the first page. This book is dark, jam-packed with mystery and slow burning romance.'
Holly Hoards Books

'*The Shadow of the Eagle* was fantastic! It has a bit of everything! A unique magic system including a sacred flame, corruptness, heresy, political intrigue, tension and the slooooow burn... definitely one to add to your tbr!'
Chapters, Tea and Me

'This has the potential to be one of the next hit trilogies.'
Christen Reads

'This was absolutely briliant, and I cannot wait for the rest of the series!'
Shelves by Sim

PRAISE FOR THE REPHAIM SERIES

'Paula Weston is the queen of cliff-hanger endings, and this one's going to blow your mind! I can't praise *The Rephaim* series highly enough.'
Speculating on Spec Fic

'If you are a fan of superbly written, action-packed fiction with interesting, brilliantly flawed characters – look no further than Paula Weston's *Rephaim* series. This is a series you won't want to put down!'
Fictional Thoughts

'As with its three predecessors *Shadows*, *Haze* and *Shimmer* Burn was completely un-put-downable and I finished it within a day. Jam-packed with action, suspense, romance, classic Aussie humour, and an ending that tied together all the loose ends and rounded out the series perfectly.'
All about UF

'The end of one jam packed, actiony, kick-arse, punch in the face YA series. It's all over and now I'm sad because there are no more *Rephaim* books to look forward to. A great ending to a great series that won't leave you disappointed.'
Dymocks

'Aussie author Paula Weston's debut is a fast-paced, sensational ride, which screams "read me" and "turn me into a movie". There are echoes of TV's *Supernatural* here, with vibrant, well-realised characters and snappy, cool dialogue.'
Adelaide Advertiser

"Angels. They're so 2009." Said nobody. Ever. After reading this book.'
Mostly Reading YA

'A fab book. One of the best angel books I've read if not the best with brilliant characters and its own take in the genre which I had previously sworn myself off.'
The Overflowing Library

'Fast-paced and action-packed, this book doesn't stop from page one.'
Launceston Examiner

'This friends is how you finish a series. Urban fantasy doesn't get any better.'
Riverbend Books, Brisbane

'It's fitting Paula Weston's *Rephaim* series should wrap up with a finale of biblical proportions. What else would you expect from the wonderfully written story of half-angel, demons, love, passion and prophecy?'
Adelaide Advertiser

'Officially experiencing major book hangover. I WANT MOOOORE. *cries* Hands down one of my all time favourite series.'
YA Midnight Reads

'I can't offer enough praise for *Burn* and *The Rephaim* series, it has been an amazing ride and I am devastated it has come to an end!'
Obsession With Books

Ignite Books (Australia)

Copyright © Paula Weston 2026

The moral right of Paula Weston to be identified as the author of this work has been asserted.

All rights reserved. Without limiting the rights under copyright above, no part of this publication may be reproduced, stored in or introduced into a retrieval system, or transmitted in any form or by any means (electronic, mechanical, photocopying, recording or otherwise), without the prior permission of the copyright owner.

Original cover artwork and design by Tiffany Munro

ISBN: 978-1-7644038-0-1(paperback)
ISBN: 978-1-7644038-1-8(ebook)

The Children of Verus Trilogy series by Paula Weston

Book 1: *The Shadow of the Eagle*
Book 2: *The Lake of Stolen Bones*

PAULA WESTON lives in the Scenic Rim in Queensland, Australia, with her husband, a retired greyhound, and a carrot-loving steer. She is the author of the much-loved urban fantasy series *The Rephaim* and the stand-alone near-future thriller *The Undercurrent*.

GLOSSARY

Amadea: Coastal and pastoral kingdom – feudal society
Angustonian: A follower of the teachings of Anguston, High Priest of Verus (executed as a heretic two years ago)
Ares: One of the old gods – the god of war – one of many worshipped by the Pyriens
Askari: Warrior class in Pyrie
Optimati: High-born families in Amadea
Porplezi: Practitioners of magic in Pyrie
Prophet: The intermediary between the god Verus and Amadeans
Pyrie: Kingdom in the mountains – predominantly nomadic society
Stonebridge Abbey: second only to the temple at Augustmount as the most sacred place in Amadea
Verus: The only god worshipped by Amadeans

MAIN CHARACTERS

Adward: Iolian warrior
Axl: Stonebridge monk, Sabine's younger brother
Dashelle: Provincial overlord of Iolia – married to Ferugo
Felix: Newly crowned king of Amadea
Ferugo: Provincial overlord of Iolia – married to Dashelle
Sabine: Young woman from the Southlands province
Pellus: Augustmount warrior favoured by the Thirteenth Prophet
Rhys: Warrior of Iolia and Tristan's cousin
Thirteenth Prophet: The current prophet
Torvus: Warrior of Augustmount, right-hand to King Felix
Tristan: Warrior of Iolia, Rhys's cousin
Ty: Tristan's squire

OTHER CHARACTERS

Abbot of Stonebridge: Leader of Stonebridge Abbey
Anguston: High Priest of Verus, Augustmount
Darius: Sabine's father
Gael: Stonebridge monk, accompanying Axl on pilgrimage
Olidus: Sabine's uncle
Marsanne: Angustonian heretic
Quintus: High Priest of Verus, Nominatia
Sabella: Sabine's mother
Tenth Prophet: Condemned as a heretic 200 years ago (also know as the Mad Prophet)
Torvus: Legendary warrior and closest friend of King Felix

OTHER AMADEAN KINGS OF NOTE

Tertius: Recently deceased (father of Felix)
Tertullian: King 200 years ago at the time of the Harvest Day massacre and first Pyrien invasion.

AMADEAN PROVINCES

Augustmount
Bloodstone
Iolia
Paramore
Southlands

PROLOGUE

The abbot of Stonebridge flattened the parchment and read it one last time. The calfskin was cheap, the words hastily written. He was in his antechamber in front of the fire, absorbing a letter from Axl written in riddles only the two of them understood. Some of the news he had heard, some of it he had not.

Torvus, the legendary warrior was dead, executed in the lower temple for treason in front of King Felix.

Ferugo and Dashelle were unwilling guests of the king and the prophet, even as the kingdom prepared to invade Pyrie. They had not been openly accused of heresy but their ties to Torvus had heightened suspicion.

Axl, the abbot's own intelligent, peace-loving young monk, was about to ride into war with the Iolian army hoping to find the Tenth Prophecy across the border.

The only reassuring news was that the blood bond the abbot himself had sealed was intact. Tristan, Rhys, Sabine and Axl would cross into Pyrie together under the Iolian banner. Most startling of all: Axl believed his sister Sabine was the one the Tenth Prophet had claimed would overthrow the prophet.

It made sense that it would be one of Sabella's children, given their family bloodline, but Sabine? The young woman who bristled with such bitterness and fury? How would she react when she understood the full truth about her heritage?

The abbot himself did not fully understand all that was in motion. His kingdom was on a dark path and his religion had been corrupted. The only way to save their world might be to break it, but without the Tenth Prophecy they were blind to the true will of their god.

He brushed aging fingers over the parchment and then fed it to the unsanctified fire, waiting for it to catch and burn.

They were in the hands of Verus now, all of them.

CAPTIVE

I

Lystra and Dex were re-strapping their wolf pelts, flushed and grinning, when an arrow buried itself in Dex's throat. He staggered back from the force, his eyes wide. Lystra shouldered him behind the cover of a tree and snatched up her spear, scanning the forest. The pine trees were washed in grey dusk light, shadows everywhere.

She'd thought they were high enough on the mountain. They were miles from the mines. Miles from the nearest Amadean infestation. And barely a stone's throw from the camp in the valley where the rest of Lystra's pack of askari were picking dried goat from their teeth. She and Dex weren't even scouting. They'd left the pack to burn off the frustration of a day without raiding. Dex had read her mood and known she'd needed to spar with someone not afraid to pin her—away from the eyes of others.

Lystra pressed her spine against the tree and checked on him. He was slumped beside her on a bed of pine needles, gasping for breath. Blood seeped from the wound, the arrow still in place. He was trying to stem the flow with his fingers. His eyes shone with fear—not for himself but for her, because she was isolated and most likely out-numbered. And they both knew how valuable she would be as a prisoner.

Another arrow slammed into the trunk. It came from a different angle than the first, so either the archer had moved or there were more than one. Lystra coaxed spit into her mouth so she could whistle for support. It took two attempts to make a noise.

The clash of iron on steel echoed in the valley below. Her pack was under attack now too.

She was their leader; she had to get to them. If she moved before she was surrounded, she might make it.

A third arrow found the tree. But it was the other sound that snatched her breath: Dex choking on his own blood. Every instinct as a fighter, every lesson beaten into her about what it meant to be askari, urged her to leave him and go to the pack. But it was *Dex*. His hand had slid from his throat, so she dropped into a crouch and pressed her own fingers where his had been. There was so much blood.

He drew a wet, ragged breath. 'Go,' he mouthed.

She shook her head. They were twenty and had barely spent a day apart since their initiation as cubs. Dex pleaded silently with her, knowing what she risked by staying, but hers would be the last face he saw, not that of their enemy.

The pulse beneath her fingers fell still.

It was a blade in her heart. She needed to howl, to mourn the loss of her pack-mate, but she would not let the scourge hear that she was wounded. Lystra closed Dex's sightless eyes, painting his face with his own blood as the violence continued further below in the valley.

She rose on numb legs and turned to face the fight. Her spear in one hand and axe now in the other, Lystra of wolf clan took a final look at Dex, swore to Ares she would avenge him, and sprang forward, burning to spill Amadean blood.

2

Sabine fidgeted as Tristan and Rhys appraised her.

'The fit is good. Plenty of freedom to move,' Rhys said, circling her. 'Nothing showing where it shouldn't.'

Tristan caught her eye. 'How does it feel?'

'Like I'm an imposter.' And not only for the buckskin vest and leather trousers she hadn't yet earned the right to wear.

It was not long past dawn and they were in Ferugo's antechamber. She'd arrived in the warrior gear Tristan had found for her.

'Sabine,' Tristan said, slightly exasperated. 'You've trained as hard as any squire. You'll prove that when we get down in the yard.'

'The cohort won't accept me.'

'We're going to war. They'll be happy for another sword.'

The call to arms for Iolia's tenants and peasants went out as soon as they'd left Augustmount two weeks ago, and Ferugo's forces were already streaming in from across the province and massing outside the city gates. They brought axes and clubs and whatever other weapons they could find at short notice. So far, there had been no reluctance to honour their duty of fealty. Word had spread that Torvus had been executed and porplezi magic had manifested in the lower temple. They could not afford to anger their god through inaction.

The Iolian army would swell on the march to the high

plains, gathering the rest of the province's archers and foot soldiers along the way.

'Once you've been blooded in conflict, we'll get that eagle across your shoulders and there'll be no argument either way,' Rhys said.

Tristan frowned. 'She's dressed to ride with us on campaign, not permanently join our ranks.'

'It would make it easier for us to stay together if she's inked.'

Sabine's skin goose-prickled at the mention of the blood bond. The warriors would revoke the rite if they understood they had pledged to protect a brother and sister descended from their enemy. Her uncle Olidus was many things—including a liar—but on that point Axl believed the swine had spoken honestly. Sabine felt the awful truth of it in the way her pulse spiked whenever she thought about her mother.

'We should be downstairs,' she said, ignoring a fresh flutter of nerves.

'You're ready?' Tristan asked.

'Yes,' she lied, although it was true she'd rather be in the training yards fending off attackers than unstitching the threads that until now had held her life together.

Adward and Iolia's nine other commanders were already in the yards when they arrived. Sabine wasn't expecting *all* of them. Word that Tristan's bed mate was joining them on campaign was clearly a too-interesting piece of news to ignore. Two dozen squires were running sword drills or wrestling in the dirt. Ty saw them arrive and held his opponent in a headlock on the ground until the other boy tapped his submission.

The fair-haired squire was yet to subdue his guilt and grief over that fateful arrow shot. He'd followed Sabine's lead and spent almost every waking moment in the training yards since their return to Iolia. She could see he was not sleeping well, haunted by the sight of Torvus dying by his hand. It had been a mercy—far quicker than the fiery death the prophet had intended for him—but the truth remained that it was Ty alone who stopped the mighty warrior's heart.

'Sabine,' Adward greeted, eying her up and down. His shoulder was finally free of its sling, but he continued to favour his left arm. A lingering gift from his encounter in the lists with Pellus. He gestured to her bare biceps. 'You're not as soft as I expected.' It wasn't the usual compliment a warrior paid a woman, but she'd take it. Even before her training, she'd been strong from a year of splitting wood, lugging grain and working the plough. Now, her body was hard from hours of combat practice and her skin permanently peppered with nicks and bruises.

Sabine gave the training yard a quick scan, relieved to see the braziers beyond the fence were black and cold. The last thing she needed was the flurry of nerves that descended whenever she neared an open flame.

The other warriors were sizing her up, trying to decide if her presence in the yard was a joke. Marcus caught her eye. At twenty-eight, he was the oldest of Ferugo's elite castle cohort and always quick with a smile.

'I hope you're tougher than your man, here,' he said and smirked at Tristan.

The warriors had all seen Tristan taken from the field at the tournament a half-moon ago—witnessed his agony and the way he'd cradled his wrist—and then saw him a day later with barely a hint of soreness. There was no doubt he'd broken bones in the tilt, but joking about Tristan overselling his injuries was less complicated than admitting he'd recovered overnight. For the same reason, nobody mentioned Torvus and how his body had disappeared before their eyes in the temple. Denial was the best defence against questions that threatened to take the ground out from beneath them.

'Test her, see for yourself,' Rhys suggested.

Sabine hid her alarm. They'd agreed she'd demonstrate her skills by sparring with Ty, show these men enough so they could see she could hold her own with a sword. But now Rhys was throwing her against a seasoned warrior without warning.

'Use practice gear,' he added, as if that made it better.

Marcus was as tall as Tristan, but longer boned and narrower across the shoulders. 'You okay with that?' he asked Tristan.

Tristan glanced at Sabine. If she refused or he intervened, it would undermine the point they were here to make. She was either good enough or she wasn't. Sabine nodded and swapped out her sword for a blunted training version and Ty brought them leather gloves and fitted training jackets. Marcus laced on his and eyed Tristan, not convinced he wasn't being played. Sabine had already warmed up, but she stretched out her shoulders and tested her knees again to make sure her joints were ready. Marcus didn't bother.

They took up position: Sabine in a high guard with the blade above her right shoulder and left foot forward; Marcus with his blade held low. Sabine took slow breaths to settle her heart rate. She wasn't familiar with the warrior's fighting style, so she did as she'd been taught and watched how he shifted his weight to prepare, noticed he favoured his right arm. She kept her distance and waited for him to attack first to see how he moved.

He came at her with a series of simple attacks to test her and she parried them with equal speed. He followed with a thrust and again she deflected it, countered with her own that found its mark. Her blade flexed as the blunted tip pressed into his jacket over his heart. There were a few murmured sounds of surprise from the warrior onlookers.

Marcus took up his position again, this time mirroring her starting guard and keeping more distance between them. He re-appraised her. Her heart beat harder now, a storm of nerves and anticipation.

This time he came at her faster and when she parried, his sword was close enough she could grab the blade with her gloved hand. Sabine struck him in the padded shoulder and kicked out his knee, sending him down on one leg. She brought her blade down on the back of his neck, stopping short of impact. It was a play she'd run dozens of times with Tristan, but he'd never gone down this easy.

'Ha!' Adward said appreciatively from the sideline.

Marcus stood up and grinned at Tristan. 'She even moves like you.'

Another warrior, Stefan, barked an incredulous laugh. 'You staged that,' he said.

Rhys gestured to the middle of the yard where Sabine was barely out of breath. 'In you go, then.'

Sabine nodded her willingness. The sword felt good in her hands and she was ready to go again. She understood she'd bested Marcus because he'd underestimated her and that Stefan would not make the same mistake.

The warrior geared up. He was as stocky as a bullock but light on his feet. He twirled his sword as he measured her. She waited in half-sword, the hilt in one gloved hand and blade in the other.

He came in with a high blow and Sabine stepped forward and blocked, letting his momentum and weight carry him forward. Her blade slid along his, and she twisted with the movement and spun around so that when it slid free, she could swing it high and strike him across the shoulders. In a real fight, she'd have aimed the blade at his neck.

Marcus clapped. Stefan grunted his annoyance and re-set.

Again, Sabine knew she'd had the element of surprise on her

side—and the fact these warriors didn't want to hurt her—but she took Stefan's annoyance as high praise.

He made her work harder in the next clash, trading a series of thrusts and parries until she found an opening, sidestepped, and struck his jacket under his ribs with a well-timed cut.

They went again. And again. Stefan scored most hits but she made him work for it. Finally, the warrior stepped back, puffing. 'I'm convinced,' he said and tilted his head in respect to Sabine. She returned the gesture, catching her breath.

'How long have you been working with her?' Stefan asked Tristan. Sabine could see Tristan was pleased and trying not to show it. Rhys made no attempt to hide his delight.

'Every day for two moons, give or take. She's a natural and she's worked twice as hard as that lot.' Tristan gestured to the squires, each now eager to earn their place in the mounted ranks for the campaign.

'She's good in a training scenario, but what about in the heat of battle where the blades are sharp?'

'It will be no different than it was for each of us and what it will be for those boys. The training will kick in or she'll die.'

Sabine let them go on talking about her as if she wasn't there.

'Can she fight on horseback?' This question from Adward.

'We haven't trained for it, but she rides well and she's a quick study.'

'Has she fought a Pyrien?'

'Brigands,' Tristan confirmed. 'Knifed one between the ribs. A quick kill.'

Sabine was grateful he didn't provide any more detail about that particular scuffle on the roadside.

'What about armour?'

'I'll have it made as we march.'

Adward turned to her. 'Who taught you to fight? I don't

doubt Tristan's ability to impart his skills, but your instincts are too sharp for someone who's newly picked up a sword.'

'My father,' she said, ready for the question. 'I was the next best thing to a son after Axl took his oath at Stonebridge.' It wasn't the full truth, but neither was it a lie. Her father had let her swing a sword, but it had been without intent. She wasn't going to tell this warrior her first real lessons in the martial arts came from the Pyrien slave who served as her blacksmith. Tristan kept silent on the matter as well.

'And where is your father now?' Adward asked.

The grief rose, as it always did when she scratched closer to the truth. 'He died on border patrol last year.'

The older warrior nodded. 'Then it is good you will have a chance to seek blood on his behalf.'

Marcus nodded his agreement. 'This brother of yours,' he said. 'He's coming with us?'

Tristan answered for her. 'Yes, to administer rites.'

'Can he fight like you?' Marcus asked Sabine.

Rhys laughed and Tristan said, 'No.'

Marcus eyed Sabine a moment longer, nodded at Tristan and turned to the waiting squires. 'Who's next?'

3

Lystra was tied to a pulley beside a slurry pond.

A cold wind swirled down the gully. It stung skin flayed raw from rope-burn and whip-bites. Chilled a scalp covered in nicks and what was left of her chopped hair. Her palms were blistered from working the crushing boulder and her thighs and lower back hurt each time she pulled the rope to lift the dead weight. Lystra released the boulder again and it fell to the ground. The impact thudded through her, bone-deep.

Haul. Thud. Haul. Thud.

She focused on the pain. Not on Dex. Not on his last breath and his blood-smeared face. She would not mourn him here. There would be a time and place and it wasn't as a prisoner at an occupied gold mine.

The rope binding Lystra's wrists was wound through a tall pulley system. The other end was knotted to a ring bolted into a boulder the size of a bullock head. When she pulled down, the boulder rose. When she released and it dropped, her arms were yanked to full stretch. She was either bearing the weight or strung up.

Haul. Thud. Haul. Thud.

Another Pyrien worked the boulder on the opposite side of the slurry pond. He was older than her, but not by much. He was covered in welts old and new. His white hair was filthy with grime, and he'd been here long enough for it to grow to his shoulder blades, well past an acceptable length for a Pyrien who was neither askari nor porplezi. He'd not allowed it to knot into ropes—as Lystra's had been before it was hacked away—so he was not askari, and she'd seen that his chest did not bear the mark of the fire-carriers either. Most likely he was a trader or herder who'd joined a border raid out of desperation and become a prisoner on his own soil.

The slave did not hide his hope at seeing an askara dragged from the wagon cell. He'd kept working while the Amadean guards wrestled Lystra across to the boulder—it took three of them and four kidney punches—never taking his eyes from her.

When Lystra understood what the scourge wanted of her, she'd hauled up the lump of granite and suspended it at the top of the pulley, defying their barks to release it—until one of the guards lost patience and introduced her to his whip. That first lash caught her across her bare neck with the sting of an angry wasp. It had taken two cuts more before she relented and let the weight pound the waiting rocks.

Her skull thudded in time with the boulder, a reminder of why she was here.

Her pack had been outnumbered in the forest. She'd killed four Amadeans before being felled by a blow to the back of the head. She'd come to in a wagon cell, trussed up and bouncing along a mountain path. The scourge had left her in there until this morning, tossing her a dead hare at dawn for breakfast like she was an animal.

Haul. Thud. Haul. Thud.

The wounds from the whip had torn wider on her neck now. She'd lifted that weight again and again, until the rocks were ground to a powder that was then shovelled by a slave into the slurry. It was replaced by another pile of rocks, carted up from the belly of the mountain by a continuous stream of dull-eyed children, and she started all over again.

It was afternoon now and a shaft of hazy light streamed between the mountain peaks. She was exhausted and aching and her legs could hardly hold her weight. In front of her, the mine entrance was barely wide enough for the single file of slaves trekking out of the darkness lugging rock-filled bags and then returning to re-fill them. Behind Lystra was the large wooden hut where broken-down warriors ate and slept when they weren't tormenting the mine slaves. They were the Amadeans' beloved *veterans*. The butchers of children. Warriors who had barely seen thirty years but whose Pyrien-inflicted injuries had rendered them useless for any task other than guarding slaves. They'd built homes on occupied land closer to the border, but here was where they spent their days and nights.

Lystra knew from the old stories that this place had once been thick with fir trees and eucalypts, teeming with goats, alpaca and hares. In those days, before the ships brought the Amadeans to the lowlands, Lystra's ancestors had collected the golden flecks and nuggets carried from the high country on the great white river. The Amadeans, though, had understood the gold was in the ground. They taught the Pyriens to go to the source. And then they grew tired of paying for it.

After two hundred years of occupation, this gully—like so many others along the border—was a scar on the landscape, all traces of green gone. It was as if Ares himself had taken a swipe out of the mountain and gouged it down to bone. Grass and fertile soil had long been replaced with pebble and shale; the songs of wrens replaced with pounding rocks and toppling trees. The great pines continued to fall in sacrifice to the veteran settlement that deepened the roots of the infestation—

The lash bit into her shoulder and the sting took her breath away. She gritted her teeth, stared ahead and pulled down on the rope.

'Concentrate,' the guard warned. He was missing an eye. It didn't affect his accuracy with the whip.

Haul. Thud.

'When this rope frays and breaks, I will snap your neck.' She made the promise between breaths in her own tongue. Lystra had long ago learned their occupier's language. Few Amadeans had bothered to understand the tongue of their slaves.

The whip-handler ignored her and instead called out to another veteran, 'Do you see that? What's on her shoulder?' Guards had come and gone throughout the day, puffing themselves up at the sight of an askara as if they'd been the one to bring her down. One of them limped closer.

'Hard to tell with all that blood.'

Like all wolf-clan askari, she wore a wolf pelt over her tunic, the pelt wrapped over the goat leather and cinched at the waist with a wide belt. The lash had broken the hide near her neck and she knew exactly what had caught their attention.

'I've never seen anything but clan ink on them.' He peered at her. 'What *is* that?'

'Clean her up and take a closer look.'

The guard with one eye laughed at the absurdity of the suggestion.

They were ignorant slugs, all of them. They had no idea who she was or what was inked into her flesh. If they did, she would not be working a boulder. She'd be dead, and her skin stretched out in their defiled mountain temple while the Great Pretender tried to understand its meaning.

A woman wearing ankle chains shuffled toward the slurry pond, the latest in a never-ending supply of quicksilver women. She kept her head down, her brittle white hair hanging forward to hide her face. The claws of a raven tattoo poked out from the sleeve of her tunic. She wore an old rope around her waist instead of a plaited flax belt, and she was stick-thin. Lystra glanced at the other Pyrien across the slurry pond. He watched this woman in a way he hadn't watched the other slaves.

Haul. Thud. Haul. Thud.

The quicksilver woman sat at the edge of the muddy water in Lystra's line of sight. She scooped slurry into a pan and another guard—this one thick around the middle and walking with the aid of a stick—limped over with his vial of poison. The woman kept her head lowered as he added quicksilver to her mix. She went to work using it to rub the grit in the water with her bare hands and pan down the contents. If there was gold in this slurry, the quicksilver would find it.

Still the Pyrien across the pond watched the woman. She was someone to him. Mother? Sister? Bonded mate? In the mountains, her stooped shoulders would mark her as being in her wisdom years, but in the mines a worn down body was no indicator of age.

The thickset guard prodded the woman with his staff. 'Anything?'

She shook her head, kept rubbing and panning. Lystra knew if the woman opened her mouth, she would be missing teeth. The quicksilver was killing her people. Slower even than the back-breaking labour in the mines but just as effectively. She could smell the poison from across the camp, burned away every afternoon until only the gold was left.

'Porplezi have cursed this place, turned the gold to rock,' the guard muttered.

Lystra barked a laugh between breaths and said in Amadean, 'When the mountains were ours, the gold did not hide from us.'

'Shut your mouth,' the one-eyed guard warned.

She was tired and aching and done with the day, so she said the one thing she knew would bring more pain—and then, Ares willing, oblivion.

'Make me.'

4

'How long has it been since you've seen her?'

Tristan knew without having to think too hard about it. 'Six moons, maybe more.'

He and Sabine were on their way north to see his mother and had slowed to give their horses a break. Tristan's family estate was only a short ride up the coast to the Midlands, but his duties rarely took him in that direction. He'd felt guilty enough about his absence before yesterday's message requesting his presence. Of course his mother had heard the rumours about Dash and Ferugo. And of course she should have heard the truth from him.

'Your mother wasn't at the planting day feast?'

'No.'

Usually, Tristan would have brought Rhys along to soften up his mother, but with the start of the march to the high plains only two days away, he needed his cousin to help Adward finalise logistics in his absence. In truth, Tristan was weary of talking about supplies; whether they had enough armourers and fletchers, and second guessing the king's plans for feeding the Amadean army once it crossed the border. Planning had always been Ferugo's domain, and Tristan and Adward had been at the periphery of decision-making, not in the centre of it. So he didn't feel as bad as he should have at handing the responsibilities to Rhys. To his cousin's credit, Rhys only complained for the time it took him to finish his scallop pie last night.

The morning had started breathless. The northern river had been cloaked in mist when they'd taken the barge across at dawn, the air cold enough for Sabine to huddle against him as they stood with the horses for the crossing. They'd first had to wait for a merchant boat to pass through on its way to Augustmount, pushing against the gentle current. They heard the drum first, that unmistakable slow purposeful beat that kept the galley slaves in rhythm as they rowed below deck, and then the long boat had appeared through the mist, its bow cutting through the water. The merchant boats of Amadea were not large, but nor did they need to be, plying their trade up and down the kingdom's rivers and coastline. Most of the boats carried gold to, and slaves from, the capital. The rest of the water-borne traffic traded in timber, grain, wool and eels.

Sea winds had greeted them when they rode up the hill on the opposite side of the river, making conversation difficult. Sabine had been preoccupied anyway, handling the warhorse that was now hers.

She and the squires had each been provided with a mount—a gift from Iolia on acceptance into the cohort. Without prompting, Adward had offered Sabine the best of them, a speckled grey gelding as tall and strong as Mina, nicknamed Trout by the stable boys for his colouring. The name had stuck. Trout was accustomed to a heavier hand than Sabine's and was headstrong on his first outing with a new rider. He'd arched his neck and pranced sideways on the muddy riverbank and it had been Sabine's suggestion to give the gelding his head. They'd let the horses stretch out to a gallop for the first mile where the road was flat and the landscape bare. Tristan suspected Sabine enjoyed the release as much as her mount. She was wearing a dress under her cloak today—more appropriate for meeting his mother than warrior vest and trousers—and the rich green fabric had caught in the wind at full gallop.

Now they were in the protection of a beech forest and the familiarity of the place loosened some of the tension across Tristan's shoulders. There were woodlands like this throughout the province but Stag Forest was different: it marked the start of the lands he called home. He knew every track, outcrop and moss-covered fallen tree. Here was where his father had taught Tristan, his youngest child and only son, to shoot an arrow on horseback. It was here that his father had shown him how to hunt boar and tell the difference between the call of an eagle and a hawk; how to spot a fox den; and when the roseberries were safe to eat.

Owen of Midlands had been a fair and generous underlord, feared enough by his peers that there were few quarrels with neighbouring optimati over wandering stock. And that was *before* his daughter became overlord at Ferugo's side and his son rose to be an Iolian commander. Owen of Midlands had been a man of swift justice, slow to anger but formidable when his blood was up. Tristan missed him most when he came home, and in Stag Forest most of all because here was where he'd had his father to himself, away from bailiffs, tenants and the constant demands of running an estate.

'It's lovely here,' Sabine said, patting Trout's neck.

Green shoots had broken through the leaf litter, new life pushing aside the old. The forest floor was dappled with golden light.

'Do you know why we call it Stag Forest?'

She gave him a sideways look, sensing it was a trick question. 'It's not for the deer that provide buckskin for your vests?'

'No,' he said. 'The wild deer are here, further in, but that's not how this place got its name.'

'How then?'

Tristan wanted her to see it even though they had other places to be.

He veered from the track and pushed Mina to a trot. It had been years since he'd visited the landmark. Maybe it had changed. But, not more than a quarter of a mile in after crossing the stream and getting the angle right, the forest namesake came into view. Sabine saw it immediately and despite the dangers they would face in the days to come, she laughed with delight.

It was an ancient beechwood that had grown misshapen from a rocky outcrop centuries ago. From this perspective it looked as if a giant stag had thrust its head from the rocks, the shape of the tree trunk giving the appearance of its shoulders, neck and head, and two gnarled branches sprouted out from its crown like monstrous leafy antlers.

'He's beautiful.' The horses were close enough that Sabine's leg pressed against Tristan's. Her expression was wistful. 'Are the chalk cliffs far?'

'You know of them?' The Midlands was a long way from Sabine's home of Greenock Hill in the Southlands.

'Dashelle speaks of them often. Do we have time?'

'We'll make time.' Who knew when he'd have the chance to share his homelands with her again?

They rode east, following a track that only someone who knew it would find, until the scent of brine carried to them on the breeze. They dismounted and tethered the horses. Tristan took Sabine by the hand and led her to the place where the forest abruptly ended and there was nothing but streaky blue sky and grey sea beyond. Her palm was warm, and her thumb brushed over the back of his hand. The beeches whispered above them, restless in the sea breeze.

'Careful,' Tristan said as they reached the drop-off. Sabine tightened her grip and steadied herself against a tree as she leant out over the edge to look down.

'Oh my,' she breathed.

Beneath them, the ground fell away to reveal steep chalk cliffs that plunged into the crashing sea far below. The clifftop was lined with beech trees for miles in either direction. Below them, a pebbly beach was littered with fallen trees that looked like kindling from this height.

Sabine stared out over the sea, cheeks flushed and loose strands of hair streaming behind her. 'I never knew such beauty existed.'

Tristan had been thinking the same thing. When she turned and found him watching her, she smiled. It was unguarded and it brought a sweet ache to his chest. He drew her back from the edge and kissed her, tasted sea salt on her lips.

They stood for a while, arms around each other and faces to the sea, not speaking.

'We should keep moving,' he said finally. 'My mother is expecting us.'

They were in the saddle and back on the path when Sabine asked, 'Did Dashelle share any news with you about your mother?'

'What sort of news?'

She guided Trout closer, so her stirrups and legs bumped Tristan's. He reached for her thigh to hold her there, the fabric of her dress soft under his touch. Sabine leaned in and for a pleasant moment he thought she was going to kiss him again.

'It seems she shares the same leanings as your sister and my brother.'

'She what?' The lingering glow he'd been enjoying evaporated. Sabine's closeness didn't lessen the blow. He hoped the forest was as uninhabited as it looked, remembering all too well Torvus's well-founded paranoia.

Sabine caught his eye. 'I didn't want to be the one to tell you, but I thought you might want to get *this* reaction over with now, rather than in front of your mother.'

'My mother is not so delicate.' He took back his hand. 'Evidently she thinks I am, though, or she wouldn't have kept it from me.'

Had he been forewarned his mother was among the heretics, Tristan would have coaxed Axl away from the Codex transcripts and brought him along. Surely, presenting the boy who might be the usurper would have distracted his mother from her anger at him. It was too late now. The monk was at Iolia Castle studying Ferugo's illicit prophecy fragments while he had the chance, because Axl would *not* be taking the writings across the border.

'What upsets you more, that your mother shares their creed or that she kept it from you?'

Tristan grunted. 'I'm happy to be in the dark about my mother's private affairs except when they put her life at risk.'

Especially when he was about to go to war and was no better equipped to keep her from the prophet's reach than he could his sister. His gut churned as it always did when he thought of Dash and Ferugo in Augustmount. They were prisoners of the prophet in all but name, and the king had done nothing to secure their release. It did not bode well for any of them.

Tristan followed the track out of Stag Forest and they rode into the heart of the Midlands estate. He knew from the bailiff's reports what to expect, but the sight still deflated him. What was once a patchwork of green crops and freshly tilled soil was now punctuated with smears of powdery black. The pestilence had blown through again and killed every leaf it touched on arable land. The surviving bean crops were ready for picking, but most able-bodied tenants had already marched south and were camped outside Iolia's walls. Which meant his mother and those left behind would have to pick the beans or the harvest would rot on the stem. The prophet had declared the pestilence was punishment from Verus for Amadea failing to crush Pyrie. The heretics believed the opposite: that it was punishment for the border occupation and slave trade. Either way, the black rot was a disaster.

Cultivated fields made way for grazing land, which at least remained viable. Here, the grass had been chewed low by the sheep that produced Amadea's best wool. They were the straightest line of descendants from the small flock aboard the ancestors' ships a thousand years ago.

Tristan and Sabine were a mile from the Midlands manor house when a scout appeared and rode near enough to identify Tristan before galloping back the way she had come. They'd barely ridden another half mile when two more riders crested the hill ahead. Tristan recognised the lead horse and the woman astride it.

'My mother has come out to greet us.' He'd wondered whether she'd have the patience to wait for him at the house. Here was his answer.

Sabine straightened in her saddle.

With his mother was Josef. He'd been Tristan's father's bailiff for many years and was now his mother's right-hand man. The pair approached at a trot and Tristan took quick stock of his mother. She wore a riding cloak with a high collar over a fine woollen house dress, but its hem was stained brown and her boots were muddy. She'd been in the fields today already.

'Have you had word from your sister?' his mother asked as she drew close, forgoing formalities. She had the dark colouring and high cheekbones prominent in the women of his family.

'A message came two days ago,' Tristan said, bringing Mina to a halt. 'It was written in Dash's hand and carried the Iolian seal. She says they have comfortable lodgings in the palace but have still not seen the king.' He glanced at Sabine, recognised nerves in the set of her jaw. 'Mother, this is Sabine of Greenock Hill. Sabine, this is my mother, Marta of Midlands.'

Sabine had agreed Tristan could announce her as optimati. He understood it was to avoid scrutiny rather than desire for status, but quietly hoped it was also a sign Sabine wanted to make a good impression on his mother.

'My lady,' Sabine said, inclining her head.

'Welcome, Sabine. I understand you are now the only woman who shares my son's bed?'

Tristan winced at the lack of tact.

Sabine, however, did not flinch. 'That would be my understanding as well, my lady.'

Tristan's mother measured her. 'It's not before time.' She collected her reins. 'Come. The kitchen has prepared for your arrival.'

Sabine widened her eyes at Tristan and then pushed Trout forward to ride with his mother. Josef reined in beside Tristan and shook his hand. The bailiff was a slight man with inquisitive eyes and soft hands.

'It's good to see you Tristan, even in the shadow of war.'

'You too, Josef.'

They let the women draw further ahead.

'How is my mother's estate?' Tristan asked.

'Income is down and will drop further with the tenants gone. But we have grain enough to support those left behind, even if we can't get the beans harvested before they spoil. We've taken the wool from the sheep early. It's a lower yield, but better than leaving it on their backs for summer for lack of shearers. Your mother has long suspected this war was coming. She's been frugal with spending, preparing for harder times.'

'My sister has missed her at court.'

'She's been needed here, Tristan. It's been hard for her to

be parted for so long from Dashelle. It was no easy decision, either, for her to not leave the Midlands with the men.'

With Tristan's father gone, it should have been his mother's place to lead the Midlands conscripts to Iolia and on to war.

'How did you convince her to stay?'

Josef was the only person beside Dash who knew how to temper his mother's steely will. Even his father never truly mastered it and Tristan had never come close.

'She knew there would be nobody left to lead the women and children to work the fields and tend the flocks. She responded to Iolia's call. She rode the fields, called the tenants all to arms and ordered them to follow Ben.'

Ben was his mother's reeve, highly dependable, and another long-serving member of the Midlands household. A good choice.

'Has she left enough men to oversee the slaves? There's no point Amadea marching to war if we have an uprising at home in our absence.'

'Your mother is not a fool, Tristan.'

Tristan had certainly never thought so. But if she was a heretic, he might need to revise that assessment.

Ahead of them, Sabine and his mother were speaking. He assumed it was about him—what else did they have in common?

'Anything else I need to know?' he asked Josef.

'About the affairs of the estate?'

'About my mother.'

The bailiff glanced at him, gave nothing away. 'I'm sure if there's something your mother wants you to know, you'll hear about it soon enough.'

Tristan grunted. 'Never a truer word spoken.'

He felt a fresh tug for home when they turned the horses into the laneway. The fields either side were dotted with freshly shorn sheep, their short white fleeces stark against the grass.

The manor house remained in good condition despite its age. Every optimati family could trace their bloodline to the ancestors on one of the six ships that followed Verus across the ocean. It was the Fourth Prophet who formalised the province borders and the land holdings within them.

Construction on the Midlands manor house began soon after, making the original sandstone section more than eight hundred years old. The home had been added to over the centuries and now had four wings facing into a large internal courtyard. It was impressive on approach, its three-storey gatehouse flanked by two-storey wings either side with steep-pitched roofs, all surrounded by a narrow moat. Tristan would have liked to have seen Sabine's reaction to it, but her back was to him.

A servant girl came out to take their horses. Tristan fell into step with Sabine as they crossed the footbridge and passed through the gatehouse. The courtyard beyond was dominated by a white marble fountain sculpted in the shape of four life-size, rearing warhorses, hooves frozen mid-paw and water spouting from open mouths that caught in the sunlight. Sabine craned her neck to admire them on the way past and Tristan gently guided her by the elbow to keep her moving.

A fire and a jug of mead were waiting for them in his mother's warming room. Marta gestured for their cloaks to be taken by a servant Tristan didn't recognise. There was then a wordless exchange with Josef before he, too, excused himself.

Tristan's mother poured three cups of mead and took her place in the high-backed chair beside the fire. 'Sit.'

Sabine sat on one end of his mother's divan, furthest from the fire. Tristan accepted the mead but did not join her. To sit in here among his mother's woollen blankets and bright cushions was to feel like a boy again waiting to be scolded.

Marta took a measured sip from her cup and watched

him for a moment. 'Do you believe Torvus was executed for treason alone?'

Tristan gave a tight smile. 'No pleasantries, then?'

'Don't evade the question, Tristan. Tell me why you think Torvus was executed without a trial and in the presence of the king.'

He grunted. There was no avoiding a conversation his mother wanted to have. 'Because he followed Anguston's heresy.'

'As do others.'

'Yes,' Tristan said, purposefully. 'As do *others*.'

They eyeballed each other for a long moment and she waited for him to do more with the bait. Tristan wished he was better equipped to deal with her thorny expectations.

'All right, mother,' he said through gritted teeth. 'How long have you counted yourself among them?'

'Since your sister and Ferugo brought Anguston here five years ago.'

'The high priest came east?' That had been kept quiet.

'Anguston's mother was ailing and the prophet allowed him to travel to the coast to see her before she journeyed to Verus.' His mother huffed. 'It was the last compassionate decision made by our Thirteenth Prophet.' She cradled her mead on her knees. 'Your sister and Ferugo had met with Anguston in Augustmount a few moons earlier. When he sent word he was travelling this way, they arranged to meet here at Midlands manor.'

She allowed a moment for Tristan to absorb the implications.

'Was my father here?'

'Yes.'

Tristan felt queasy.

He remembered his father's mood on that last fateful Pyrien campaign. It had been Tristan's second tour to the border and his place had been at Ferugo's side, not his father's, but he saw enough to know his father had been distracted. Tristan had assumed it was being on the border—crossing into Pyrie did strange things to even the most fearless of men—but now he wondered if something else had plagued him.

He could barely voice the question, but he needed to know.

'Did my father follow Anguston's heresy?'

His mother exhaled, and he caught a glimpse of the depth of grief she still carried. 'No.'

The relief was overwhelming. 'But he allowed you to?'

'He didn't *allow* anything,' she snapped, but the sting of her annoyance passed quickly. 'Your father wasn't pleased about my interest in Anguston's teachings, but he promised to hold his tongue on the matter providing I did not bring transcripts under our roof. I respected his wishes and he respected my choices.'

That was something, at least. If his mother had no fragments of the Codex, it would be harder to brand her a heretic.

'You have pages now, though,' Sabine said. It wasn't a question.

Tristan looked to his mother for the denial, but all she offered was a grim smile. 'She's a sharp one, isn't she?'

He stared at her. 'You could not be so foolish.'

'They are well hidden.'

His anger was instant. 'Anguston is dead. Torvus is dead. Your daughter and her husband are imprisoned in all but name, and the prophet is scouring the kingdom for these transcripts. Verus has not protected them so why would she protect you?'

He paced to the window and back, frustrated at his inability to keep his temper. He didn't want to make the same mistakes he'd made with Ferugo: blurt out every thought in his head, only to be separated from his lord and overwhelmed with guilt and remorse. But he needed to know his mother had not taken leave from her senses.

'Are you going to free your slaves?'

His mother gave him a pointed look. 'I don't support slaughtering Pyrien women and children, here or anywhere. That doesn't mean I'm naïve about what those we have enslaved would do to us if given the chance.'

'Is that not what Anguston taught? That they should be freed?'

'He taught what he found in the Tenth Prophecy fragments: that a terrible fate would befall Amadea if we invade Pyrie. He also believed that if we did go to war, a usurper would rise who would receive the power of the First Prophet and end the tyranny of the final prophet. Anguston believed the usurper would rise in this generation.' She turned to Sabine. 'It appears he was right on that count.'

Sabine paled. 'You mean my brother?'

'Are you aware of anyone else?'

She didn't answer.

'Have you not read the transcripts at Iolia, Sabine? It's not only the Tenth Prophet who talks about him. The Seventh Prophecy says one will come and they will be marked by ritual, have no possessions and be hidden to the prophet. It's no surprise *that* passage has not been taught to Amadeans in our generation.'

'I'm aware of the prophecy,' Sabine said. 'My brother doesn't believe it refers to him.'

'Then he is truly the right man for the job.'

Tristan grunted. 'He's not a man, he's a boy in Stonebridge robes.'

'Which fits the prophecy.'

Tristan scrubbed a hand over his beard. He heard the

conviction in his mother's voice and knew there would be no dissuading her.

'Tell me, mother, how is it you know so much about this usurper when you've not been to court in Iolia in two years?'

His mother took a sip of mead before she answered. 'Your sister and I devised a code for corresponding after Anguston's visit. We also occasionally meet midway in the ale house run by your cousin, Sacha.'

Tristan shook his head, incredulous. His mother and sister had been exchanging coded letters about a heresy, and they'd been doing it for *years*. If he hadn't found Axl with that transcript in the castle temple, would they have ever told him?

'You are so much like your father,' his mother said, watching him struggle. 'But you have what he did not.'

'What?' he demanded, ready to argue because his father had lacked nothing.

'Evidence.'

Tristan scoffed but found he couldn't look at Sabine. He couldn't deny he'd been witness to *something*. They both had. She too had seen Axl use unsanctified fire to stop a spear; had taken a share of Tristan's pain when the monk invoked a lost rite to hasten the knitting of Tristan's bones; had herself been strengthened by the monk to break free from her uncle's binds.

'The monk you speak of has no idea what he's doing.'

'That's why you must help him find the Tenth Prophecy in Pyrie.'

'How can I do what Ferugo asks of me and not condemn him and my sister in the eyes of the prophet? You are talking about *treason*.'

His mother set down her mead. 'Do you love this kingdom, Tristan?'

'Of course I do.'

'Then do what must be done or there will be no kingdom to come home to.'

'You can't believe that. Where is the evidence Amadea is on the brink of destruction?'

'It is in the prophecies, son. Open your eyes.'

Tristan shook his head, cursed under his breath and finally sat beside Sabine, defeated. These conversations about heresy were more exhausting than a day in the training yard. He'd so much rather be swinging a sword right now.

'Tristan,' his mother said, softening. 'Ferugo and your sister know the choices they have made and what is at stake. They're risking everything in the belief you will do what needs to be done when they cannot.'

'I know, mother. That doesn't make it any easier.'

'You must believe.'

Tristan worried at the scar on his palm. His hands were stained with leather oil and hardened from training. He was a warrior whose creed was violence, obedience and blood oaths. What did he know of belief?

5

They returned to Iolia Castle mid-afternoon, the sea breeze gusting at their backs as they rode through the inner gates.

In the courtyard, Sabine dismounted and handed Trout's reins to Ty, well aware Tristan's dark mood had followed them home. She'd known better than to press the warrior for conversation on the journey, giving him space to chew over the visit with his mother. She saw Tristan was caught up in his own thoughts and failed to notice Ty's downcast eyes; made none of his usual attempts to lift the squire's spirits when he saw the boy wallowing in guilt again.

Sabine wished she could read Tristan better, wished she had the words to reassure him. But there was nothing she could say that would undo the knots she could almost *see* tightening in his neck and shoulders. There were other ways she might unwind him but she doubted even her touch would still his troubled thoughts right now. Not when he needed to rejoin Adward and help lead the very army he'd been ordered to abandon.

Tristan threw back his hood and glanced her way, his dark eyes distracted. 'You should check on your brother.'

Sabine tried to hold his gaze but his attention shifted to the keep behind her. The tender moment on the clifftop this morning seemed a lifetime ago and the distance between them hollowed her out a little.

'And *you* should work off your frustration in the training yard.' She walked away before waiting for a reply. Of course she had no words of comfort for him. What reassurance could she offer that wouldn't be worthless the moment he learned the truth of her bloodline?

She entered the castle through the kitchen, the warm air heady with the smell of roasting pheasants. Dashelle's cook acknowledged her with a nod, accustomed to Sabine using the servant entrance to get to and from the yards. Sabine took the narrow back stairs and made her way to Ferugo's antechamber, where Axl had spent every waking hour since their return to Augustmount. She knocked twice. 'It's me.'

Her brother was quick to unbolt the door, his tired expression softening at the sight of her. He stepped aside so she could enter and then closed and re-bolted the door behind her. Ferugo's illicit transcripts—the source of so much of Tristan's unease—were still fanned across the table by the window. 'How did Tristan take the news about his mother?' Axl asked as he returned to his seat.

Sabine managed a tight smile. 'About as well as I'd expected.'

He gestured for her to take the divan near the hearth, saw her glance at the fire. 'And Marta? What is she like?'

'Formidable. As direct with her speech as Dashelle says. She doesn't pull her punches, not even for Tristan. *Especially* for Tristan. The visit hasn't made him any more comfortable about Ferugo's orders. If anything, it's made things worse.' Her gaze flitted back to the hearth. The fire was down to coals, barely enough to take the chill from the room. 'And, no, I haven't said anything to him about the *other* matter.'

Axl gave a weary sigh, disappointed but unsurprised. He wore one of those expressions that gave him an air of maturity far beyond his sixteen years. Most days it comforted Sabine. Today was not one of those days.

'We need more than a theory Axl.'

'Yes, Sabine, we need the blood bond to test it.'

She shook her head, frustrated they had to have this conversation every time they spoke alone.

'We must trust in Verus,' he pressed. 'She has a plan.'

Sabine gave a sour laugh. 'It's a poor one if it involves the fire of the First Prophet in *my* bones.' Saying it aloud made her skin prickle. Axl was watching her closely and she knew what was coming next.

'Why don't you get the fire going?'

There were a dozen reasons why Sabine didn't want to build up the flames, and all were laced with fear: fear that Axl was right and their illicit bloodline had condemned her with a terrifying destiny; fear that she might one day hold the fate of Amadea in her hands—*that* idea was so big, so beyond her imagination, she could not even give it shape—and that she would fail; and fear that Axl might be wrong and there was nothing beneath her skin but blood, bone and marrow.

'You need to try again,' he coaxed. The golden glyphs on the right side of his scalp gleamed even in the grey afternoon light. 'While we still can.'

He was right of course. There would be none of these moments once the Iolian army was on the march.

Nerves fluttered as she knelt on the ancient floorboards and reached for the kindling basket. She tossed a handful of sticks on the coals, blew on the embers until the wood caught, and then added larger pieces until the flames were big enough for a split log. Satisfied, Sabine sat back and crossed her legs. Axl's robe rustled as he joined her on the floor. She'd only tried this twice before, and each time the fire had been well established and the flames lazy. This would be her first attempt with a new flame. She watched the log catch, tendrils of smoke curling out the end of it like catfish whiskers.

'What do you feel?' Axl prompted.

Sabine took a shaky breath. If the flames of the First Prophet were part of her, surely she would have sensed them long before now?

'Take your time. Concentrate on the memories.'

Sabine focused on the inexplicable fire-related *incidents* that had occurred since the Stonebridge abbot bonded her to the warriors.

'Remember what you felt in each moment.'

The recollections came easily enough.

The terror for her brother during the brigand attack on the campsite. Anguish for Tristan lying broken in his bed. Hatred at the sting of her uncle's fist in the warehouse and blind fury at allowing herself to be paralysed by her fear of him. The feelings were all there but they were dusty and faded, softened by hindsight. The flames before her flickered unaffected, just as they had the other times she'd focused on them in this room.

Sabine blew out her breath and closed her eyes. Did she need to dig deeper? To the fire that burned down her home? Her mouth instantly went dry. But that was before the blood bond and she *really* didn't want to dredge it up—

The memory rushed in before she could shut it down, and she was back there in that kitchen, smashing the jug into her uncle's face. Then came the blow of the fire iron across her shoulders and legs, the cruelty of uncle's fingers around her throat as he shoved up her skirts—

A blast of heat sent her scrambling backwards.

Sabine snapped open her eyes in time to see flames roaring up the chimney.

'Praise Verus!' Axl exclaimed. His face blazed with the sudden brightness. He'd barely spoken the words before the fire shrunk back to normal. 'What did you do differently?'

Sabine was trembling and panting, waiting for her body

to remember she was safe. Her heart thrashed and her palms were clammy. She couldn't look at her brother, couldn't bear for him to see her like this. So vulnerable. So *raw*.

'You controlled it,' Axl said, staring at the fire as if she might do it again. 'The flames *reacted* to you, Sabine. I saw it with my own eyes.'

Her heart rate steadied enough for her to take a deeper breath and force down her unease. She tried to ignore the all too familiar buzzing in her ears. 'That was the opposite of control, Axl.' She said it quietly, needing him to understand what the moment had cost her.

But when Axl looked at her, his face was alight with hope. He only saw what he wanted to see. 'It's proof, Sabine. Praise Verus, it's the sign we've been waiting for.'

*

The buzzing grew louder as she hurried to the training yard. She was taking her own advice. She didn't dare stop to change out of her skirts for fear the madness that had gripped her at Stonebridge would take hold again. The yard was deserted, thank Verus. She snatched up a practice sword without warming up and struck the training dummy with so much force she split the hessian sack and bit her tongue. She swung again and again, frightened and furious, all at once.

What was she supposed to do with what just happened?

Sabine attacked the dummy until her hands bled and the noise in her head fell silent. Shaking and exhausted, she made her way back to the keep and the wash basin she'd requested be waiting for her in her room. She was sweating and her shoulders ached, and she hoped she wouldn't meet anyone and have to explain the state of her hands. She was careful not to get blood on the handle when she opened her door and was so preoccupied with her thoughts that it took her a heartbeat to realise she wasn't alone.

The fire was blazing and Tristan stood in front of it. He turned as she walked in, using a damp cloth to squeeze water across his neck and chest. The room smelled of lye and rose-scented water and he was naked from the waist up.

'Ty was to keep an eye out for you,' he said, almost apologetic. 'He should be on his way with a fresh pitcher.'

Sabine clasped her hands together, ignoring the hungry flames in the hearth. 'Why are you using my water?' It wasn't an accusation; she was genuinely surprised to find him here. They spent every evening together in his room or hers, but this was the first time he'd bathed in her quarters.

'Your room was closer than mine,' Tristan said.

Sabine was momentarily distracted by the water dripping from his wet hair onto his collar bone and tracing a path over his chest and stomach. He caught the drops with a deft flick of the washcloth before they reached that soft trail of fine hair further down.

Tristan hadn't missed where her attention had gone.

His eyes softened. 'And I wanted to see you.'

A fresh wave of exhaustion washed over her. 'I wanted to see you too.'

He took in the state of her. 'You were in the yard? In those clothes?'

She nodded and sank onto the bed. She kicked off her boots, wished she had some way to clean her hands without him noticing the mess she'd made of them.

Tristan finished bathing. For a while, the only sounds in the room were the crack of the fire and sloshing water. The lye scum was growing in the bowl and Sabine was grateful when Ty arrived with fresh water. Steam wafted from the pitcher, and Ty had had the sense to also bring a clean basin and extra cloths. 'Thank you,' she said. 'I prefer not to smell like Tristan after I bathe.'

Ty's eyes flitted to hers and he almost smiled—the squire of old most certainly would have, given he was often second or third in line for a bath or basin—but he couldn't keep a grip on it. He carried the pitcher and basin to the side table where Tristan was now drying himself, and then left with the used water, careful not to slop it over the sides. Sabine bolted the door behind him. She started unlacing her dress on her way back to the hearth.

'I smell better than *you* do right now,' Tristan said when she drew closer.

She gave him a tired smile. 'That's not difficult.' She really should have changed. Now these clothes would need to be laundered before she could wear them again—*if* she got the chance to put on a dress again before the march to the war.

Tristan leaned against the side table, made no move to get dressed. He watched her fiddle with the side of her dress. Her fingers were stiffening as they cooled down and she was struggling with the fine touch required. The blood on her palms at least had dried.

'I'm sorry about the ride home,' he said quietly.

Sabine let her hands drop. 'I can't tell what you're thinking when you get like that.'

He conceded a nod. 'I'm not like Rhys. I need to think things through, not talk my way into understanding. You're not so different, yourself.'

Sabine let out a surprised huff, realising he was right. 'Maybe we need to try talking for a change.'

'You go first.' Tristan poured out the water. 'But let's get you washed while you talk. Don't waste this warm water.' He gestured for Sabine to turn sideways and took over undoing her dress, gently tugging at the lace. She busied herself winding her plait on the top of her head and thought carefully about what she wanted to say.

'I'm well aware of how you feel about the heresy,' she started, her eyes flitting to the flames, alert for even the slightest change in them. 'Axl is part of it, which means I am, and I know you didn't ask for the blood bond—'

'Sabine, my frustration with this madness has nothing to do with you. *Nothing*.'

She swallowed, wished with all her heart that were true.

'I'm not angry at you or Axl.' He frowned, struggling for the right words. 'I'm frustrated because *nothing* is in my control. I'm powerless to protect the people I care about.' He placed his hands lightly on her hips and turned her around to face him. 'I have never regretted being bonded to you, not for a heartbeat, and I never will.'

'You can't make that promise,' she whispered, her throat threatening to close over.

'I can. And I do.'

Sabine felt a tear slip down her cheek. Tristan wiped it away with his thumb and then took her hands in his.

'Sabine—' He faltered when he realised the state of her palms. 'Didn't you wear gloves in the yard?' His frown deepened. 'Did I make you so annoyed that you forgot to change your clothes and protect your hands?'

She hesitated for only a moment. 'No, it wasn't that. Axl and I were talking about the fire...*incidents*,' she said carefully, not wanting to lie to him anymore than she had to. 'He thinks my state of mind might have had some influence over what happened each time.'

A muscle in Tristan's jaw twitched. He was well aware of the type of memories she was talking about, even if he didn't understand the specifics. Sabine didn't want him thinking about it too deeply, especially when he was bare-chested in front of her—and there were other things she'd prefer he think about. She quashed thoughts of Olidus, too. She refused to let him rob her of her own desires and needs.

'I'm all right, Tristan. *Fine*,' she conceded in response to his raised eyebrows, 'I'm all right now that I've worked up a sweat and I'm here with you.'

He was watching her carefully. 'Are you sure?'

She understood what he was asking. 'Adamant.'

Tristan waited a beat and then, slowly and tenderly, he washed the blood from her chafed palms and wrapped them with strips of linen.

'Let's get you out of these clothes.'

He helped her undress with hands far more familiar with the task than that first, fraught time in a tiny washroom on the pilgrim's road. And this time, of course, he did not look away. Sabine sensed him check himself, as he always did when she was naked. He might exert power in the training yard, but he always let Sabine set the pace when they were alone no matter how aroused he was. And it was obvious the effect she was having on him right now. Tristan's desire for her, paired with his restraint, never failed to set Sabine's skin ablaze. And yet again he gave her the power, even when he could easily take control with a look or a touch.

No wonder she was falling in love with him.

No wonder she was afraid she would lose him.

She handed him back the wash cloth, her skin warmed through by the fire, and he began to bathe her. Firstly with enough attention to clean the sweat and grime from her, and then his focus shifted from hygiene to pleasure. Finally, when she was clean, dry, and burning with wanting, Sabine led him to the bed so they could finish what he'd started.

With the hearth fire still blazing, they lost themselves in each other while the light faded across Amadea.

6

The mornings were the worst.

Daybreak offered Lystra her best chance of overpowering her captors. That was when she was rested, fed (with a tepid broth of barley and pig fat), and her limbs were not as sore as they would be later in the day. But for seven days now, her Amadean guards had come for her in numbers. Each morning, one of them hauled her from her cage, the leather collar and wrist binds chafing her skin, and dragged her to the slurry pit. Another five shadowed her with swords and whips, ready to draw fresh blood if she resisted.

Lystra would only get one chance at escape, and she'd either be free or dead at the end of it. So she was biding her time, waiting for her moment. But every lost opportunity was a nettle in her side, needling her for the rest of the day. She could bear the aching muscles, welts and gnawing hunger—an askara was trained to live with such discomforts. It was the feigned submissiveness that ate at her. The Pyrien working the other boulder had warned her from an escape attempt on the second morning after her capture, the alarm in his eyes enough to quell her bloodlust and restore her senses. He understood why she had not fought back since that first day, but she hated that the overfed veterans believed they had crushed her so easily.

They'd understand their mistake soon enough.

Escape would not be easy, but it was not impossible if she could take a weapon from one of them. She'd be quicker with her spear, but she had some skill with the sword. Enough to slow down this pack of crippled warriors. Already, she could see their wariness hardening into resentment. Complacency would follow.

Lystra and the Pyrien on the other boulder were kept in cages far enough apart they couldn't speak without raising their voices and alerting the guards, limiting them to eye contact and hand signals. Lystra had counted twenty-four slaves working the mine. They spent each night in cramped quarters built from mud and straw. The low-roofed hut had been hastily constructed, lacking straight lines and proper wall height. But it must have been built by Pyrien hands—*slave* hands—because it still stood. If Amadeans had attempted to build a mud hut in the Pyrien way, it would have dissolved back into the mountain after the first heavy rain.

Every afternoon, the slaves who worked underground were herded inside it, grimy and shuffling, and locked behind its iron gate. The hut was inadequate for so many, but at least they had shelter. Lystra's cage offered no protection from the elements, which didn't matter so much this time of year, but would be deadly for anyone left outside in winter. She'd been given a blanket to ward off the night-time chill. Horsehair wasn't as warm as her bearskin—abandoned where she'd left it to spar with Dex—but it was better than nothing, given the state of her pelt and tunic. And at least by night she was too exhausted to think of anything but sleep.

Today was her eighth morning as a captive.

As soon as she woke, she felt the change in the valley. The bitter tang of quicksilver smoke hung in the air from yesterday's burning, but there was an overlay of pine and eucalyptus and loamy soil. It was the scent of the high country, as if the mountain that crouched at her back was stirring and reclaiming its breath.

Ares was telling her to be ready.

Dawn crept into the valley and Lystra's eyes adjusted to find the Pyrien in the other cage sitting up, alert. Their eyes met and he nodded: he felt it too. She dipped her chin in response. When she was free, she would release him and the others. She rubbed her arms and legs, coaxing blood back into limbs numb from the cool night.

Two guards stood by a fire to warm their hands, bleary-eyed after a night of sentry duty. They were oblivious to the shift in the air. A sharp whistle came from the Amadeans' hut and the pair straightened to attention. The cook appeared, lugging his pot and balancing a stack of wooden bowls wedged between the lid and his chin. A stout Amadean, he listed as he walked, his apron hitching up with each step. This one was no veteran.

The cook looked Lystra in the eye, though, and grunted a greeting as he placed one of the bowls on the ground, just out of her range. He ladled in broth and inched it close enough for her to reach. She leaned out and took it with calloused fingers. The blisters from the pulley rope had worn down to hardened skin and it took a moment to be confident of her grip. She couldn't fit the bowl between the cage bars, so she pressed her face to the iron and awkwardly sipped the cooling broth. It was fatty and salty and stung all the raw places inside her mouth. She tried not to gag on the barley—Pyriens neither grew nor ate it—but Lystra chewed the swollen grains and forced them down, needing the sustenance.

The cook repeated the process with the other caged Pyrien, and then left the pot, ladle and remaining bowls outside the mud hut gate. Slender hands reached through the bars and started scooping broth into the bowls, dragging them through a gap under the gate and passing them back into the hut. The hands belonged to the woman who panned for gold at Lystra's feet again yesterday; the slave her caged companion couldn't take his eyes from. There weren't enough bowls for the number of Pyriens crammed in the mud hut, and the woman refilled the empty ones as they returned to her, serving herself last.

Lystra sat back and waited.

The guards always came for her first. They wanted her secured to the boulder before they released the others. The men on daylight duty strolled out of the timber Amadean hut, soft-bellied and lazy. In the lead was her one-eyed tormenter, already unfurling his whip. Lystra knew him by name now: Janus. With him was the shorter one, Matteo, who favoured his left leg and was never without his sword, and Sisto, the one whose nose had been broken so often it was permanently crooked. Sisto drew a dagger and absently spun the hilt as he approached. He was the oldest, and whenever he came out of the hut the others snapped to attention. Behind Sisto came two more guards: the one called Caius was missing three fingers on his right hand. The other, Virgil, had lost his left arm from the elbow. Both men wore swords low on their hips. Caius also carried a staff and he used it to prod and beat slaves as the mood took him.

Lystra watched for the sixth guard but nobody else appeared from the hut. Her pulse picked up. They were down a man today, either because the veterans believed five was enough to manage her after seven days of exertion and whippings, or the sixth had failed to roll out of bed yet. Either way, this was her chance.

She slumped against the bars and watched the Amadeans through heavy-lidded eyes; let out a faint, despondent grumble as they neared.

Virgil was already complaining.

'You cheated, Janus.'

'How could I cheat a coin toss?' The whip-wielder barked a laugh. 'And look how Verus smiles on you. If your turn had come even two days ago, I'd wager you'd have lost the use of your other arm. We've softened up the mangy wolf for you.'

Virgil huffed, unconvinced. Lystra ignored the jibe at her clan and kept her eyes down, tracking their boots in her peripheral vision. The men surrounded her cage. Matteo drew his sword. Lystra briefly lost sight of Caius and felt the jab of his staff in her lower back.

'Up.'

If it was Virgil getting her from the cage he would need his good arm, which meant his sword would stay in its scabbard, and Caius couldn't hold a staff *and* a sword with any skill, not missing those fingers. That left the whip, the dagger, and Matteo's blade to deal with.

Virgil used the stump of his left arm to hold the padlock while he unlocked it, and the gate swung open with a high-pitched whine. Lystra kept her breathing slow and willed herself to relax. She couldn't tip them off before she was out of the cage or Sisto and Matteo would stab her to death while she was trapped inside. Their blades were already trained on her through the bars. Janus stood back, ready with the whip.

'Wrists.'

Lystra lifted her wrists and Virgil slipped a noose over them, deftly tightened it one-handed. She dropped her chin, drawing him further into the cage to hook the lead on her leather collar. He fumbled and swore, and she caught the stench of last night's ale on his breath. Virgil yanked on her collar and she resisted, not lifting her eyes for fear he'd read her thoughts. 'Move,' he growled.

Every other morning, she'd resisted at least twice and then let them drag her out on her hands and knees, intentionally leaving herself off-balance. Not today. When Virgil tugged the second time, she started to move and then rocked back, getting her feet beneath her. Impatient, he jerked again, and this time she was ready.

Lystra launched herself at him. He staggered backwards at the sudden lack of tension, making it easy to drive him out of the cage. Blood flowed into her legs, hot from her thundering heart. She used her bound wrists to bat away his good arm, grabbed the hilt of his sword two-handed and kicked him hard in the gut. The blade came free from the scabbard as he fell backwards. There were shouts of alarm as she swung the sword in Matteo's direction, knowing Sisto would be on her in a heartbeat. Her grip was wrong because her bound hands were too close together and the weight not what she was expecting, but she was quick enough to take Matteo by surprise. He parried, startled, but he'd taken his weight on his bad leg and it wouldn't hold him. He hobbled to right himself and Lystra attacked with an ascending cut that sliced him open from hip to sternum. She was turning to face the other guards when the whip bit across her exposed neck. The skin there was flayed raw, and fiery pain forked down her arms. She gritted her teeth and used her momentum to slash at Virgil as he fumbled for his dagger with his good arm. He fell and she spun around, expecting a rushed attack from the other men. Instead, she found Janus, Sisto and Caius circling her. It was controlled and tactical, a reminder these men had once done more than torment slaves.

'On my command,' Sisto ordered. 'Maim but do not kill. King's orders.'

Caius had discarded the staff and now held the longsword in his one and a half hands, its tip pointed at the ground. His nostrils flared and his eyes darted to Matteo. The fallen veteran was crumpled on the ground, not moving. Virgil sat in the dirt a few paces away, clutching his shoulder and blood soaking through his tunic. She'd cut him deep enough to deter him from re-entering the fray. The remaining three, though, had her covered. Sisto scooped up the staff and held it out to one side, the dagger out to the other, as if herding a goat. Lystra kept her feet moving, whipping her head from side to side, measuring the distance and picking Caius as the weakest—

Their eyes locked and he attacked before Sisto gave the order.

Caius came in fast and Lystra barely had time to defend herself. With her wrists still bound, her grip on the sword was awkward and her instinct was to counter with a thrust, as if wielding her spear. Caius deflected, knocking her off her line. He darted in and palmed her wrists with his disfigured hand as she swung back, used the other to strike her hard in the face with his pommel. White-hot pain forked from the bridge of her nose and reunited at the base of her skull. She kicked out and caught Caius above the knee before he could repeat the blow. He staggered sideways and she steadied to capitalise, but the whip bit into her neck again and Sisto slammed the staff across the back of her legs, driving her to her knees. Caius was already recovered and swinging his blade, and it was only Sisto blocking with his dagger that stopped him burying it in her neck.

'Stand down!' The older veteran ordered. Lystra was in a world of pain. Her flayed neck stung, her skull throbbed and blood gushed from her nose—and then Janus was there, kicking Virgil's sword from her hands. She panted and spat blood as Caius stepped back, red-faced and with spittle on his lips, his blade held high over his right shoulder, ready to strike again.

Sisto trapped Lystra's head against him and pressed his dagger to her exposed throat to keep her still while he dealt with his men.

'I told you to stand down.'

'You brought a dagger for a reason,' Caius said. 'Kill her!'

'No.'

'Matteo is dead and Virgil's bleeding out,' Caius shouted. 'She's a rabid wolf and if you don't have the balls to put her down, I will.'

'End her life and I'll end yours. She is an *askari hostage*, you idiot. Since when do we have authority to execute them?'

'When we're defending ourselves.'

'Have you forgotten what she's worth? We get nothing if she's dead.'

Lystra's throat worked to avoid choking on her own blood. Vaguely, she wondered if the Amadeans knew who she was, or if she was simply worth something because she was wolf clan and her pack members were so hard to capture.

Caius grunted but kept his distance. 'We'll never see that gold.'

'All we have to do is keep her alive until the king sends men to collect her.'

'Nobody is coming. Every warrior in Amadea is massing on the high plains. That's why she was dumped on us in the first place and not taken straight to Augustmount.'

'Pellus knows she's here.'

Lystra couldn't see Sisto but she had eyes on Caius and he faltered at that name. The half-handed veteran swallowed but kept his chin up, the defiance not yet cooled. 'He needs reminding, then, that our job is not babysitting askari.'

Sisto barked a laugh. 'Do you want to ride across the border and explain that to the prophet's warrior?'

The prophet's warrior? It wasn't a title she'd ever heard.

'If that's what it takes to get the wolf out of our camp.'

Sisto paused as if considering the offer. Lystra eyeballed Janus and then Caius, aware of urgent footfalls as the sixth guard belatedly rushed to the scene.

'I will see you all dead,' she managed in their tongue, even with the blade at her throat.

Sisto scoffed.

'Put her back in the cage. She'll be useless for anything else today.'

7

The march to war was surprisingly tedious.

'Sweet Verus, we're getting slower,' Rhys muttered.

Sabine looked at him sideways. She was stiff from the day's ride and longing to be out of the saddle. 'We're going uphill. What did you expect?'

It was impossible to get an army of five thousand foot soldiers to move faster than a walk, and progress over the past ten days had been excruciatingly slow. Iolia's tenant farmers and peasants trudged behind ranks of archers and the eighty-strong warrior cohort, carrying axes and clubs and whatever other weapons they could gather or fashion at short notice. Bringing up the rear were armourers, blacksmiths, supply wagons and the non-combatants who would keep the soldiers fed and clothed. The army had gained size as it crossed the province, heralds travelling ahead to call in the fealty owed by the men and women of Iolia to their overlords.

Nervous energy had rippled up and down the line on the morning the troops set out from Iolia Castle, and it fluttered again each time the numbers were bolstered. The rear of the Iolian army had now cleared the provincial border and the column was marching through greater Augustmount. There were no more additions, no more excitement. The process of march, camp, sleep, break-camp, march had quickly become monotonous.

Sabine and Rhys rode together at a walk near the head of the warrior cohort. Tristan was up front with Adward and the standard bearer, again discussing logistics. The lead party was deep in the sprawling forest that separated the capital from the high plains. The army was reportedly two days at most from joining King Felix and the rest of the Amadean forces. The road took them between pine trees so tall Sabine could not see their tops and the breeze that blew between them was cold, even mid-afternoon. Summer might be close in the east, but it felt far away now they were almost in the shadow of the border mountains.

For all her saddle soreness, Sabine was in no hurry to reach the high plains and the uncertainty that awaited them there. The downside to the pace, though, was that the more miles she spent riding Trout with a slack rein, the more time she had to think about Axl's mission beyond the border, how they were going to get him away from the army—and what it might mean for her if he actually found the Tenth Prophecy.

'These days are killing me,' Rhys said. 'And the nights aren't much better.'

Sabine wasn't interested in hearing yet again about his lack of nocturnal diversions, but Rhys was bored and in a sharing mood.

'There are a few pleasant distractions among the cooks, but they're three miles back and by the time they reach camp every night and finish feeding us, I'm half asleep and they're exhausted. The lovely Ravenna is always eager enough for a weary tumble, but it's never the *complete* experience I like to deliver. Don't shake your head at me. It's fine for you and Tristan. The rest of us have to take our pleasures where we can find them.'

Sabine huffed a laugh. She and Tristan might bed down beneath the same blankets each night, but there was no passion to be had in a tent shared with Axl, Rhys, Ty and three other warriors. They found privacy when they could beyond the camp and out of earshot, but their encounters were no less of a weary tumble than Rhys's and usually meant risking ant bites or bark-grazed skin. At least her lacerated palms had healed—aside from the bond mark. That never seemed to fade.

Sabine's need for those moments with Tristan was about more than desire. Without him, she was untethered; with him, there was nothing else. No heresy, no usurper and no nightmares. Increasingly, though, when they returned to their shared tent flushed and satisfied, Sabine would lie awake plagued by the knowledge his hunger for her would quickly wane when her mother's bloodline was dragged into the light. She had to tell Tristan, she knew that, but marching to war while he was at the head of Iolia's army did not seem the best time.

At the front of the column, Adward called a halt to the day's march. There were hours of daylight left and they'd need it for the remainder of the army to reach them and make camp by dark. The warriors dismounted and the squires went to work unsaddling horses and leading them to the river to drink. Sabine stretched her spine and looked for Tristan, but he was already riding off with Adward to check perimeters.

As she had every day, Sabine helped Rhys pitch their tent. In truth, she should have the rank of a squire, but none of the warriors treated her as such. Axl, who'd kept close to her all day, gathered wood and built the fire at the centre of the warriors' camp.

By the time Tristan joined them it was dark, and she and the men were seated around the brazier, honing their blades with whetstones. Tristan sought her out in the firelight as he dropped his saddle with the others.

'Drink?' Rhys offered.

Tristan held out a hand and caught the wineskin. He drained it, found Sabine again. 'Where's Axl?'

'He went with Ty to see the blacksmiths.'

Tristan frowned and Sabine saw he was tense. 'I need to speak with him. I assumed he'd be here.'

'Where are the forges set up?' she asked.

'Not far away.'

Iolia's blacksmiths worked through each night while the rest of the army slept. Every day at sunset they set up forges on wheels away from the main camp, beat farm implements into spear tips and billhooks, and hammered out arrowheads. When the camp broke at dawn, they packed up and slept on carts for the next leg of the journey, ready to do it all again the next night. It was the same for the armourers.

Sabine wiped down her sword, stood up and sheathed it. 'I'll come with you.'

'Do you two need me?' Rhys asked as if he was offering his services in inappropriate ways, when instead, Sabine realised, he was referring to the blood bond. She'd been so keen to be alone with Tristan she hadn't considered the possibility their connection might be needed.

'Thanks for the offer, cousin,' Tristan said and tossed the wineskin back to him. 'We'll muddle through.'

Rhys grinned. 'If you come across that pretty red-headed cook with the long legs and she asks after me, send her this way.'

Tristan waited for Sabine to skirt the brazier and then they walked together through the camp. Neither spoke as they made their way between clusters of tents and the smaller make-shift shelters shared by the archers. Further down the column were the Midlands forces, led by a man named Ben. Tristan had ridden some of yesterday's march with him.

Sabine heard the ring of steel on anvil in the trees away

from the main camp and Tristan led her in that direction. In the dark proper, he laced his fingers through hers.

'Has something happened?' she asked when it felt safe to do so.

'Your brother would not look me in the eye today.'

Sabine marvelled that Axl had been perfectly happy to keep secrets from the warriors when they belonged to the Stonebridge abbot, but now they were hers he was uncomfortable.

'It's the robe,' she said, trying to be dismissive. 'He's playing the part.'

Axl had swapped his green Stonebridge robe for the more common dark grey version favoured by the mendicants who served the border communities. There, the servants of Verus had no abbey or temple, relying on veteran settlers and optimati on border patrol to feed and shelter them. By the very nature of their service, they were renowned for their piety and humility.

'It's not the robe. Something is going on with him.'

He squeezed her hand and let go as they entered the blacksmith's camp. It was busy with activity, men and women hammering white-hot steel while their apprentices worked the bellows to keep the coals blazing. Even in the open night air it was hot and noisy work. Sabine had never seen so many blacksmiths in one place: blade-smiths beating out steel for swords and daggers that were handed to cutlers; village and farm smithies shaping iron into arrowheads for fletchers. The sounds and smells brought back memories of Bryn in the forge at Greenock Hill. She hoped the old slave was safe wherever he was in Amadea.

'Over there,' Sabine said, finding Axl and Ty by a forge at the far end of the cluster. The coals were contained in an iron box on wheels, and the monk and squire sat on the ground far enough away to be safe from sparks. They were boys, the pair of them, her brother not yet seventeen and the squire only fifteen, listening intently to whatever the smithy was saying between hammer strikes.

Ty saw them coming and his eyes widened with alarm. The smithy stopped and turned. His face was hidden under a full beard and soot, but there was no missing the flare of panic in his eyes. His apprentice, a girl of about ten, stopped pumping the bellows and stood stiff with fright.

Sabine's heart sank. They were Angustonians. There was no other reason for the reaction.

The smithy was wiry and loose-limbed, and he recovered quickly. He set down his hammer and the pike he'd been working and wiped his hands on his leather apron. The tunic beneath it was scorched in parts and stained with soot. He stepped forward to meet Tristan.

'Greetings, warrior. I am Galen of Whytes Hill.'

Tristan radiated fury. 'Come with me. All of you.'

He strode deeper into the trees and was swallowed by the shadows. Sabine tried to catch Axl's attention in the firelight, but her brother stood and walked with the smithy, patting the older man's arm as if in reassurance. Sabine fell into step with Ty and the young apprentice. 'This is Galen's daughter,' Ty said, as if that somehow made the situation better.

Tristan whistled sharply and they followed until they found him far enough from the forge camp to be out of earshot. The din from the anvils helped. Tristan kept his voice low anyway, forcing them to huddle close.

'Tell me this is not what it looks like.'

Axl cleared his throat. 'Galen shares the creed.'

'Are you working your way through camp looking for heretics?' Tristan's tone was dangerous. 'How did you know you could trust him?'

'We've met before,' the blacksmith said, answering for Axl. 'At Stonebridge.'

'And what purpose does it serve for you to find each other now?'

'I wanted to reassure Galen that hope was not lost,' Axl said.

Sabine's stomach dipped. 'By telling him what?'

'That Verus is guiding us.'

She wished she could see her brother because she needed to know that he hadn't mentioned their search for the Tenth Prophecy or his theory on the identity of the usurper.

'Are you trying to get yourself executed?' Tristan hissed.

'Men and women across the kingdom continue to risk their lives for the truth. They need to know that Verus has not forsaken them.'

'That's yet to be seen. Tell me neither of you brought anything incriminating with you.'

'No, Tristan, of course not.'

Sabine's brother was capable of lying when it suited him and she hoped he spoke the truth now. Surely even his faith was not such that he believed he could carry forbidden Codex translations in the king's army?

'And you, Ty,' Tristan said. 'Torvus told me about your father. You share this creed too?'

The squire hesitated. 'I don't know what I believe.'

'Then believe this: any whiff of heresy will end you. There is no need for a monk to keep company with blacksmiths on a march to war. These gatherings end now. Sweet Verus, Ty, use your head.'

The squire swallowed loud enough for Sabine to hear.

'What?' Tristan demanded, knowing the boy well enough to sense his reluctance. 'What about this situation is unclear to you?'

The squire hesitated and then said, barely above a whisper: 'Who is my enemy?'

'Anyone who attacks you,' Tristan snapped. 'I don't care

what side of the border they're from or who gives the order—if they're trying to maim or kill you, they are your enemy. Enough of this.' He stepped away from the huddle. 'You and Axl come back to camp with us, now. Make sure you bring enough arrowheads to justify the visit. And you, Galen, get back to work and keep your head down.'

There was no holding of hands on the walk back, nor any chance of Tristan and Sabine finding time alone. Back at the camp, they ate a meal of pottage mixed with salted fish brought from Iolia. Rhys read Tristan's mood and asked no questions. Sabine suspected he preferred not knowing what had happened at the forge.

When they bedded down for the night, Sabine and Tristan lay side by side, not touching. She sighed and closed her eyes, assuming Tristan was stewing over Axl's recklessness. But then he rolled over and gently turned her face to him so he could kiss her. It was slow and tender and her body turned to him like a flower to the sun, forgetting for a moment they were not alone. His hands, however, did not find their usual path. Instead, he rested his forehead against hers.

'I'm afraid,' he whispered, and those two words were like shards of ice.

'Of what?'

'That I can't keep you safe.'

'My safety is not your responsibility, it's mine.'

'I made a blood bond—'

'Three of us made that oath, Tristan. We all have responsibilities to each other.'

He kept his face close, his breath warm on her lips. 'You could have rebuilt your home by now. You'd be safe in your own bed and the underlord of your father's estate if I'd had the strength to let you go.'

'If that's what I wanted, I'd be there.' Even with her uncle dead, the thought of Greenock Hill did not call to her as home should. 'And it's not as if I'd go just because you thought it was the best place for me.'

That surprised a small laugh out of him, and he kissed her again. His hand slid to the small of her back and drew her closer. 'I'm glad we fight on the same side.'

'Me too,' Sabine said, and desperately hoped they would find nothing over the border to change that.

8

'My prophet, do you not wish to speak with the king?'

'Did I ask for Felix?'

Pellus dipped his chin, chastened. It pleased the prophet how little it took to humble his warrior.

'When and how I converse with Felix is of no concern of yours unless I deem it so.'

The glow from the sacred flames almost hid the flush in the warrior's bared neck. Unlike most warriors, he wore no beard, and his long blond hair—almost golden in this light—was pulled back in its customary neat plait.

'Of course, my prophet.'

The young priestess, Gwinny, knelt behind Pellus in the otherwise empty pavilion, her eyes downcast and her narrow shoulders hunched in reverence. She had accompanied the king and Pellus as the keeper of the flames they had carried from Augustmount. The lick of fire dwelled in a chalice the prophet himself had blessed, and only when he reached out through it, as he did now, did it grow large enough to hold his presence.

The warrior and priestess were at least forty miles from where the Thirteenth Prophet stood in the mountain temple, and yet he felt their devotion as if they were on their knees before him.

'The Iolian forces draw close.'

Pellus nodded. 'Scouts have confirmed they will reach us before nightfall tomorrow.'

The prophet had seen truly, then. It was not always so when it came to Iolia. He told Pellus what he expected of him, and the warrior again nodded, this time more slowly. Uncertain.

'Have you not bested both men who lead the Iolian contingent?'

'In the lists, yes, my prophet, but that means little on the battlefield.'

'You are my chosen warrior and now the right hand of the king. They will do as you say.'

Pellus opened his mouth, then closed it again without voicing the question. But the prophet easily sensed what troubled him. What he was ordering Pellus to do was a dangerous move, one that would inflame the rage he sensed simmering among Iolia's warriors and test Felix's trust in his prophet. But the prophet needed to know how far he could push the king before the combined Amadean forces crossed the border. It would be too late then to discover Felix harboured rebellion in his heart. In the weeks since Torvus had died, there had been no sign of it—only a dark, bitter grief—and the prophet had sensed the king's anger was towards those who had poisoned his friend's mind, not the one who had lashed him to the pyre. But the bond between Felix and Torvus had been forged in fire and blood, and the prophet understood how easily the tide of the king's sentiment might turn. It would only take a certain look in the wrong company.

'Keep a close watch on Ferugo's commanders,' he said. 'Don't hesitate to separate them if their influence stirs dissent. Your task is to bring glory to Amadea and Verus and to deliver me Xanthe's head. Nothing is more important.'

The prophet watched as Pellus fully understood what he was being asked of him. 'And what of the Stonebridge monk?'

The prophet hid his surprise. 'Gael remains in the service of the mountain temple,' he said, well aware that was not who the warrior meant.

Pellus did not press the point. If the warrior had been physically in the temple, the prophet would have delved into his mind to understand his interest in that other Stonebridge monk. The one Gael had said she'd travelled with on pilgrimage from Stonebridge Abbey, who had tarried at Iolia Castle at the overlords' request.

The monk the prophet could not see.

It unsettled him that the hidden monk was at the forefront of the warrior's mind.

'Gwinny is serving you well?' the prophet asked, changing the subject.

'Yes, my prophet. She is a great comfort to the king.'

'She serves Verus faithfully. Keep her safe and the sanctity of the pavilion intact.'

Only the king and his right-hand warrior were permitted to be alone with her, and then only in the presence of the flame. But even the most faithful of servants could be distracted so far from the mountain temple. Gwinny was young and beautiful and the prophet had chosen her for the task knowing Pellus's preferences lay elsewhere. It was unlikely the warrior would seek to seduce a servant of Verus, even one more to his taste, but the prophet knew better than to ignore the risk. He had seen how focused the warrior could be when he sought loyalty, and it was through pleasure, not pain, that he was most effective. The king was no concern at all. Felix liked his women with more curves and far less modesty.

'Go, dine with the king,' the prophet said to Pellus. 'We will speak again when the Amadean forces are assembled.'

The high temple was bathed in morning sunlight when the prophet withdrew his consciousness from the flames. The expansive floor was a sea of gold, the tiles warm beneath his bare feet. His skin tingled as it always did after communicating through the flames.

Novices had been in during the night, scrubbing soot from the sacred flames from the white marble walls. There was a time when the flames gave off no smoke, when the walls did not need washing. The prophet understood those days would not return until he cleansed the flame, and that meant cleansing the hearts of his people.

It was time to visit the Iolian overlords. He would go now, while the sacred fire was fresh on him and his powers of discernment sharp. He searched for a sense of the pair and found them in the king's library.

While the temple tiles were sun-warmed, the stone floor beyond them was cold. On the other side of the great door, he stepped into slippers for the walk to the palace. The prophet decided to take the route along the parapet rather than inside the mountain and drew on his cloak. His old bones felt the cold too easily these days. The breeze from the west was a reminder there was snow year-round in the Pyrien high country. All going to plan, the Amadean army would not need to push that far to defeat Xanthe and seize her lands.

The prophet stood for a moment to scan the plains beyond the pine forest. From his mountain-top vantage, he could see with his own eyes the gathering Amadean army, a mass of men and women, warhorses, pack animals and wagons, punctuated by tents and pavilions, all specks from this distance. Smoke trailed up from hundreds of campfires, as if Verus herself were drawing their faith to the sky. The Pyriens would see it and know they were coming. It mattered not. An army this size would crush all resistance, no matter how much warning Xanthe and her clan chiefs were given.

The prophet continued along the parapet and re-entered

the mountain at the other end, following a torch-lit passage until he reached a door used by king and prophet alone. It was made of oak and marked on both sides with the sign of the prophets, a flame seared into the wood by the sacred fire itself when the palace and temple were carved out of the mountain a thousand years ago.

The prophet pressed his hand against the image of the fire, felt the carving warm beneath his hand. The door creaked open with a sense of ceremony.

The passage beyond gave no hint it had been built from solid rock. Its walls and ceilings had been hewn straight and rendered smooth, and were painted with frescoes of Verus: the towering god appearing in the storm waist-deep in the ocean, leading her newfound children across the sea to their promised land; watching over them as they settled their animals and tilled the soil; building the great structures of Stonebridge; ascending back to the gods wrapped in storm clouds and fire; watching on as the Amadeans brought their new god to the savages in the mountains; and then raging when those same savages massacred Amadeans and defiled the temple. It was the history of Amadea and her enemy, all within twenty paces. A bare stretch of wall remained for the next great era, and the Thirteenth Prophet knew it would be his likeness that dominated the scene.

He entered the library without knocking and found the overlords of Iolia on opposite sides of the room. Dashelle sat on a couch near the fire, a small calfskin-bound book open in one hand. Ferugo stood in the doorway to the balcony, facing the high plains just as the prophet had moments ago. Dashelle gasped at the unexpected sight of the prophet and snapped the book shut. Ferugo turned and exchanged a startled glance with his wife before they both lowered themselves to their knees and bowed their heads.

'Most High Prophet,' Ferugo greeted, framed by a crisp blue sky behind him.

The prophet had meant to surprise them, so the spike of fear he felt in the room was not unusual. Even those who had nothing to hide fretted they were mistaken when they were in the presence of the one who knows all. Or, the prophet thought bitterly, the one who *had* known all and would again once Xanthe's head was at his feet.

'You may be seated.'

The prophet had not yet granted the overlords permission to look at him and so neither lifted their eyes as they returned to their feet.

Ferugo crossed the library to sit beside his wife, confused by the prophet's presence. It was understandable. The kingdom came to the prophet, not the other way around, and it was unprecedented in this generation for the prophet to meet privately with overlords without the king in attendance. The prophet could not summon overlords to the high—or low—temple without cause, and so far the sacred flames had given him no clear sign of heresy at Iolia. Yet Ferugo had been on close terms with Torvus, and he had ties to a Stonebridge monk the prophet could not see. Porplezi interference had masked the high priest Anguston's treason *and* that of the king's warrior. It was not inconceivable the Pyrien priests might also now be hiding the dark hearts of the kingdom's most powerful overlords.

To summon Ferugo and Dashelle before the sacred flame was to accuse them of a crime, and the king had forbidden it without proof or a sign in the flames. The prophet had allowed Felix to flex such authority over him, partly in deference to the throne, and partly because the prophet was not ready to bring others into the presence of the sacred flames after what had happened with Torvus. He did not like the unexpected. To say it was a surprise the flames consumed the warrior's corpse in such spectacular fashion would be an understatement.

The prophet let the silence in the king's library stretch out, allowing the tension to squeeze the overlords' hearts and fuel their uncertainty. This part of the palace extended out from the side of the mountain, and its walls were almost as tall as those in the high temple. They were lined with thousands of scrolls and books, the largest collection of writings in Amadea. On the ceiling high above, a blue-painted sky swirled with sea wrens.

The prophet gave them a moment longer and then said, 'You may look upon me.'

The overlords of Iolia raised their faces to him. Though more than a decade apart, they were a formidable pair. As with all optimati unions, theirs was arranged, but it was also a love match and the marriage had brought stability to the Iolian province. Dashelle was young, but her insight and empathy had tempered the hot-headedness that had typified Ferugo's early years. There had been no children in five years of marriage, though, which did not bode well for the bloodline.

'You honour us, my prophet,' Ferugo said.

The prophet took up a position between the couch and the balcony, and made no move to sit in one of the library's many chairs. He was not a tall man but it was not his stature that made Amadeans tremble in his presence.

'You are comfortable here in the palace?'

Ferugo was a storm of barely repressed frustration. 'I would be more comfortable sleeping on the ground with my army. I can see for myself the troops are massing near the border. Iolia will be well on the march.'

The prophet did not confirm nor contradict him. 'Do you understand why this test of your loyalty has been required?'

'Truly, I do not.' There was a short beat, in which the overlord reconsidered his answer. 'I respect that my understanding is irrelevant if this is the will of our god. We live but to serve her and her anointed servant.'

Anointed servant. It was an interesting choice of words, yet the prophet could not find fault in them.

'You are guests of the king in the royal palace. There are worst ways to prove your loyalty.'

Ferugo did not disagree, but all in the room knew that while they were not prisoners, neither were they free to leave without the king's consent.

'My prophet, do you believe we are heretics?'

Ferugo had become skilled at diplomacy in recent years, but clearly frustration and impatience had resharpened his edges. It was tempting fate and the prophet could not help but wonder if a guilty man would ask such a question of him.

The prophet brushed his consciousness across the overlords' minds, first Ferugo's and then Dashelle's, gentle enough they would not notice, and found no more hint of heresy than he had through the flames. There was great love for Verus within them and a fierce loyalty to Amadea. But he'd found the same virtues in Torvus not many moons before the warrior attempted to kidnap the king with a band of heretics.

'I trust Verus will reveal the truth to me in her time.'

The prophet had many questions—about the monk Axl, and who it was that had prematurely stole the life from Torvus with an astounding arrow shot—but to do so would reveal too much about what was hidden from him. For now, he would play the longer game.

'Your army will reach the high plains tomorrow. If your warriors obey the orders given to them and prove that Iolia continues to serve the king and our god without question, you will be free to join them across the border and your wife may return to your home.'

Ferugo absorbed his words, found the catch in them. 'Orders given to them...by the king?'

The prophet kept the smile from his voice when he said, 'By their new general. I have given your army to Pellus to lead in your absence.'

9

Tristan had always believed that marching to war under Iolia's banner would be the greatest honour of his life. How was he to know that when the time came, he wouldn't be marching towards glory. Instead, he was leading the Iolian forces onto the high plains with the sole purpose of deserting his brothers-in-arms at the earliest opportunity to help heretics find a lost prophecy written by a madman.

The forward party had arrived at the gathering site at midday and the remainder of the Iolian army streamed in across the afternoon. The routine was the same, but the mood among the infantry was heightened and jittery. Foot soldiers quickly made camp, checked weapons and ran training drills with renewed fervour.

It was hard not to be daunted by the occasion. The king's army filled the high plains, yet the Amadeans were as ants at the foot of the border ranges. The mountains crouched over them, the sheer cliffs and steep inclines even more formidable up close. The slopes were covered in granite outcrops the size of castles and forests too thick to penetrate. The only way into Pyrie was through the Blood Pass: a swathe the Amadeans had cleared two centuries ago to better access the mines and establish the veteran settlements. Even with the pass, the king's combined army would only be able to march no more than twenty horses abreast.

It was not such a risk on the border, where Amadea controlled the area, but it would make the army vulnerable further in without a plan to counter ambush.

War was barely a breath away, and Tristan still had no sense of what his role in it would be.

Over the past week, travelling at the head of the warrior cohort, there were moments when he'd almost convinced himself he didn't have to desert. His blood oath was to protect Sabine and Axl. He could achieve that by doing exactly what they had marched across the kingdom to do: go to war against Pyrie. It would prove Iolia was loyal to king, god and prophet, and surely Tristan had a better chance of keeping Axl safe in the company of warriors rather than on the run in enemy territory, being hunted by Pyriens *and* Amadeans? Barely a handful from the cohort knew the monk was from Stonebridge. They believed he'd changed into grey mendicant robes out of humility, not to hide his identity, so the risk of him being discovered was low.

Away from Iolia Castle, Tristan had almost convinced himself he could live with Ferugo's fury at his disobedience. At least the overlords of Iolia would be alive to punish him.

And yet.

No matter how many ways he plucked and picked at it, he'd promised Ferugo he would help Axl find the Tenth Prophecy. And he couldn't do that without leaving the king's army. That meant betraying the Iolian warrior cohort and the king, and the bruise of that truth spread each time he prodded it.

'Why can't we stay with the army until you have a better sense of what you need to do?' Tristan had asked Axl two nights ago.

The monk had pressed his palms together in front of his heart. 'Once we're on Pyrien soil, I'll call on the blood bond to seek our god's will. Do you want me to use unsanctified fire to do that flanked by warriors and a stone's throw from the king's pavilion?'

Tristan had ground his jaw by way of response.

Sabine had weighed in with a more practical argument. 'The warriors think Axl is here as their sacred guide. They will expect him to administer rites to them before battle. How long until word gets out you've brought a monk and Pellus comes to pay tribute?'

Rhys grunted his agreement. 'The pious prick won't be able to stay away. I guarantee he'll remember Axl from the tournament and have questions we can't answer.'

The conversation played on Tristan's mind now as he rode the full perimeter of Iolia's camp. It was not yet widely known Ferugo was absent—even his mother's man, Ben, was unaware—and the warriors in the castle cohort had agreed to keep it that way in the hope their overlord would join them before word got out.

And now they'd reached the high plains.

The royal banner flew in the midst of the massing Amadean army. Just below it flew the banner of the prophet, which could only mean Pellus shared the king's tent.

Tristan's mood had further darkened by the time he joined the warriors in the make-shift training yard marked out with stakes and ropes.

As always, Axl was out of sight. Sabine was in the thick of it, sparring with Rhys and having to frequently adapt as he changed sword hands. She fought with more confidence since she'd been training with a wider range of fighters, and even Adward lined up to test her with his good arm whenever the opportunity arose. True respect from the warriors, though, would only come after seeing her level of skill and courage in the face of the enemy. Something else he didn't want to think about.

Tristan was still watching Sabine when Ty sprinted into the training yard, openly distressed. 'The king is coming.'

Startled, Adward ordered the warriors into formation. Tristan shared an urgent glance with Sabine and she found a place deeper in the ranks.

The king and six Augustmount warriors appeared between the tents. Felix's rust-coloured hair and beard were longer and wilder than when Tristan had seen him in the mountain temple nearly a moon ago. He was dressed in bearskin vest and trousers, and only the broad gold bands on his fingers marked him as Amadea's ruler.

Striding beside him was Pellus, as if it was his rightful place. Tristan seethed at the sight. That position belonged to Torvus, and to see the prophet's attack dog in his place was a cruel twist of the blade. Pellus met his gaze, unblinking.

'Majesty,' Tristan said purposefully before dropping to one knee and bowing his head. He loathed taking a knee before Pellus. Adward and the others did likewise and Tristan was doubly relieved Sabine was not in the front ranks.

'Warriors of Iolia,' Felix said. 'Arise.'

Tristan kept his eyes on his king as he stood. 'The hearts, hands and steel of Iolia are at your service, my king.'

'Thank you, Tristan.'

He was startled the king knew his name and then understood Pellus must have told him on the walk here. So, Pellus was advisor, now, as well.

'You called in the fealty and led Iolia here?' Felix asked.

'Adward and I did, yes, sire.' Tristan nodded to the warrior at his shoulder.

This was not news to the king either. 'I trust your march from the coast was trouble-free?'

'As trouble-free as five thousand troops can be without their general.'

A tight smile from the king. Pellus did not speak and the mood was strange among the king's men at his back.

'My scouts tell me Iolia's force is as large and strong as we had hoped.'

'The people of Iolia live to serve Verus, king and prophet,' Tristan said, unease creeping in.

'That is good news. Ferugo will re-join you soon enough.' There was barely a beat before he added, 'In the meantime, you need a general. I have appointed Pellus to the post.'

Tristan stared at his king. Muted outrage rippled through the warriors behind him and Rhys hissed loud enough to draw a glance from the newly appointed general.

Adward was the first to recover. 'Sire, Ferugo has entrusted that responsibility to Tristan and me—'

'That may be so, but a two-headed beast will only tear itself apart.'

A prick of ice penetrated Tristan's rage. That sounded like something the prophet would say, which meant the prophet had seen something of them in the sacred flames. Maybe it was not Pellus after all who'd told the king who was leading Iolia's forces.

'Then appoint one of us, and the other will serve as second in command,' Adward pressed. 'Our warriors have never been led by a general not of the House of Iolia, and we now have our entire army behind us—'

'Enough!' the king said, not hiding his frustration. 'I can see this is a bitter tonic for you but if you continue to argue I will assume your dissent is a symptom of something more insidious.' He let those words settle, not needing to explain what he meant.

'Your new general will return in the morning to take up his post. Prepare your cohort and your troops. We cross the border the day after tomorrow.'

Through it all, Pellus stood silently at Felix's side, unreadable. Mostly, he watched Tristan, but his gaze occasionally shifted to Adward.

The king and his company left the Iolian camp and were barely out earshot when Rhys demanded, 'What the fuck?'

Tristan and Adward exchanged a long, bitter look. It was bad enough that anyone outside of the castle cohort had been handed Iolia's army. But Pellus? The man who had captured Torvus and escorted the overlords of Iolia to be confined in the palace? It was the most insulting choice possible. And the king well knew it.

'This is about more than a test of loyalty,' Adward said.

Warriors were gathering around them grumbling. Tristan caught a glimpse of Sabine heading into the tent to tell Axl the news. Fresh dread stirred. It would be impossible to hide Axl from Pellus or explain why a Stonebridge monk was embedded with Iolian warriors wearing the robes of a mendicant.

Adward was waiting for Tristan to respond. The older warrior rubbed his own left shoulder—another insult from Pellus.

'The king is not himself,' Tristan said, which was not far from the truth. Felix wore his grief for Torvus like a shroud.

Rhys spat on the ground. 'It's horse shit is what it is.'

Sabine took Axl with her when she left for an armour fitting. Tristan and Adward spent the next few hours going over the ledgers, making sure they were well prepared for Pellus in the morning. No doubt their *general* would have questions about supplies, weapons and troops. More than once, Tristan felt Adward watching him, a question on his lips, but the other warrior did not give it voice. Tristan had avoided outright lying to him and wanted to keep it that way.

The brazier fire had been lit and Rhys was checking the dents in his breastplate when Ty again sprinted into the clearing.

Tristan had him keeping watch in case there were more surprise visits.

'Pellus is coming,' he panted. 'Alone.' The squire was nowhere near as distressed as he'd been at the sight of the king.

Tristan bristled.

'The bastard can't wait until tomorrow?' Rhys asked, setting his armour aside.

Adward was on his feet, keen to intercept Pellus before he came too far into the Iolian camp. They had yet to break the leadership news to the wider warrior cohort.

Pellus was unsurprised by the intercept.

'Can we help you, *general*?' Adward asked.

The Augustmount warrior stopped in front of him. They were the same height, though Adward was broader in the shoulders, and older by a year or so.

'I need two warriors to go ahead into Pyrie and retrieve a high value prisoner from Mine Five.'

'What sort of prisoner?' It was Rhys who asked and Pellus answered without taking his eyes from Adward. He was yet to acknowledge Tristan or Rhys, even though they flanked the other warrior.

'An askara with unusual markings,' Pellus said. 'Wolf clan.'

Tristan sensed Rhys's interest sharpen despite himself.

'What's this got to do with Iolia?' Adward asked.

'I am sending Tristan and Rhys.'

Tristan opened his mouth but Adward spoke first. 'I will find you two others.'

Pellus raised his eyebrows at the challenge so early in his Iolian leadership.

'They will not cause you strife, Pellus. They are loyal to the king and as much it stings to have anyone but Ferugo lead us, we respect the king's orders.'

'This is not a request.'

'We march into Pyrie in two days—'

'The going will be slow once we move beyond the mines. If the weather holds, it should take these warriors no more than a week to collect the askara, deliver her to Augustmount and re-join us.'

'They can return?'

'Of course.' Pellus frowned, as if offended. 'You can do without them until then.'

'Why must it be these two?'

'They are among your best and this prisoner is a handful. She's killed one veteran and maimed two others. I need men with the skill to contain her without killing her.'

'Should I be insulted you're not sending me?' Adward asked.

'I want you as my second-in-command. You cannot possibly find that insulting.'

Adward grunted.

In any other circumstance, Tristan would be livid at the task. Instead, he understood the opportunity it offered. 'We are at the king's mercy,' he said.

Pellus shifted his attention and Tristan felt the weight of his interest. 'A wise attitude. And your cousin?'

Rhys offered a tight smile. '*I* look forward to subduing the wolf and returning to the king's army to spill Pyrien blood.'

The prophet's warrior heard the truth in Rhys's words. He turned to leave and then paused. 'I met a Stonebridge monk in Iolia. Did he complete his pilgrimage?'

Tristan's heart gave a hard thump. He frowned, feigning confusion. 'A monk?'

'We crossed paths at the healers' tent the day of our tilt. He was waiting to see you, I believe.'

'I have no idea who visited me in the tent that day.' It was the truth.

'He declined my escort to Augustmount because he'd been

asked to tarry in Iolia. I'm interested only in how long he stayed.'

Tristan felt Adward's effort *not* to look at him.

'You think we spend our time worrying about monks?' Rhys said, saving him from lying.

'It is our sacred duty to protect the servants of Verus.'

Rhys huffed out his breath as if bored. 'When do we leave to get your wolf?'

Pellus seemed to consider pressing his question but instead said, 'I will bring the veteran Caius at first light. Be ready.'

It was the second time Pellus had enquired after Axl; the first had been on the day of Torvus's execution. Tristan couldn't read the blond warrior. Did he know Sabine's brother was different? Did he know Axl was here?'

Tristan risked a glance at Rhys and saw his cousin understood what they had to do next.

They needed to get Axl out of the camp. Tonight.

10

'What are you going to tell Adward?' Sabine asked Tristan, skittish at what she had to do. She'd thought there was more time.

She and Tristan stood with their heads together, speaking quietly as Axl gathered up his bedroll. The three of them were alone for the moment in the tent. Night had fallen and the time had come.

'I'm hoping Adward will have more pressing matters to worry about than the fact Axl is elsewhere come morning.'

'Even after you openly lied to Pellus about him?'

'If Adward wanted to know, he would ask. He hasn't.'

Sabine checked her dagger and sword for the fifth time. 'What if he notices my absence?'

She knew Axl needed to be gone before Pellus returned in the morning and that she had to go with her brother and keep him safe—Pyrie was no place for an Amadean monk travelling alone in any colour of robe—yet a small part of her fretted what Adward would think of her disappearance. The warrior's respect was new and fragile and she'd hoped to keep it a while longer.

'He'll assume you've chosen me over a place in the warrior cohort and followed us to the mines. He'll get over it.' Tristan blew out his breath and rubbed her arms. Of course he understood her reticence. 'It won't matter until we see Adward again. *If* we see him again. Ready?' he asked Axl, effectively ending the conversation.

Her brother nodded, resolute. He'd interpreted the assignment as the hand of Verus and believed their god would protect them on their journey. Sabine didn't share his conviction, but the unexpected side mission was certainly a better option than crossing the border under Pellus's command.

'How do we avoid being seen?' Sabine asked.

The Blood Pass was guarded by garrison towers, and the way beyond it was lined with torches to the first mine a mile into Pyrien territory.

'You'll take the scout trail.'

Her pulse tripped. Had he forgotten she'd never been on border duty? 'Tristan, I don't know what that is.'

'I'll take you there.'

'If we're discovered at this hour it will look like desertion.'

'Then let's not get caught.'

The three of them managed to leave the tent without drawing attention and quickly moved beyond the pools of light cast by the braziers peppered through the camp. There was no tree cover on the plains and Tristan frequently checked the night sky as they walked. The blanket of stars stretched from the hills in the east until they were blotted out by the mountains. 'The moon won't be far away,' he warned. They'd need its light once they were on their way, but for now it would only expose them.

They avoided the royal enclave and skirted the Southlands troops until they were at last clear of the camped army. The inky wall of forest loomed before them and Tristan let out a short whistle. It was met with a three-note reply and Ty struck a flint to reveal his position. The squire was waiting on foot with Trout and Mina, packed and saddled.

'Mount up,' Tristan said.

'Wait.' Sabine reached for him, a mess of nerves. Regardless of which kingdom's blood pumped through her heart, there would be no safety for her or Axl in Pyrie. No guarantee this plan would work. Tristan drew her close, one hand in the small of her back, the other on the nape of her neck.

'Follow my instructions and we'll cross paths tomorrow.'

'What if something happens and you can't come?'

'I'll send Ty.'

'What if we don't make it to the meeting point?'

'This is what we came here to do, Sabine. You have to make it.' His hands were gentle, familiar, but he spoke to her as a warrior. 'There won't be askari on the track, it's too close to the border. It doesn't divide or deviate and the only place it will take you is to a higher point in the Blood Pass about five miles in. You have your sword and dagger. Don't hesitate to use them if you need to.' He brought his face closer, traced the line of her jaw with his thumb. 'You can do this.'

Tristan kissed her, even with Axl and Ty barely an arm's length away. Sabine leaned into him, pushing down the fear that fluttered whenever she thought of what might await them in Pyrie. What might await *her*. Tristan broke contact first. 'We have to go,' he whispered.

Panic flared, more insistent, but she took Trout's reins and mounted. Ty had strapped a bedroll to the front of the saddle, and she fixed her sword to it with trembling fingers. Tristan helped Axl up behind her. He took Ty with him on Mina and they rode along the face of the forest. The trees were a mass of shifting shadows that creaked and rustled beside them.

Tristan rode close enough to squeeze Sabine's knee through her trousers. 'The scout track is about a quarter of a mile away.'

Sabine squinted and found a single torchlight in the distance.

She shivered. 'Is it guarded?'

'It won't be when we get there.'

Tristan lifted his face to the sky and howled. A beat later there was an answering howl from deep in the forest.

It had to be Rhys.

'What's he going to—'

Sabine's question was cut short by a blood-curdling shriek from the trees.

'What was that?' Ty breathed, fear getting the better of him.

Tristan waited for it to come again. 'That, Ty, is the call of the yapa.'

'They're real?'

'Very much so. *That*, though, is not. Yapa have never come this far east, but everyone on border duty frets they might.'

The cry came a third time and Sabine shuddered. Real or not, the sound was bone chilling and did nothing to settle her nerves.

'Have you seen one?' Ty asked, and for a brief moment he was the curious squire Sabine had met on the road—the boy he'd been before the guilt of a dead-shot arrow stripped him of joy.

'Only once,' Tristan said. 'It was miles from the border and half-rotted, but that was enough. I have no keenness to encounter one alive.'

Sabine had only seen drawings of the bird-like creatures. They were said to be as tall as a man, and even though they had wings, they ran instead of flying. Their legs and their long neck were covered in thick, tough scales and they had sharp clawed feet large enough to grip a man's skull. Their beak was long and hooked, equally as dangerous as their claws, and a deadly spur jutted from the back of their head. The stories said that no matter which direction they slashed, they drew blood. The thought of meeting one on the dark path ahead drained the feeling from her legs.

The shriek came again.

'Will the guard go after it?' she asked, nervous for the sentry because *they* didn't know it was Rhys making that god-awful noise.

'No chance, not at night, and they won't wait around to see how close it might get.'

Sure enough, the torch was already moving away, hoof-beats carrying on the breeze.

'There's a veteran settlement half a mile ahead.' Tristan glanced at the far horizon again. 'We haven't got long.' He urged Mina into a canter, and Sabine hoped Tristan had the skill to find the scout track now the torchlight was gone. She needn't have worried. When they reined in, she caught a whiff of lingering pitch smoke from the now-departed torch and there was a break in the brambles.

Rhys emerged on the track.

'I'm almost disappointed it was that easy,' he said, patting his gelding on the neck.

'This is our path?' Axl asked. He'd been quiet until now and the waver in his voice hinted at a new uncertainty. Was he doubting the hand of Verus now that he was on the edge of the unknown? Sabine could make out the track in the gloom. It was barely wide enough for a single horse, but it was passable.

'Trout will stick to the path,' Rhys said 'The brambles and vines make it impossible for him to stray off it. And the pine trees are tall, but they're sparse further in and there's not much of a canopy. I could see well enough by starlight and you'll have more light shortly.'

The first hint of a bone-white moon had appeared over the hills in the east.

Tristan brought Mina in close until his leg crushed against Sabine's. 'There's a clearing about two miles in. Ride until you find it and take turns sleeping when you get there. Keep it short. You need to get moving again while there's still moonlight. The track joins the Blood Pass in the next valley. Get there as soon as you can. If we leave at dawn as planned we should reach you mid-morning, but if our escort wants to ride hard, it might be earlier.'

Sabine thought about all the things that could go wrong. 'Are there guards at the other end of the scout trail?'

'If there are, stay out of sight until you see us and I'll handle it.'

There was no kiss, but Tristan found her fingers and squeezed reassuringly. Her palm itched and she fleetingly wondered if the blood bond would hold once they were in Pyrie.

'Go,' Tristan said.

'Verus will guide and protect us,' Axl said. He sounded as if he was trying to convince himself as much as them.

Sabine hoped he was right because, in only a few steps, Trout carried her and Axl and their traitorous blood across the border and into enemy territory.

ENEMY
TERRITORY

II

Pellus was thinking about the Stonebridge monk again.

He was lying on his bedroll, his arm bent under his head as a pillow, watching the sacred flame. He'd taken to sleeping here rather than in the king's tent proper, finding greater comfort in the glow of his god's light. Felix had not missed his company.

It was deep into the night and the camp outside was silent. Thoughts of the monk had returned these past few weeks, worrying at Pellus like a splinter. What had happened to the one who called himself Axl? Had Tristan of Iolia lied about the boy's whereabouts? If so, why had Pellus been unable to discern it?

His new gifts did not allow him to delve into others' minds the way the prophet could, but Pellus could usually sense heightened emotion—like Adward's anger towards him. *That* was incendiary, even if the Iolian warrior hid the full heat of it. Pellus, though, had not seen signs of rebellion from any in the Iolian cohort, only wounded pride from Adward and Tristan, the two he'd bested in the lists. Disappointingly, Tristan felt he'd received a double insult in being sent to the mines. It was true that Tristan and Rhys were influential among the Iolian commanders and their absence would make Pellus's new rank easier, but he had spoken honestly about why he was sending them to retrieve the askara. The prophet wanted the Pyrien alive, and the Iolian cousins had the skills and reputation to get the task done.

So, yes, he'd sensed resentment. What he hadn't sensed was duplicity in their answers about the monk. Yet the fact remained that Axl had not completed his pilgrimage—and the prophet had known nothing of him until the other Stonebridge pilgrim, Gael, mentioned Axl and his extended stay at Iolia. All of which was at odds with the impression Axl had made on Pellus at the tournament: that he was a faith-filled servant of Verus with nothing to hide.

Across the tent, the tendril of flame flickered as if affected by a draught. Pellus blinked. It was impossible, because the sacred flame was impassive to the elements. It reacted only to the presence of the prophet, and it seemed unlikely he was about to make an appearance given Gwinny was in a deep sleep at the foot of the makeshift altar. The gold-ink glyphs on her bare scalp shone in the light of the flames, breathtaking in their beauty.

When the army was on the move, the young priestess rode in a covered wagon with the golden bowl on her lap. Each night, Pellus set up its stand in the tent he now shared with her. He would push its clawed feet into the earth to anchor it, and Gwinny would gently place the bowl atop it, nestled into fine-boned fingers beaten from iron. Whether the flame rested in human or iron hands, though, it did not flicker without the prophet's face arriving moments later.

Perhaps the flames were reacting to the closeness of Pyrie. The Codex taught that the flames of Verus refused to burn in the land of the heathens. It was why the fire on the stolen rib bone was snuffed out the instant the thieving porpleza stepped across the border two hundred years ago. The Thirteenth Prophet, though, was convinced the flame he had sanctioned and sent forth with Felix would not be extinguished. This border crossing was different—this was an invasion with the full blessing of their god.

Pellus watched the chalice and wondered if he imagined the movement.

The flame flickered again.

Gwinny remained oblivious, her breathing soft and deep, and a new awareness crept over Pellus. He was alone with the sacred fire of Verus. It thrilled and unnerved him in equal measure.

He sat up slowly, not wanting to wake the priestess, and resisted the urge to trace the pattern seared into his skin. It mapped where Verus had marked him, a finger-width scar that coiled around his chest and limbs, branding him as the prophet's warrior. That agonising encounter had been punctuated with a solitary burn in the shape of a fingerprint at his temple. He touched that scar now and the flame began to sway as if moving to music Pellus could not hear. Was the prophet reaching out? No, the prophet arrived with barely any warning and the flames swelled, not danced. This was something else.

Pellus rose to his feet, trembling. He had an irrational urge to strip naked before the altar. Would the flame touch him again without the prophet here to command it? Blessed Verus, he craved that intimacy, that sense of acceptance, even accompanied by pain. Perhaps he had been celibate too long. He missed the comforts of the flesh and would need to take a lover soon so it did not become a distraction. Was that what this was, a misdirected longing for pleasure and connection?

Tonight would be his last in Gwinny's tent. From tomorrow he would train, eat and sleep with the Iolian warriors as their general. He may never again find himself alone with the flame of Verus. He could not let the opportunity pass.

Assured Gwinny was asleep, Pellus unlaced his bearskin

vest and stepped out of his trousers. He ignored the cold air that bit at his exposed flesh and stepped closer to the altar. The golden bowl stood at chest height and he watched the flames twisting and curling at its centre. Without Pellus uttering a word, a tongue of flame rose up like a serpent and weaved its way towards his chest. He halted his breath; felt his pulse beat at his temples and in his fingertips. He held his arms out from his sides and braced for the pain. But this time the fire did not touch him. Instead, it followed the path marked on his body, travelling a finger-width above the scarred flesh, as if reacquainting itself with him. His skin goose-prickled at the warmth as it passed. The fire snaked around his chest and travelled down one leg and up the other and vined around each arm. And then it retracted to the bowl and the fire returned to stillness. It was again a single flame drawn upwards like a candle in a breathless room.

Pellus stood for a long moment, barely breathing, his entire being humming with joy. He found himself thinking about the stolen rib bone. Surely no bone from the First Prophet could be truly destroyed. Even extinguished, it was a sacred relic and needed to be found and returned to Amadea.

He exhaled and sunk to his knees, knowing the prophet must be pleased with him. Pellus had communed with the blessed god of Amadea, and there was no access to Verus without her prophet. He sat back on his heels, overwhelmed with love for his king, his prophet and his god, and filled afresh with gratitude for the opportunity the prophet had given him.

The one who had begun life as a bastard son to an absent and indifferent warrior was now Pellus of Augustmount, chosen warrior of the Thirteenth Prophet of Verus, and general of the Iolian army. He would help lead Amadea to glory in Pyrie and win his king's love and trust.

The comfort he craved settled on him, along with a certainty he would save Amadea from the darkness that threatened it. He would bring the prophet the head of the Pyrien ruler. And then he would find the monk, Axl. If the boy had since been corrupted by heretics, Pellus would bring him back from the brink. But if he was a wolf in sheep's clothing, if he'd stood before Pellus that day at Iolia with lies in heart, the warrior of the Thirteenth Prophet would end his life.

12

'You have to tell Tristan when we rejoin them.'

Axl hadn't spoken since they'd entered the path and this wasn't the conversation Sabine wanted to have. She didn't answer, instead focusing on the moonlit track in front of Trout. They'd been riding for what felt like half the night and they still hadn't found the clearing Tristan promised. Maybe they'd missed it? The going had been slower than she'd expected. She'd had to keep Trout to a walk because the way was so narrow and winding between the vine-choked scrub.

'*Sabine*,' Axl pressed in a whisper. His arms were still around her, even though the ground had momentarily flattened out.

'Tristan is a warrior, Axl. His loyalty will not be to me if he knows our blood ties us to his enemy.'

'Tristan and Rhys are not the same men we travelled with from Nominatia. They have witnessed too much, seen the power of Verus in new ways. They won't turn their backs on the blood bond, not when they've been commanded by Ferugo and Dashelle to protect us. And you know that order was not given in ignorance.'

Sabine remembered the kindness Dashelle had shown after the warehouse revelation and then how readily the overlord embraced Axl's rushed declaration that it was Sabine and not he who might be the usurper. That belief, more even than illicit Codex trafficking, was what would undo Dashelle if she failed to hide it from the prophet. Anxiety swelled for her friend and Sabine pushed it down with all the other fears clamouring at her.

'Dashelle and Ferugo are a long way from here, Axl. Once the warriors are on Pyrien soil—'

She faltered. There was a gap in the vegetation ahead and Sabine lost interest in their conversation. *Sweet Verus, let this be it.*

The space was not large, but it was the first and only break they'd seen since they'd left the high plains. There was barely enough ground to unroll their beds without Trout stepping on them, but it was flat and it would have to do. The soil had been churned up by others and there was horse dung not older than a day or so. Sabine brought Trout to a standstill and they waited, breathless, listening for movement.

'Verus watches over us, Sabine. We are safe.'

She waited a moment longer, heard nothing but the creak and sigh of the pines, and exhaled. They dismounted and Axl walked about stiffly. Sabine tore away vines to find a branch sturdy enough for tethering Trout and then unsaddled the warhorse, gave him a quick rub down and tied on a feedbag. Axl rolled out the beds and they huddled in their cloaks. A fire was not an option.

'I don't think I can sleep yet,' Axl said. 'You should rest first, Sabine, you're exhausted. I can hear it in your voice.'

Sabine knew she should argue but if there were threats ahead she'd need her reflexes sharp. 'Wake me if you hear *anything*.' She used her saddle as a pillow like she'd seen Rhys do, and listened once more for sounds in the darkness, knowing how easily they could be discovered here, but as soon as her eyes closed she sunk into oblivion—

—and jolted awake with Axl's screams in her ears and her arms on fire.

Sabine flung off her cloak, slapping at herself and twisting around frantically for her brother.

'Sabine!'

Axl clamped his arms around her and she tried to push him away—*she would set him on fire!*— but his grip tightened and now she realised he wasn't screaming, he was trying to calm her.

'Shh, shh. You're safe.' He held her with surprising strength, his fingers interlocked and his cheek pressed to her shoulder. 'Sabine, slow your breathing.'

Her breaths came in shuddery pants. The flames were gone but her skin fizzed and stung where they had been. The air tasted of pine needles and the wood-ash beaten into Axl's robes. 'How did you put the fire out?' she rasped.

'There was no fire, Sabine.'

She breathed in and out. In. Out. Breath by breath, she steadied herself. It wasn't the first time she'd had the nightmare but it had never felt so real. The forest loomed over them, threatening to suffocate her. Trout had backed away as far as his tether allowed.

'Hey, hey boy, it's all right,' she soothed. The gelding didn't believe her. He stamped a hoof and snorted and Sabine could see the whites of his eyes.

Axl unclasped his hands and sat back, keeping a light touch on her elbow. His fingers were clammy and trembling. It felt like she'd closed her eyes for only a moment but the moon had moved further west in the sky. The memory of Axl's anguish lingered and she broke into a fresh sweat. Her brother drew her cloak around her and it was enough to keep her there with him and not tumbling back into the nightmare.

'Tell me what you saw.'

She didn't want to think about it.

'Sabine, please.'

'I never *see* anything,' she said, exhaling. She touched the hilt of her dagger and then her sword, needing the comfort of iron and steel. 'I hear things. Feel them.'

Axl handed her the wineskin from his saddle pack and she took a long drink. The wine was sweet and watery and quenched a thirst she hadn't known she had. She scanned the dark shapes that ringed their camp and wished it was dawn. Only daylight would drive back the shadows lingering at the edge of her vision.

'Tell me,' Axl urged.

She tapped her sword hilt with her thumb, agitated. 'I'm in darkness. You're screaming my name. I can't see you, but I know that you're,' she hesitated before rushing on, 'burning or terrified or both. And I'm on fire. My arms and hands. That's when I wake up.'

It was a long moment before her brother spoke. 'When did the nightmares start?'

'The night we spent in the fuller's cottage.' The memory was vivid. So too was the moment that followed when the embers in the hearth inexplicably burst into a silent raging fire.

'This power you carry could spark all manner of dreams and visions until it fully manifests.'

'So which is this, a nightmare or a vision?'

Axl thought for a moment. 'The First Prophet received her power direct from Verus and wore the living fire on her skin. Anguston believed that when the usurper comes into full power, they will do the same, but I don't know if he meant that literally.'

Sabine ignored the deeper implications of what he was saying.

'But is something going to happen to you? And why show me if I can't see enough to know how to stop it?'

Axl took her hand. 'If I am to suffer, it will be the will of Verus.'

'Then Verus is cruel and I want nothing to do with any power that comes from her.'

'Sabine!' Axl said, shocked. 'There will be meaning in whatever fate is ahead of us. We will find the Tenth Prophecy, and if the first power *is* within you, you must be ready for it.'

There it was again, the hope that blinded him to everything else, even his own safety. Sabine took back her hand and returned the stopper to the wineskin. 'We need to travel further before the moon sets. You should sleep now.'

Her brother hesitated long enough for her to know he had more to say, and then he exhaled his resignation. 'Wake me when you're ready to move.'

Axl lay facing Sabine as if worried she might disappear if he put his back to her. His breathing slowly lengthened until she knew he was asleep.

If the first power is within you…

It still felt impossible. She was a murderer and an arsonist. She'd been beaten and defiled, ready to throw herself from the Stonebridge pinnacle in a fit of madness not so many moons ago. The buzzing that had driven her across the abbey field and to the training yard at Iolia barely half a moon ago was never far away. It stirred to life even as she thought about it. Her heart gave a hard thump. She had not crept into Pyrie in search of power. She had crossed the border to keep her brother safe while he searched for answers.

Nothing else, no matter what Axl believed.

13

Tristan slept fitfully and woke before dawn with dread heavy in the pit of his stomach. He roused Rhys and Ty, and they saddled the horses in silence.

Adward came to watch.

'Where's Sabine?'

Tristan shook his head and Adward didn't press the matter. Let him think what he would about the fact she wasn't here to see him off.

Rhys looked up from checking a shoe on his horse. 'You might want to tidy yourself up for our new general.' Adward wore his hair long and loose and his beard was untrimmed—unlike Pellus who somehow stayed as clean-shaven as a monk even on campaign and unfailingly kept his hair neatly plaited.

The older warrior grunted. 'I would hope the butcher of Black Valley cares more about my battle skills than how I keep my hair.'

'I think he prefers *prophet's warrior* as his title these days.'

Adward's eyes hardened. The only way Pellus had beaten him, Iolia's tilt champion, was because the prophet had strengthened his body. 'Let's hope that status proves useful on the battlefield.'

Across the yard, Ty was already mounted. The sight of the grieving king yesterday had been a form of torture for the squire and he was as restless as Tristan to get moving. Adward stepped in close to check Mina's girth. 'Is there something I should know about the monk?'

Tristan rested a hand on the mare's rump. As a squire, he'd watched a then-seventeen-year-old Adward terrorise men from across Amadea in the lists. Later, when Tristan joined the castle cohort, it was Adward who first knocked him into the dirt at training—and who first helped him up. Adward was the warrior he'd most wanted to impress on his first border tour. Tristan knew how well Ferugo loved him. The overlord might well have trusted Adward with Iolia's secret if he'd had more time.

'Are you loyal to Ferugo and Dash to death, no matter what?' Tristan asked, keeping his voice low.

'Of course I am.' Adward said it without hesitation, just as Tristan had when life was simpler.

'Then trust that it's their desire to keep Axl away from Pellus.'

Adward considered that. 'Why?'

'Does it matter?'

'It would help.' Adward waited for an answer and when none was forthcoming said, 'How do you expect me to hide him from our new general?'

As if summoned, Pellus arrived at the mounting yard and Tristan took a risk. He leaned in close and said, 'The monk won't be a problem for you.' He led Mina away to meet Pellus, hoping Adward wouldn't ask what he meant now they had an audience.

The prophet's warrior rode with a second man: the veteran they would travel with. Neither dismounted and Pellus introduced his companion as Caius. He was older than all of them, closer to thirty, burly, and missing three fingers on his right hand. He carried a sword though, so Tristan assumed he could still use it.

'I hear you need a hand to manage your wolf-clan askara?' Rhys said, deliberate in his choice of words. 'Remind me: what is it the king pays you to do up there?'

Caius gave him a flat look. 'Let's see how smart that mouth is when you've been across the border for more than a moon.'

Pellus skimmed his eyes over the three horses, his gaze landing on Ty. 'The boy stays.'

Ty stiffened in his saddle.

'He is my squire,' Tristan said.

'You have no need of one,' Pellus said. 'This task will take you five days at most.'

Tristan looked to Adward, who was clearly weighing up whether or not to get involved.

Pellus did not miss the silent exchange. 'This is the boy's first campaign, yes? Then he must cross the border with the army. You should not rob him of such a moment because you're too lazy to unsaddle your own horse.' His tone suggested jesting, but he meant what he said. 'If you are concerned your absence will mean a loss of status for him, I will take him into my own retinue.'

Tristan's mouth turned to dust. They couldn't leave the boy behind, not given his state of mind.

'Come on, Pellus,' Rhys said. 'I know he's pretty and of age, but surely you have plenty of strapping young lads to share your bed roll with?'

Caius ducked his head to hide a smirk.

'Enough,' Adward said. 'Pellus has been appointed as our general until Ferugo returns. Show some respect.'

Tristan saw that it stung Adward to acknowledge it, but Ferugo's warriors could not be seen to oppose an appointment made by the king and prophet. Pellus, impassive as always, showed no signs of insult. He nodded to Adward. 'The matter is settled.'

Ty looked to Tristan, his eyes wide and nostrils flared like a spooked colt. It wasn't Ty's fear that worried Tristan. It was the fact the boy knew truths that could get them all killed, and they were leaving him to eat, sleep and fight beside the prophet's most loyal warrior.

14

The point where the scout track met the Blood Pass was deserted. There were no guards, no scouts and no sign of the warriors. It was too early to have missed them, but Sabine's nerves were frayed regardless.

'I guess we wait,' she said.

The winding trail had brought them down to the floor of a forested valley. The ground was littered with pine needles, so Trout's progress was muffled, but the vines and shrubs had thinned out between the trees and there was little to hide them from sight. The Blood Pass itself was wide and hard packed from two centuries of traffic between Augustmount and the mines strung along this part of the border ranges. Soft morning light filtered through the branches, making the setting unexpectedly lovely.

'We need the veteran to think we came this way yesterday and spent the night here,' Sabine said and urged Trout onto the road. She pushed him to a gentle trot until she found a fallen tree that would have offered protection if they'd spent the night here. She and Axl dismounted and scuffed up the ground near the trunk, laid out their bedrolls.

'We should have a fire,' Axl suggested.

Sabine's pulse skipped, but he was right. Nobody would believe they'd spent the night here without a fire.

She gathered kindling and Axl built a fire, loading it with

larger branches in the hope they would have coals by the time the warriors and the veteran appeared. If nothing else, it was nice to be warm. They sat together in front of the flames, palms held out to soak in the comfort. Sabine kept her attention on the warmth and tried not to let her mind wander.

Axl touched her knee.' Do you want to—'

'*No,*' she said. 'I most certainly do *not*.'

'We are in Pyrie—'

'Even more reason not to tempt fate.'

'I'm not talking about the fire,' he said patiently. 'I need to ground myself.'

'Oh.' Her surprise overcame any embarrassment at misreading him. 'You remember how to do that?' They had spent so little time together since he went to Stonebridge. She'd assumed the teachings there had blotted out anything she'd taught him as a child.

His smile was sad. 'It's one of the few things we have from our mother.'

That was Sabine's fault. She'd destroyed the last of Sabella's possessions when she'd set fire to their family home. A hand-carved bird, drawings of animals on parchment, timber bowls her mother had haggled for at the market, the small knife she always carried on her belt—all of it gone.

'I could do with grounding too,' she admitted.

They dug their fingers into the cool forest dirt and Axl closed his eyes and spoke the words Sabine usually recited silently to herself.

'*No matter where I am, the sky will remain above me and the earth below. The moon will wax and wane as it always has. And I am not in this world alone.*'

His whispering filled the space between them, knitted them together in ways both familiar and new, and Sabine felt Axl's longing for the mother who had taken her last breath bringing him into the world. Sabine's own ache rose, and with it a fresher, sharper grief, because she and Axl *were* in this world alone, and no mantra would change that.

Axl opened his eyes before she could mask that particular pang. He spoke the words again, holding her gaze. 'No matter where *we* are, the sky will remain above us and the earth below. The moon will wax and wane as it always has. And *we* are not in this world alone…because we have each other,' he added.

They sat for a long moment, eyes locked.

Rather than contradict him, Sabine said, 'That's not something other Amadean mothers taught their children.'

Axl nodded. 'Because our mother was not Amadean.'

Sabine studied her brother. She had always seen Sabella in him, in the shape of his lips and the slight upturn of his nose. Their father had always said it was Sabine who took after their mother—her colouring and something about her eyes—but in the rare moments she stood before a mirror she could not see it.

'When did she teach it to you?' Axl asked.

'Not long after she knew she was carrying you.'

'Do you think…' Axl faltered and in his hesitation she saw the depths of the loss of a mother he'd never known. 'Do you think she knew she would not survive my birth?'

Sabella might very well have descended from a line of porplezi priests, so it was possible she might also have had their abilities—whatever they were. But that meant she would have had to conjure dark magic in an unsanctified fire, either in the manor house or somewhere in the hills behind it. The thought sent a shiver through Sabine.

Axl placed his palm on his chest. 'Maybe she knew we might one day discover the truth of our bloodline. Perhaps this ritual was to prepare us and remind us we would always have each other.'

Sabine considered the possibility. She'd relied on the mantra when she fled Olidus in the hope of reaching Axl at Stonebridge. There had been no logic in going to her brother—he could not have claimed the estate on her behalf or evicted their uncle—but she'd *needed* to see him. So much so, the news of his absence had driven her to the brink of madness. Only Tristan's intervention had stopped her running off the edge of the pinnacle and plummeting to a certain death.

'Or, if we found out the truth, did she want us to remember we have kin across the border?' Axl wondered.

As Sabine sat with that thorny possibility, the sound of cantering horses carried to them. She and Axl locked eyes. What if it wasn't the riders they were expecting?

The approaching horses slowed to a walk and there was a burst of a drinking song from a familiar voice.

They exhaled together. *Rhys*.

Sabine helped Axl to his feet and dusted off her hands, Pyrien soil now caked beneath her chipped fingernails. 'Ready?'

He nodded. Sabine glanced at the fire. There were barely coals but as long as the veteran didn't get too close, he might assume it had been rekindled this morning.

They waited beside Trout. The gelding stood tall, ears pricked, and he whinnied when the riders came into sight. Mina called back in response and Sabine frowned—there were three riders, not four. Even from this distance, she saw Tristan relax at the sight of her. Despite all his assurances before they'd parted company, he'd been worried. But where was Ty? The stranger riding between Tristan and Rhys was a short, stout man who was wary at the sight of her and Axl.

Her brother raised his hand in greeting.

'Are you lost, monk?' the veteran asked as he reined in.

'Not at all. I travel west to offer blessing to our beloved veterans.'

'And you?' he asked Sabine, signalling for Tristan and Rhys to stop with him. 'Why are you dressed like a warrior?'

'Because she *is* a warrior,' Tristan said. 'She may not yet be inked but she belongs to Iolia.'

'What's she doing skulking about with a monk instead of preparing for war with your army?'

'The mendicant asked for an escort,' Sabine said, answering for herself before Tristan got too carried away in her defence. 'A warrior cannot refuse such a request.'

'I'm aware of a warrior's oath, woman.' The veteran picked at something in his nose and flicked it away. Sabine realised he was missing three fingers on his right hand. 'I'm surprised your new general gave you leave from the king's army.'

Rhys snorted. 'You think Pellus would deny a request from a servant of Verus?'

The veteran looked sideways at Rhys. 'He's as pious as they say?'

'More so.'

The older man glanced at the campfire smoke rising from behind the fallen tree. 'You slept on the road last night?'

Axl nodded. 'I had intended to reach Mine Five before dark, but we did not make time as I'd hoped.'

The veteran rubbed at the stump on his hand where fingers should have been. 'Verus smiles on you today, my friend.' He sat up straighter in the saddle, finally remembering the protocol required of him. 'I am Caius, veteran of the borderlands, and we are on our way to that very mine. It would be an honour to accompany you. We could do with a change in fortune there.'

Sabine's brother bowed his head in gratitude. 'Thank you, Caius, I am Axl of...the borderlands.' He caught himself in time. 'This is Sabine of Iolia.'

Caius brazenly eyed her up and down. 'I'm sure there are

ways *you* can bless the men of the settlement, too. It's rare to find a woman who wields a sword *and* stirs a man's blood.'

She raised her eyebrows at him. 'And it is rare to find a man so quick to insult a woman who wields a sword. My blade will be happy to *bless* any man who asks for it.'

Rhys laughed, and Caius lifted his eyes from her breasts, only mildly chastened. Tristan watched on in stony silence.

'Ignore him,' Rhys said, as much to his cousin as to Sabine. 'Caius has spent too long in the company of slaves.'

Sabine kicked dirt over the fire and prepared Trout. The big gelding was unimpressed having a saddle on again so soon and pranced around until she jerked the reins and growled at him to stand still. He did as he was told, and she and Axl were soon mounted and falling in line with the riding party. She rode close enough to Tristan for them to brush knees. It was as close to a reunion as she dared.

'No squire?' she asked, trying to sound conversational.

A muscle twitched his cheek. 'Pellus did not want to deny the boy the honour of crossing the border with the army. He's taken him into his own company until we return.'

Their eyes briefly met. Sabine felt a stab of fear for the squire, and then another for the members of the blood bond if the boy's guilt overcame him.

'We'll follow the road for a few miles and then take the goat track,' Caius said. 'It gets us there in half the time if we pick up our pace. The borderlands are well patrolled. It's as safe as the pass.'

It was a mild morning and Sabine had to remind herself she was no longer in Amadea. Pyrie was feared as a place of dark magic and savages, yet there was no sense of either as they rode under a clear blue sky. Trout kept his ears relaxed, untroubled by the land beneath his hooves. As promised, Caius led them onto a narrower track and the going quickly became steeper, forcing them into single file.

The landscape changed over the next mile, pine trees thinning out to make way for rocky outcrops and moss-covered boulders taller than Trout. Up front, the veteran slowed his mount to a walk. Rhys was behind him, followed by Sabine and Axl, with Tristan bringing up the rear. Axl loosened his grip as they weaved between the great stones. To their right the mountainside rose steeply. Beyond the boulders on their left was open sky and a treacherous cliff-face passable only by the goats they'd heard bleating further below. At one point, Sabine felt an odd sensation in her ears as if they were filled with water, and then they cleared and she could hear properly again.

They kept ascending, boulders now crowding either side of the track. The monoliths loomed close. It was like being in a narrow back alley in Augustmount—

Axl grunted as his light grip was ripped away. Trout skittered sideways and Sabine twisted around to see her brother being dragged wide-eyed and kicking into a gap between the boulders, a pale hand clamped across his mouth.

Every other thought evaporated as she leapt off after her brother, further startling Trout. Tristan shouted at her but she was already scrambling between the boulders where Axl had disappeared. In her haste she'd left her sword strapped to the saddle, so she drew her dagger and ducked beneath an overhanging slab of granite, catching a flash of movement ahead. What if there was more than one attacker? She was aware of Tristan coming after her but couldn't risk slowing to wait for him. Whoever had Axl knew these mountains and if she lost them now, her brother would be gone for good. The buzzing was back in her ears, a swarm of frenzied wasps. Sabine vaulted a waist-high boulder one-handed and was almost on them. The Pyrien—it had to be a Pyrien with that white hair—was the same size as Axl but wiry. He was dragging her brother, being rough with him.

Axl was struggling against the hold when Sabine attacked. She came at the Pyrien from the side, leaping on him without breaking stride and grabbing a handful of matted hair. It hung in filthy ropes and was *spiky*, but her blood pumped so hot she barely registered the sting as she ripped his head back and drove her dagger down between his collarbone and neck. It was more luck than precision that she missed striking bone. The man—no, boy—instinctively threw an elbow and connected with her cheekbone. Pain forked through her skull but she hung on and twisted the dagger as all three of them toppled sideways. They met the ground in an untidy heap and Axl scrambled out of the way. The Pyrien grunted and tried to roll over but Sabine had clamped her legs around his hips and rolled with him, still clinging to his back.

'End him.'

Tristan was circling her, his eyes sharp.

She wrenched out the blade and stabbed the Pyrien again, this time in the jugular, and all the fight went out of him. He collapsed face-down in the dirt. Sabine pulled the knife free and readied her grip to strike again but the boy was dead. His pale blue eyes were open, his mouth slack. His blood was everywhere, on his goat-hide tunic and up his neck. In his spiky hair. Soaking into the dirt beneath him. Sabine's hands and arms were sticky with it, and she could taste it on her lips. The noise in her head quietened and all she could hear was her own ragged breathing.

Axl.

She untangled herself from the body and crawled the short distance to her brother.

'Are you hurt?'

He'd flattened his spine to a boulder and was clutching his knees to his chest. He was still in the moment, his body not yet able to let go of the terror. One hand was pressed over his chest where he wore porplezi markings. Had he expected Pyriens on this side of the border to treat him differently? She checked him over and found no injuries and then realised not all of his reaction was about the Pyrien.

She had horrified him. Again.

Tristan stopped circling, satisfied they were alone, and held out a hand. Sabine let him help her to her feet, smearing blood on his wrist where she held onto him. Her legs were uncertain and she briefly wobbled like a newborn calf.

'Who taught you *that*?' he asked, gesturing to the dead boy.

She had no answer. The savageness of it still coursed through her.

'I've never seen anything like it from an unblooded warrior,' Tristan said. 'You fought like one of them.' He took her hands and turned them over. One was covered in the blood of the dead boy, the other peppered with new punctures that were only now starting to again sting.

'The askari weave nettles into their hair before they attack,' Tristan explained. 'Another weapon.'

Sabine blinked, belatedly understanding who she had just killed. 'He's askari?'

Tristan rolled the boy over with his boot and helped himself to the axe hanging in the Pyrien's plaited belt. 'This one's an initiate. Askari don't cut their hair and his is not yet past his shoulders.' He took a closer look at her. 'You were on him like a mountain lion. Your ability to adapt...' He shook his head. 'Incredible.'

It had all happened so quickly. All that noise in her head, all the fear for Axl. Would she have done what she did if she'd known the attacker was askari, boy or not?

Tristan touched her jaw. 'I'm glad of it.'

A three-note whistle carried from the track. Tristan gave a two-note reply, reassuring Rhys the situation was under control. 'We need to move,' he said.

Sabine helped Axl to his feet. He was ashen and trembling, still finding his way back to her. Tristan took the dead initiate by the scruff of his tunic and when Sabine saw he meant to take the body with them, she led Axl ahead so he didn't have to see the dead boy slung over Tristan's shoulder.

Rhys and Caius were waiting, swords drawn.

Tristan dumped the bloodied body in the dirt. 'I thought you said this track was safe?' he accused the veteran.

Caius stared first at the body and then at the blood on Sabine's hands and face. Rhys understood first and found a cloth in his saddle pack. He tossed it to Sabine and she wiped down the blade and then her face and hands, trying to hide her shaking.

'You did this?' Caius asked her.

She sheathed the dagger, avoided looking at the subject of their conversation. 'He took my brother.'

'Your brother?'

Too late, she realised her mistake.

'Her *monk*,' Rhys said, as if her meaning was obvious. And then, to Tristan: 'What clan?' Sabine had not checked inside the askara's wrist, but Tristan must have because he answered without needing to look.

'Wolf.'

Rhys nodded, satisfied. 'Bandage that,' he said to Sabine, gesturing to her nettle-pricked left hand. The tremors were easing and Sabine needed to be back in the saddle. She couldn't bring herself to look at the corpse as she dressed her palm. She took Trout's reins from Rhys and gave Axl a boost, then mounted the gelding, aware Tristan had slung the body across

Caius's horse. A dead askara was worth a bounty and Sabine had no interest in claiming it.

'Is that usual?' Tristan asked Caius of the attack.

'On this side of the mines? I've not heard of it in my time.' The veteran sniffed the air. 'We're barely half a day's ride from the border. The promise of war has made them bold.'

Sabine and Tristan met eyes. Was this about the prisoner at the mines, or something else? Sabine gathered the reins in one hand and reached behind her for Axl. He understood what she wanted and wrapped both arms around her, locking his fingers together in a desperate grip.

'Thank you,' he whispered, and in those two words she knew he finally understood where they were.

Sabine squeezed his wrist as they moved off again.

'Don't let go.'

15

Verus, guide me.

Pellus briefly touched a fingertip to the scar at his temple as he and the Iolian squire walked to the king's pavilion. Felix had called what would be the first and only war council on the high plains, and Pellus hoped to arrive early enough to provide counsel to the king before the overlords and their generals arrived.

The squire had barely spoken since Tristan and Rhys left with the veteran at dawn. Ty had listened while the other squires explained how Pellus's armour fitted together and had helped assemble it with minimal instruction. He'd worked Pellus's warhorse with skill and stayed focused during combat training. The other squires were full of bravado, eager to elevate themselves in the hope of riding closest to Pellus on the battlefield. The Iolian boy, though, was guarded and careful not to draw attention. Pellus did not sense shyness in him, nor did he detect resentment. Perhaps it was simply Pellus's own history with the Iolian household that kept the boy distant in his company. Ty was a handsome lad, yet there were no signs he traded on it. Not that it mattered to Pellus: his preference was for men, not adolescent boys, regardless of what Rhys thought he did with his squires.

He'd opted to take Ty with him to the war council on a whim, even if he was a not a warrior prone to spontaneity. He needed the boy to understand he was not being punished, that the separation from Tristan was an opportunity to shine in the service of Verus. Pellus sensed a quiet piety in the squire and would draw him aside and speak to him more on the subject once the duties of the day were complete.

It was mid-morning and a minstrel was already roaming the camp, singing a rousing battle song to inspire the king's men. He was slender and lithe, his lute worn high as he walked between the tents singing of the glory awaiting the victorious. He spied Pellus and raised his volume, and offered a confident wink as he passed. Pellus ignored him. Willowy minstrels were not his type either.

Every provincial banner now flew on the high plains: the attacking mountain lion of the capital; the swooping eagle of Iolia; the two rearing stallions of the Southlands; the prowling bear of Paramore; and the red deer of Bloodstone in the far north. Pellus wished he had time to find a vantage point high enough to take in the sight of Amadea's entire army assembled for the first time in the kingdom's history.

As the prophet's warrior, he had the authority to enter the king's tent unannounced—though he was yet to take advantage of the privilege, knowing it would do little to endear him to Felix. Reaching the royal pavilion, he nodded for the duty guard to inform the king he had arrived. The guard disappeared, returning a few moments later to hold the entrance open for him. Pellus had to duck his head on the way in and when he straightened, he found Adward had beaten him to Felix. The pair stood in the middle of the tent by the brazier, obviously mid-conversation. Pellus hid his surprise and directed Ty to wait inside the entrance.

'Majesty.' Pellus bowed. 'Adward.'

'Pellus.' The Iolian warrior's anger at him continued to simmer.

Pellus attempted to read the mood between Adward and Felix. Had Adward gone to the king to complain about Pellus and his leadership? The idea stung, not because he expected loyalty so soon into his command, but because he expected more from a warrior of Adward's reputation.

'Do you have news from the prophet?' Felix asked, misreading his early arrival.

'The flames have slept thus far today, sire. The priestess remains on watch and will alert us if that changes.'

The king used his thumb to turn the rings on his finger, studying Pellus as he so often did. Pellus understood that to break the silence would be a sign of weakness, so he waited, unflinching under the king's scrutiny. Smoke from the brazier rose lazily between them, escaping through the opening above. Ten chairs had been draped in deer hides and assembled around the brazier—two for each of the four regional provinces and two for the king and his warrior.

The latter would once have been filled by Torvus.

Pellus would have taken the seat if he'd not been appointed as Iolia's interim general, and he couldn't help but wonder if that was why the king so easily agreed to the arrangement. For now, the chair beside Felix would remain empty.

'I received news this morning from Augustmount,' Felix said, breaking the silence. 'Word from the overlords of Iolia. I sent for Adward and Tristan to share it with them, only to discover Tristan is no longer on the high plains. Nor his cousin, for that matter.'

There was no question from the king, so Pellus did not respond. His shoulders relaxed though at the news Adward had not actively sought to undermine him.

'Did these two warriors refuse to serve you?' Felix demanded.

'No sire.'

The king had given Iolia's forces to Pellus to lead as he saw fit. He was not explaining himself unless ordered to do so.

Adward was trying to catch Ty's attention by the door, but the squire had fixed his gaze on the grass-littered carpet. The king noticed Adward's distraction.

'Something special about this boy?' he asked.

Adward raised his eyebrows at Pellus to answer.

'I have taken him into my retinue until Tristan returns.'

'He is Tristan's squire?' Felix's interest surprised Pellus. 'Step forward boy.'

The lad should have been brimming with pride at being spoken to by the king, yet he hesitated a beat before obeying.

'Ty is the best archer I've seen for a lad his age,' Adward said. 'He's got a better eye than most of the cohort.'

'Is that so?' Felix watched the boy come forward and stop a few paces away. 'I lack a good archer among my lads.'

The king had entire ranks of archers; he did not need a boy who could not yet grow a full beard. Pellus chose not to point that out.

'His colouring is fair for an Iolian. Where were you born, son?'

The squire swallowed loudly. 'My family is from the Southlands, sire.'

'How is it you're serving in the Iolian ranks?'

Ty glanced at Pellus, who nodded for him to answer.

'My father was separated from the Overlord of the Southlands in a skirmish on border patrol, sire. He finished his campaign under the banner of Ferugo of Iolia. He did not make it home and his dying wish was that I serve with the Iolian household when I came of age.' He delivered it as a story he'd told many times.

'How long have you been with the House of Iolia?'

The squire hesitated. 'Five moons, sire.'

Pellus found Adward watching him, looking for a reaction to the king's interest. Adward had striking eyes, but there was no warmth in them, certainly not for the warrior who had taken his place at the head of the Iolian army. Pellus met that gaze with cool detachment because of course he understood where this conversation was going.

Pellus was honoured to carry the prophet's mantle but, in moments like these, he wished he had gained his elevation to the king's side under different circumstances. Being sent into his confidence by the prophet was not the same as being chosen by the king, and it was inevitable Felix would find opportunities to humble the prophet's warrior. This was about to be one of them.

'Fetch your gear and your horse,' Pellus said to the squire.

Ty blinked, confused. The boy was naturally off balance: he was changing command for the second time in a day.

'Do you not want to serve your king?' Adward asked, only half-teasing.

'Yes, of course—'

'Then get your gear,' Felix said to him. 'Take your horse to my quartermaster and then return and wait outside.'

'Yes, sire.' Ty left without a sideways glance at either Adward or Pellus.

Satisfied, the king sat in the largest chair in the circle. He rested a boot on his opposite knee, drummed his fingers on the arm rest. His hair was dishevelled and the lines around his eyes were deeper. The king was yet to reach his thirtieth birthday, yet the strain of the death of his father and then that of Torvus was taking its toll.

'How are the Iolian troops?' the king asked Pellus as they waited for the parties from the Southlands, Paramore and Bloodstone.

'They're training hard and ready for battle.' It was true.

Pellus had been quietly surprised by how well Adward and Tristan had organised the Iolian army in Ferugo's absence—logistically and militarily—and kept up the spirits of peasants who'd left behind families and land that would likely succumb to the black rot in their absence. Pellus had neither family nor land to return to. He hoped this campaign might provide opportunities to change that. He remembered, then, that the king had mentioned word from Ferugo.

'I trust the message from the Iolian overlords was good news, sire?'

Felix measured him, searching as he always did for malice or ill intent in his interest. 'Ferugo and Dashelle are comfortable and in good health. The prophet has asked them to stay a while longer in the palace.'

Pellus found himself relieved Ferugo was not yet on his way. The overlord's absence gave him the opportunity to win the king's favour legitimately and prove his worth as a general. There was also still the position at the king's side to be earned, and it would be the greatest honour of his life to be offered that place.

16

The girl was skin and bone even by slave standards, all angles and hollows, moving listlessly with a sack of rocks slung across her shoulders.

Lystra was back working the boulder at the slurry pit. She kept track of the child from the corner of her eye, careful not to give away her interest. The guards watched Lystra with heightened intensity, always looking for an excuse to punish her. There were no more jokes about who would get her out of the cage. Sisto, the one with the crooked nose and quick dagger, had taken on the responsibility. The head guard might want to keep her alive for whatever reward the scourge-king paid for askari captives, but she knew he would not hesitate to add to her injuries. The fresh cuts and staff-shaped bruises were a testament to his diligence. Two days after her failed escape attempt, though, and she'd been able to move well enough to be put back to work.

The veterans had buried Matteo the same day Lystra killed him. The Amadeans were always swift to put their dead in the ground, as if the sight of a lifeless body reminded them of their own fragility. They buried him out of view from the mine, yet still within the settlement, convinced that planting corpses on Pyrien soil strengthened their claim to the mountains. The veterans lit no fire, offered no tokens, and showed no outward signs of mourning beyond bleary eyes and the stench of ale leeching from their skin. Such restraint did nothing to honour their dead. It was as meaningless as every other Amadean ritual. Lystra thought of the totems she and Dex had traded as children, the responsibilities they had pledged to each other should they die fighting. The tiny wolf he had carved had been taken from her by her captors, along with her spear and axe. She would get them back. She *would* honour him.

Beyond the slurry, the slave girl was making slow work of it from the mine entrance. Her hair was matted and her plainspun tunic filthy. Janus shadowed her with his whip. 'Move it.' He prodded her in the backside with his boot and she stumbled forward. Lystra hauled on the rope to lift the boulder, took a glance. The girl was young, less than ten at a guess, and her legs and arms were mottled with bruises. She'd been up and down the mines three times already this morning and each time she was getting slower. It was going to be a long day for the child if she survived it.

Another slave came out of the mines, a boy not much older than the girl but taller and stronger, carrying a larger load. He quickly caught up with her, though he was hardly walking with urgency.

'That one,' Janus ordered, directing the pair to Lystra's side of the pond. She'd already pounded her last load of rocks and rubble into dust.

'Hold.'

Lystra pulled the boulder up to its highest position and leaned back so her weight could keep it there. The boy slung off his bag and dropped to his hands and knees beneath the suspended rock. Hastily, he scooped the powdery dust there into the slurry. These were the moments Lystra hated most, because if her body gave out or she lost her grip on the rope, there would be Pyrien flesh and bone between granite and dirt.

'Hold,' Janus repeated, as if she needed to be told.

Done scooping, the boy emptied his bag and then the girl's in front of Lystra. The girl stood listless, eyes downcast and trembling. The boy didn't dare look up for fear of Janus's whip, but Lystra sensed his anxiety for the girl.

'Off you go.' Janus herded them back toward the mine, his whip unfurled and ready to bite. Lystra saw the welts on the back of the young ones' legs as they left. She let the boulder drop, imagining it was the veteran's head beneath it.

The morning wore on. Sisto allowed Lystra a brief respite—long enough to sit in the dirt and drain a sheepskin full of the fruit-water the Amadeans favoured—and he was ordering her back to her feet when the sound of hoofbeats carried up the valley.

The energy of the camp instantly sparked.

'Janus,' Sisto called, moving away from the slurry with purpose. 'Stay on watch.'

Lystra kept working, hiding her interest.

Haul. Thud. Haul. Thud.

Caius must have returned and had brought others with him. Were they here for her? If she was being taken for interrogation, it would mean travelling through the mountains. Another chance to escape. She strained to hear between her breaths and the thuds. The riders had stopped somewhere beyond the guard hut. Three, maybe four mounts, and at least two of them sounded heavy enough to be war horses. Janus doubled back on the track between the slurry pit and the mine entrance, eager to see the new arrivals. He fiddled with his whip handle and picked his teeth with a fingernail until the Amadeans finally appeared on foot.

There were four others with Sisto and Caius, two of them warriors. Lystra could glean enough from the corner of her eye to recognise the build and the way they moved. These were not veterans. They were loose-limbed, spines straight and whole. And they were coming for her. The flesh across Lystra's shoulders tingled as if the ink there had been touched by fire.

'You put her to work?' The voice was young and not at all like any warrior Lystra had heard.

'She's askari,' Sisto said. 'What else was I supposed to do with her?'

'She's injured.'

'And one of my men is dead, another now useless. You forget where your sympathies lie, monk.'

Monk?

Lystra's head turned mid-haul. She immediately caught herself and looked away, but not before she confirmed that a follower of the Great Pretender had crossed the border. It was the first time Lystra had seen a monk with her own eyes, and this one was either stupid or brave because the porplezi hated the Amadean servants of Verus even more than they hated warriors.

This one was barely a man, which meant he would piss himself when he was inevitably captured and the porplezi brought him before their fire. Then he would either recant the lies he had been taught or would be set alight to appease Ares for the insult.

'The wolf understands our language.'

The observation came from one of the warriors. He ambled closer. He was armed with a sword, worn low on his left hip, and he was strong from wielding it. His hair was the colour of dirty honey, grown long and worn loose. The familiar stench of the enemy carried to her: stale ale and horse sweat. She ignored him as he walked a slow circle around her. She took quick stock of the others and realised the fourth rider was a woman, armed and dressed like a warrior.

Lystra had fought and killed Amadean warrior-women and they had been taller and bulkier than this one. There was blood on her, though, so she knew something of violence. Three warriors and a monk. Strange company.

The warrior circling Lystra stopped in her line of sight. 'She's a mess,' he said to Sisto. 'Did you inflict this damage before or after you bound her?'

The guard grunted. 'She tried to escape.'

The warrior eyed Lystra with cold curiosity, one hand resting lightly on the hilt of his sword. 'That was two days ago. Some of these whip marks are older than that. Where is the honour in *this*?' The warrior gestured to the cuts on Lystra's neck, the bruises on her face, arms and legs, and then her chains.

'You come live and work in this shit-hole and see how long you cling to the notion of honour,' Caius said as he reached him. 'We're here for gold, Rhys, not glory.'

Lystra hauled up the rope and when she let the boulder drop, found the breath to threaten: 'If I were not bound, you would be lying in a pool of your own blood.' Her voice was scratchy from lack of use, her Amadean rough.

The warrior Rhys scoffed at her. 'You might find I'm a bit more trouble than these old men.'

'Unchain me. I will fight you now with my bare hands.'

He laughed without humour. 'I want you dead, wolf, make no mistake, but there would be no satisfaction killing you in the state you're in.' He stepped closer and dropped his voice. 'There would be *some* satisfaction in it, but not enough to lower myself to your level.'

She bared her teeth at him, felt her dry lips crack. 'I am ready when you run out of excuses.'

'You think honour is an excuse?' He laughed as if she'd made his point for him.

Lystra hauled up the boulder again, aware he had moved within striking range. 'You do not know the meaning of honour,' she said to keep him close.

'I know it's not butchering women and children in the streets.'

'Your *children* grow up to kill and enslave my people, and your women give birth to them—' Lystra dropped the boulder and kicked out as the rope lifted her shackled wrists. The warrior read her intent and skipped sideways, easily batting her away with a double-palm strike to her shin.

Goat rutter!

The effort had ripped open a half-healed whip bite on her upper back. She grimaced and waited for the warrior to take advantage of her hanging there at full stretch. Instead, he offered a cool gaze and lifted his eyebrows. 'I'm not taking your bait. I need you to heal so we can do this properly.'

Over at the mine entrance, Janus cracked his whip.

The bony girl had re-emerged from the mountainside, her back bent under the weight she lugged. There had been a steady supply of slaves dumping rocks but Lystra had not seen this girl since this morning. Her knees were grazed from an earlier fall and the dirt stuck to bloodied skin.

Janus shadowed her to the slurry pond. 'I said, *move.*' He flicked his wrist and the whip caught the girl on the back of a bare calf. She stumbled, not uttering a sound. Lystra grunted her fury as she hauled up the boulder, keeping an eye on the approaching child. The girl kept coming, limping now. Janus lashed her again, this time across her backside. She jerked involuntarily and the weight of the rocks dragged her to the ground. Janus growled his annoyance and stepped forward to strike her a third time when the warrior Rhys strode over and snatched the whip out of his hands.

'What the fuck?' Janus spluttered. 'Have you never seen a slave being trained?'

The warrior didn't answer and didn't hand back the whip.

'And what do you think *you're* doing?' Janus demanded.

The monk was hurrying to the girl. Janus tried to get around Rhys to intervene, but the warrior shoved him backwards.

'Touch him and we will have a serious problem.'

The warrior continued to block Janus, seemingly unfazed that the monk had squatted in the dirt beside the girl. Lystra did not look away as she kept her rhythm. Haul. Thud. Haul. Thud. The boy-monk's head was tattooed on one side with golden symbols she half-recognised, though she did not know how. His skin was soft and the fingertips on his right hand were stained with ink.

Sisto moved as if to get involved and the other, taller, warrior stopped him with an outstretched hand.

Haul. Thud. Haul. Thud.

'I mean you no harm.' The monk spoke quietly to the girl, and it took Lystra a moment to register that he did so in their tongue. The girl kept her eyes on the dirt as he helped her to her feet. He dragged the sack two steps and held it out for her to do the same, rather than attempting to lift it.

'Your stay here won't see out the day if you place slaves ahead of your own people,' Sisto said. He was angry, but not enough to test the warriors with violence. The fact the veteran—easily the best fighter among the guards—was so quick to bend to the will of warriors a decade younger said much about who wielded the power in this company.

The girl dragged the sack the rest of the way to Lystra, favouring her injured leg. The monk helped. 'How do you hope to find gold if you injure your slaves?' he asked over his shoulder.

'It's the only way they learn,' Janus said. 'And it's not like they're in short supply.'

Lystra lifted and dropped the boulder again. When she was free, she was going to cave in the guard's skull with the blunt side of her axe.

'The method works. Look at her.' Janus pointed to Lystra. 'She hates us, yet she does what she's told.'

Rhys clicked his tongue. 'You're an idiot. Every time she lifts that boulder, she's building strength. She'll use it against you again the first chance she gets.'

While they were arguing, Lystra held the boulder above the ground to give the girl time to tip out the sack. Concentrating on the task, it was a beat before she realised the monk had drifted closer, and another before she understood he was studying the parts of her tattoo visible on shoulders through her shredded tunic. She eyeballed him, panting from hoisting the boulder, and then he startled her by lifting his fingers to his chest out of sight of the others.

The girl finished her task. She took her empty sack and shuffled back in the direction she'd come. Lystra watched only the monk. He put his back to her and re-joined the warriors as if nothing had happened.

'Wolf mange,' Janus yelled. 'Get on with it.'

Lystra realised she was still suspending the boulder above the new pile of rocks. She'd forgotten to let it go. She did so now as Rhys walked by on his way back to the others. 'Don't be so quick to waste your energy,' he said, looking her dead in the eyes. 'You'll need it soon enough.'

Lystra didn't growl or bare her teeth. She was too preoccupied thinking about the signal from the monk and what it meant.

17

Tristan walked around the wagon.

'We'll need a beast to pull it,' he said. The iron cage had seen better days and he tested the gate with a quick rattle. He saw Sisto glance at the stables behind the hut where Sabine was rubbing down Mina. Annoyance flared.

'I am not hitching a wagon to a war horse.'

'I wouldn't suggest it if I had a mount to spare.'

'Find one.'

Sisto pretended to think about it. 'I may be able to spare an ox. But I'll need it back, along with the wagon.'

'My job is getting the prisoner to Augustmount. You can sort the rest out with the prophet or buy another with the gold Pellus gave you.'

Sisto huffed. 'It's a shame to waste the wagon on a single prisoner, but you won't get her there without it.' He shifted his attention to the slurry pit. 'Is he always this obsessed with askari?'

Rhys was back with the askara, the third time since their arrival, and the pair were exchanging increasingly creative insults.

'The wolf clan chief took his father's head.'

The veteran watched Rhys with new understanding. 'She's in for a tough time, then. Good.'

Tristan searched for the monk and found him sitting on

a rock not far from the mine entrance, watching the slaves come and go. Axl had been foolish to intervene with the girl earlier, but he'd promised to perform a rite of blessing before the veterans' meal tonight and it seemed to appease them.

'When will you leave?' Sisto was clearly keen to see the back of them.

'First light.'

Tristan would ride out now if he could get across the border before dark, but there were not enough hours left in the day and he was not travelling with an askari prisoner in the dark.

He should have felt vindicated being here. The mines were at the heart of Amadean life. Gold was what Amadeans lived and died for; it was central to worshipping and pleasing their god. And yet, now that he was at the source, he was utterly uninspired. Beaten children. Emaciated men and women with dead eyes and missing teeth. Amadean veterans now shells of their former selves, their honour and pride ground down by the cruelty required of them.

None of it roused even a flicker of pride for Tristan's kingdom.

And the smell was something else again.

'What is that stench?' he asked Sisto.

'That, my friend, is the smell of gold.' The veteran saw Tristan didn't find him amusing. 'We dig the rocks out of the mountain and pound them to dust. That dust goes into the slurry and our panners over there use quicksilver to draw the gold together into lumps. To get to the gold, we have to burn the quicksilver away.'

And by 'we', he meant the slaves.

'We do it further down the valley, but the wind sometimes blows this way. The guards at the burner wear masks.' He tapped his front teeth. 'We prefer to keep these.'

Tristan looked in the direction of where he'd gestured, saw

a haze of smoke through the trees. 'I thought the gold came out of the ground in great lumps?'

The veteran shook his head. 'Not for a hundred years or more.'

Tristan whistled sharply to catch Rhys's attention and nodded towards the stables. He moved in that direction himself. 'We'll join you in the hut shortly,' he said to Sisto.

'Take your time.'

Tristan caught Axl's eye, indicating he was needed too.

In the stables, the three warhorses had their heads in a feed bin. Trout was rubbed down and Mina was almost done but Rhys's gelding, Lager, was still damp where her saddle blanket had been. Tristan found another cloth and went to work.

'This place doesn't quite match the stories we've been told,' Sabine said when he joined her.

'No,' he conceded. 'It does not.'

They hadn't had a chance to talk further about the attack on the road, and he suspected her offer to rub down the horses was to cover her persistent trembling. The blood might be washed from her hands but she would feel it on her skin for days. Tristan could not shake the sight of Sabine pouncing on that askara and felling him like he was prey. He would not have believed her capable of such wild violence if he'd not seen it for himself.

Rhys smiled as he joined them. 'This is more fun than I was expecting.'

Tristan tossed the towel to him. 'Rub your horse down while we talk. Axl, come in and act like you're helping.' He checked the yard and saw Sisto had gone inside the guard hut. 'As soon as the blessing is done, Axl, you tell Sisto that you and Sabine will head out tomorrow, too. We'll leave in opposite directions, and you can double back and catch up with us.'

Axl heaved his saddle from the fence railing. His outrage

over the conditions here had drawn him out of his bruised silence. 'What is it you're planning to do with the prisoner?' Even after being snatched by an askara he could find sympathy for the enemy.

'Take her to Augustmount,' Tristan said. 'Verus willing, it will be enough to appease the prophet and we can ride back across the border with Ferugo, and Dash can go home. And then—' he raised his hand before Axl could protest—'we'll resume this folly of yours, as commanded.'

Axl hung the saddle over a peg on the wall and wiped his hands on his robes. 'We're already in Pyrie. We must perform the ritual and let Verus guide us.'

'We will, after we get Ferugo. Taking the askara to Augustmount is the quickest way to prove Iolia's loyalty and get Ferugo back at the head of his army.'

'We *cannot* deliver her to the prophet.'

Tristan glanced around, annoyed the conversation was taking so long. Sabine moved around Mina to be closer to her brother. 'Why not?' she asked him.

'She can take us to the Tenth Prophecy.'

Rhys's head appeared from behind Lager. 'The wolf? You said nobody knows where it is.'

'That's not necessarily true on this side of the border.' Axl shot an apologetic look at Sabine. This was news to her, too. 'The Tenth Prophet received his revelation in Pyrie and wrote it here. He understood it would not be well received in Augustmount, so he made a copy—'

'Yeah, yeah' Rhys interrupted. 'It was the copy that was destroyed in Amadea and the original is here somewhere. You've told us the story, Axl. What's it got to do with the askari out there?'

'Anguston taught that the Tenth Prophet not only hid the original prophecy here, but that he protected it somehow—'

Rhys's eyes hardened. 'You mean with dark magic?'

Axl glanced at Sabine and rushed on. 'The Tenth Prophet could only have created that protection with a porpleza, or it would not have held.'

'Anguston believed that?' Rhys shook his head. 'Then the high priest was as deluded as the mad prophet.'

'Rhys,' Axl said, exasperated. 'It means the porplezi will know how to break the ward. They've kept and protected that secret for two hundred years.' The monk tilted his head in the direction of the slurry pit. 'The askara wears *something* on her shoulders. I believe Verus brought us to this awful place for a reason, and that ink is important.'

'It could be anything.'

'Have you ever seen a tattoo on a Pyrien other than a clan mark on their wrist?'

Sabine could hear her brother's growing conviction. 'But, Axl,' she said, 'if what you say is true, the Pyriens would have accessed the Tenth Prophecy long before now.'

'Yet they haven't. We would know if they had.'

We. The Angustonian heretics.

'I need to understand what those marks are and what they mean.'

Tristan moved closer to Axl. 'You want us to leave here with an askara in a wagon cell and never arrive at Augustmount?' he hissed. 'You might as well sign the death warrant for Ferugo and my sister.'

'How is that any different from deserting the army?' Axl demanded, and then swallowed hard, immediately aware he'd misstepped. He took a shaky breath, tried again. 'Tristan, Verus has brought us to the askara and if I'm right, it stands to reason she knows where the prophecy is hidden. This is the will of our god.'

'No.' Tristan said, his jaw tight. 'If Verus has led us to her, it's to free my lord and my sister.' He did not look at Sabine, afraid she might side with her brother.

'We need this askara,' Axl said. 'She's the reason Ferugo sent us here.'

Tristan closed the space between them. 'Are you telling me Ferugo knew about her?'

'No...not her specifically, only that someone in Pyrie would have answers. She's who we came to find, Tristan—'

'You said the blood bond and your fire ritual would guide you. Shouldn't you at least consult Verus before deciding your search is already done?' He knew he was standing over the monk. He didn't care. 'You can do it just as easily heading east as you can heading west.'

Axl took a nervous breath and steeled himself. 'What was Ferugo's last command to you?'

Tristan wished he didn't remember the words so clearly, spoken in haste while Pellus waited outside in the street.

Protect those to whom you have bound yourself. Let them guide you when the road becomes dark.

The road was not yet so dark he needed to take orders from a monk.

Tristan looked to Rhys.

'It's your call,' Rhys said.

Irritation flared at the ease with which his cousin deflected responsibility.

'Why is it always up to me?'

Rhys widened his eyes in mock disbelief. 'Because you're the responsible one, remember? You always take charge. It's what you do. It's not my fault you don't like the choices this time.'

The fact he was right only rankled Tristan further.

'The wolf stays our prisoner though, either way?' Rhys added.

Tristan ignored him. He risked a glance at Sabine, but

instead of giving him a sense of her opinion, she nodded at something behind him. 'Caius is coming.'

'Tristan...' Axl was pushing for an answer before the veteran was in earshot.

Tristan had no idea what he was supposed to do and that unknowing muddied his thoughts.

'Let me sleep on it.'

18

Dashelle woke alone.

Still half-asleep, she felt Ferugo's side of the bed and found it cold. She sat upright, panic coursing through her.

'I'm here, Dash.'

The fire had burned low and the room was dark and chilly. He was in the doorway to the balcony, silhouetted by the full moon hanging low in the western sky.

'I didn't mean to wake you,' he said.

Her heart gave a painful thump and settled back in her chest. Fully awake now, she found her boots by the bed, wrapped herself in a blanket and joined her husband. Ferugo drew her to him and kissed the top of her head. 'I couldn't sleep.'

He'd been watching the high plains again, anxious about how their warriors were responding to Pellus and frustrated he couldn't be in his rightful place to lead Iolia's troops. The plains were peppered with pinpricks of flickering light from campfires, soon to be extinguished when the Amadean army mobilised and crossed the border.

Dashelle was desperate to tell Ferugo about Sabine. She'd been biding her time, needing to confirm their conversations remained hidden from the prophet. The fact they were alive meant the prophet had no evidence they'd been trafficking Codex transcriptions for three years. But they were on the sacred mountain, closer to the temple and the flames he commanded, and Dashelle was wary of dropping her guard. She'd tested the waters on their first night, whispering the news about Sabine and Axl's bloodline. She mentioned no names, only that it confirmed what they'd long suspected: that the usurper would have a connection to Pyrie. There had been no repercussions, but Ferugo had urged her not to speak of it further.

The moon had waxed and waned since then, and she had to risk telling him the rest of it. Ferugo needed to know the fullness of what Axl now believed and Dashelle needed to talk to her husband about what it all meant. It was the way of their marriage. From the early days of their courting, they had discussed everything from Augustmount politics to whose mother was more formidable. When Dashelle had become Ferugo's wife, he'd elevated her to his own status. They were not overlord and wife. They were *overlords* together, and he had made sure that standing was widely understood and acknowledged, especially when she was yet to produce an heir. Ferugo had known that in giving her status he also put her at risk. That status was the reason they were both here in Augustmount, prisoners in all but name.

'Ferugo.'

He was moving his hand in comforting circles between her shoulders. 'Yes, my love.'

'Before we left the house, our friend shared something with me.'

'Dash—'

'The gifts we believe he's bearing may, in fact, be the property of his sister.'

Ferugo's hand fell still. He considered the news for a long moment. 'Why do you think that?'

'Our friend's own conviction and the evidence.' She'd told Ferugo about the flames in the warehouse the night it happened.

But until Axl reframed that moment, Dashelle, like everyone else, had assumed it was the work of the blood bond.

Her husband took a long moment to absorb the idea. 'What does *she* say?'

'I only had a moment with her. I don't think she believes it yet.'

'Do you?'

Dashelle had replayed the moment in the wool store in her mind repeatedly: Sabine railing against her uncle, thrashing to avoid his touch, and then the flames from the torches arcing past him and burning her binds away. Devouring them without harming her skin.

'Yes. That night...' She stopped herself before she said too much.

Ferugo understood. 'Does anyone else know?'

He meant Tristan and Rhys. 'Not when we last spoke. I'm not sure if that's since changed.'

'They are blood-bonded to her, they should know—'

He was interrupted by two light raps on the door. Polite, tentative, and completely unexpected at this hour. They turned towards the door together.

'If we were being arrested there would be no warning,' Ferugo said to reassure her, and then, louder: 'Enter.'

The door opened and soft light spilled in.

'Please excuse the intrusion.'

The visitor was so unexpected it took Dashelle a moment to realise she recognised the tall figure.

'Gael?'

'My lady. My lord.' The monk bowed. The sight of Gael brought a strange quiver in Dashelle's chest that at first she didn't understand. Ferugo had not moved from the balcony and she resisted her natural response to go to her guest in greeting.

'We always welcome a visit from a servant of Verus,' her husband said. 'It is unusual, is it not, for a pilgrim to visit a guest of the king, and at such an hour?'

Gael lifted her lamp and came further into the room until its light reached them. 'We live in unusual times, my lord,' she said. 'The Most High Prophet has bid me come to you, as a friend and familiar face.'

The sensation came again, like a plucked string, and now Dashelle understood: Gael had been on pilgrimage with Axl. She would know by now he did not complete the journey alone as promised. Gael also knew Axl was travelling with his sister.

'Before dawn?' Ferugo pressed.

Gael shifted her weight. She was as restless as a novice. Dashelle had always thought her unusually built for a servant of Verus and she seemed even more imposing in a room filled with shadows.

'I have been on vigil since the midnight service in the lower temple. The prophet sensed you were awake and restless and came to me in my meditation; bade me come to you.'

Dashelle flashed hot, then cold.

'It is understandable,' the monk continued, her gaze fixed to the left of them. 'It would be difficult for you to be separated from your warriors and your army.'

'We do as our prophet and king bid,' Ferugo said, and the words sounded as hollow as he meant them.

The monk changed the lantern to her other hand. 'Shall I send for warmed mead? Would that help you sleep?'

'A kind offer but unnecessary.'

Silence settled, strained and heavy with uncertainty. Dashelle's heart thudded against her ribs. She made no move to light candles. It was best for the monk to not see the tension she could feel in her face.

Gael cleared her throat. 'I wanted to thank you again for

your hospitality at Iolia. You were most generous hosts for Axl and myself.'

'Pilgrims are always welcome in our home, especially those from Stonebridge,' Ferugo said.

'I trust your extended time with Axl brought the guidance you sought?'

'Very much so. It was timely, given the events that would follow.'

Ferugo made no comment on the fact Gael had been among the monks to light the pyre beneath Torvus.

'Axl is well?' Ferugo asked.

Gael blinked. She thought for a long moment. 'I have no reason to believe otherwise.'

The monk and Ferugo watched each other, both readying for a question that would test their willingness to outright lie. The silence stretched out. It went against every instinct in Dashelle to not rescue Gael from the awkwardness of the moment.

'You are sure there is nothing I can send for, for either of you?'

'Thank you, Gael, no. There are enough hours of the night left that we should attempt to find sleep again.'

The monk nodded, relieved. 'That is wise, my lord. I shall leave you to it then.'

'Thank you,' Dashelle said before she could help herself. 'We appreciate the visit.'

The monk touched her inked scalp self-consciously as if to remind herself she was a servant of Verus and then turned and left the room, taking her pool of light with her.

Ferugo exhaled. 'If the prophet could see us in the flames, he would not need to send his servant.'

'He felt we were restless, though. We must be vigilant.'

'Come.' He led her to the bed and they climbed in together. Dashelle found his face in the dark, felt an overwhelming rush of love and longing for him. She kissed him deeply, her hands sliding under his shirt to caress the skin she knew as well as her own.

Ferugo murmured his approval and gently pulled her on top of him.

'Let's be restless in a way that will make the Most High Prophet blush.'

19

Lystra was awake when she saw it. Or at least she thought she saw something. The flickering light was so fleeting she might have imagined it.

She pressed her face to the cage bars, straining to make out the gouged mountainside and the patch of remnant forest on the ridge. The moon was hidden behind cloud, drawing down the sky and blanketing the world in darkness. Lystra shivered. She was wrapped in a horse-hair blanket that stank of stale sweat and dried blood and did little to warm her aching bones.

There. Her heart gave a hard thud. That had to be real.

She'd known that if askari came for her it would be under the cover of night. The mine camp was so bereft of trees there was no chance of a stealth attack in daylight. Even at night it was fraught, given the stretch of bare ground between the ridge line and the camp—and if her people made it this close to the mines they'd already evaded sentinel towers deeper in the valley. But askari would not bring light, which could only mean they had a porpleza in their company because *they* went nowhere without their pyr staves. Lystra lifted her head and sniffed the breeze. It blew towards the mountain not away from it, offering no answers.

Sisto, Janus and Caius patrolled the torch-lit perimeter a hundred paces apart. Ram-horns hung on their belts to raise the alarm when needed, but the veterans would not be expecting an attack, not this close to the border and not with the Amadean army on the march.

Caius approached. Lystra curled back up into a ball and feigned sleep, keeping one eye open. He stifled a yawn as he passed and continued on his way. She would be unwatched now until Janus limped by. Lystra sat up and scanned the forest, trying to locate the light—

Movement by the guard hut snagged her attention. Someone was heading her way, staying out of the torchlight. Lystra strained her eyes to see who it was. The figure was narrow in the shoulders and moved like a nervous hare. *Fool*. It could only be the monk.

She tracked his dark form, and when he stopped well short of the pool of light around her cage, she realised he did not want to be seen by the guards.

'Did you see?' he whispered. 'They come in the trees.' He said it in Pyrien and his voice shook. 'You must warn them not to kill the warriors in my company.'

Lystra growled. What did she care who her people slaughtered? Her blood called for vengeance. As soon as she was out of this cage she would join in with the killing.

'If they die,' the monk rushed on, 'all hope is lost for your people.'

She spat her disbelief.

'I speak the truth. I am not your enemy.'

'Now I *know* you are lying.'

'You have seen for yourself.'

'It means nothing.' He might know the sign of the porplezi, might show compassion to a slave girl, but he belonged to the Great Pretender. Who knew what deceptions an Amadean was capable of?

'Please. The warriors who travel with me are the key to your future.' He was panicking. Of course he was. This camp of desecration was about to be swarmed with askari and none but her own kind would survive.

'I cannot stop what is coming.'

The monk shifted his weight and she sensed he was peering into the darkness. 'Then I must convince them myself.'

'You will die.'

'If that is the will of Verus, so be it.' With a rustle of robes, he was gone.

Lystra squinted to see him but he had melted into the night. The breeze meant she could not hear his footsteps and track his progress. She heard Janus limping closer, though, and had enough time to lay back down and steady her breathing before he passed, trying to mask the eager beat of her heart against her ribs.

*

Sabine jolted awake to the sounds of horn blasts.

Tristan and Rhys jammed on their boots and she fumbled to do the same with her bandaged hand.

'What's happening?' She was light-headed from sitting up so quickly.

'Trouble,' Tristan said. 'Where's Axl?'

The bunk room the four of them shared was lit by the guttering torch outside the window and her brother's bunk was unoccupied. Sabine's insides knotted. 'I didn't hear him leave.'

She followed the warriors' lead and strapped on her sword on her way out the door. Tristan placed his hand on the nape of her neck as they stepped into the night. 'Whatever this is, you've trained for it.' He was focused, ready for a fight. Sabine drew her blade and they ran for the mine, rounding the corner of the guard hut—

Her heart faltered at what was unfolding at the camp perimeter.

Sisto, Janus and Caius stood on one side of the torches, brandishing weapons. Opposite them were four wild-looking Pyriens with ropey hair, dressed in wolf-pelts and woollen leggings and armed with axes and spears. It wasn't the sight of the askari that had seized Sabine's heart, though: it was that the tallest of them had her brother in front of him, a dagger pressed to his throat.

'Axl!' Sabine ran two more steps before Tristan pulled her up by her elbow. 'Wait,' he growled as the three of them skidded to a stop. 'We don't know what this is yet.'

She felt the buzzing before she heard it building in her ears; the overwhelming urge to *do* something.

'Stay there or he bleeds.' The newcomer's Amadean was heavily accented but there was no mistaking the threat.

'Sabine,' Axl managed, careful not to move too much. His eyes were locked on hers, desperate. 'Trust me.'

She heard Tristan suck in his breath between his teeth. *What had Axl done?*

The wolf-clan askara rattled her cage and yelled at the other askari. Sabine had learned enough Pyrien from the blacksmith Bryn to understand she wanted the askari to kill every last one of them, starting with Sabine's brother. Janus kicked the bars to silence her and when she snarled at him it was more wolf than woman. The slaves pressed against their gate, jostling to watch the stand-off.

'You're outnumbered,' Sisto said to the Pyriens. He gestured toward the sound of running boots and Sabine cast an urgent glance over her shoulder to see Virgil and three other guards on their way. Numbers were irrelevant. If fighting broke out, Axl would be dead before anyone could reach him.

'What do you want?' Tristan asked.

The askara threatening Axl shifted his attention to Tristan, unblinking. He seemed at war with himself and Sabine understood that he truly wanted to slit her brother's throat. There was a reason why he hadn't. The askara looked from Tristan to Sabine and then Rhys, his eyes cold with hatred in the guttering torchlight. At last he blinked, turned his head and whistled sharply. For a moment, nothing happened and then a light appeared in the trees on the ridge and began moving downhill.

'Reinforcements,' Janus said to Sisto, urgent. 'We need to end this, now.'

'Move,' the askara urged. 'And the monk *will* bleed.'

Sabine looked from Axl to Sisto. Was the veteran willing to risk her brother's life? The buzz in her head was so loud she could barely think. 'What do we do?' she asked Tristan. He still held her by the elbow, frustration radiating from him.

'It's not more askari,' he said.

'No,' Rhys agreed. 'It's worse.'

The light was closer now, less than fifty paces away. It was an orb, perfectly round like a tiny sun, and about the size of a man's skull. It glowed pale orange, with a lick of blood-red swirling at its centre. It gave off no sparks and no smoke and bobbed over a long stave carried by a hooded figure. There was no visible means of attachment. The orb threw off enough light to reveal a shorter hooded figure accompanying the stave bearer.

'Who are they?' Sabine whispered, knowing the answer but needing to hear it. Tristan's grip on her tightened and the hairs on the back of her neck lifted.

'Porplezi.'

As the hooded pair reached the torchlight, Sabine saw the light wielder wore a robe covered in midnight-blue feathers so glossy they looked wet in the firelight. Their companion wore mottled grey fledgling feathers, with a leather bag slung across their shoulders and a rolled mat strapped to their back.

Here they were, the practitioners of blasphemous dark magic.

Her mother's people.

The knot tightened in Sabine's belly. The slaves were deathly still in their hut, and even the wolf-clan askara had quietened in her cage. The mine veterans, though, grew increasingly agitated, hissing and muttering and urging Sisto to act. Their restlessness frayed Sabine's nerves.

The askara pressed the dagger blade into her brother's throat and Axl grit his teeth as it dug into his flesh. Blood dribbled down his neck, his eyes wide with understanding at how close he was to death. There was fire within reach if Sabine knew how to use it—if she *could* use it—but these were porplezi. Even if she was able to command the flame, she would be a flea against mountain lions.

'On your knees.'

The voice that came out from under the hood gave no hint of gender or age, only that its owner was a Pyrien who held no fear in the moment. Nobody moved. Sabine's legs shook, threatening to betray her.

'On your knees, *scourge*, or the monk dies right now in front of you.'

20

Tristan's heart thrashed in his chest. He knew a dozen ways to kill a man, but he didn't know how to fight dark magic. He'd never seen porplezi, knew them only by terrifying reputation, and his dread stoked an irrational urge to charge the priest and see if he could snap their neck before he himself was killed. Tristan would rather die fighting than be cursed with sickness or madness—but what then of Sabine? And what would happen to Ferugo and Dash if he couldn't get their prisoner to Augustmount?

Sisto and the veterans were already on their knees, trembling and speechless in the presence of an enemy they too had most likely only heard of. Tristan, Rhys and Sabine followed their lead.

The flames of the torches blurred and the night sky pressed down. It was unimaginable the Pyrien priests would come this close to the border and risk capture. The last time porplezi were known to have ventured this far west was two centuries ago, when they snatched the First Prophet's rib bone from the sacred flames in Augustmount.

The askara was making demands in her own language and whatever the tall porpleza said in reply infuriated her. She gripped the cage bars and raised her voice, but when the priest barked a single word at her, she sat back on her heels as if slapped.

The priest turned their hooded head towards Axl and continued to speak in Amadean. 'These warriors are the bonded three?'

'Yes,' Axl managed.

Tristan locked eyes with the monk. Had he betrayed them?

The priest pushed back their hood and for the first time in his life, Tristan saw Amadea's *true* enemy. Xanthe and her askari might be brutal, but without the priests and their blasphemous fires, there was nothing that could not be defeated in these mountains with enough arrows and steel.

The porpleza's age was hard to tell because their long face was painted with wide black stripes. There was a sharpness to their jaw and cheek bones, as if they had been starved, and their moon-white hair was not worn in long ropes in the way of the askari, but wound up around their head, matted and woven like a bird's nest. The eyes were the worst, though. At first, Tristan thought they were on fire, but then he realised that, no, their irises were so dark they reflected the burning orb.

'We came for the guardian and our people,' the porpleza said. 'We will leave with the monk and you three as well.'

'God's arse you will,' Rhys said. His voice was rough with rage or fear or both.

The porpleza raised their arm as if Rhys hadn't spoken, and deliberately pointed a bony finger at Tristan, then Rhys and then Sabine, and clicked their tongue three times.

For a long, fraught moment nothing happened.

And then the breeze carried the crunch of gravel shifting under sprinting feet, a heartbeat before half a dozen more askari appeared out of the darkness. Sisto and his men leapt up instinctively and rushed to meet them.

'Axl!' Sabine screamed and Tristan and Rhys were already on their feet—they would be slaughtered if they didn't move—and took three steps before Tristan felt a sharp sensation in the side of his neck. A sting, as if from a bee or a wasp. He stumbled as something hissed past him and lodged in Rhys's neck. His cousin spun, confused, slapping himself, but his knees were already buckling.

This was new.

Tristan took two more steps before his own legs gave out and he fell sideways, dropping his sword as he went. His hip and shoulder hit the ground, hard. Tingling warmth spread across his chest and shoulders. Confused, he tried to roll over, but his arms and legs were dead weights. Boots and steel rushed past him and there were sounds of shouting and fighting all around. The warmth was in his legs now. He couldn't get up. His heart hammered. Rhys was on the ground beside him, eyes wide with panic.

Sabine.

With enormous effort, Tristan rocked himself over to see Sabine fending off an axe-wielding askara. She too had been shot with whatever had felled him and Rhys—the dart stuck from her neck—but she was at least on her feet. As he watched, though, he could see her reactions slowing. And then she stumbled, and the Pyrien tackled her to the dirt.

'Sabine!' Tristan managed to form her name, even though he could no longer feel his face, but the askara did not bring his axe down on her neck. Instead, he kicked away her dropped sword, rolled her onto her stomach and pinned her hands behind her back. The Pyrien now sat astride her, panting.

Sabine was within reaching distance of Tristan, facing him, confused and afraid, and there was not a thing he could do to help her.

21

'Release me!' Lystra demanded.

The oracle ignored her. He stood as stone with the acolyte beside him, both protected by the two askari who weren't butchering mine guards. The monk was still being used as a shield, wall-eyed and panting with fear.

'They are *mine* to kill,' she insisted.

Perhaps they were saving the warriors for her, but Lystra's blood howled for the guards. It was they who had whipped and beaten her, caged her like a beast; they who'd ground down the mine slaves for no other reason than for being Pyrien. In a moment, though, there would be none left alive to punish. The crippled veterans were no match for askari. The warriors might have been, but they'd been taken down with darts. There was some satisfaction in that. Whatever the oracle had in store, it would be a slower death than by axe or spear.

Lystra wondered what the monk had said to keep the warriors alive. He'd somehow survived his encounter with the porpleza and he now watched on in horror as askari cut down the mine scourge with ruthless efficiency.

'Oracle!' Lystra shook the bars of her cage. She had been told to wait, but the fight was on and she needed to be part of it. 'Free me!'

The mine slaves rattled their gate, chanting Xanthe's eternal command to her people:

'Death to the maggots who feast on our flesh.
'Death to the invaders who give us no rest.
'Drive them back to the sea, let them drown in the cold.
'Take back our mountains, our children, our gold.'

Their voices grew louder and more confident as each Amadean fell. By the time they had recited the words three times the veterans were slain. Lystra sat back on her haunches, furious at the insult of it. The oracle held up a hand and the slaves fell quiet. The askari fell in line behind him, barely out of breath.

'Guardian, I will release you on the condition you do not harm the warriors.'

'What happened to "Death to the maggots who feast on our flesh"?'

The oracle's eyes hardened. 'You question me?'

Lystra turned on her haunches and lifted her hair to reveal her flayed skin. 'I have earned the right to ask why you would show mercy to our enemy.'

That gave the oracle pause. 'Are the symbols intact?'

Were they, after Janus's whip?

'Yes,' she said, hoping it was the truth and well aware she was of less value to the oracle and Xanthe if they weren't.

'Where are your weapons?'

Lystra tilted her head in the direction of the veteran hut.

'Fetch them,' the oracle ordered one of his askari, and said to another, 'Release the guardian.'

The first sprinted off and the other wiped clean his axe and used it to smash open Lystra's cage. None of the askari here were familiar to Lystra, but she would forever be in their debt. The oracle turned to the slaves. 'Beloved of our gods, you will soon be free. First, I must deal with our hostages and I need their full attention.'

Lystra crawled from the cage on stiff legs and stood to her

full height, giving no hint of how much effort it took. The askara who'd freed her stepped back to give her space. Only now did Lystra realise the magnitude of what had happened. The oracle—who had long ago forsaken the comforts of his home to live in the mountains—had dared come to the border. For her.

The oracle was watching the spared Amadeans now with something close to hunger in his eyes. 'You,' he said to the monk. 'Sit the warriors so they can see me.'

The monk was shoved towards them. All three lay in the dirt, motionless except for flitting eyes and heaving chests. Lystra watched as the monk struggled to lift the ink-bare warrior into a sitting position. He hooked his arms under hers, clamped his hands together across her chest, and dragged her to the veteran hut. He whispered urgently to her and the words were stolen by the breeze. The oracle was unconcerned. The monk propped her against the wall and stood for a moment to catch his breath. He was not built for this. At this rate, the poison would wear off before he got them all upright.

Next, he tried to lift the taller of the inked warriors but his hands and body were too soft and the weight was beyond him. At the oracle's signal, an initiate with matted hair barely to her shoulders moved in to help. She was not as gentle as the monk had been, dumping the taller warrior against the wall hard enough to knock his head on the timber. He sneered and his nostrils flared but he could not spit out the curse on his tongue.

The first askara returned then and presented Lystra with her weapons without making eye contact. 'Your fight continues, Lystra, Guardian of the True Path'.

Lystra nodded, long weary of the title.

She hooked her axe through her belt and took up her spear. She walked on aching legs to stand over the honey-haired vermin Rhys, the one who had mocked her and promised violence when she was fit for it. He glared up at her, spittle pooling in the corner of his mouth. She used her boot to lift his face so he could see her fully. 'I look forward to fighting you, scourge.' She smiled at him as he was hauled upright, not caring that the effort again cracked her split lip.

The monk huddled beside the ink-bare warrior and took her paralysed hand in his. The oracle watched and then met Lystra's gaze. 'What is your question for me, guardian?'

Lystra blinked, surprised.

'Speak the invaders tongue when you ask it.'

Lystra stretched her neck from one shoulder to the other and decided not to ask why, in case that counted as her question. Instead she asked, 'Why may I not bleed the life from these four?'

The pyr atop the porpleza's stave flared bright and the oracle bowed his head as if acknowledging permission only he could hear.

'Because, guardian, this monk may be the one promised to us, and these warriors are bonded to each other—and to him.'

Lystra laughed her disbelief. The monk had told a dangerous lie to save his skin. 'You have been deceived, oracle. The usurper will come to us in the flesh of a mighty leader. This one is a weedling!'

'The usurper will wield power that requires strength of mind and spirit, not muscle. The monk before you walked the fire at Stonebridge *and* he wears our mark. No other has done both.'

It was an effort not to revert to her own tongue. 'Have you seen this mark?'

'My acolyte did the work by his own hand.' The oracle nodded at his companion, who remained hidden beneath their hood. Lystra had heard the rumours but had not laid eyes on the oracle's pet until now.

'Not so many seasons ago, your acolyte was a servant of the Great Pretender. There is deception here.'

'See for yourself.' The oracle caught the monk's gaze. 'Show her.'

The monk shot a nervous glance at the inked warrior beside him—not Rhys, the taller one—and faltered. Lystra clicked her tongue and held out her hand for the dagger that had been at the monk's throat moments ago. The boy shrank from her as she knelt and grabbed the cowl of his robe. She slit the fabric, then put the blade between her teeth and tore a hole with her bare hands. There was *something* on his skin, but she couldn't tell what in the shadows, so she took a fistful of fabric and hauled him to his feet, turned him to the light of the pyr.

Godstrike.

The sign of fire was inked over his heart, rising and falling with his rib cage.

'Impossible,' Lystra said to the oracle. 'No Amadean-born filth can bear the mark of the porpleza. Not even your acolyte.'

The oracle replied without lifting his gaze from the tattoo. 'Tell her.'

The monk closed his eyes, trembling under Lystra's grip. 'My mother was not Amadean.' He said it in Pyrien.

'Say it in your own language, or I will cut the tongue from your head,' the oracle warned.

The monk opened his eyes and took a shuddering breath. 'My mother was not Amadean.'

The ink-bare warrior made a strangled sound.

The oracle smiled to himself. He raised his free hand and slipped it between the pyr and the gold-capped stave. Lystra's mind resisted as it always did when porplezi handled fire. The oracle moved his hand and the pyr moved with it, leaving the stave and hovering over his palm. He stared into the swirling fire a long moment—the lick of red within it darkened and bled until the ball of fire was almost entirely purple—and then it left the porpleza's hand. A wingless bird, moving on its own.

The warriors, still unable to move or speak, sucked in their breath in unison. The pyr moved as if floating on calm water, unaffected by the persistent breeze. It reached the still-standing monk and hovered at the same height as his bare chest. He stared at it, eyes wide and nostrils flaring. Lystra could see he was afraid and yet he did not cower from it. The darkness swirling within the pyr shrank and the orb flared orange again.

Lystra expected the fire to return to the oracle's stave, but it floated lower to illuminate the warriors. If the move surprised the oracle, he gave no sign.

The pyr passed by the warrior-who-wasn't-Rhys, and then Rhys, barely pausing. The pair followed its progress, wide-eyed and barely breathing. When the pyr reached the ink-bare warrior, it stopped. She recoiled, tried to turn her face away, but the toxin from the dart still flowed in her blood. The pyr hovered before her, its light casting her features in patterns of soft orange. For a long moment, nothing happened. The breeze stilled, as if the night itself held its breath. And then the pyr flared so brightly that Lystra instinctively raised a hand to shield her eyes. A heartbeat later the light was gone, and when the spots in her eyes faded, the ball of fire had returned to its usual state.

In all her nineteen years, Lystra had never seen it do that.

'Who is this woman?' the oracle demanded. The monk's gaze followed the pyr on its path back to the oracle and Lystra saw his mind working. The oracle saw his hesitation.

'Lie to me and I will kill her.'

The monk was stricken. 'She is my sister.'

Lystra peered at the young woman in the torchlight. She could not deny there were similarities in the shape of their mouths and the line of their cheekbones. Was this one a warrior or not? Her body was hard but why was she not inked?

'Does she too wear the mark?' the oracle asked.

The monk shook his head.

Whatever the oracle thought about the warrior-sister, he kept it to himself. 'Return him to them.'

Lystra pushed the monk to the ground between the warriors. He huddled against his sister, made no attempt to make eye contact with the other two.

'Guardian,' The oracle said in their own tongue. 'The monk comes with us and those who are bonded to him will remain alive until I am convinced they no longer serve a purpose.'

'Where will you take them?'

'*We* will take them to the lake.'

'My place is in Xanthe's army.'

'If this is the fulfilment of your destiny, she will come to us.'

Lystra's skin prickled in understanding. *No.* 'This monk is not the one to break the wards.'

'If he is the one promised to us, it will be the least of what he can do.'

The oracle purposefully scanned the mine camp and the carnage the Pyriens had wrought and turned to the waiting askari. 'Free our people and burn down this blight on our soil.'

The slaves stumbled out of the hut and as one fell at the oracle's feet. Skeletal men, women and children, bruised and dressed in rags. The oracle touched each of them on the head and promised them their suffering had earned great blessings from the gods.

The slave hut, built in the Pyrien way, would not succumb to fire, but the thatched roof burned well enough. The veterans' quarters went up like dry straw. Lystra tried not to think about Dex's wolf token that been taken from her and kept in the hut now consumed by flames.

'Leave the bodies in the open. I want the Great Pretender to know what happened here.'

The monk gasped. 'Sacrilege!" He grabbed at the hem of

the acolyte's fledgling robe. 'You can't leave them here to be devoured by beasts! They will never be acceptable to Verus.'

The acolyte did not respond, but the oracle glanced around at the now-empty slave hut, the slurry pit, the chains, the gaping mine entrance and the stripped mountainside.

'That, monk, is the point.'

22

The call of the flames woke the Thirteenth Prophet.

For decades, he had slept at the foot of the chalice in the open-air high temple, nestled in a sumptuous couch brought out by his priests each night and draped in woollen blankets and furs. But over the years his old bones had increasingly complained about the cold. After the high priest Anguston's execution two years ago, the prophet had ordered a proper bed be added to the Codex scroll room so that he could sleep in greater comfort *and* guard the most sacred of texts.

He'd sensed no particular urgency from the flames this morning, only the usual warm sensation beneath his breastbone. So there was no haste as he stretched out his stiff back, splashed water on his face, relieved himself in the water closet and allowed a priest to help him into his robe.

The prophet walked barefoot from his room into the temple, saw the flames slowly undulating in the chalice. He took the walking stick he kept out of sight behind the urn by his door and used it to climb the twelve steps to the dais. He stood before the golden chalice and the fire brightened in recognition. The prophet had only the vaguest stirring of unease as he pushed his face into the flames and waited for what his god wanted to reveal to him.

What he saw there chilled his marrow more than any winter's night on hard tiles.

Mine Five had been destroyed. The veterans' quarters were a smoking ruin, the slave hut without a roof and empty, and the mine entrance collapsed. Anything that could burn had been set alight. Cages had been pushed into the slurry pit and the boulder-pounding pulley systems toppled sideways.

The true horror was the tableau of brutality laid out on the ground in the smoky morning light. Bodies and limbs strewn about in the dirt, left to rot under the open sky. The most profane of insults.

Rage swelled. The wolf clan askara the prophet had been promised was gone, and the damage would set back the mine operation by moons, if not a full season. And he'd lost valuable leverage with the overlords of Iolia. He willed the flames to show him the faces of those who had been slaughtered, seeking out the two warriors Pellus had sent to retrieve the askari hostage. One by one, he studied them. The dead men were disfigured, dismembered and bloodied, but he could see enough of each enough to realise the Iolians were not among the corpses.

'Attendants!'

Four temple priests and two monks appeared through opposite doors. Gael was one of them and it was to her he gave the order.

'Bring the overlords to me. Now.'

23

Sabine had thrown up twice.

Once when the feeling returned to her body—it came back in a rush and the first thing she did was eject the greasy pottage from the night before—and then again right before being shoved into the prison wagon intended for the wolf-clan askara. It was too much to keep in her body. The massacre of the veterans. The nauseating after-effects of the poison. The stark reality of her family shame being thrust into the light at the worst possible moment. All of it had left her trembling and wrung out.

That final scene at the campsite haunted her.

She'd cared little for the mine veterans but she would not wish such defilement on any man or woman. Without burial rites, none could enter into the world that awaited where Verus would vouch for them with her brothers and the elder gods. And while Sabine was no stranger to the sights and sounds of death, it was infinitely worse watching while lying useless in the dirt and waiting to die by poison or axe, or for the dark-eyed porpleza to slit Axl's throat.

But their lives were spared. All four of them.

Given the frenzy that followed, it was a testament to the power of the one the Pyriens called oracle that the askari butchers obeyed the order. Instead, she, Axl, Tristan and Rhys were dragged to the wagon, alive only because of her brother's confession. Sabine had regained partial feeling in her body but her head ached and her limbs were as heavy as iron. Tristan had managed a wayward kick and Rhys swung a sloppy punch at the wolf-clan askara when she hauled him across gravel and stones. Sabine had barely had the strength to resist, let alone strike out.

The Pyriens were not done with the horror: there was a corpse waiting for them in the prison wagon. It was the askari initiate who'd snatched Axl on the mountain track. He was laid to one side, skin waxen, his sightless eyes fixed open and his slit throat gaping. Sabine had gagged at the stench of dried blood and shit, and then she'd retched until there was nothing left.

The night sky was lit orange when they'd rolled out of the mine camp, five of them in a cage made for twice that number. Sabine and Axl huddled together at one end, as far from the corpse as possible; Tristan and Rhys stretched out at the other, ignoring their dead companion. The warriors' legs took up a lot of space. Sabine had caught a glimpse of Tristan in the torchlight, his features a storm of accusation and confusion. As the wagon lurched forward and carried them into full darkness, she'd sensed an unmistakable thirst for violence from the warriors. What she couldn't discern was how much of it was aimed at her and Axl and how much at their captors.

The wolf-clan askara, the one the porpleza called 'guardian' in the Amadean tongue, had been with the wagon since they'd left the camp. She stalked alongside in silence, coiled with fury and pent-up violence. She was nothing like the initiate had been. When Sabine had first seen her at the slurry pit, she'd known the Pyrien was askari even with her moon-white hair chopped to her scalp. She was as tall as a warrior and *strong*, despite being beaten and injured. When the askara had come close to sneer at Rhys, Sabine was surprised to find she was not monstrous to look at. Beneath the blood and bruises were the kind of cheekbones and lips considered beautiful on Amadean women.

The freed mine slaves took turns to join the wolf-clan askara in the moonlight. Some spat at Sabine and the warriors, others cursed them in Pyrien. The waif girl simply walked beside the wagon. It was Axl who had helped her from the ground and repacked her rocks, but it was Rhys she reached out to touch through the bars. The askara repeatedly shooed her away, and each time the child returned, wordless but determined.

Surprisingly, the Pyriens had spared the warhorses. Sabine saw them strung together in silhouette when the column crested a rise: Mina, Trout and Rhys's bay gelding, Lager, trailing behind the wagon along with six smaller horses from the mine camp. The askari had also found the two oxen in the yards and put them to work to pull the cell wagon.

'The horses are alive and with us,' Sabine said to nobody in particular. Her mouth tasted sour and the observation earned a jab from the butt of the askara's spear. Tristan's head turned to her—a reflex action no doubt—but the moon was not so bright that she could see his expression. He turned away without speaking.

For the next few hours, they bumped over rough, steep terrain as the path the Pyriens followed twisted and turned between tall dark trees. The scent from the leaves was sharp, tangy and unfamiliar. Worn down by fear and exhaustion, Sabine fell into an uneasy sleep against her brother. There were no dreams and she woke with a start to the sound of the wolf-clan askara speaking harshly in her own tongue. The second voice was male and the response in perfect Amadean: 'I come with the oracle's consent.'

The forest was bathed in murky grey light—dawn had come—and when Sabine sat up, she recognised the mottled cloak made from fledgling feathers. It was the oracle's acolyte keeping pace with the wagon. His hood was up, hiding his features, and his hands were beneath his cloak. Axl slid across the cage to be closer to him. There had been something familiar about the acolyte's voice, something about how the askara had insulted them earlier—

Understanding came to her in a rush.

'Alba?' Sabine blurted.

The acolyte turned and ink-stained hands pushed back the hood.

'*Traitor!*' Tristan hissed.

It was the mendicant monk, the one who had been with her brother at Iolia Castle when Sabine—and then Tristan—discovered Axl was a heretic. Dark curly hair now covered the sacred tattoos on his scalp, and his broad face was striped with ash. He was as far from a servant of Verus as an Amadean could be.

The askara bared her teeth in a way that could have been a smile.

Sabine's chest tightened in understanding. The mendicant had been more than a trafficker of illicit Codex transcripts: he was in league with the enemy. And Axl was in league with him. She'd known her brother had Pyrien sympathies—it was inherent in the Angustonian belief—but she'd convinced herself he was loyal to Amadea. Even now, even knowing their blood connection to this godforsaken place, it jarred.

'And you,' Tristan said to Axl. 'You are the greatest traitor of all.' He didn't look at Sabine as he ground out the words. Her brother glanced at the askara, wary of the butt of her spear.

'I am not your enemy.' Axl said it slowly, purposefully.

Rhys grunted. 'You wear their mark.'

Axl took a steadying breath.

'The abbot believed I would have a part to play in the rise of the usurper.' He held up his hand before Rhys could interrupt.

'He never said it was me, but he saw signs I was involved. He knew Alba was in contact with the porplezi, so when he last visited Stonebridge—'

'The abbot allowed this traitor to cross the bridge to the pinnacle?'

'The leader of Stonebridge Abbey does not see borders as you do, Rhys.'

'As the *king* does, you mean?' The warrior seethed. 'And then *you* let him remain under the Iolian roof undetected, knowing his ties to dark magic?'

The traitor in question cleared his throat. In the temple scriptorium all those moons ago, there had been little remarkable about him. But here, under a Pyrien sky, with his hair grown out unnaturally and his face painted, he was frightening. 'I have not forsaken Amadea. I have apprenticed to the oracle to save it.'

The askara gave a low growl but kept her eyes ahead.

'Save it how?' Tristan demanded.

Alba gripped the cage so he could keep himself steady as he answered. 'By being the bridge between our people when the line of prophets is thrown aside.'

Tristan eyed Alba's ink-stained fingers for a long, furious beat. '*You* put that tattoo on Axl?'

'Yes, at Stonebridge, and at the abbot's request.' Alba allowed a moment for that to sink in. 'The fact I could mark his chest at all was as momentous as the sun rising in the west. Never in the history of our people has an Amadean been able to bear the mark of the porplezi.'

Rhys grunted. 'It's not such a big deal if he's Pyrien.'

'*Half*-Pyrien,' Alba said, as if correcting a mispronunciation. 'And *any* drop of Amadean blood should have made it impossible.'

Tristan locked eyes with Sabine. 'Did you know?' The

question came out more confused than angry and it undid her another notch.

'Not until the warehouse.'

'How...?'

Sabine drew her lips between her teeth. She didn't want to have to say it. Axl saved her the trouble.

'Olidus.'

The wagon hit a rut and bounced violently and the corpse jumped with it. Sabine bit the inside of her mouth as she landed. She instantly found the cut with her tongue, tasted copper.

'He told Sabine our mother was Pyrien.'

Tristan's expression darkened. 'Your uncle was a smear of eel shit. How could you believe anything that came out of his mouth?'

Axl answered by placing his hand inside his ripped robe, over his tattooed chest. 'Because nothing else makes sense.'

Sabine watched Tristan's jaw work. 'And you never suspected it?' He was asking her, not Axl.

She held his gaze, needing him to believe her. 'Her hair was dark like mine and her eyes were green. She didn't have a clan tattoo. Why would I ever think it?'

Sabine barely remembered her mother. Yes, there were stories years later of how Sabella would grow restless and moody before disappearing into the hills. That she would come home days later, her eyes bright and calmer in spirit, and that Darius always greeted her with joy as if he'd not expected her return. People said Sabella was wild and Darius too indulgent of his wife. But not even Greenock's most bitter gossips accused her of being Pyrien.

'Do you not see that Axl and Sabine have the blessing of Verus?' Alba pressed. 'Verus has bonded Amadean blood to them to protect their safety.' He pointed to Tristan and then Rhys, as if they might have missed the connection. 'And our god has honoured that bond and kept you safe by bringing you to the porpleza I serve. If anyone other than the oracle had been waiting in the darkness last night, you would all be dead.'

Tristan resumed grinding his jaw and looked away. Sabine pressed her thumb into her bandaged palm, feeling queasy again. She flinched when Lystra rapped her spear on the cage.

'What is your mother's name?' she asked Axl.

'Her name *was* Sabella of Greenock Hill.' He paused and then added, 'She died giving birth to me.'

Lystra shook her head. 'Say-bella is not a Pyrien name.'

'Her mother might be called Nyomi?' Axl said.

The askara actually stumbled. She recovered quickly, her expression unreadable.

'Do you know her?' Sabine's brother asked, sitting forward.

Lystra rapped the cage again to discourage his nearness. 'If what you say is the truth, monk, you are going to wish you died at the mine.'

It took everything in Sabine not to throw up again.

24

When the full heat of anger burned through his confusion, Tristan allowed a moment for it to consume him.

They had all kept him in the dark.

Axl.

Sabine.

Dashelle—Tristan's sister was there with Olidus when the accusation was made—and even Ferugo, because Dash told *him* everything.

And now he and Rhys were captives in enemy territory for a cause neither of them believed in. Rhys was directing his rage at the askara, itching for the violence brewing between them. Tristan needed something more—he needed purpose, but that was fast evaporating. Right now he'd settle for a fight.

The prison wagon rocked and bounced, jarring him to the marrow. His jaw ached from him clenching it. He worried at the scar on his palm, wished he could rub it away and with it the storm of guilt and rage woven into the hardened skin.

Protect those to whom you have bound yourself. Let them guide you when the road becomes dark.

Those were Ferugo's last words to him in Augustmount before he and Dash were taken away by Pellus. And they were fine words when Tristan thought he understood what they meant.

But what if those he was sworn to protect were the ones who had darkened that road?

And what did it mean if his lord and sister had even deeper ties to that darkness than he'd been told?

25

The high temple floor gleamed, even under the overcast dawn sky.

The golden tiles, crossed only in bare feet, were wiped clean twice daily by a novice whose heart thundered to be so close the source of the sacred flames. In the centre of the open-air court, the fire gifted from Verus a millennium ago still burned on the bones of the First Prophet. The true flames.

Here was where the Thirteenth Prophet was at his strongest, where his gifts were the most reliable. Here, the flames bended to his will, even if it required increasing skill because the fire's purity had been diluted by the darkness tainting his kingdom. He understood it was a warning he was running out of time. The prophet had seen that he would wield original power as the First Prophet had, but only when the head of the Pyrien ruler lay at his bare feet. The time for a measured response to the heresy had passed.

He felt the overlords of Iolia before they appeared. Their dread was palpable. They understood a summoning to the high temple was unprecedented. Since the theft of the First Prophet's rib bone two centuries ago, this place had been accessible only to prophet and priests. The Thirteenth Prophet had made several exceptions of late: he'd sacrificed a Pyrien slave here and set alight a heretic shepherd. But optimati? None had set foot in here in living memory.

Ferugo and Dashelle had been allowed to change from their nightwear and appeared wearing the clothing they'd arrived in almost a full moon ago. The prophet noted the small bound copy of The Sacrifice of Antigonus he'd gifted the overlords was hanging from Dashelle's belt. He could not fault the show of piety.

Gael, dressed in her green Stonebridge robe and standing half a head taller even than Ferugo, bade them stop and remove their footwear and then led them into the sanctuary. The Iolian overlords crossed the tiles shoulder to shoulder, their spines straight. Despite the presence of the prophet, they had eyes only for the true flames. The prophet did not speak as they made their way to him, the soles of their feet leaving ghost prints on the tiles. The high temple was at least a quarter of the size of the lower public temple and bereft of adornment, yet it thrummed with power. Here, there was no need for statues or colonnades to glorify Verus as there was in the lower temple. Her true fire was more than enough to steal the breath from any who crossed her threshold. Every sacred flame that burned in public temples and private altars across the kingdom originated from here. These flames held more power than all of those fires combined.

Yet, even now, the prophet sensed the change in them. He'd first felt it at Anguston's execution two years ago and then again when he commanded the flames to immolate the heretic shepherd.

Resistance.

It was enough for the prophet to not risk failing when it was the great warrior Torvus at the stake. That trial was held in the lower temple, and the prophet had sent the sacred flames to the dying warrior only once the unsanctified flames had already taken hold. And still they consumed Torvus in a manner the prophet had never before witnessed.

In the high temple, Gael placed cushions on the floor, gestured to where the overlords should kneel, and moved to leave.

'Stay,' the prophet commanded. The Stonebridge monk had spent time with the overlords, and her connection might help him distil their thoughts and memories. Gael bowed her head and obeyed.

A long and deliberate silence passed. The prophet knew he had crossed into unchartered waters by delaying his part of the greeting ceremony. He felt outrage spark and catch, most likely from Ferugo—it was difficult to separate the overlords' energy—and finally said, 'You are worthy to look upon my face.'

They raised their faces to him. Dashelle's expression was one of trepidation; Ferugo's schooled and calm. The Iolian overlords knew better than to speak first. Now that they were before him on their knees, the frustration and impatience that had been clawing at the prophet subsided. For as long as he kept the overlords in the high temple, they were his, not the king's. He looked from one to the other, settled his gaze on Ferugo.

'Yesterday, two of your best warriors were sent into Pyrie ahead of the king's army. Their orders were to fetch an askari prisoner from Mine Five and bring her to me.' He pursed his lips by way of pause. 'Last night, the camp was attacked and burned to the ground. Every veteran was slaughtered.'

Ferugo stared at the prophet unblinking. 'May I ask which warriors were sent?'

'Tristan and Rhys.'

There was a beat as the news took hold and then Dashelle let out a single, devastated sob. Ferugo did not avert his gaze. 'You said every *veteran* was slaughtered?'

The prophet had to admire the man's sharpness of mind considering the moment. 'Your warriors were not among them,' he conceded.

Dashelle groaned her relief and slumped back on her heels. 'There were also no Pyriens among the dead.'

Ferugo understood the inference before his wife. He met the prophet's gaze. 'My warriors were taken captive?'

'That has been hidden from me.'

The air around the overlord pulsed with uncertainty and... was that a tendril of relief at the prophet's blindness? Or was the relief about the warriors' survival only? The prophet kept them on their knees, planned his next move.

'Dashelle, I am told you do not approve of the way slaves are treated in our kingdom?'

She wiped tears from her cheeks and stayed sitting on her heels. Her relief was such that all tension had momentarily drained from her. In a pinch of regret, the prophet understood he should have let them believe the warriors were dead a while longer.

'My prophet,' she began. 'I have on occasion, and only among our peers, expressed my wish that the king would order all optimati to feed their slaves, not starve them to save coin.'

'Is that because you are concerned about the welfare of those we have enslaved?'

Dashelle hesitated only a moment. 'Yes,' she admitted. 'In the same way I am concerned for the beasts in the field; they cannot adequately serve us if they are sick and underfed.' It was not the fullness of her feelings, but her words contained truth.

'So you are not sympathetic to our enemy?'

The tension snapped back. The sensation was enormously satisfying.

'No, my prophet.'

'Tell me, then, how could your warriors be captured without ending at least one Pyrien life?'

Ferugo grunted his indignation. 'There is no way we can answer that given we were not there.'

The prophet turned the full force of his gaze on him. 'Is there any reason your brother-in-law and his cousin would not kill our enemy?'

A muscle in Ferugo's jaw twitched beneath his beard. 'None. They were either outnumbered or incapacitated.' His mind was racing now. 'Perhaps they did kill their attackers. The askari would take their dead with them, would they not?'

The prophet sensed a spike of anxiety from Dashelle. He lightly dipped his consciousness into hers—not deep enough that she would feel it—and found a swirl of colours that were different from those more clearly visible when she'd been thinking about the warriors. Flashes of vivid green and fiery orange.

'Did you expect others to be with them?' he asked.

The colours spun faster and blurred to grey. Dashelle was trying to hide her thoughts.

'Tell me about the Stonebridge monk, Axl.'

The prophet sensed the effort it took for husband and wife to not look at each other. It was Ferugo who answered.

'Axl accepted our invitation to stay at Iolia Castle when he and Gael were on pilgrimage.'

'Why did you ask the boy to stay longer and not Gael?'

The overlord shot an apologetic glance at the tall monk. 'Axl may be younger in years than Gael, but his ink is older.'

'What troubled you both so much that you required a servant of Verus to interrupt their sacred pilgrimage?'

Ferugo locked eyes with the prophet. His defiance was growing. 'Like all provinces, our lands have not been spared from the pestilence destroying crops across the kingdom. We have struggled with the great questions of how we lead our people in these times; how we keep our lands viable and those who rely on us, fed.'

'And what advice did this boy monk give you?'

'Axl offered no advice, of course. That is not his place. He spent time with us in meditation in the presence of the sacred flames, reconnecting us with our rites and strengthening our bond with Verus.'

The prophet felt his own impatience stirring. These were acceptable answers of course, but why then could he not *see* the monk? 'Did you have cause to suspect he is a heretic?'

The shocked gasp that followed came not from Dashelle, but Gael. The Stonebridge monk immediately blanched under the prophet's withering gaze and averted her eyes, but not before he saw her utter confusion at the accusation.

'No,' Ferugo said, and frowned. 'Do you, my prophet?'

It was the first time Ferugo had used the term of respect since the start of the conversation.

'The boy is hidden from me, which can only mean he is wrapped in porplezi magic.'

The prophet attempted to skim the overlords' thoughts as they absorbed this momentous news and found nothing but a maelstrom of swirling grey. He would need help from Verus to probe deeper.

'What does this have to do with Tristan and Rhys being taken captive in Pyrie?'

'That, Ferugo, is what I am trying to understand. Your warriors are missing in Pyrie and you are hiding your thoughts from me. I must know why.'

Dashelle's eyes flicked to the chalice, where the flame had begun to dance in anticipation.

'You leave me no choice but to use the fire of Verus to burn away the veils you have in place.'

'That is forbidden,' Ferugo said, outraged. 'The king will not allow it.'

'I do not answer to the king!' the prophet snapped, louder than he'd intended. 'I answer to Verus, and she has commanded me to root out this heresy and free Amadea from its snare.'

'No.'

The overlord made as if to rise, reaching for his wife. In fury, the prophet summoned the flame. The resistance was there but it read his intentions and bent to his will. A tendril of the fire left the chalice, split in two and rippled through the air. Ferugo and Dashelle froze on their knees.

'We have nothing to fear from the living flame of Verus,' Ferugo told his wife, but his shortened breath betrayed him.

The tendrils drew further apart as they approached the overlords. In unison, the flames formed a circle around each of their heads, covering their eyes but not quite close enough to burn. Dashelle was panting with fear and Ferugo clutched her hand. They were trapped beneath the bind of the flame.

Now the prophet could delve deeper. He focused his efforts on Ferugo. Women were always better at protecting what mattered most to them. He'd found that men, especially those who wielded power, were less guarded when angry.

The prophet pushed through Ferugo's most recent memories of his wife—he had no interest in their moments of passion—and paid little attention to a host of other memories that had taken root closest to his consciousness: the grief of watching his men die in a border campaign; the warmth of a newborn lamb he'd helped deliver in a storm; the shock and horror of Torvus's death...

He dug deeper.

There.

A memory shimmered, came into focus. It was an image of two monks in Stonebridge robes, sitting cross-legged before a private altar. *At last!* This was the elusive Axl, cloaked in Gael's memories and buried deep in Ferugo's.

How did the overlord feel about this monk? The prophet held onto the thread, felt the overlord's emotions float tantalisingly within reach, swirling...whatever it was, it was strong, but the prophet could not sense if it was light or darkness behind it. He tugged harder. It was like trying to wind in a fish on a pole—

The thread broke.

The prophet pulled back his consciousness to find the overlord slumped on the tiles, his eyes rolled back in his head and blood trickling from his nose and ears. The flames whipped back to the chalice as if summoned and Dashelle's eyes snapped open.

'What have you done?' she gasped, falling over Ferugo and frantically feeling for a pulse, first in his wrist and then at his throat. She listened for his breath and pressed her ear to Ferugo's chest. He remained as still as a stone. Desperate, she slapped him across the face and her hand came away bloodied. There was no response.

'Do something!' she screamed at the prophet.

The prophet could see there was nothing to be done but he probed again anyway, found only darkness and void. 'Dark magic has taken Ferugo before he could yield his secrets,' he said, and felt the conviction of the declaration taking root. 'Your husband is gone.'

Dashelle of Iolia began to wail.

REUNION

26

The dead initiate started to stink on the third day.

Lystra was tempted to leave the stench unabated and prolong the Amadeans' discomfort, but it would be disrespectful to the fallen initiate. That was why before they set off on the final stretch to the lake, she sent the freed children in search of flowers and herbs.

The young ones—bellies full on the boar they'd speared and spit-roasted themselves on the second night—were still battered and bruised, yet they were eager to go into the trees, returning with bunches of wild lavender, juniper and jasmine. The silent girl—the others called her Indy—remained fixated with the warrior Rhys. He was tethered by the waist to the other three Amadeans, beyond the wagon, and she offered her flowers to him. The warrior eyed her with mild irritation and when it looked like he might accept the offering, Lystra snatched the bunch away.

'They are for our dead, girl,' she snarled. 'Not the dogs who killed him.'

The oracle's pet hovered behind the child. 'We must bind and burn the body before five days have passed since death.'

'I know our customs, acolyte.'

'Apologies, guardian.' Alba glanced at the monk, *Axl*, and Lystra understood with annoyance the information had been for his benefit. The monk was barely listening. His sister had not spoken or eaten for a day and a night now, and his attention was on her, not the corpse.

Alba was right: the death rites should have started long before now. They could have stripped bedding from the guard hut before the slaves set it alight—it would have been better than nothing for the binding—but they hadn't known the initiative's corpse was waiting strung up in the stables until the hut was already burning. They had now cleared the lower ranges of the border mountains and would reach open ground later today. Trees were already sparse, and the morning sun would further deteriorate the corpse.

'Be quick,' she said to the waiting children.

Alba hovered at her side as the young ones repositioned the dead initiative in the wagon and gently placed armloads of herbs and flowers on top of him. They were not offended by the state of his body. They were well acquainted with what happened to flesh and organs after death.

The Pyrien who had worked the boulder opposite Lystra was approaching, holding something in his closed hand. His name was Styx and he'd been preoccupied until now with the reunion with the quicksilver woman—his troth-mate.

'This was found in the hut with your weapons,' Styx said when he reached her. 'I thought it might have belonged to the initiate.'

He held out a small wooden token and Lystra's throat closed over. It was a wolf carved from sycamore.

'No,' she said, her voice thick. 'It is my pack mate's. Dex.'

'He is with Xanthe?'

For a moment she was back in the forest, pressing her fingers to his neck, trying to stop the bleeding; seeing the life leach out of his eyes.

She felt Rhys watching her. She swallowed her grief, tugged on the strands of her hatred for the warrior to ground her. 'He was killed when our pack was ambushed. I thought this was lost to me. Thank you.'

Styx placed a hand over his heart, understanding the significance. 'I will stand with you when the time comes.'

Lystra nodded her gratitude. She would otherwise stand alone at the ceremony. She was a pack leader without a pack, an askara marked by whip and chains. She had shamed her clan and her people, and the only way for redemption was through bloodshed and victory. Until then, she was a lone wolf reliant on the generosity of others.

The dead initiate was now covered in sweet-smelling offerings. The children had picked so much that the entire floor of the cell was strewn with purple and white flowers. Lystra tucked the wolf where it belonged, in the pouch on her belt beside her axe loop, and turned her attention to the Amadeans. The monk had been translating the conversation for the warriors.

'Get them into the wagon,' she said, bristling that Rhys understood the depths of her loss.

Styx helped untether the Amadeans from the tree. They were stiff from sitting all night and he pushed each of the warriors forward to keep them off balance, even though they were flanked by a dozen askari and posed little threat. Rhys was in the lead, shaking out his arms as if readying to fight, and he eyeballed Lystra as he approached. Lystra set aside her spear so she had both hands free and waited for him to get closer.

'Let him go,' she growled and nodded for Styx and the others to release him.

The warrior shouldered Styx aside and charged at her.

'Mine alone!' Lystra called and let the warrior barrel into her. She was ready, grabbing him and twisting as they fell. They landed hard and rolled as she'd intended, but then he hooked his legs around hers first, stealing her move and the advantage. She'd wanted him on the ground so he'd lose his height advantage, and now he was on top of her pinning her wrists either side of her head, grinning.

Scourge.

Lystra bucked her hips and swung her arms down to her side in a burst of speed. It threw Rhys forward and forced him to throw his hands out to stop himself from face-planting in the grass. She turned her head before he landed on her and bear-hugged him, pressing the side of her face to his chest. He was pushing up to take his weight on his hands again and swore as she came with him. Before he could steady himself, Lystra let go with one arm and pulled in the weight-bearing forearm, rolling him sideways. As soon as she was out from under Rhys, she punched him high in the gut, driving all the wind out of him. She quickly capitalised, shoving him on his back, straddling him and pressing her forearm to his throat. Her face was inches from his. His eyes were hard and his beard was rough against her arm. He grabbed her shoulders and tried to dislodge her, but he was winded and out of air. The warrior bared his teeth and passed out.

'You've had your fun, guardian,' the oracle said, irritated.

Lystra hadn't realised the porpleza had been so near. 'Let him breathe.'

Lystra lingered a moment longer and then sat back, still straddling Rhys as she waited for him to come to. She wanted to be the first thing he saw.

'Off,' the oracle said. 'You are done.'

'I have earned this.'

'He is not your prisoner, guardian. He is mine.'

She stood up and stepped away, grinding her jaw. Rhys started to stir and two askari moved in and dragged the warrior to the wagon. It was only now Lystra saw the monk's sister and the other warrior were pinned face-down to the ground.

The grass around them was churned up as if there had been a separate scuffle.

Indy stood beside the stunned monk, staring at Lystra with something close to disapproval.

Lystra took up her spear and banged it on the cage as she passed Rhys. His bleary eyes found her and she gave him a triumphant smile. She licked her lips and tasted blood. The welts on her neck were again bleeding and her face throbbed, but it was the best she'd felt in days.

27

'Thanks for the back up.'

It was the first thing Tristan had said to Sabine in more than a day and it brought a flare of relief. He'd landed beside her when they were shoved back into the wagon and even though they were moving again, he'd made no attempt to create distance between them. He hadn't touched her and his tone gave nothing away, but his closeness took some of the chill from her blood.

'It didn't achieve much,' she said.

'It did,' he said, meeting her eyes. 'It showed me something.'

Her relief dissolved. 'You didn't think I would follow your lead?'

Had the two warriors taken on the askari to *test* her? No, Rhys's attack was born of hatred, and Tristan reacted in the only way he knew how.

'I wasn't sure what you would do.' He said it honestly, without malice, and it cut her to the marrow. It was the eviction from Iolia Castle all over again, only this time Tristan's readiness to believe the worst of her was so much harder to bear.

'I forgot how quick you are to judge,' she said, pressing on her reddened knuckles until she found the sorest spot.

'Sabine—'

'After everything we've been through, I thought I'd earned your trust.'

'You kept the news about your mother from me.'

She met his gaze again, letting him see the truth. 'I didn't *know*. And once I did, I didn't know how to tell you because I knew you'd react like this.'

'So, I hadn't earned *your* trust?'

It stung because it was true. She hadn't trusted his feelings for her to see past the tainted blood pumping through her heart.

'And I was right, wasn't I?'

They fell into a bruised silence as the wagon rocked along.

The wolf-clan askara paid them no attention. She was preoccupied keeping pace with the rear of the wagon where Rhys was slumped against the bars glaring at her balefully.

'I expected more,' Lystra goaded him in her thick accent.

Rhys grunted. 'I'll keep my feet next time.'

'It will not matter. I beat you when I am hurt. Imagine what I will do when I am healed.'

'Let's see how you go when I don't have your poison working its way through my blood.'

'Always excuses with you.' She tapped her spear tip on the bars. 'I will let you breathe longer next time.'

Rhys gave a dark laugh. 'I'm a fast learner.'

Axl had squeezed himself into the opposite corner of the cell, keeping as much distance from the corpse as he could. He kept peering through the bars, waiting for Alba to return rather than engaging with anyone in the wagon. He sneezed once, twice, and pressed part of his torn cowl over his nose to mask the smell of the body and its new, sickly floral overtone.

The column pushed on over increasingly uneven ground. Lystra and Rhys exchanged insults and Sabine and Tristan went back to ignoring each other. Sabine fixed her gaze on the passing forest. There were trees and shrubs she'd never seen before, some with leaves twice the size of her hand and berries the colour of dried blood, yet even the strangeness of the vegetation couldn't quieten the thoughts chasing each other in ever-tightening circles.

She had to tell Tristan what Axl believed, whether she accepted it or not.

But what was the benefit of Tristan knowing she *might* have a connection to the power the heretics believed was coming? It would either further widen the distance between them or raise false hope she was a match for the porpleza. The first thing Tristan would ask would be how long Axl had believed it, and her answer would heap insult on injury. As would the fact she understood Pyrien as well as Axl did—not because of her mother's bloodline, but because a slave had taught her during the time she spent in the smithy hiding from her abusive uncle.

Sabine closed her eyes, desperate for rest. She was exhausted from lack of sleep, lack of food and constant, gnawing anxiety. Until the mine attack, she'd thought she'd proven herself worthy to ride beneath Iolia's banner. That she'd earned her place at Tristan's side and had some semblance of control over her life. None of it had been true. Everything Sabine had worked for had been for nothing. She might be stronger and a better fighter than the day she fled her uncle, but she was just as powerless. The unfairness of it ached beneath her ribs.

The caravan kept a steady pace through the day and there were no signs of stopping, even to eat. The mine slaves, accustomed to working on meagre rations, shuffled on without complaint, helping each other up if one fell. Sabine, tangled up in her own misery, envied their solidarity.

Mid-afternoon, the column left the protection of the wooded mountainside and crossed open rolling hills. Here, wild grass grew knee-high and swayed with the breeze. Goats were scattered across the landscape and it was only when Sabine heard the tinkle of bells did she realise they belonged to a tended herd. It shouldn't have been a surprise. The blacksmith

Bryn had told her there were Pyriens who were neither askara, porpleza nor slave, but this was the first she'd seen evidence of it.

Sabine's situation would have been slightly less fraught if her mother had been a goat herder. There was no 'good' way to be Pyrien, but porplezi was by far the worst. Her mother had not looked Pyrien. How was that even possible? How did her father, an Amadean underlord, meet a porpleza? Did it happen in Pyrie or Amadea? How did they come to fall in love and marry?

Sabine's memories of Sabella were faded, but her mother and father had loved each other deeply and her father never truly recovered from the loss. Sabine had long believed that was why Darius had made the reckless decision to volunteer for border patrol last year.

It was that, or whatever the Stonebridge abbot said to him on his last visit to the abbey.

Ahead of the caravan, rugged mountain peaks grew large and then disappeared when the column entered a birch forest. Less than a mile in, when the way grew steeper and the light turned golden, the Pyriens finally stopped and made camp. The slave who had taken responsibility for the oxen had quickly become adept at hitching and unhitching the yoke. He stroked each beast on the head and whispered praise in their ears; fed them handfuls of sweet grass and got them moving each morning with the promise of more. It was far more kindness than the Pyriens extended to the Amadeans.

The prisoners were ordered from the wagon one at a time, allowed to relieve themselves (at spear-tip) and were then chained up for the night. Sabine and Rhys were tethered at one tree; Tristan and Axl at another. As he had every evening, Alba brought them dried goat for dinner. Sabine assumed it was goat because it had a far stronger flavour than lamb. She managed to keep it down, along with a few gulps of water from an animal skin she didn't recognise.

Rhys, who rarely held back on commentary, slumped in brooding silence beside her. The air was cooling quickly and Sabine wrestled with the chain around her waist so she could wrap herself more tightly in her cloak. Wearied by the effort, she rested her head back against the tree and looked up at the sky. Beyond the branches, thin clouds were streaked with pinks and oranges. It cast unexpected beauty in an otherwise bleak day.

'Sweet Verus, what is it with this kid?'

Sabine followed Rhys's gaze to see the waif girl approaching. She was carrying something round and pale that might have been a piece of fruit, but it was so big it took two of her hands to hold it. The girl walked with tired legs, eyes only for Rhys. Like Sabine, Rhys was chained and shackled at the waist and ankles but his arms were free.

Rhys shifted position. 'You come to poison me?'

The waif walked right up to him, unblinking.

Sabine's heart sped up, afraid for the girl. 'Don't hurt her.' It was out before she'd considered how it would sound.

He grunted. 'If I wanted to hurt a Pyrien, I've got one right next to me.'

Sabine pretended to ignore the barb, but it found its mark.

The girl held out her offering to Rhys. He made no move to take it from her.

'It's an aprycot.' Alba said from his place on the grass near Axl. 'It's quite tasty once you get used to the tang.'

'If I take it will you go away?' Rhys said, gruff but not cruel. The girl kept her arms outstretched, waiting. 'Fine.' He took it and turned it over his hands a few times. 'How do I eat it?'

Thie girl must have understood because she mimed biting into it. She sat down beside him, cross-legged and waited for him to follow her instructions. Her bone-white hair was matted and her face streaked from the day's travel but those pale blue eyes were full of expectation.

'You first.' Rhys handed it back to her and she bit into it without hesitation. She returned the fruit to him, wiping juice from her chin as she chewed. Rhys shrugged and took a huge bite. His eyes widened, and then he screwed up his face and coughed. 'Tangy, all right,' he managed, and kept chewing until it was all gone. His eyes shone with tears as he cleared his throat, and then took another bite, smaller this time, and handed the fruit to Sabine.

She sniffed at it, hungry enough to give it a try. The tart flesh made her eyes water too, but the nectar was surprisingly sweet. She handed it back to Rhys, who tossed the half-eaten aprycot to Tristan. He passed the fruit to Axl without trying it. Once Axl had spluttered his way through a mouthful, Tristan lobbed it back and Rhys ate the remaining flesh. The waif watched as he sucked the last of the flavour from the pip at its core.

'Thank you,' the warrior conceded.

'Whelp!'

The wolf-clan askara was crossing the clearing, furious. The child sprang up and ran past her back to the other freed slaves.

Rhys tossed the aprycot pip to Lystra and she caught it without thinking.

'Delicious,' he said and licked his lips. His beard glistened with nectar.

Lystra realised she was holding something that had been in his mouth and threw it away in disgust, then disappeared into the darkening forest wiping her palm on her wolf pelt.

'Where are we going?' Axl asked Alba, drying his hands on the insides of his sleeves.

Alba glanced to where the oracle was now speaking with the freed slaves. Raw-boned men and women sat at his feet listening intently, most of the children already curled up in the grass asleep. The oracle's orb hovered over the stave, the dark swirl at its heart barely visible. Sabine didn't look too closely. Her scalp crawled if she focused on it for too long.

'The oracle is taking you to the lake.' Alba said it with reverence.

Axl frowned. 'The lake?'

'The Pyriens have many holy places in these mountains, and the lake is among the most sacred.' His eyes slid to the oracle again. 'It's where the oracle is meant to live. I have followed him for three moons and we have never been, but I can see his heart calls him there.'

'What makes it sacred?'

Alba lowered his voice so it was almost a whisper. 'I've heard there is a shrine to the old gods there.' He tilted his head as if there was more.

'And?' Axl pressed.

Sabine felt the hairs on her arms lift at the hunger in her brother's voice.

Alba waited a beat and then said, 'I think the Tenth Prophecy is there.'

28

'Brute force and weight in numbers are not enough. We need a new tactic.' Adward's hands balled into fists on his armrest as he addressed the war council. Pellus could feel the Iolian warrior's frustration growing—and not only because Adward had been forced to sit at his new commander's right hand in the king's pavilion.

Carmine, Overlord of Paramore province, shook his head. 'We already have a tactic: destroy everything in our path. It has been working so far.'

'With significant losses,' Adward argued. 'We are too vulnerable in the valleys, we need to find high, flat ground and make the askari come to us so we can fight on our terms.'

Pellus watched the exchange, unsettled by the king's silence. It was dark outside and the shadows cast by the fire danced across Felix's features. It made him harder than usual to read, even with Pellus's heightened intuition.

Carmine shook his head. 'You underestimate our warriors, Adward.'

'Our *warriors* are adapting. Our foot soldiers are not. They are terrified of an enemy they can't see coming.'

'Speak for your own men. Those of Paramore do not flinch in the face of the enemy.'

Alicia, Overlord of the Southlands, scoffed. 'Take your hand from your trousers, Carmine. Your men have been hiding behind mine, shitting themselves and jumping at shadows.' She was a long-boned woman with sharp features and a sharper mind. She wore her long hair tied high on her head so it cascaded down her back like a glossy black horse tail. Her helmet had been customised to allow for it and her entire warrior cohort had adopted the same style.

Carmine's finely shaped eyebrows bunched together in a scowl. 'Your army is too slow and too lazy for anyone to hide behind.'

Pellus contained his impatience. It hadn't taken long for old rivalries to surface between the overlords. He would need to redirect the argument before they started re-litigating the rights to the river that separated their provinces. He glanced at the king, but Felix's attention was on the squire standing to attention by the entrance. The king's mood had been dark since he'd spoken alone with the prophet this morning.

'If we increase our pace,' Pellus said, commanding the generals' attention, 'we will reach the scouted valley in less than a week. It remains the best place for us to make our stand and means we won't have to cross the Great Spine.'

'It might take *three* weeks,' Adward countered. 'We don't know this terrain.'

'Our ancestors didn't know the border lands two hundred years ago, and yet they were victorious in subduing the Pyriens and securing the mines.'

'True—against a handful of rock crushers and before the rise of the askari.' Adward cracked a knuckle. Pellus had come to recognise it as a sign of rising agitation. 'Xanthe knows we're coming,' Adward continued. 'She'll throw everything she has at us to diminish our forces while she has the upper hand. We have no idea of the true size of her army. How many more foot soldiers can we afford to lose before we give away the advantage of numbers?'

The war council had known there would be losses once they were beyond the mines and into territory that had only been mapped from the highest peak of the Border Mountains. But the death toll was higher than anticipated so early in the campaign and it was true that troops up and down the Amadean column were in constant fear the forest would spring to life with charging askari. The fleas picked off the weakest fighters with brutal efficiency and then melted back into the trees, barely uttering a sound. Amadean battle tactics had been tested and refined in border skirmishes, but never on a scale like this.

'If we take too long, we'll run out of food and the troops will starve before we get a chance to set for battle,' Carmine countered. 'The supply wagons will be empty in under a week and these forests offer little by way of meat except for wild goat.'

Alicia was not done baiting him. 'We need to adapt and eat what the Pyriens eat.'

'I will not ask my warriors to defile themselves with goat flesh!'

Pellus grit his teeth. It was enough of a challenge to lead an army the size of Iolia's. Did he have to sort out this petty squabbling too? He'd expected more from overlords. He and Adward had more restraint than the lot of them.

Gregori, Overlord of Bloodstone in the far north of Amadea, cleared his throat. He, like the king, had not yet waded into the argument. Unlike the king, though, Gregori had been listening.

'It concerns me that Xanthe is yet to throw herself into the fray.' He glanced around the circle. 'The only reason she has not joined the attacks is because she is elsewhere gathering her forces.'

'If that's true, it's even more reason we push forward,' Carmine said. 'We need to be at the battleground of our choosing when she crosses our path.'

The brazier fire in the centre of the pavilion popped and

sent a shower of sparks out through the opening above them. Adward sat back in his chair and huffed out a breath.

'What would you have us do instead, Adward?' Pellus asked.

The Iolian warrior fixed him with those stone-grey eyes, measuring the question, and Pellus. 'I'll gather a group of warriors from each province and a dozen archers at dawn. We'll dress as foot soldiers, hide our ink and weapons, and act as if we're deserting, drawing the askari away.'

Pellus nodded at the strategy. 'They won't be able to resist the sight of you fleeing on foot. They will take chase, and when they catch you—'

'We'll be ready.' Adward gave a grim smile of satisfaction. 'If we can reduce the size of the pack shadowing us, the next leg of our journey will be less fraught.'

'It's risky. You won't know the numbers coming against you.'

'Do we ever?'

They locked eyes, in agreement for the first time.

Gregori nodded. 'It's a valid plan.' He held up a palm before Carmine could jump in. 'Unless it takes more than a day for the askari to attack you and they leave a large enough pack behind to continue ambushing us, only now we'll be under-manned. It will give the Pyriens a chance to hem us in if they have the numbers. We could be trapped for weeks. Months.'

The king's head jerked up. 'Unacceptable.'

Everyone looked to Felix. There was something new in his expression; something nearing urgency.

'It's only a chance,' Gregori said, frowning. 'I'm not against Adward's proposal, we simply need to think through the possibilities—'

'There is no time. The prophet has commanded Xanthe's head be delivered to the Mountain Temple by the Day of Atonement.'

The news shocked Adward and the overlords into complete

stillness. Pellus absorbed the fact the king had not shared it with him in advance. Adward glanced at Pellus and caught his moment of surprise.

It was the overlord of the Southlands who broke the silence. 'Sire, that's less than a moon away.'

'I am well aware, Alicia.'

The overlords exchanged glances. Pellus was the first among the gathering to recover. 'What are your orders, sire?' he asked.

Felix chose not to look at him when he answered, focusing his gaze on the brazier fire instead.

'We double our pace. We need to be in that valley within four days.'

29

Tristan felt the tug back to the border like a rope around his chest. The farther he travelled from it, the harder he found it to breathe. Everything here was wrong: the tangy smell of the trees, the shrieks of unseen birds, the constant dampness in the air, the utter isolation of the mountainside. His gut clenched and his hands craved violence.

This is what it felt like to be a captive.

And it was worse now because they were travelling in the dark.

Yesterday, the journey had been constantly uphill, the column snaking back and forth as they'd climbed the Great Spine. Trees and brambles had grown thick and the way had narrowed. The track wasn't meant for oxen and cart, and the porpleza Alba referred to as *oracle* had frequently ordered the askari to widen the path so the beasts and wagon could fit through. The butchers grumbled at blunting their battle axes on saplings—but not within earshot of the spindly porpleza.

The slaves struggled with the climb. A handful of toothless women hung on to the wagon to let it pull them along and most of the children dragged their feet and fell behind. Pyriens this side of the border did not ride, so it didn't cross their minds to use the warhorses. Still the oracle drove them forward. He was so impatient at the slow progress that their sleep had been cut short and they had resumed the journey through the night.

Tristan had been awake when the askari came in the darkness and forced the Amadeans back into the wagon by torchlight. There had been no sign of the traitor monk Alba, so there was no-one to ask what was happening. Whatever it was, the askari were wary of something other than their prisoners. Six of them flanked the wagon as they set off with torches.

Not too far into the journey, the track started its descent. The air quickly became damp and the night breathless. A mist crept in to cast halos around the torch flames, giving an eerie glow to the wagon. Dread stirred in the pit of Tristan's belly. Sabine sat with her brother, gripping the bars as the wagon rounded another switchback. Tristan felt her eyes on him. She was looking for a sign from him, either as warrior or lover, but his pride burned from her mistrust and he was confused about how he should feel towards her. No matter how he poked and scratched at it, though, the anger that threatened to suffocate him sprang from the shitty situation, not Sabine. The way he felt about her was far more tangled.

Sweet Verus, he needed to *do* something with this storm of confusion under his ribs.

He only had to lock eyes with Rhys to know his cousin would rather die fighting at his side than they be taken into the heart of Pyrie like lambs to the slaughter. Their weapons had been bundled together and strapped to Trout. If he or Rhys could somehow get to them they would at least have a fighting chance. But of course it wasn't that simple. Nothing was, not since Ferugo and Dash had upended his world. He'd been told to trust Axl, and Axl believed they were where they were meant to be. That much was obvious in the way the monk found sleep every night. It was Alba's presence that had done it—convinced Axl their predicament was part of Verus's plan.

Tristan couldn't see how that was possible, and he'd played it out in his head a dozen times. *Maybe* they were being taken to the Tenth Prophecy. *Maybe* they could get their hands on it. Then what? They had to get back to Amadea, but to whom? Torvus was dead, Ferugo and Dash were prisoners. It all came down to Axl unlocking a power he didn't believe he possessed and then what? The boy would face down the prophet? The idea was laughable.

The scar on Tristan's palm tingled and he yet again cursed the Stonebridge abbot for the bond that had robbed him of choice.

His hand was still bothering him when the darkness shifted to something murkier. The first signs of daylight revealed a world shrouded in grey. Mist cloaked the wagon cell and its guards, shrinking the world to a suffocating closeness. With the newly risen sun hidden, it was impossible to track time as they continued downwards, twisting and turning until the ground finally flattened. The askari moved carefully, eyes scanning the deepening mist, and when a high-pitched keening carried through the shroud, the Pyriens flinched as much as the Amadeans. They muttered among themselves and the wolf-clan askara's hand strayed to the long-handled axe in her belt.

Shadows flitted in Tristan's peripheral vision and one of the oxen snorted and propped, forcing the other beast and the wagon to an abrupt halt. The silence was unnerving. The keening came again, this time from behind, and his cousin's tormenter spun around, axe in her hand.

Somewhere ahead the oracle barked a command in Pyrien and the slave in charge of the oxen got them moving again. The cell rocked sideways as it lurched forward. Tristan caught Sabine's eye and saw naked fear there.

The keening continued, louder still, and then the wagon bounced across a stream and the awful sound ended as abruptly as if a door had slammed shut. Rhys grunted his relief and the wolf-clan askara let out a nervous laugh. Their eyes met on reflex and her expression immediately hardened. She jabbed him with her axe handle for good measure.

Slowly, the fog lightened enough to see the lower part of trees either side of the wagon. They were as wide as ale barrels and instead of bark, they had skin as smooth and pale as a river stone. The caravan resumed a winding descent and when the path next levelled out, they were hemmed on one side by a rock face and on the other by a vast expanse of water.

How far had they travelled? There was no hint of salt in the air so it had to be the lake Alba spoke of, although its true size was hard to judge given the far shore was hidden by fog. Tendrils of mist rose like steam from its surface.

They rounded a bend and Tristan frowned at what was ahead. 'Where are we?' He tried to make sense of what he was seeing through the mist.

'Huh,' Rhys said. 'I didn't know these fleas had villages.'

Lystra grunted. 'The world could not hold all you do not know about us.'

Breaks in the mist revealed a cluster of timber huts on the lower part of the mountain slope, bunched tightly together right down to the water's edge. It was as if the buildings had sprung up out of the ground like flowers and the mountain forest had grown around them. Bright squares of fabric hung down from the apex of steep roofs: shades of orange, yellow and purple in stark contrast to the wind-blasted timber. The buildings perched over the water were on a pier. A retaining wall made of timber slabs stretched out in either direction beneath it, with the rest of village growing up the mountainside. It was not at all what Tristan had expected this side of the border.

As the caravan drew closer and the angle changed, he saw the village gate was wide enough for the oxen and wagon—but barely. They entered on a paved street lined with huts. Unlike Amadean homes, these were raised on stumps, with steps up to a narrow deck that ran the width of the house. Men, women and children emerged from each as the group approached. Tristan braced for abuse but when the villagers saw the oracle, they dropped to their knees and lowered their faces to the timber decking.

Tristan had never seen Pyriens like these.

Like askari, the men wore a knee-length tunic belted at the waist and their pale arms were bare. Unlike those worn by askari, these tunics were made of spun wool and dyed blue, and the men wore another piece of fabric pinned at each shoulder and shot through with golden thread. The women's tunics were longer, and their belts were braided with wool a dozen shades of pink and orange. Their moon-white hair was so clean it shone; the men wore theirs tied at the nape of their neck, the women, in two coiled braids. They too had bare limbs, but their ankles and wrists tinkled with shining bracelets, and when they sat back up to stare at the Amadean prisoners, Tristan saw they each wore broad decorative circlets around their neck. It was more gold than he had seen outside of Augustmount.

Each of the onlookers placed a palm over their heart as the group trudged past. Axl raised a hand in tentative greeting and Rhys slapped it down. The gesture wasn't for them. It was for the men, women and children who had been freed from the mines.

Ahead, the street forked. Veering right would take them on an even narrower way that snaked its way upwards between the terraced huts. The oracle led them left and onto to more even ground, travelling parallel with the lake. Tristan could see glimpses of the water between the fishing huts.

Sabine sniffed the air. 'Is that...?'

'Smoke,' Tristan confirmed and a beat later heard the unmistakable crackle of a roaring fire. This could not be good.

The street opened into a wide square and Tristan

straightened to get a better look. In the middle of the space was a towering bonfire. It was ringed by a knee-high stone wall blackened from soot and ash. The flames reached higher than the huts framing the square and Tristan could feel the heat, even at this distance. Fresh dread stirred beneath his ribs, a beat before hooded figures appeared from either side of the blaze. It was as if they had stepped out of the fire itself, their faces hidden under cloaks of black feathers.

Tristan exchanged an urgent glance with Rhys. Askari they could fight. What weapons did they have against more wielders of dark magic?

The porplezi joined up to form a single line in front of the bonfire and lowered their heads. Sabine drew her cloak tighter and Tristan saw she was shaking.

One of the porplezi stepped forward and pushed back their hood. The woman's face was free of the ash stripes the oracle and Alba favoured. She was younger than the oracle, and her white hair was cut close to her scalp. She approached as the wagon entered the square, a goat horn strung across her chest, and the slave leading the oxen brought the beasts to a halt. The other slaves did not wait for instruction. As one, they dropped to the hard-packed dirt, utterly depleted.

The oracle and the short-haired porpleza met halfway between the bonfire and the wagon. The young woman lowered her face and the oracle let her keep her head bowed for a long moment. Tristan sensed tension among the porplezi and saw the moment it eased when the oracle spoke and the younger one replied. The air was still and their voices carried as they conversed in Pyrien.

'What are they saying?' Rhys asked Axl, and for once the ill-tempered wolf-clan askara did not punish him for speaking.

The monk listened, his face a mask of concentration. 'The porpleza seems surprised to see the oracle...The oracle is giving instructions for these slaves to be fed and...' he focused before translating aloud, 'prepared for a ceremony.'

The oracle inclined his head in the direction beyond the fire and said four words. The younger porpleza shot a nervous glance over her shoulder.

'He wants someone summoned.' Axl pressed his palm to his chest. It was an unconscious gesture and one Tristan recognised, only now it made his skin crawl.

'*Bone witch?...*' Axl frowned.

The oracle turned, pointed to the wagon and spoke again. Axl and Sabine locked eyes. Whatever was said, Sabine understood enough for it to shock her. Tristan should have guessed she knew at least a little Pyrien given it was a slave who'd trained her to use her dagger.

'What is it?' Tristan demanded.

Sabine's eyes widened and he caught a hint of the wildness he'd seen at Stonebridge—the flare of panic that drove her to the brink of the abbey pinnacle. Axl swallowed and touched his chest again, unable to repeat whatever was said.

It was the wolf-clan askara who provided the translation.

'The oracle says we have two half-breeds who claim to be the bone witch's grandchildren.'

30

The short-haired porpleza lifted the horn she wore and blew a single, deep note. A prickly heat washed over Sabine, a dizzying assault of dread and anticipation that was even worse than the energy of the bonfire. It pushed and pulled at her, a living, breathing beast of a thing.

A breeze arrived as if summoned, fanning the bonfire and pushing back the lingering mist to reveal the base of a broad stone structure at the far side of the square.

'What is *that*?' Rhys hissed.

The sight brought a quiver in Sabine's chest, the strangeness of it stirring something deep and dark within her. It looked like the base of a castle keep—except Pyriens didn't build castles. The mist continued to lift, and it was obvious this was something altogether different. The structure had huge, stepped terraces that grew smaller and narrower the higher they went and a steep flight of stairs had been built into its face. Sabine craned her neck but the highest point was still hidden in cloud. Whatever this was, it was as tall as the outer curtainwall of Iolia Castle and extended into the mountainside behind it.

'A temple,' Axl said, barely breathing.

Rhys pressed his face between the bars. 'Pyriens hate temples.'

'They hate ours. This is not that.'

'These fleas don't have the skill to build something like this.'

'That's what we've told ourselves, Rhys. It doesn't make it true. This looks as old as Stonebridge. Older, even. A temple for the old gods...' Axl gripped Sabine's wrist. 'Look.'

A lone figure had appeared from the mist at the top of the stairs. The wolf-clan askara moved to the front of the wagon as if commanded and Axl spoke to her without turning his head: 'That is Nyomi?'

Lystra grunted confirmation.

The woman, faceless from this distance under a black-feathered hood, slowly descended. All feeling drained from Sabine's legs. She'd clung to the fraying hope that Nyomi had been a fabrication of Olidus's ale-soaked imagination, but this woman—this *bone witch*—was very real.

'There must be many women with that name?' Her brother's voice shook now.

'No,' Lystra said. 'There is only one.'

The waiting porplezi separated into two lines either side of the bonfire and each of them turned to face the descending woman. The porpleza who had called for Nyomi walked to the base of the steps, hidden behind the bonfire. The oracle did not move.

'*That's* meant to be your grandmother?' Rhys's voice came from far away. Sabine kept a grip on the cage as the blaze swam in and out of focus.

The two porpleza emerged on the lake side of the fire, the bone witch walking a step ahead of the other. Sabine could barely breathe. Beneath Nyomi's hood, wide bands of ash were smeared across her eyes and mouth. A long bone-white plait hung over one shoulder, stark against the black feathers of her cloak. She stalked towards the oracle and pushed back her hood.

'You return without notice and *summon* me?' Her Pyrien was raw and guttural.

The oracle, taller than her by a head, stared at her unflinching. 'You forget your place, Nyomi.'

'No, you have forgotten *yours*. It is here, not roaming the mountains like a wild goat.'

'I go where the gods lead and they led me to your kin.'

The bone witch finally acknowledged the wagon and locked eyes with Sabine. The effect was as paralysing as the dart. Nyomi barked an order. The askari guarding the cell did not react until the oracle echoed it. Sabine heard the wagon gate open, heard scuffling and swearing, but she couldn't take her eyes from Nyomi. Was she under her thrall?

'Sabine...' Axl was pleading for her to move, but the askari were already there, pulling her out of the wagon and dumping her belly-down on the ground beside the warriors.

She and Tristan were nose to nose. 'I'm sorry—' It was all she could manage before a spear tip pressed into the flesh beneath her ear and silenced her. Tristan could see her fear and confusion, though, and that was enough.

Nyomi let them lay in the dirt, soaked in dread, before Sabine and Axl were hauled up to their knees before her. The bone witch stood barely two arm's lengths away. She measured them, first Axl and then Sabine. There was a flicker of recognition in that cold stare.

'You are the spawn of the scourge who stole my daughter.'

Sabine and Axl locked eyes. *Stole*?

Nyomi's pale eyes flared at their confusion. 'Sabyl did not abandon her destiny willingly.' Her Amadean was heavily accented but there was no missing the venom in her words. She stabbed a finger at Axl. '*You* are the one who killed her. I would know it even if I had not seen it in a vision. I can sense her suffering all over you.'

Axl's face crumpled as the witch tore open his deepest wound.

Sabine loathed this woman for her careless cruelty. 'Our mother *loved* Axl,' she said between clenched teeth. 'She lived long enough to hold him and name him and bade me to protect him always.'

'You lie. You cannot remember that. You would have barely seen four winters yourself.'

Sabine didn't know if it was a real memory or one that her father had shared so often she'd come to believe it as her own. It didn't matter. 'They are the last memories I have of my mother and they are woven into my flesh.'

Nyomi registered a moment of surprise and then let out a bitter laugh. 'I see she had time to infect you with her love of pretty words.'

There was something so familiar about this awful woman. The height of her forehead, the fullness of her mouth. The pang Sabine felt had nothing to do with Nyomi and everything to do with the child she once was. The lonely girl who missed her mother.

'Our father did not *steal* my mother. She was not a slave.'

A grunt. 'There is more than one way to enslave a Pyrien.'

'No, there's not. There is only one way in Amadea and my—'

'Silence!' Nyomi snapped. Here eyes flared and she turned on the oracle. 'Why did you bring them to me?'

The oracle stepped in and pulled down the torn flap of Axl's robe. Like Nyomi, he spoke in Amadean. He wanted the warriors to understand.

'The boy wears our mark. He is the one.'

Nyomi's eyes narrowed as she absorbed this news.

'I doubt that but keep him if you want. Kill the others. I'll have their bones for the temple.'

Sabine's heart seized as the askari guarding the warriors lifted their spears for the death blow, looking to the oracle for confirmation. She reacted with thinking. She spun on her knees, palmed aside the spear inches from her own neck and launched herself to her feet. Tristan and Rhys rolled in opposite directions and took the guards' legs out from under them.

'Do not kill them!' the oracle cried.

The resistance was short-lived. Sabine and the warriors were immediately surrounded by more askari and again hemmed in at spearpoint. Without weapons of their own they had no chance. Axl was panting with fear, trying to see over his shoulder to reassure himself Sabine had survived.

'They are not your prisoners to execute,' the oracle said, furious. 'They are mine and I need them alive. They are bonded to the boy.'

The bone witch scoffed. 'Amadean bonding is a meaningless ceremony.'

'It was performed in the grove on the pinnacle under the trees and sky. The Great Pretender was not involved.'

'Is that true?' Nyomi demanded of Axl. He stared at her mutely, unable to hide his horror at the ease with which she was so willing to shed blood.

'Yes,' Sabine answered for him, her eyes flitting to the askari in case one of them decided to break ranks and lunge at her. 'I am bonded to the warriors, and they to him through me. Whatever Axl is, he cannot fulfil that destiny without us.'

She felt Tristan's eyes on her and was unsure if he was grateful or resentful that she'd spoken for him. Right now, her only concern was keeping the four of them alive.

'We will not know until we test the boy's blood.'

Test? Sabine waited for Axl's reaction, but her brother had dropped his chin to his chest and was somewhere else right now. The reality of the moment was too much for him.

Nyomi's gaze skimmed the faces of the askari and found Lystra. She did not seem impressed by what she saw.

'Guardian.'

The wolf-clan askara stepped forward.

'Has your skin been broken?'

'No.'

That was clearly untrue. Lystra still bore the wounds from the mine.

'You were enslaved by our enemy. They took your hair.'

The askara seemed to steel herself and Sabine understood with a start that Lystra feared the bone witch.

'Captured. Not enslaved.' She held out her wrist to show her clan tattoo was intact.

'You must earn back your honour before you are of any use to me.'

Lystra nodded and glanced towards the lake. Only now did Sabine see the mist had cleared to reveal the full landscape beyond the village. The lake was bordered on three sides by steep mountains and, thrust up in the middle of the watery expanse, a lone mountain stood taller than the rest. Its peak was not jagged like the others; it was a mass of smooth bare rock, as if one of the old gods had tried to push their way out of the ground, taking the earth with them.

'First,' the oracle said to Lystra, 'we will honour the dead and cleanse those we have brought back with us.'

'You best hope you are right about this boy,' Nyomi warned him. 'Xanthe does not forgive false hope.'

'She will see the truth with her own eyes.'

'You will need that evidence by the time she arrives.'

'Xanthe is coming here?' The oracle looked to the orb and frowned. 'Why has she left her forces?'

Nyomi lifted her ashen eyebrows, as if surprised he did not know. 'Xanthe has not left them. She brings her army with her.'

31

'Why are the scourge here?'

Lystra gestured with her chin to the Amadeans. All four were sitting on the ground by the wagon with their wrists bound. They had been positioned a stone's throw from the bonfire, giving them an uninterrupted view of what was to follow. 'This is not for their eyes.'

The oracle made a small noise of derision. 'That is not for you to decide.' He had been in a dark mood all day. He glanced down at the token in Lystra's hands. 'Your only concern is what you must do. Have you prepared?'

Lystra had bathed in the lake and washed the blood and grime of the mines from her body. She had allowed her wounds to be tended by the healers. And she had cleansed the carved wolf in her palm with her tears. 'Yes.'

Soon, she would pay her tribute to Dex. First, though, the porplezi would remove the symbol of bondage from those who'd been enslaved by the enemy, and then honour the sacrifice of the dead initiate.

It was mid-afternoon, though it felt later with the sun hidden behind a low bank of clouds. This time of year the greyish light lingered longer, and now that the breeze had completely dropped there was barely a ripple on the water's surface. It was as if the lake itself was waiting for what was to come. Lystra ran her thumb over Dex's wolf, tracing its tiny nose and ears and then following its spine down to the tip of its tail. A lump rose in her throat.

Not yet.

To distract herself she looked to Rhys and found him watching her, a forearm resting on his bent knee as if the sacred rite was a mere curiosity. He raised his eyebrows in challenge and her hatred for him flared enough to fleetingly smother the heart-crushing grief. Lystra took some satisfaction that Rhys and the other warrior had positioned themselves apart from Nyomi's half-breeds; that the so-called bond was being tested.

The warrior-sister sat hunched with her face in her hands. The monk-brother watched Nyomi, wall-eyed with fear. The bone witch stood with her back to them as if they meant nothing to her, but Lystra could see the lie of it in the way she clenched and unclenched her fingers, staring at the bonfire unseeing.

'Why won't you let her kill them?' Lystra asked the oracle.

The oracle offered a humourless laugh. 'You fight well, guardian, yet you do not listen. Do you not feel the shifting weight of the ink you bear on your shoulders?'

Irritation sparked but she was careful not to show it. 'My duty is to carry the marks. It is for others to understand them.'

'And yet you ask why the Amadeans live.' He moved away and took his place on the dais beside the fire.

Lystra huffed. Surely, the oracle could not believe that any among the enemy would be able to decipher the glyphs on her shoulders when generations of porplezi had not? She was the sixth askara to wear them, and every generation found new meaning in them. None had been correct.

An acolyte—not the Amadean—brought the oracle his stave. The orb had been returned to the bonfire on his arrival as was required by the gods. Before he accepted the stave, the oracle took one of the three ceremonial knives from his belt and nicked his palm. He tilted his head back and held his fist over his mouth, letting the blood drip onto his tongue. Lystra heard a hiss from one of the warriors. The oracle smiled at them, his teeth smeared with his own blood, and then he sprayed the mouthful into the bonfire. The flames roared in response, stretching for the sky as thick ribbons of dark red wove their way through the fire. The oracle accepted his stave and pointed it at the cluster of slaves sat in the grass.

Styx and his troth-mate, the quicksilver woman, were the first to step forward. They knelt in front of the oracle and presented their clan tattoos, now marred with the red-ink slash of slavery. The oracle gestured for the Amadean acolyte Alba to kneel beside them, and then he thrust his stave into the coals of the bonfire.

'Hold them,' the oracle said when the gold-capped tip was hot enough.

Alba took Styx's wrist and held it tightly as the oracle pressed the heated gold into the slave's tattooed skin. The unmistakable stench of burning flesh tainted the afternoon air. Styx grimaced but made no sound. When it was his troth-mate's turn, she hissed through her gums but did not cry out.

'This day, you are reborn,' the oracle pronounced. 'You no longer belong to the clan of your birth. You are now bonded into a new clan, the clan of the libertini. What will you do with this freedom?'

Styx and his troth-mate lifted their heads and said together, their voices tight with pain, 'Whatever Xanthe requires of us to please the gods.'

'Go, seal the mark.'

The pair rose, each cradling their wrist, and hurried to a circle of porplezi with large wooden bowls. As soon as the new libertini sat, the porplezi began pouring water over their burns, emptying one bowl into another over and over again.

One by one, each of the slaves who had trekked from the

mines stepped forward and had their new lives seared into their flesh. Acolytes refilled bowls from a cask of water as needed.

Indy stepped forward and Lystra registered the slightest movement from Rhys. The child walked alone to the oracle. She held up her bony wrist and lifted her chin, her jaw clenched, bracing for the pain. She closed her eyes and bared her teeth when the brand sizzled on her skin, but no sound escaped her. The oracle repeated what he'd asked each slave and the whelp met his gaze, unflinching.

'Speak, little one,' the oracle commanded.

Indy lifted her chin higher. Tears streamed down her face—from the agony of the burn inside her wrist or a deeper wound, Lystra couldn't tell.

'For fuck's sake, let her be treated,' Rhys muttered from where he sat on the ground.

Lystra held up a hand to silence the warrior and called out, 'The girl does not speak.'

The oracle looked at the child more closely. 'Is she dull-witted?'

'No.' Notwithstanding her obsession with Rhys. 'The scourge have stolen her voice.'

The oracle considered this for a long moment. 'Will you do whatever Xanthe requires of you to please the gods?' he asked the child.

She nodded, tears streaming down her cheeks.

'Go, seal the mark.'

The girl fled to the porplezi. Rhys watched as the wound was washed and wrapped, and when his eyes met Lystra's again they were full of accusation. Did he not see the irony of his outrage?

Next, four askari carried forward the body of the dead initiate brought from the mine. He was properly wrapped now, head to toe. 'Ares, honour the sacrifice of the wolf clan,' they intoned. The askari lifted the body above their heads and, with the skill born of endless loss, swung and tossed the offering to near the top of the flaming pile. The shroud caught and the oracle called forth the weeper. With none of the initiate's own pack mates present for the initiative, it was left to a stranger to mourn for him. A small porpleza stepped forward. She held her arms wide, threw her head back and began to wail.

Lystra did not have Dex's corpse to offer to the fire, only his token. She felt hollow beneath her ribs as she stepped forward gripping the wolf tightly, preparing herself. Once she let it go, Dex would be gone. She should have hidden the token, kept it with her even if it meant Dex would be in exile from the gods until she died and—

'It is time.'

Styx had joined her by the flames as he had promised he would. His left wrist was wrapped in flax and his mouth pinched in discomfort, but he was there.

Lystra's bruised heart ached for her fallen friend.

She raised the wolf to her lips and kissed its head, let the rush of memories wash over her: Dex as a boy, putting corn husks on his head to make her laugh; catching her eye to distract her from the agony of a whipping when she missed a target; burying his axe in the head of the warrior who'd run her down with his warhorse in their first settlement raid. Dex had trained against her and fought beside her, each making the other stronger, and he'd respected her ascension to pack leader even when he could just as rightfully been given the honour.

'Ares, mighty god of war, honour the sacrifice of Dex of wolf clan. He served you well.'

She lobbed the wolf as gently as she could into the flames. She watched it flare before sinking into the inferno, and then she threw back her head and let loose the grief she'd carried since that day in the forest. Styx joined her, his voice cracking, and she knew it wasn't for Dex alone. It was for all those he'd lost to Amadean steel and iron. The weeper added her voice and the dying afternoon was heavy with their lamentations.

32

The wailing was almost worse than the smell of burning flesh. Almost.

The keening burrowed into Sabine and snaked around her insides. She hugged her knees to her chest, desperate to convince herself she had no connection to these wild people. How could she when they repelled her so utterly?

'They drink blood and burn their dead.' She whispered it to Axl as if he'd not just witnessed the same defilement. The death ritual was no secret but hearing the stories and witnessing it were very different things. Her brother sat on his heels, his gaze skittering between Nyomi, Alba and the oracle. Sabine risked a glance at Tristan and there weren't enough shadows to mask his revulsion.

'We are not them,' Sabine insisted. Tristan didn't answer, but he didn't disagree either.

At last the wailing stopped. The afternoon was again silent except for the crackling fire and the spitting and hissing body Sabine had robbed of life four days ago. The wolf-clan askara walked away from the pyre with heavy steps. Sabine wondered who it was she mourned, this Dex of wolf clan.

Nyomi pointed to Axl and then Sabine.

'Get up,' Sabine said, hauling her brother to his feet as best she could with bound wrists. She would not give Nyomi the satisfaction of having them dragged before her again.

'Kneel,' Nyomi said when they reached her.

Axl obeyed but Sabine stood firm, aware now of her height advantage over the witch. Her heart knocked against her ribs.

'*Kneel.*'

A kick to the back of her right knee took her to the ground and she was beside Axl before she had time to counter.

The woman who'd given birth to their mother looked down on them. Her pale blue eyes were shrewd, her lips flattened in disdain. She smelled of smoke and death. Beneath her black feathered cloak she wore a plain tunic, belted at the waist with tightly braided flax. A dagger and a paring knife were sheathed on her hip. The dagger hilt was shaped like Sabine's, except where hers was unmarked, Nyomi's carried the unmistakable clan mark of the raven.

My mother was a raven. And her name was Sabyl, not Sabella.

Nyomi scowled. 'My daughter wasted her gift to bring you two into the world?' She shook her head in disgust. 'If not for you and your father, Amadea would be in chaos and my people would have driven yours back into the sea.'

The words made no sense to Sabine.

'Your father took her from me,' the bone witch continued, 'and then he put her in the ground instead of returning her to the flames where I could find her.'

'You saw that?' Axl asked, his voice wavering.

'I see everything, *scourge*. I saw your father, a wretched excuse for a man.'

Hatred flared. 'If you truly saw him, then you know that's a lie,' Sabine said.

Nyomi smiled without humour. 'I saw that he crossed the border looking for me.'

That wasn't news. Sabine's uncle had told her as much. It's what got her father killed.

'Yes, and he died on the border because of it.'

'No, he was *injured* on the border and brought to me.'

Sabine blinked. Irrational hope flared so intensely it hurt her heart. 'My father is alive?'

Nyomi threw back her head and laughed. 'Your *father* stole the gift of Ares, and you think I let him live?' She drew the dagger from her belt, her blue eyes shining. 'I ended his life with this very blade and let the wolves feed on his carcass. Then I fashioned a chair out of his bones. Every day I sit on them and thank the gods for the honour.'

There was a dizzying beat while those words took their full, monstrous shape, and then the night ground to a halt. The bonfire blurred and the orange-streaked sky pressed down. Sabine swayed on her knees, vaguely aware Axl was retching. Wild thoughts spun and tumbled.

This witch murdered her father. She let his body be desecrated.

She sits on his bones.

Sabine's world narrowed to Nyomi. For the first time in many moons she had clarity of purpose. She wanted to hurt this woman. No, more than that: she wanted to burn her alive.

Sabine focused on the bonfire and pictured a lick of flame separating from the blaze and arcing through the air at Nyomi, now walking away. She clenched her hands and her jaw in fierce concentration. *Burn her!* Sabine felt heat rush along her arms and for a heartbeat the bonfire blazed brighter and a flame thrust out of it like a serpent—

'Sabine!'

Axl's panicked cry tore her concentration.

'*Sabine!*'

Her attention snapped to her brother. An askara was dragging him by his bound wrists after Nyomi.

Sabine forgot about the fire. She was on her feet and to

Nyomi in four steps, her speed taking everyone by surprise. She snatched the dagger from the flat-footed witch and looped her bound wrists over Nyomi's head, pulling her close as a shield.

Tristan and Rhys lunged at their own guards and the lakeside erupted into chaos. Axl barely made it out of arm's reach before the askara who'd been holding him grabbed his cowl and jerked it hard, ripping him off his feet. Sabine's brother met the ground with a thud, and the askara pressed her spear to Axl's chest to keep him there.

'Stop!' the oracle shouted in Pyrien and the askari fell back into a loose formation around the warriors. Tristan and Rhys were back-to-back and ready to fight, surrounded yet again on all sides by askari. Two more Pyriens were picking themselves up from the ground. Tristan held an axe that he'd taken from one of them. He was cut above his right eye, blood trickling down the side of his face. He risked a glance at Sabine.

'What do you want to do?' he panted.

Sabine kept Nyomi close and angled the dagger at her throat. 'I want to kill her.'

'Do it.'

'That would be a death sentence for *all* of you,' the oracle said in Amadean. His mouth was smeared with blood from the ritual and his eyes were black.

'You have more porplezi,' Sabine said.

'None like her.' The oracle very intentionally shifted his gaze to the top of the temple beyond the bonfire.

On the ground, Axl lifted his head, desperate. 'Is the Tenth Prophecy up there?'

The oracle did not answer. He was studying Sabine as if seeing her for the first time. 'Do not harm Nyomi.'

'She bragged of murdering my father and was about to kill my brother.' Sabine dug the tip of the dagger into Nyomi's throat. The blade felt so familiar she forgot for a moment it wasn't her own.

'Were you?' the oracle asked. 'Speak their language.'

Nyomi grunted. 'I was going to test his blood.'

The oracle gave her a withering look. 'We agreed we would wait for Xanthe.'

'I am impatient.'

'And now you have your own blade at your neck.'

Nyomi had no answer for that.

'Child of Sabyl, we will not break the blood bond until its meaning has been revealed,' the oracle said.

'That's not much reassurance.'

The oracle glanced at the sky. 'Do you wish to die before the sun finds her rest? Or did you come here with a purpose yet to be fulfilled?'

Sabine felt the bonfire at her back, knew these monsters would not hesitate to throw her onto it if she was of no value to them. She locked eyes with Tristan. She knew his instinct was to fight, but that instinct was at war with the promises he'd made to Ferugo and fear for his sister's life. Sabine shifted her focus to her brother.

'Do you still believe this is where Verus wants us to be?'

His chest rose and fell, and she saw how much he needed the horror here to have meaning. For Sabine to find the destiny he imagined for her. 'Yes.'

Lystra stood by watching it all, impassive, weighed down with her grief. The stench from the fire was worse now.

What choice was there? Either they were here for a reason, or they weren't.

'Argh,' she grunted and shoved Nyomi away. Her grandmother had stumbled only a few steps clear when a familiar sting flared in her neck.

Sabine dropped to the ground, barely able to soften the

fall with her hands. As her head met the dirt and the world receded, she hoped the answer was worth giving up the only advantage they'd had since they were captured.

33

Felix woke to darkness, his thoughts thick and slow as he surfaced from the murky depths of sleep.

He'd dreamt of Torvus again.

It wasn't the nightmare that came most evenings. The one where he again watched on, powerless, as the flames of the pyre reached the warrior's boots; when he endured Torvus's screams, first at the betrayal, and then in agony; and then came the knee-buckling relief when an anonymous arrow ended the cruelty. Felix always gasped awake soaked in sweat and grief at that moment.

Tonight, though, was different.

Tonight, he'd dreamt Torvus had come to him here, in his pavilion. The warrior had sat, not next to him in his rightful place but across the brazier, his right ankle resting on the opposite knee, tankard in hand. He'd repeated the words he'd uttered in the cells beneath the high temple, so softly Felix had needed to lean forward in the dream to hear them.

You will never fulfil your destiny if you choose to live in blindness and let a power-hungry prophet lead you around in the dark.

The words cut deeper now and the magnitude of the loss crushed the breath from him.

Torvus was dead.

Worse, Torvus was *gone*.

According to the Codex, the dead must be returned to the earth in thanks to Verus. Only then, with the proper rites, could they pass into to the world beyond where Verus dwelled with her brother and the elder gods who'd abandoned Amadea a millennia ago. But Torvus had not been buried. Torvus had been *consumed*. And in the belly of night, Felix was terrified that meant he would not see his friend in the afterlife.

The king felt Torvus's absence like he would a missing limb. He was no longer whole—and that was a dangerous state given he had now brought his kingdom to a point of no return.

The Amadean army had reached the valley in four days as ordered. As the scouts had promised, it was an expanse of grassland eaten low by livestock, positioned between steep mountains. The only way in for Xanthe was the pass at the northern end. The Amadeans had total control of the southern access. The troops were bloodied, bruised and foot-sore, yet Felix had made it further into Pyrie than any Amadean king before him.

The prophet was pleased.

Felix's army was less than two-thirds of the size it had been when it crossed the border, but his men had left a trail of dead Pyriens in their wake: mostly the herders who'd hurled spears at them, but also their children who'd thrown rocks and stones.

Why had Torvus come to him now in his dreams? Did he disapprove of the killings? No, the warrior would not begrudge Felix what had to be done on the battlefield. Yes, Torvus had grown tired of routine bloodshed in the borderlands, but the warrior understood what was required in war. What Torvus would rail against, if he were here, was how easily Felix had bent to the prophet's will. Alive, Torvus would not have sat calmly across the fire and whispered uncomfortable truths. He would have paced the pavilion and raged at Felix, slamming his fist into his palm to drive home his point.

Unlike Pellus, who, despite his clear desire to please the king, was the prophet's warrior first and always. Or Adward, who could barely meet the eye of the king who had allowed Ferugo and Dashelle to be imprisoned. Even the overlords, so quick to bicker among themselves, acquiesced to their king, but it was of out fear and greed, not love.

Damn Torvus and his pride.

Away from the prophet, Felix had to work harder to remember it was Torvus who had betrayed *him*; chosen Anguston's heresy over his own life; over Felix.

A muffled sob reminded him he was not alone.

In the gloom, he could make out the Iolian squire beside the brazier. Ty was sitting with his head between his knees and hands clasped around his neck. He'd let the fire burn to embers and was so caught up in his own misery he hadn't heard Felix sit up.

'Boy.'

Ty's head came up so fast his neck cracked and he was on his feet in an instant, chest heaving and eyes again down.

'Get the fire going and be quiet about it. I don't want a visitor.' He meant Pellus. That man likely had eyes everywhere.

The squire hurriedly wiped his cheeks with the back of one hand and got to work with sticks from the kindling box. Felix stood stiffly and made his way to his chair, refusing to feel pity. The boy's suffering was necessary. The king hoped he had time to make it count. Pellus would come to him at the first flush of dawn and this was not a conversation for an audience.

When the fire had caught again, Felix ordered the squire to sit. 'Beside me,' he clarified when the boy started to lower himself to the ground.

Ty hesitated.

'It's a chair, not a promotion.'

The squire sat down warily beside the king as if he expected the seat to bite him. His face flickered in the firelight, his breathing quick and shallow.

'Did you spend time with Torvus?'

The question took the boy by surprise, so much so that Ty looked the king in the eye. Horrified, he snapped his attention back to the fire.

'Answer me.'

'Yes, sire.' It came out barely a whisper.

'When?'

'We rode to Augustmount with him.' Ty pulled on his thumb until a knuckle popped. First his right, then his left. 'Two nights after planting day feast,' he added.

'Ferugo travelled that week?' It was unheard of for an overlord to be anywhere but his own lands a moon either side of planting day.

'No sire...Tristan.' His voice broke on the warrior's name. 'And me.'

'Why?'

Ty swallowed, took a shaky breath. 'To find Sabine and Axl and bring them back to Iolia.'

'Who are Sabine and Axl and why was Tristan sent to find them?'

Ty squeezed his eyes shut and tapped a knuckle against his forehead in reprimand. Yes, there were secrets here, all right.

'I don't have the patience for this dance, boy.'

The squire exhaled, thought long and hard before he recounted what Felix recognised was a hastily adapted version of the story. 'We met Sabine on the road in the Southlands...'

In fits and starts, Ty told him that Tristan and his cousin Rhys had escorted a young optimati woman to Stonebridge Abbey to reunite with her brother who was a monk there. The boy, though, had not long left on pilgrimage for Augustmount, and when the girl desired to follow him the warriors continued the escort. They caught up with the monk at Nominatia and the party continued together on to Iolia, where they remained for planting day feast. And yet, within days of reaching Iolia, the siblings were in the capital and Tristan was sent to find them, with Torvus keeping him company. There was only one reason Torvus would involve himself in Iolian affairs.

'What's the monk's connection to the heresy?'

Ty bent forward and linked his hands over his neck again, distressed.

'Tell me,' Felix growled.

'It doesn't matter, he's dead.' A small sob. 'He and Sabine.'

'How do you know?'

Ty raised his face to his king, cheeks shining in the firelight. 'You said nobody survived the attack at the mine.'

It was a beat before Felix understood. 'This woman and the monk were *with* them?'

The boy squeezed his eyes shut, realising his mistake. Felix reached over and clamped his hand around Ty's neck, yanked him closer.

'Why did Torvus care about the monk?' He tightened his grip. 'Look at me.' The king saw the squire's turmoil—anguished with grief and his imminent act of betrayal. 'I command you to tell me.'

Ty swallowed hard, blinked back tears, and whispered, 'He believed Axl was the one promised by the Tenth Prophet.'

Felix let go and sat back, flashing hot and then cold.

Torvus had said it himself. *The usurper may already be in our kingdom.*

Felix felt it then, a small spark. Of what, he couldn't yet say, but it filled his lungs and sharpened his mind. There had been no mention of a monk or optimati woman among the dead.

And given Tristan and Rhys were, in fact, alive, it meant all four were most likely together somewhere in Pyrie.

34

Lystra should have slept soundly.

She'd paid her tribute to Dex and sent him on his way to the gods. It should have been enough to bring her peace, but she'd been a captive and there was a price to be paid for that shame. She could not relax until her honour was restored.

She'd spent the night with the oracle's askari. Ordinarily she would have been given the place of honour by the hut door, yet it was Lystra who had slept against the far wall as if she were the weakest among them and needed protection. It stung. As did the fact the askari were forbidden from sharing a meal or fighting beside her until she'd earned back those rights. Given who Lystra was, only their ruler could determine what was required of her. Just the thought of what Xanthe would do with that power made her insides twist.

Grey light filtered through timber shutters, casting stripes across the stirring askari. Lystra threw off a borrowed blanket and gingerly sat up. She was a mess of aches and pains, each injury further proof of her failure: welts on her neck and legs; fading bruises on her thighs and shoulders; back muscles still stiff from the boulder. There were so many sore points she almost missed the usual quirks of her body. Lystra rolled her wrists and flexed her fingers, hoped Rhys would give her an excuse to fight him again today. Since Dex's death, her only triumph had been closing his throat and watching him pass out.

The askari nervously met her gaze before each one filed out of the hut ahead of her. They at least believed she would regain her honour and that she'd remember how each had treated her while she was without status.

Lystra hooked her axe through her belt and headed out into the mist-shrouded morning. At the foot of the temple, the acolytes were building the bonfire back up, readying for Xanthe's arrival. The prisoners were in the wagon cell where they'd spent the night. The oracle had ordered alpaca fleeces be thrown over the top of the cage to ward off dew and given each of them blankets. It made Lystra's teeth itch that he was treating them with a consideration Amadeans *never* extended to Pyriens. It meant he believed the lies the monk had spun.

The sister-warrior, Sabine, had been unconscious when Lystra left the fire last night. The warrior who was not Rhys— Tristan—had carried her to the wagon, threatening any askara who got too close. She was now awake and groggy and the warrior was giving her space. The stories about Nyomi's seat of bones were legendary, but it had been a misstep for the porpleza to taunt Sabine. Hatred was a sharper weapon than fear.

Without consciously making the decision, Lystra approached the prisoners. Rhys had his back to her, his face pressed against the bars as if looking at something on the ground. She rounded the cell wagon and found the whelp, Indy, sitting against one wheel, her freshly washed face turned up to the warrior.

What was *wrong* with this child?

'What poison are you pouring into her ears?' she demanded in Amadean.

'I'm telling her how I will beat you when we next fight.' He smirked, but the dark circles under his eyes undermined his attempt at arrogance. He'd not had a restful night.

Lystra scoffed. 'The child does not understand you.'

'She understands enough.'

Styx approached with a clay bowl filled with mussels from the lake and offered it to Lystra.

'You should not bring me food.' She said it quietly, not wanting the monk to hear and translate for Rhys.

'*I* am not askari. I am libertini,' Styx said. 'I am free to do as I will.'

Lystra's stomach rumbled, so she followed Styx down the laneway to the water's edge. They sat together on the pier, their bare feet in the clear, cold water. He watched her crack each shellfish and suck out the flesh. The mussels were plump and creamy, a delicacy she did not deserve.

'When do you go?' she asked when she'd finished slurping the last traces of flavour from the shells. The libertini would each start the journey home now they had been cleansed. Most stayed loyal to the clan of their birth, even if they could no longer live among their own people.

'We leave for the flatlands tomorrow. We were herders there. Perhaps we can take up the crook again.'

Lystra frowned. The flatlands were at least a ten-day walk from the border. 'How were you captured?'

He gave a rueful smile. 'Five winters ago, when Xanthe reunited the clans, we followed our chief east. I saw the truth: that we could only defeat the enemy through weight of numbers. Those of us in the flatlands could no longer pretend the troubles at the mines belonged only to wolf and raven. Not when generations of Pyriens had been enslaved on both sides of the border.' He smiled ruefully. 'I was captured in my first mine raid.'

Lystra was still thinking about the distance to his homeland. 'Are there libertini so far west?'

'There were when we left. We will join them if they will have us.'

Even among the libertini there were politics and prejudice.

'Get word to me if they treat you poorly. I will come and remind them we are one Pyrie now.'

He glanced at his wrist. Lystra could smell the honey smeared on the burnt skin beneath the bandaging. 'I am branded, Lystra. I am not cleansed. I will never be free from this shame.'

Lystra shifted her gaze to the lake proper. The sky was cloudy and the water was the colour of quicksilver. Would that be her fate, too? That she would do whatever Xanthe asked of her but it would never be enough. Was the weight of captivity so heavy it could never be cast aside?

A horn blast carried from the northern watchtower.

'Xanthe is coming,' Styx said, instantly breathless.

Icy fingers grazed Lystra's heart. This was it. She tossed the empty shells into the water and handed the bowl back to Styx. 'Thank you.' She said it so he understood her gratitude was for more than the meal.

When they reached the temple forecourt, Styx went to find his woman and Lystra hastened her pace. She needed to be in position when Xanthe arrived.

The army flowed down from the mountains like a river, more than a thousand askari, four abreast and spears held upright stabbing at the sky as the pack moved at jog. Never had so many fighters been gathered. Not herders and weavers and growers: askari.

Lystra's blood sang.

What a terrifying sight we will be when we descend on the Amadeans.

The army did not come via the Forbidden Way as Lystra had been forced to yesterday—the shrieks of the angry gods still thrummed in her marrow—but from the high pass further north. That track linked to the heart of Pyrie, and every askari initiate who trekked to the lake came that way.

Even from this distance Lystra could pick out Xanthe at the front setting the pace. The ruler of Pyrie wore no special markings, had no standard bearer. Anyone who knew her recognised her, though, even from afar. It was the way she carried herself, as if Ares himself ran at her shoulder. Immediately behind her ran four of the five clan leaders. They wore the head-dress of their people: black feathers for raven; curled horns for goat; woven reeds for weaver-finch; and tusks for the tapyr.

Wolf clan, then, must be shadowing the Amadean army. As it should be.

On the ridge above the village, Xanthe raised her fist and the askari in the front line did the same, slowing to a walk and then coming to a halt. The signal rippled backwards through the ranks and within moments the army began to spill out either side of the track, spreading across the face of the mountain. Xanthe continued down to the village alone.

The oracle was on his way to the dais.

'Does she know I'm here?' Lystra asked him as he passed.

The oracle answered without taking his eyes from the approaching ruler. 'I sent word yesterday.'

Acolytes had loaded fuel onto the fire and it now blazed high, pushing out scorching heat. Nyomi took her place on the first step of the altar, slightly below the oracle but higher than the rest of the porplezi. The libertini sat at the foot of the porplezi, fidgety with nerves. The monk and the warriors were out of the wagon and on their knees, hands bound in front of them, and their askari guards stood to attention with their spears dug into the ground. Lystra choose a patch of dirt between the libertini and the askari. She planted her feet and lifted her chin, resenting the nervous thud of her heart.

Xanthe was a hundred paces away now. The horn blew a

second time and Lystra dropped to one knee and bowed her head in unison with the other askari.

'Welcome, Xanthe, blessed of the gods, ruler of the five clans and blade in the neck of Amadea.' The oracle's voice carried across the forecourt. 'How may the lake be of service to you?'

Xanthe continued her approach as she gave her required response: 'I seek the will of the gods and for my askari to draw strength from the waters.'

Lystra's skin prickled. Xanthe had barely seen twenty-two winters, yet her voice was deep and husky and resonated with authority. Lystra felt the faint, familiar, sting of envy.

'I was pleased to hear you had returned to the lake, oracle.'

The oracle did not respond and Lystra wished she could lift her eyes and see the exchange.

'The enemy will soon reach the plains beyond the spine,' Xanthe said, closer now. 'They have been fooled into thinking they have the advantage but they will not expect the askari pack that will devour them.'

'Gods willing, we have an even greater weapon for you to wield,' the oracle said.

'So you claim.' A beat. 'Where is the guardian?'

Lystra's eyes were fixed on the hard-packed dirt in front of her and she could *feel* the moment Xanthe saw her. Her pulse beat hard in her throat. She risked a glance. Of course Xanthe was coming over to deal with her before the Amadeans.

Mud-splattered goat-hide sandals stopped within striking distance. The ruler of Pyrie smelled of sweat and lanolin and dried goat.

'You failed to protect your pack.' Xanthe's voice was cold, not intended to carry. There was no performance. Not yet. There was also no question, so Lystra did not speak or lift her head.

'You were a slave to the enemy.'

Lystra thrust out her wrist to show her clan tattoo was unmarred.

'You worked the mines, Lystra,' Xanthe hissed. 'You had to be *rescued*. Look at me.' Lystra lifted her head and met her ruler's stony gaze. Xanthe leaned closer. 'Your bare head is a disgrace. You've brought shame to our bloodline.'

Of the all the indignities forced upon Lystra at the mine, the loss of her hair was the worst. It would be a reminder of her shame long after the welts and bruises were gone.

'How in the name of Ares did you get caught?'

'It was an ambush.' Lystra said between clenched teeth. 'Dex is gone. I watched him die.'

Xanthe blinked. She hadn't known that. 'Have you paid tribute?'

'Last night.'

Xanthe nodded and for a moment she was not the ruler of Pyrie, but the older girl Lystra had followed around as a child like a whelp.

'It is good you survived, sister.'

Lystra's breath hitched in surprise. 'I am pleased you think it.'

'How can I not? You are worth nothing to me dead.'

The humiliation was instant. Lystra burned with it. She took a moment to swallow it down before she spoke again.

'How can I regain my honour, my ruler?'

Xanthe sniffed, a habit she'd picked up from their late father, the wolf king. 'I will confer with the oracle. But if you fail me again, sister, I will end you myself.'

The ruler of Pyrie put her back to Lystra and strode toward the dais, gesturing for the oracle to come down from his ceremonial position. Nyomi joined Xanthe without invitation. The three spent a long moment with their heads bent together.

Lystra couldn't hear what was said, but Xanthe raised her

eyebrows at Nyomi at one point and then finally acknowledged the prisoners.

'Askari, get them on their feet!' the Pyrien ruler ordered.

The guards by the cell wagon rose from their knees. Lystra took her place among them, daring Xanthe to challenge her right to do so. The ruler crossed to the Amadeans as they were hauled upright. The monk put his chin to his chest, shoulders folding inwards as if willing himself to disappear. The sister-warrior lowered her eyes but not her face. The other two warriors refused to even do that.

'Drop your gaze,' Lystra growled at them.

Tristan ground his jaw and lowered his eye line to Xanthe's throat. Rhys ignored the order and glared at Xanthe in open defiance. Xanthe spat on him. Rhys continued to eyeball her, even as spittle dribbled down from his forehead. Lystra felt a twinge of satisfaction that his disrespect extended beyond her.

Nyomi was arguing with the oracle. 'Ares would not allow Verus to put power in the hands of an Amadean again, let alone a servant of the Great Pretender and three warriors.'

The oracle lifted upturned palms outwards from his chest and around, indicating it was not his place to question the gods. 'The signs are clear.'

Xanthe, apparently, agreed. 'Bring them to the cave,' she ordered.

Lystra grimaced. Her humiliation was not yet complete.

The Amadeans were prodded forward, toward the lake. As Rhys passed Lystra, he faked lunging at her in an attempt to make her flinch. She scoffed at him. 'I will do more than spit on you, scourge.'

Xanthe watched the exchange, amused. 'Let me see if the wolf still has teeth. Untie him and let them fight.'

Lystra's blood hummed as Rhys was unbound. She turned side-on and balanced her weight, waiting.

Tristan reached out to Rhys with bound hands. 'Don't—'

The warrior charged.

Of course Rhys was stupid enough to use the same tactic as last time.

But then the warrior seemed to falter, almost tripping over himself, and Lystra was taken completely by surprise when he *leapt* at her and tackled her in a bear hug. All she could do was stagger back, shocked—this was not how Amadeans fought—before he used his momentum to fling her to the ground. And then he was on her chest, pinning her with a forearm to her throat the same way she had pinned him not two days ago.

She was almost out of breath when Xanthe ordered three askari to intervene and drag him off. They drew blood in the process but it was a small consolation. When Lystra sat up, Rhys was grinning at her with bloodied lips.

'You remain a disappointment, sister,' Xanthe said, and walked away.

35

Sabine's head thudded and the dull buzzing was back in her ears. It might have been the lingering effects of a second dose of poison or her hatred for Nyomi. The witch was far enough ahead to deter another attack, but that didn't stop Sabine from planning what she would do when the opportunity came.

They'd been walking beside the lake for a good half-mile, navigating a narrow ledge. It was barely above the waterline and the going forced them to travel in single file. There were fifteen in their party, strung out like beads in the still, grey morning. Nyomi was third in line behind the Pyrien ruler and the oracle. Then came Indy, Lystra, Alba, Axl, Rhys, Sabine and Tristan. A twitchy askara had a spear tip at the base of Axl's skull as incentive to keep the other Amadeans in check and four more askari brought up the rear. Indy trudged in front of Lystra, her earlier attempt to fall back to be closer to Rhys having been thwarted.

Tristan had spoken little today, but he'd kept close to Sabine and intentionally put himself between her and any Pyrien who came too close. Last night, he'd carried her to the wagon and held her, wordlessly, while the poison worked its way through her blood. Sabine had felt his agitation in the tremble in his fingers and the rapid rise and fall of his chest. And then Axl had taken her hand and pressed it to his forehead, rocking himself back and forwards and weeping quietly. In the dark, she couldn't even comfort him with her eyes.

'Were you expecting a loving reunion?' Rhys had asked last night, not entirely cruelly.

Axl hadn't answered. *Had* he expected that? If Sabine had been able to speak then, she might have pressed her brother—and in the midst of their trauma he might have spoken the truth—but by the time her voice returned, the moment had passed and Axl had retreated behind blind hope. Sabine kept imagining her father being dragged here, injured, realising he was going to die. It was an itch that hurt to scratch and she dug her nails in anyway.

'Breathe, Sabine,' Tristan muttered quietly from behind her. 'You don't fight well when you're tense.'

His energy towards her had changed since last night. He was guarded, yes, but the heat of his anger was gone and when she met his gaze at first light she found a new question there. One she didn't yet understand.

Over her shoulder she murmured, 'You're wound tighter than me.'

'Maybe, but I'm aware of every Pyrien in front and behind us. You're obsessed with only one.'

She couldn't argue with that.

'I didn't know you spoke Pyrien,' he added. It wasn't quite an accusation.

'I can't, not really,' she said, watching where she put her feet. 'I *understand* more than I expected to.'

There was a beat and then: 'How much time did you spend with that slave of yours?'

Sabine thought of the old blacksmith, his ash-blackened hands and the pale blue eyes that always held kindness for her. Bryn's life had been reasonable under her father, not so much under her uncle.

'It was Bryn or Olidus.'

Tristan dropped the subject.

In front of Sabine, Rhys had fallen back to listen to their conversation. Their guards appeared to be paying them no attention. Either their voices weren't carrying or the askari were hoping the Amadeans were conspiring and would give them an excuse for more violence.

Rhys glanced over his shoulder. 'What's so important about the wolf?'

Wherever they were going, Lystra had been included when the clan chiefs had not. Sabine considered what Axl had said at the mine about Lystra being connected to the prophecy, and then the oracle's interest in the askara's markings. It had to be the ink on Lystra's shoulders. She said as much now.

'And Indy?' Rhys pressed. 'Why is she with us?' They'd all seen the oracle call for the child to join them.

'No idea.'

The cliff face crowded further onto the track, forcing Sabine to duck beneath an overhang. When she straightened she saw that the ledge ended at an impassable rock wall not far ahead. They would have to get into the water to keep going in this direction. Her heart gave a panicked thump. Sabine's mother had taught her to float on her back in a shallow rock pool, but she had never learned to swim properly. She glanced down. The water was clear and she could see the sandy bottom but she couldn't tell how deep it was.

In the lead, the oracle stepped off the ledge…and disappeared only as far as his knees. He steadied himself with his stave and waded out of sight with the orb. Axl was already in the water and Sabine had no choice but to follow. She climbed in gingerly and the shock of cold snatched away her breath. Water filled her boots and soaked her trousers. She shivered and tried to concentrate on where she put her feet, her sloshing sending ripples across the otherwise calm surface. The lake grew deeper the further they went, all of them feeling their way around the cliff-face. Sabine's teeth began to chatter. She was thigh-deep by the time they rounded another outcrop and saw a small cove with white sand. Beyond the beach was a gaping mouth at the base of the cliff.

Sweet Verus, were they going in there?

Not even Xanthe spoke as they emerged from the water, wet and shivery. The cliff opening was low and wide, like a grimace. Their entire number could have stood elbow to elbow and not filled the width, but its clearance was barely enough for the oracle to pass beneath without dipping his head. Dull sunlight penetrated no more than two paces inside.

The oracle disappeared into the blackness without hesitation but the askari faltered. A sharp glance from Xanthe and they were moving again, warily prodding the Amadeans ahead of them. Tristan ducked his head as they entered and Sabine crowded close to him. It was like being swallowed whole. Her heart was insistent against her ribs as they shuffled forward. The ground became hard under her boots and then the oracle's orb flared bright and lit the yawning space around them.

Sabine propped and Rhys stumbled into her.

They were inside a mouth.

Menacing-looking teeth sprouted down from the roof and there were more at ground level sprouting up.

'What is this place?' Rhys hissed.

'A cave,' Alba said to Axl. 'They are all over Pyrie. Nothing here can hurt you—'

'*Silence*,' the oracle ordered and Alba's mouth snapped shut.

The snarling ceiling was high above but Sabine felt it pressing down even when she tore her gaze away. A jab in her hip from the blunt end of a spear got her moving again. She crept forward tentatively, as if the granite jaws might snap shut at any moment. She looked back to reassure herself the opening was still there—it was—and Nyomi hovered at the entrance. The bone witch's cold gaze was fixed on the oracle where he waited with Xanthe and Lystra.

Sabine carefully wove her way between the teeth on the floor. She instinctively reached for one of the growths to steady herself and was surprised when the rock crumbled beneath her fingers.

'What is *that*?' Tristan asked.

On the rock face beside the oracle was a single glyph about the size of Sabine's hand. She had a niggling sense she'd seen it before. A few paces away was a ring of blackened stones, ominous looking in the glow cast by the oracle's orb. The black-eyed Pyrien waited for the Amadeans to reach him. Xanthe exhaled loudly. She was not as comfortable as the oracle being in the belly of the mountain.

'The one you call the Tenth Prophet came to steal the rib bone our ancestors took from the Temple of Lies,' the oracle began in Amadean. 'Eolis, the mighty god of tempests, brought rain, wind and lightning against him. As your prophet hid from his wrath, he stumbled upon a porpleza, Kyana, who had sought shelter on her faith-trek to the gods-touched falls.' The oracle gestured around the cave. 'This is the place their paths crossed and your prophet became her prisoner.'

Sabine saw that Axl was transfixed by the story. It did nothing to settle her unease.

'Kyana needed to know how this Amadean had found the lake without a guide. She lit her fire and called to the gods with her blood, and then she *and* the invader fell into a vision-trance. When they returned to themselves, they each recorded what they had seen on this wall, painting it in ochre and their own blood.' The oracle paused for effect. 'They soon realised they had been shown the same thing.'

'What was it?' Axl whispered.

'Nothing,' Nyomi snapped. She'd crept closer now. 'Kyana allowed the Great Pretender to flee and—' The bone witch caught the look from the oracle. She huffed and fell silent.

Xanthe flicked her fingers twice, signalling for the oracle to continue.

'Kyana hid the markings with a ward so that none but she could see them.' He saw Tristan shift his weight and gave a dark smile. 'The porplezi access powers well beyond those of Verus.' With his accent, it came out as '*Ver-oose*'. 'The clans had not yet united,' he continued, 'and it was the wolf clan chief who heard rumours of Kyana's prisoner. But by the time he arrived, there was no sign of your prophet. Kyana refused to break the ward and would not share what she had seen. Instead, she scratched glyphs into the sand that she promised would have meaning when Pyrie was ready. Such was the wolf chief's rage that he ended her life by his own hand.'

Xanthe sniffed her approval.

'The porpleza serving the wolf chief had the wisdom to tattoo the marks in the sand onto one of the men with them for safe keeping.'

Sabine glanced at Lystra. The askara was listening, impassive. She'd heard this story before.

The oracle continued, 'The best fighter from each generation of wolf clan is chosen to wear the symbols until the ward can be broken.

'The best fighter?' Rhys mocked. 'Then why does she have them?'

Lystra bared her teeth at him.

'The glyphs shift and change on the flesh of the one carrying them,' the oracle continued, 'but their command remains constant.'

Axl's face was lit with fascination. 'They change? How often?'

'Whenever the gods will it.'

'And what do they command?'

The oracle smiled and the sight of those blood-blackened teeth made Sabine's skin crawl. 'Breaking the ward requires the blood of an Amadean and a Pyrien, and no Amadean blood has worked in two centuries.' He did not take his gaze from Axl. 'But you'—his eyes flared and the swirling orb brightened with them—'have Amadean *and* Pyrien blood. You alone wear the symbols of both kingdoms.'

Nyomi uttered a string of curses in Pyrien and the oracle inclined his head as if conceding the point.

'Some believe Kyana and your prophet were driven mad and the glyphs are meaningless. Others say there is nothing on these walls except what we can see.'

Axl glanced at the bare rock. 'What do you believe?'

'I believe the blood and the flames and the shifting ink on the guardian's shoulders. And all promise me there is truth hidden here.'

Axl's fingers strayed to the ink on his chest. He moved closer to the oracle, beyond Sabine's immediate reach.

'Must I die?'

'Axl, no!'

The oracle held up his free hand up to silence Sabine and then extended it to Alba. The traitor monk produced a small clay bowl from inside his feathered cloak and sat it on the blackened stones. It was not unlike the one the abbot had used at Stonebridge for the bonding ritual.

'I need enough of your blood to recreate the glyphs on the guardian's skin onto the wall. No more. He nodded to Alba and the traitor monk hurried outside, returning a moment later with an armload of driftwood and kindling. Sabine's breath shortened as he prepared the fire pit and lit the tinder with flint and stone. Alba added larger pieces of driftwood and the smoke rose, twisted and disappeared upwards. There had to be a rift in the ceiling—enough to draw the smoke away and carry it outside.

The oracle slipped his hand between the orb and guided the swirling fireball from the stave towards the new fire. It left his palm and became one with the flames. He drew his dagger and warmed each side of the blade, all the while murmuring to himself.

Sabine couldn't bear it. 'Let me stand with my brother.'

The oracle withdrew the blade from the fire and eyed her closely. 'I will kill him if you interfere.'

'And I will kill *you* if you if he dies today.'

The oracle made a sound that might have been a laugh. He gestured her forward and Sabine moved up beside Axl. Her brother gave her a quick, frightened smile and she put her arm around him, ready to wrench him aside if need be. Axl offered his trembling hand to the oracle, holding his palm upwards as was required for an Amadean blood ritual. But the oracle took his wrist instead. 'Oh—' was all Axl managed before the oracle dug the tip of the blade into the soft flesh inside his elbow and then turned his arm over. Axl leaned his weight against Sabine as his blood dripped into the bowl. She felt ill watching it pool.

When the oracle was satisfied, he guided Axl away from Sabine to Alba, who deftly wrapped the wound with flaxen cloth and bent her brother's elbow to stem the bleeding. The oracle dipped two fingers into the bowl—*sweet Verus is he going to put it in his mouth?*—and flicked Axl's blood into the flames. When the fire flared, it wasn't with the dark red stain of the bonfire, but tendrils of blue, vivid like a warm summer sky. Or Pyrien eyes.

The oracle stared into the flickering colours for a long moment, his black irises shining. He held the bowl toward the flames—not too close, he was no prophet—and a lick of blue kissed the vessel, swirled into a ball and hovered over it.

Carefully, the oracle turned to the rock wall, the blue orb moving with him.

'Guardian.'

Lystra hesitated for only a moment and then removed her cloak. She unwrapped her wolf pelt and then pulled the tunic over her head, shrugging out of it to stand naked from the waist up. Sabine tried not to stare. The askara, who was surely no older than her, was a map of scars and welts and bruises. Sisto and his guards were responsible for the freshest of them but there was a legacy of injury that was much older.

Lystra faced Sabine and the warriors, putting her back to the firelight. She eyeballed Rhys, unflinching in her near nakedness. Sabine saw the moment his gaze dropped to her breasts—involuntarily—and when he looked up, it was to elsewhere in the cave.

The oracle dipped his forefinger into the warmed blood and began to paint on the wall, referring to Lystra's shoulders frequently.

When he was done, he stood back and waited.

Sabine's heart thudded.

The fire crackled.

Xanthe squinted at the wall.

'Pah,' Nyomi spat. 'There is nothing to see.'

The oracle's dark gaze skimmed across the Amadeans, his brow furrowed in thought. 'We must need the blood bond.'

The askari came for Sabine first. She considered resisting, but the thought of another dose of poisoning was a strong deterrent—that and the dagger pressed under her chin. She clenched her arm but her blood flowed anyway, and then it was she who was putting pressure on her wound and it was Tristan's turn, then Rhys's, both of them rigid with fury.

When the oracle was satisfied, he stirred the bowl with his index finger. This time he could no longer resist and ran their blood over his gums and teeth, then licked his finger clean. The oracle's gaze grew distant. 'I taste the power.' He swayed a little as if drunk.

'Lystra,' Xanthe ordered and the askara, still half naked, took the oracle by the elbow and guided him back to the wall. She held the bowl while he dipped his finger again and began repainting the symbols created in Axl's blood. The oracle was slower this time, and when he was finished, he stood back in triumph.

Sabine had no idea what the chief porplezi was expecting, but nothing changed inside the cave. The orb returned to the fire and Nyomi laughed without humour. 'There is no hidden truth and the blood bond is worthless.' She said it in Amadean to make sure her grandchildren understood. 'Let me kill them now. They serve no purpose but to tear open my wounds—'

Xanthe slapped her so hard it knocked the older woman off her feet. 'This is not about you.'

Nyomi gathered herself, seething.

The oracle stared hard at the granite wall, willing it to give up its secrets. If their blood had no value he would no longer need them.

Axl moved closer to the wall. 'These are Amadean glyphs,' he said carefully.

Lystra shot him an accusing look. 'You lie.'

'They may not always be, but they are today. Look,' he said to the oracle. He pointed to one of the symbols and then to a section on his own inked scalp. The gold tattoos given to Axl on his initiation at Stonebridge had never had meaning to Sabine beyond being part of the abbey's ancient rites. The oracle stood over Axl to get a better look in the firelight and then gestured to Alba's own scalp, now covered in curly hair.

'They are different to yours.'

'We are each given our own from Verus,' Alba said. 'She guided the hand of the monk who first inked Axl, just as she guided mine when I tattooed the flames over his heart.'

The oracle continued to check each of Axl's markings against those he'd painted on the wall. 'Only that one is the same.'

'Yes,' Axl said. 'To us it means peace.'

The oracle did not seem pleased with the news. 'What else do you see?'

Axl wet his lips, nervous. 'To break the ward...I think it's more than blending the blood of a Pyrien and Amadean. It requires the blood of sworn enemies who have found peace. See this glyph? This is about reversal. And this one is unification.' His eyes shone. 'That's how the Tenth Prophet and your Kyana were willing to work together to create the wards: whatever they saw in that vision made the enmity between them meaningless.'

Sabine didn't understand. But Alba did.

'Oracle, we need a warrior from both kingdoms to make peace. And I believe one of them has to wear the glyphs left to your people.'

Lystra huffed out a laugh. 'Then these wards will not be broken in my lifetime.'

'They will if you want to be cleansed of your shame,' Xanthe snapped.

Both she and Lystra had reverted to Pyrien. The ruler pointed a finger at Alba and continued speaking in her own tongue. 'Do you trust this one?' She asked the oracle.

'I trust his fear. He has seen what I do to those who attempt to deceive me.'

The oracle signalled for Lystra to cover up and then thought for moment. His gaze passed over Tristan and Sabine and landed on Rhys.

'You will make peace with that one.'

Lystra laughed as she tied on her under tunic, but the sound died on her lips as she realised he was serious. 'Impossible.'

'You will make it possible,' Xanthe said.

'I cannot cease hating our enemy simply because you and the oracle will it.'

'It is your path, Lystra, and the only way you can take your place at the head of another pack. If you fail, you are of no further use to me. You can live out your days here serving the oracle.'

'I am a pack leader, not a pet!'

'I have spoken it before the oracle. You are bound.'

Sabine felt the anger pulse between them, saw there was no love lost between the wolf clan sisters. Tristan and Rhys understood enough without a translation.

'How do you expect me to do this thing?' Lystra said, snatching up her wolf pelt.

Xanthe raised her eyebrows at the oracle and he gave another blood-stained smile.

'I have an idea.'

36

Tristan did not fully understand what Xanthe and the askara were arguing about, but it involved Rhys and his cousin was readying to fight his way out of whatever this was.

'Hold position,' Tristan said out of the corner of his mouth.

'I can take her.'

The fearless idiot meant Xanthe.

'*Hold.*'

The Pyrien ruler was not as tall as Tristan had expected, but she was muscled and wiry and moved like a mountain lion with a grudge.

'What are they saying?' Tristan whispered to Sabine.

'Xanthe wants Rhys and Lystra to make peace.'

'*Peace*? How?'

'We're about to find out.'

Lystra finished tying on the goat-hide with quick, jerky movements. Tristan watched the oracle approach, but it was not the warriors he sought. It was the wolf child, Indy. She'd crept to Rhys's side sometime after they entered the cave. The oracle gestured her forward and the child obeyed without hesitation.

'Ares has seen you,' Sabine translated for Tristan and Rhys.

Ares. The only one of the old gods whose name Tristan remembered, and only because he was the god of war.

Sabine continued in a whisper, 'The enemy has robbed you...

of strength and skills...there remains a path to being askari if you are willing to walk it.'

Rhys stared at the oracle, incredulous. 'The girl is skin and bones. Are you that desperate for fighters?'

The oracle indulged a private smile and Tristan sensed Rhys had stepped into a trap. The chief porpleza continued speaking to Indy.

'Will you answer the call?' Sabine translated for the warriors.

Indy nodded, her eyes alight.

'Good.' The oracle reverted to Amadean. 'Come. All of you.'

Tristan had never been so happy to see daylight, even under a Pyrien sky. Fresh air filled his lungs and sharpened his senses. The oracle guided the wolf child further onto the beach with a hand at the nape of her neck and nodded for Lystra and the Amadeans to follow. Tristan caught Rhys's eye to deter his cousin from an impulsive attack. The askari had the advantage of numbers and were already on edge.

'You see the son of Gaia?' the oracle said to Indy.

Tristan followed the oracle's pointed finger to the mountain in the middle of the lake.

'You will climb him and bring me back the egg of a yapa.'

Indy blinked, swallowed hard. Nodded. Sabine translated.

'How the *fuck* is she going to do that?' Rhys demanded.

The oracle finally acknowledged him, speaking in Amadean. 'You and Lystra will guide and protect her.

The askara was already shaking her head. She and Xanthe began arguing again in Pyrien, so rapidly Sabine didn't have time to translate. It was over quickly and Lystra fumed in her defeat.

The oracle jabbed a bony finger at Rhys. 'The child has two days to reach the nesting ground on the summit, steal an egg, and return here to this cave. She will be tested in combat on her return so you must also teach her basic skills in that time.'

'No,' Tristan said. It was suicide. If the stories were true, a yapa was more than a match for even askari. This was not what they came for—

'Can I take my weapons?' Rhys asked.

The oracle nodded and Rhys smiled as if he'd won an argument.

'You can't kill Lystra,' Axl said, understanding Rhys's willingness. The monk stood near Sabine, still holding the bandage in the crook of his elbow.

Rhys locked eyes with the askara in question. 'Why not?'

'For the same reason she can't kill you. This task is to force you to work together. *For enemies to find peace.* If you succeed, your combined blood should break the ward.'

'And if *you* die,' Sabine said, giving Rhys a meaningful look, 'all of this will have been for nothing.'

Xanthe barked a laugh. 'You don't think he could finish off my sister?'

Rhys raised his eyebrows at Sabine.

'That's not what I mean and you know it,' she said.

There was a long beat in which Rhys considered the risks without the reward he'd hoped for.

'It's the only way to the Tenth Prophecy,' Axl said quietly.

Tristan scoffed. 'Rhys doesn't give a shit about the Tenth Prophecy. His only motivation is to best the askara.'

His cousin shrugged. 'Two birds, one stone. I assume we can still fight?'

The oracle led them back to the village pier and the boats moored there. Nyomi slunk off between fishing nets strung out to dry. Tristan was glad to see her go and not only because his blood ran cold whenever he looked at her. It was one less distraction for Sabine, and he needed her focused.

'Is there a track to the summit?' he asked Alba as they reached the jetty. 'Or will they have to climb sheer rock?'

'That knowledge is for initiatives and askari alone. Only they are permitted to cross the lake to the mountain...until now.'

Tristan took that to mean there would be a track, which would make Rhys's task slightly easier. First, though, his cousin had to get across the lake.

'You want me get in that?' Rhys was staring at a long narrow boat made from what looked like birch bark and tanned hide. It was only wide enough to sit single file, with cloaks and bedrolls crammed in at either end. Two porplezi acolytes knelt down and held the vessel steady. 'After you,' Rhys said to Lystra.

She shot a black look at Xanthe, huffed, and climbed in with her axe in one hand. From the way she wobbled and sat down quickly, she hadn't spent much time on the water either. She accepted a spear and Indy took the middle spot. The boat barely rocked when the wolf child stepped into it.

Another acolyte came forward with Rhys's sword and dagger, both sheathed and bundled with his belt. Tristan fought the urge to lunge for them.

'Give me those before you hurt yourself,' Rhys said as he snatched the bundle from the Pyrien. Ever the quick study, he climbed into the boat slowly, knees bent and sat his arse straight down. He actually flashed a quick grin at Tristan, pleased with himself.

Xanthe ordered the acolytes to step back and launched the boat with a push of her boot. Rhys and Lystra grabbed a paddle each as the boat drifted sideways. Indy sat perfectly still in the middle, facing forwards.

'Work together,' the oracle suggested as the pair struggled to point the front of the boat towards the mountain. Tristan had no advice to offer. This was not a skill a warrior acquired. The only people who propelled water craft in Amadea were fisherfolk and slaves on the oar-boats that traded along the kingdom's coastline and rivers.

'Let it straighten,' Rhys said, lifting his paddle from the water. Lystra scowled and did the same, and they waited while the bow of the boat lined up with the mountain.

'Now,' the askara said and they thrust their paddles into the water at the same time. 'Again'. It took a few more strokes before they found their rhythm, and then they were cutting through the water and putting distance between themselves and the jetty.

'It begins.'

The oracle watched their progress for a moment longer and then turned to Sabine. Not Axl. *Sabine*. He studied her for a moment—Sabine weathered his gaze without flinching—and the oracle's mouth softened as he turned away. The knowing smile brought a sickening quiver beneath Tristan's ribs. It was proof he hadn't imagined what he'd seen at the bonfire last night.

Because the oracle had seen it too.

37

Pellus was not a man for impatience but his disposition was being well and truly tested on this campaign, so when an opportunity came to engage with the enemy he was the first to step forward.

A pre-dawn raid had left two food wagons ablaze and at least twenty foot soldiers dead. The wagons smouldered in the first strains of light, a dozen bags of flour, barley and peas gone; nine sides of salted venison ruined. It was food they could not afford to lose so deep into Pyrie. There had been a heated argument in the king's pavilion about being an easy target in the valley, and Pellus had seized the opening to avoid the row by volunteering to find and punish the raiders.

He hadn't realised how exhausting it would be keeping provincial egos in check. Is that what Torvus had done every time the overlords gathered, or was his brooding presence alone enough to keep them under control? Either way, Felix left it to Pellus to deal with the grumblings and he was not so deluded as to think it was a compliment.

Pellus and Adward had gathered eight warriors and half a dozen mounted archers to track the askari responsible for the brazen attack. Adward was at his side now, watching the archers assemble their bows and test the weight of the draw. The Iolian warrior was as impatient as Pellus for action, absently massaging his shoulder with the heel of his palm.

Adward caught Pellus's sidewards glance. 'It works fine when it's warmed up.'

'I've watched you, Adward. I'm aware of your skills.'

'I'm not as *skilled* as I was before the Iolian tournament.' He gave a small grunt. 'I wonder if you would have been so quick to incapacitate me if you'd known I'd be the one covering your back within a season?'

Pellus measured him. Was that a threat? Or was this the sort of banter Iolian warriors favoured? Adward kept his attention on the archers but Pellus sensed he was waiting for a reaction.

'No,' he admitted. 'I imagine I would have unseated you slightly less spectacularly.'

Adward's eyes slid in his direction. '*I* imagine facing you in the lists before you became the prophet's warrior. That outcome would not have been such a forgone conclusion.'

Pellus warmed a little at the idea of Adward thinking about him at all, no matter the context.

'Shit,' the other warrior said. 'Here comes the windbag. You deal with him, *General*.'

Pellus opened his mouth to order Adward to stay, but the approaching overlord of Paramore had caught his eye and the Iolian warrior was already on his way to the horses. Pellus wouldn't risk calling out to Adward and being ignored with an audience.

'Pellus.'

'Carmine.'

The overlord's gaze skimmed the party. 'Is that enough men?'

Pellus hid his frustration at having to yet again explain his tactic. 'Quality over quantity.'

'Yes, but what if you *do* run straight into the entire Pyrien horde hiding out in the next valley?'

'Then you can execute the scouts who provided the false report.'

Carmine huffed and stroked a curly chestnut beard that remained well manicured even on campaign. 'Where is Xanthe, then? How do we know she isn't storming across the border and invading Amadea while we're sitting here with our thumbs up our arses?'

'We know, because the prophet sees all.' Pellus said it as he always had, with complete conviction, even if part of him had come to wonder if that was entirely true.

Carmine waited, seemed to weigh the mood between them. 'Why won't Felix take an audience with me?'

Adward was fussing with his warhorse but his head was half-turned in their direction, listening.

'The king has much on his mind.'

'He is unfocussed, Pellus; distracted. What does the prophet say?'

Pellus raised his eyebrows.

'What would you expect the prophet to share with me about the king of Amadea? I am the prophet's warrior, not his confidante and certainly not part of his intimacy with Felix, but I will be sure to pass on the concerns of Paramore about our king's choices on campaign.'

The overlord visibly paled. 'That won't be necessary.' He waited for the heat to go out of the conversation. Above them, pennants bearing the Iolian eagle snapped loudly in the breeze, and the sound of clashing steel carried from the training yard. Carmine tried a different approach. 'You are the only one Felix listens to, Pellus. You should not risk your life for anything less than a battle.'

A small part of Pellus—the bastard child who craved approval—wanted to believe that was true. But the man he wanted to become could not allow himself to be led by such false flattery. If Felix truly trusted him, the king would not prefer the company of his new squire.

'What sort of general would I be, Carmine, if I sent the best warriors Iolia has to offer to fight and warmed myself at the brazier waiting for them to return?'

'You would be like every other.' The overlord gave him a knowing look, as if Pellus really was one of them now. *Optimati*. Odd that it should feel like an insult.

'Iolia's cohort is accustomed to Ferugo riding ahead of them into the fray. How can I ask his men to respect me as his proxy if I—a warrior no less—refuse to do the same?'

Carmine held up a hand. 'Of course, of course. My apologies, Pellus.' The overlord saw there was no point in pressing his position. 'Ride safe and Verus be with you.'

Pellus watched him stride back the way he had come, disappearing between pavilions.

Carmine wasn't entirely wrong: there was something different about the king. He *was* distracted. Now that Pellus had moved into the Iolian pavilion, he was out of touch with the king and any news coming from the prophet. Gwinny would send for him if the prophet demanded an audience, which he hadn't for several days. If there was news about the task he'd given Tristan and Rhys, he was yet to hear it.

Adward finished tightening the girth on his saddle and when he locked eyes with Pellus his expression was less hostile than usual. 'Let's find and kill these vermin,' the Iolian said.

They rode from the smoky camp into the northern pass and the next valley, chest armour in place and shields strapped to their arms. Pellus and Adward were in the lead, trailed by warriors, squires, and archers. Pyriens were notoriously tricky to track because they rode no mounts to churn up the ground, and they spread out to disperse their footprints. Marcus, the lanky warrior and oldest among them at twenty-eight, was able to pick up the trail each time they lost it and then found the place where the askari formed a single file to pass through a narrow ravine. The warriors and archers left the warhorses with squires and continued on foot, treading carefully so as not to give away their approach.

Adward spotted the Pyriens first and held up a fist to bring them to a halt. As Pellus had predicted, it was a raiding party not a full pack, and they were reasonably matched in numbers. The askari had assumed the Amadeans would not give up their mounted advantage to come after them on foot. The Pyriens were off guard, cleaning axes and spears in a shallow stream, keeping only a cursory eye on the trees around them. It had been too much to hope a clan chief would be among them.

Adward signalled to the others and then remembered he was no longer in charge. He raised his eyebrows at Pellus and Pellus saw the misstep was driven by the fire in his blood, not disrespect.

Pellus gave the sign for the archers. It was unlikely an askara would flee from a fight but, just in case, the bowmen were there to ensure no Pyrien survived. This pack would not be too far from a larger force.

The archers split off in opposite directions and Pellus gave them time to get into position before he and the warriors fanned out and crept closer. The askari were strung out along the stream. They had darkened their bone-white hair with river mud for the night-time assault, but there were no nettles woven into the ropey strands; another indicator they had not expected immediate reprisal. By the time they saw the Amadeans, they barely had time to snatch up a weapon before the warriors were on them.

Pellus led the charge, the point of the arrowhead formation, and immediately drew two spear-wielding askari to him. They were fast and accurate, quick to react despite the surprise attack. Pellus would have backed himself against two of them even before he became the prophet's warrior, but the guarantee of always being at his strongest and best was a gift he willingly embraced.

He kept the first askara at bay with his shield and directly engaged the second, batting away the spear with a deft flick of his sword and then running the Pyrien through. The first attacker came at Pellus again from a wider angle and he barely had time to defend the spear thrust before he caught the flash of a sharpened askari axe blade rushing at him end over end. An Amadeanshield came up and blocked the weapon. It struck so hard the warrior wielding it was forced back two steps.

It was Adward.

Pellus pushed back his remaining opponent, aware of Adward wrenching the axe from his wooden shield and hurling it at another charging askara.

It was over quickly. All twelve askara were dead, ten by blade or axe and two riddled with arrows. Without being told, the warriors positioned the bodies in a row, leaving them as a provocation for whoever came looking for them.

Pellus sat on his haunches at the edge of the stream to clean his blade. Adward did the same less than two arm's length away. The other warriors were further upstream.

Pellus glanced at the Iolian warrior, trying to figure him out.

'What?' Adward asked, catching him.

'You protected me. Thank you.'

'You are my general.'

They stood up together.

'Yes, but...'

Adward wiped his sword on his trousers and sheathed it. Met his gaze. 'Ferugo and Dashelle are prisoners of the prophet and under a cloud of suspicion because they were loyal to Torvus. You have been elevated to Ferugo's place at the head of his army, so I imagine that your death would not bode well for my overlords.'

Pellus nodded, hiding his disappointment. 'So it was not out of loyalty to me.'

'Of course it was. Being *loyal* to you on this campaign is the greatest show of fealty we can offer Ferugo and Dashelle.' Adward measured him and Pellus felt seen in ways he did not want to be.

'You have our loyalty, but what you *want*, Pellus, is our love. And that you will never have.'

It was a truth he'd not even admitted to himself, and the fact this warrior with his piercing eyes saw it and mocked him for it cut deep enough to bleed.

38

Lystra's shoulders and lungs were burning from exertion by the time they reached the mountain shore.

She had enough strength left to haul the canoe with Rhys up the pebbled beach, gratified that he was sweating and panting as hard as she was. He dropped to the ground and sat with his head between his knees, recovering. Lystra was determined to stand tall while she caught her own breath, but her legs were having none of it and she ended up on her backside, bent forward like Rhys. Indy positioned herself between them, cross-legged, looking back across the water to the temple.

'The boulder should have given you condition,' Rhys taunted between breaths.

'What is your excuse?'

'I'm not a slave.'

'Neither was I.'

He coughed a laugh. 'Tell that to your sister.' Rhys was already breathing easier, giving her that hard smile of his that made her blood roil. He leaned back on his hands and kicked off his boots. The soles of his feet were pale compared to the rest of him, and soft like a baby's. He stood on steady legs and hobbled barefoot back to the water's edge, splashing into the shallows. The warrior squatted and scooped water over his head and neck, and then cupped his hands and drank deeply, letting the rest of it run through his beard and drip onto his vest.

Indy raised her eyebrows and Lystra nodded. She would quench her thirst now that Rhys had gone first and shown his weakness.

Lystra kept her eyes on the warrior as she drank and cooled herself.

'Now what?' he demanded.

Her plan when they reached land had been to break at least one of his bones. There were plenty of ways she could hurt him and he'd still be able to climb. But she was tired and sore from paddling and he might best her again if she attacked now.

A new thought startled her: did the oracle plan it this way? Was he that cunning?

Of course he was.

'Now,' she said, wading out of the water, 'we climb.'

They retrieved their cloaks from the canoe, eyes locked on each other while Lystra tucked her axe into her belt and Rhys strapped on his sword belt. When he was satisfied she was not an immediate threat, the warrior craned his neck so he could see the bald rock of the summit.

'Have you been up there before?'

'I am askara. We all make the climb.'

He made a sweeping gesture. 'After you, then.'

'I am not having you at my back. You first.'

'And have your axe between my shoulder blades before midday? No chance—'

Indy clapped her hands together in rapid succession and they both faltered, surprised at the vigour of the interruption. The whelp pointed to Lystra, then herself, then Rhys. She was going to walk between them. As if that would stop the scourge from running her through from behind at any point of the climb.

Lystra held the child's gaze. 'There is more at stake than your future if he kills me.'

She nodded, solemn.

Annoyance flared. This child knew nothing of the burden of the ink on her shoulders or of being Xanthe's blood-sister. Indy did not feel the weight of losing Dex and her pack or now having to trust her future to a whelp and an Amadean warrior. It was beyond humiliating.

'Stay close to me,' she muttered and set off.

Lystra quickly found the track and the going was easy for a while, switching back and forth across the base of the mountain. And then the incline steepened and the path gave way to rocks and loose shale. She could hear Indy starting to labour but there were no complaints from the girl. Nor should there be if she wanted to be askari. But initiatives usually came to these shores after years of training and preparation, not malnourished and bone weary from enslavement.

The clouds had thinned enough for Lystra to track the journey of the sun. It had not long passed its zenith when Indy fell for the first time.

'Stop,' Rhys said, panting. 'It's too much for her.'

Lystra propped and turned around, the relief immediate in her own legs. 'Just because you are useless without a horse does not mean she is.'

'*I'm* doing fine.' The hands on his knees spoke otherwise. 'This girl crossed a mountain range on foot only a day ago—'

'While you rode in a wagon.'

He gave her a flat look. 'Not by choice.'

'Look at her. She is tougher than you.'

Indy was on her feet again, exhausted, unsteady and ready to push on. Lystra felt a swell of pride. The child was giving the warrior a lesson in persistence and far be it from Lystra to deny her. She set off again, ignoring the protest from her own burning thighs.

They had climbed no more than a hundred paces when Indy fell again and this time a small sob escaped the child.

'Enough,' Rhys said. 'She's bleeding.' Indy sat on her backside, her knees and palms grazed and bloodied, the bandage on her wrist filthy. 'She can barely pick up her feet.'

Indy lifted her eyes to the warrior and Lystra saw gratitude. This attachment to him was an insult to every other Pyrien who had suffered at Amadean hands.

'And whose fault is that?' she snapped. 'Who put her to work in a mine? Who put rocks on her back and whipped her when she faltered?'

His eyes darkened. 'That wasn't *me*.'

'It was done in your name.'

He flexed his fingers and she knew he'd be charging by now if he wasn't so exhausted. Like her, though, he would not attack without an advantage.

'She needs water.'

'*She* has a name,' Lystra countered.

'I don't hear you using it.'

On the ground, Indy coughed until she retched and Lystra silently chastised herself for her own negligence.

'There is a stream soon,' Lystra promised Indy in Pyrien.

The warrior didn't understand but he stepped forward anyway. 'I'll carry her.'

Lystra blocked him. 'That is my job.'

'How?' He pointed to the crusting wounds on her neck and throat. 'Where do you think she's going to hang on?'

'I am willing to bleed for her.'

'Yeah? I'm not willing to fail because those wounds open up and slow us down. Or you damage that cursed ink on your shoulders.'

Lystra narrowed her eyes at him. 'She will not feel safe with you.'

The warrior raised his eyebrows. *Challenge accepted.* He squatted down and gestured for Indy to climb onto his back.

She did so without hesitation, wrapping her tiny legs around his waist and looping her arms around his neck. He smirked at Lystra and it was only the child on his back that kept Lystra from taking out his legs.

'Okay, *Indy*, I'm going to teach you something to make the wolf here feel better.' Rhys turned his neck so he could partly see the child. 'This is a choke hold.' He positioned Indy so her upper arm was pressed against his windpipe and the other hand gripped her elbow to apply extra pressure. 'When I say, squeeze my throat as tight as you can. When I tap your elbow, release the pressure. Ready?'

She nodded, concentrating on his words.

'Now.'

Lystra watched as Indy applied pressure with her entire body. Rhys's eyes widened with surprise and he tapped her arm three times in quick succession. She eased off immediately.

'There's not a lot of you, kid, but you've got a death grip. I reckon if you had to, you could choke me out before I could shake you off.'

It wasn't true, but Indy was pleased with herself, relaxing against him with her arms looped loosely across his chest.

'Happy?' Rhys said to Lystra, all the warmth leaving his eyes.

She huffed a laugh. 'Only if she does the job properly and chokes you out.'

39

Sabine could *see* Tristan's mind working.

His agitation wasn't all about Rhys being across the lake with the askara. She frequently found him watching her, not with recrimination or suspicion, or even worry—this was something new.

His scrutiny was almost as unsettling as the presence of Xanthe's army camped above the village. The askari were scattered across the mountainside like goats, more Pyriens than Sabine had ever seen. There were so many that she, Tristan and Axl were no longer confined to the cell wagon. Orders just had been given that if any one of the Amadeans tried to leave the village by foot or boat, all three would be killed. And the first askara to reach them could choose and deliver the method of execution. In the beginning, packs of askari had taken turns to prowl the ridge above the village, calling down to Tristan, goading him to stray from safety and prove himself. But Tristan wasn't Rhys and he didn't rise to the bait, even if it stung to ignore them.

Xanthe's mandate gave them a freedom of a sorts. They were not permitted to enter huts or climb the steps to the temple or get too close to the bonfire. All places Sabine was happy to avoid.

Alba had been ordered to stick close and they were also shadowed by the oracle's guards, so with the lake on one side and an infestation of askari on the other, all they could do was wait until Rhys returned. And Tristan was not good at waiting.

'Walk?' Sabine suggested.

Tristan's eyes skimmed the forecourt and then the ridge. To move away from the wagon meant trusting they wouldn't be killed the moment they set foot outside the temple precinct.

His nod was wary. 'Lake?'

The deep water beneath the pier frightened Sabine, but not as much as the bonfire. It felt different to the fires in Amadea, more *alive*, and it's sheer size made her heart quiver.

She and Tristan made their way down the stepped alley to the water. Axl trailed behind, deep in conversation with Alba. There was a studied focus to her brother's questions, a quiet desperation to stay distracted from the horror above them in the temple.

The alley was lined with tubs of shellfish and striped perch that had been salted and placed in rows to cure. The fishy air here was better than the stench of burning flesh lingering in the temple forecourt. The waterside was busy with men and women mending nets, gutting fish, and checking ropes made from flax and what looked like Pyrien hair. Sabine caught snatches of Pyrien names in the animated chatter—*Xanthe... Nyomi...Sabyl*—and then the villagers caught sight of them and the pier fell silent. She felt exposed as they passed the wide-eyed fishermen and women. It was strange to see Pyriens so fresh-faced and well-fed, dressed in tunics and leggings without holes and frayed hems.

Sabine felt all those pale blue eyes following them. She concentrated on putting one foot in front of the other, not trusting her feet to know what to do otherwise. For a long beat, all she could hear was the gentle lapping of water against the pylon and the empty shells strung to dry clacking in the soft breeze.

Tristan's knuckles brushed against hers.

'Sabine,' he said when she missed the cue. He gestured for her to walk with him out onto the jetty where the remaining long boats bobbed on their moorings. She was wary about venturing out over the water and her nerves only intensified when Tristan signalled for Axl and Alba to stay on the pier.

His touch was light on her elbow as he guided her to the end of the jetty. The water was barely a hand's span below the timber boards, and it was too deep to see the bottom. The sun had emerged from behind a cloud and turned the lake to shining silver, and Sabine shielded her eyes, pretending to focus on the mountain Rhys should now be climbing.

'I wonder if they've hurt each other yet?' she said, her mouth turning dry.

Tristan followed her gaze. 'Guaranteed.' He shifted his weight, scratched at something on his vest. Whatever it was he wanted to say, he didn't know how to start.

'Sabine,' he managed, and waited until she turned to face him. 'I saw you at the fire.' He spoke quietly, even though Axl and Alba were out of earshot. 'It was as if...' His gaze shifted to somewhere behind her and he shook his head. When his eyes returned to her, he took a breath and tried again. 'It was as if you were trying to command the flames.'

Sabine couldn't read Tristan's mood; couldn't tell if this was an accusation or an observation. Either way, she wasn't going to lie to him.

'I wasn't able to, though, was I?'

His eyebrows rose, surprised he was right. 'But it worked in the warehouse in Augustmount. When the flame burned through your binds?'

It was her turn to be surprised. *This* is what he'd been thinking about?

'It had to have been you,' he said. 'I just didn't want to consider it at the time.'

Sabine closed her eyes, remembered the hot rage coursing through her when she'd been at the mercy of her uncle, desperate to be free so she could use the skills Tristan had taught her to punish Olidus and protect Dashelle.

'And now?' she asked carefully.

'I don't have the luxury of ignorance.'

Neither did she.

'Whatever happened that night in Augustmount, Tristan, it wasn't intentional.'

He was studying her again and she could see him thinking. 'At the campsite when the fire saved Axl...That was you, too?'

Her pulse skipped. 'I don't know. I didn't *do* anything then, either.' How did she explain something she didn't understand herself? A flock of long-necked birds Sabine didn't recognise flew over the lake in an arrowhead formation. Her eyes followed them until they were specks in the distance.

'Is it you?' He said it so softly she hoped she'd misheard. 'Are you the usurper?'

Sabine's heart banged hard once against her ribs. She searched Tristan's eyes, wished she could read him better in this moment.

'I can't be.'

'How did you not get burned when your binds were destroyed in the warehouse?'

'You forget,' she said bitterly, 'I'm the child of a porpleza—'

'Even the oracle doesn't touch fire, Sabine, because it burns him like it does the rest of us. And the prophet can only touch the sacred flame, not any fire.' He ran his thumb over the scar on his palm. 'The abbot bound Rhys and me to you for a reason.'

And there it was.

'Does it make me being half-Pyrien easier to swallow if I have the power to storm the palace and save Dashelle and Ferugo?'

Tristan flinched enough that she saw there was some truth to it.

'Don't get too attached to the idea, Tristan, because I don't *feel* powerful, and if you saw me last night then you know that even if some power is hiding within me, I have no clue how to awaken it, let alone use it. Because believe me when I say that if I could have burned Nyomi to the ground last night, I would have.' She was trembling now, furious and hurt.

'It has to be true,' Tristan said, and Sabine saw how much he needed the blood bond to have meaning. He was a man being swept down a river looking for a branch to cling to. It was far from a consolation.

'Because coupling with me would not be such a defilement if I'd been chosen by Verus to carry the power of the First Prophet? Without it, all you've done is lain with a half-breed porpleza.'

The honesty of it was more than she'd intended and it flayed her to the bone.

Tristan breathed deeply through his nose, jaw clenched. 'No, Sabine, it would mean the abbot is as mad as the Tenth Prophet, Dash and Ferugo are deluded heretics, and I'm a traitor.'

They stared at each other, nostrils flaring and breathing hard.

'Sabine—' Tristan said then stopped as something caught his attention behind her. She turned, dreading it would be Nyomi or the oracle and in no state to cope with either of them.

Instead, a wiry Pyrien with a slightly bent back was moving along the jetty towards them. He held out his hands to show he was unarmed. His loose white hair was cropped to his shoulders and there was something familiar about the way he favoured his left knee. Sabine stared at him until recognition struck.

Bryn.

For a heartbeat her head swam and she had to reach for Tristan to steady herself. How could he be *here*. The last time she'd seen Bryn—the morning of the fire—he'd been in the smithy, hammering out nails to repair the kitchen shutters. The slave had been far from her thoughts when she'd fled the burning manor house, her hands bloodied and her thoughts wild. Guilt and shame washed over her, dousing her anger at Tristan. She stared wordlessly as the old Pyrien warily closed the distance between them. His pale blue eyes shone with tears.

'Are you *kidding* me?'

Bryn lowered his gaze at Tristan's outburst and then lifted his eyes almost immediately, remembering he no longer had to defer to an Amadean. Sabine saw the moment the slave recognised the warrior. 'You.' It was not quite an accusation.

'I thought you were handing yourself in to the bailiff?' Tristan accused.

'I could not find him. So I kept walking.'

'On those "bad knees"?'

Bryn gave a small defiant smile. 'They had some life left in them after all.'

Axl was hurrying towards them, on the verge of breaking into a run. 'Bryn,' he said, breathless. 'How in the name of our blessed Verus are you *here*?'

That was the question Sabine had been trying to voice.

The old blacksmith directed his answer to her as if she'd been the one to ask it. 'Each of us who have been enslaved must bathe in the waters of the lake and be marked by the oracle if they wish to return home.'

The skin under his nails was no longer black, but his fingers were calloused from years at the forge. Burn marks scarred his forearms and disappeared under the sleeves of his tunic, evidence of where Olidus had turned her father's signet into a brand. Her uncle had used it to remind Bryn to whom he belonged whenever he caught Sabine in conversation with him.

'I'm so sorry,' she whispered. 'I should have come for you.'

His forehead creased. 'You had to leave. I was happy to stay and watch the manor burn.'

'Speak Amadean,' Tristan growled.

Bryn repeated the start in their tongue and this time said, 'I was sorry to watch the manor burn.'

Sabine did not correct his amendment. She was still light-headed, so she lowered herself to the weathered boards and sat cross legged in her filthy warrior trousers. Bryn did the same, bad knee and all, and Tristan stood over them both, deeply unimpressed.

'Bryn,' Axl said, sitting with them. 'It's Axl.'

The blacksmith finally looked at him properly. 'You have your mother's eyes.'

Her brother's chin wobbled and Sabine weathered a storm of emotion—for her mother, for Axl, and for this man who had served her family from before she was born.

'Is it true she came from this place?' Sabine asked.

Bryn pressed his lips together, nodded.

'And are my father's bones in that witch's temple?'

The blacksmith looked past her to the water, the lines in his brow deepening.

'Answer her,' Tristan ordered, old habits dying hard even this side of the border.

Bryn met Sabine's gaze. 'This is the story the porplezi here tell. That Nyomi's daughter disappeared many years ago and the loss drove her insane. When your father was brought here, injured and muttering her name, he told Nyomi that Sabyl had been his wife and she had died not many years after leaving the lake. He did not get the chance to tell her how her daughter left this life.'

'Nyomi already knew,' Axl said. 'She saw our mother die giving birth to me. She said she had a vision.'

Bryn's narrow nostrils flared. 'She does not have visions. She has me.'

'I don't understand.'

'When I fled Amadea, I made my way here as we all must,' Bryn said. 'Nyomi questions anyone who been across the border, be they askari, slave or prisoner, seeking information on your mother. I was the first to bring her news since your father, and she had not let him survive long enough to tell her about either of you.'

The jetty pylon creaked beneath Sabine. 'You knew who our mother was?'

'No,' Bryn said quickly. 'Your mother understood me far too well for an Amadean, but I know of no magic that can hide hair and eye colour. I could not ask how she knew my tongue. It would have meant death if I had given insult.' He paused for a beat. 'I told Nyomi I had been in the Southlands, under Darius of Greenock Hill. It was only then that I heard the truth about your mother's origins.' He picked at a thumbnail. 'I told Nyomi about you both because I thought it would comfort her to know her bloodline lived on. It did not.' Bryn held out his wrist to show his slave mark was unburned. 'She will not permit me to be cleansed and return to my homelands. I must first serve as her attendant for as long as she requires it.'

Axl gripped the front of his tattered robe. It was grubby where he kept touching it. 'Do you know what Nyomi means when she says our mother was the hope of Pyrie? That she had a gift?'

Bryn grunted. 'Nyomi loves to speak in riddles.'

'Did our father know our mother was Pyrien?'

The old slave considered the question. 'All I know is they both treated me well.'

'And now you are the bone witch's slave,' Tristan said.

Bryn bristled but didn't correct his use of the term. 'I serve as she wills.'

'So why did she send you to us?'

The question startled Sabine. It hadn't occurred to her that this was more than a coincidental reunion. But of course it was. Look where they were.

'I am to offer to help you escape,' Bryn said.

Tristan nodded, his expression bitter. 'So we can die in the attempt. How would it happen?'

Sabine glanced from the warrior to the slave and back again. Tristan wasn't seriously considering it, was he?

'I am to hide a canoe for you along the cliffs. You will be seen as soon as you are in the water. But first, I will take you to your weapons in the temple sanctuary. Nyomi wants you to see what she guards there before you die.'

Sabine's blood chilled. 'Our father's bones.'

He nodded. 'She also wants you to know what she keeps at the altar.'

Axl sat forward, wary hope in his eyes. 'Tell us, Bryn. What is it she keeps up there?'

Bryn picked at his torn thumbnail and his fingers trembled. When the old slave locked eyes it was with Sabine, not Axl, and the hairs on her arms lifted.

'It is the flame of Verus.'

40

The climb was as taxing as Lystra remembered and long-buried dread stirred at the memory of what awaited at the summit.

She pushed on under a cobalt sky, stopping to rest whenever she reached one of the streams that criss-crossed the mountainside. The first part of the ascent had been the quickest, with a clearly marked switchback trail, but when dirt turned to rock and shale their progress slowed. The three of them clambered over boulders beneath giant banyan trees, scrambled up rocky gorges and edged along cliffs with heart-stopping sheer drops. Lystra's nerves were strung tight. Ahead were sharp beaks and deadly talons; at her back, Amadean steel. Lystra imagined what she might have done if Rhys hadn't had Indy on his back. All that yawning sky might have been too much temptation for her, regardless of the consequences.

The hard going meant she had no spare breath to bait Rhys as a distraction. Soon, she would need to stop and tell Indy the things the child needed to know as an initiate. But for the first two legs of the climb, there had been satisfaction in withholding information from Rhys. The higher they went, the more wary he grew. But his unease was unsettling Indy, so when Lystra reached the rock pool on the eastern plateau she caught her breath and broke her silence.

'The yapa have their nest near the summit,' she said

grudgingly in Amadean. 'The hens lay their eggs in the same nest and the dominant female—the domi-hen—sits on them. We will make camp close by and raid when the others go hunting.'

Rhys swung Indy down from his back. His face shone with sweat and he'd tied back his hair with a strip of leather. He stretched out his shoulders and Indy did the same, mimicking his movements.

'We only have to contend with one of them?'

Lystra focused on Indy as she explained. 'Yes. She will protect her own egg with her life. She will fret less about the eggs at the outer edges of the nest.'

The warrior walked a lap of the clearing, checking the perimeter. 'Why haven't we seen any sign of them?'

'They hunt at night.'

He looked around at the sheer rock faces and precarious tree outcrops dominating the mountain slopes. 'Where? They don't fly. Do they?' He couldn't hide his alarm and Indy's eyes widened with fear.

'No. There are goats, weasels and hares in the forest on the other side of the mountain. Yapa and harpies hunt together there.'

Rhys raises his eyebrows. 'Yapa and...?'

'Harpies,' she repeated. 'Birds of flight that also hunt at night. Almost as big as the yapa.'

The warrior's hand strayed to the hilt of his sword and Lystra took her time taking a drink from the rock pool. Telling him the truth was even more satisfying than keeping him in the dark.

'Why do they hunt together?'

'It should not surprise me that you do not understand cooperation.'

'I understand *animals*. And one species does not help another without a reason.'

Lystra rankled at having to explain things every Pyrien

child understood. 'The harpies on this mountain are lazy. The night hunt is easier when prey comes to them. The yapa drive the quarry out of the trees into a clearing and the harpies keep them there. Together, they feed in a frenzy.'

As an initiate on this mountain, Lystra had heard the night hunt. It was not something she'd been in a hurry to hear again.

'This place...' Rhys shook his head and turned east toward his own kingdom. There was nothing to see except more Pyrien mountains.

Lystra re-shouldered her pack. 'We need to keep moving.'

Rain-heavy clouds hugged the mountain when they finally reached the initiate campsite mid-afternoon. The cliffside clearing offered a rare stretch of flat ground. It was protected by an overhanging rock that hid it from the summit, hemmed in by granite on three sides and an open, threatening sky on the other. The rock walls were scarred with carvings of clan symbols, spears and axes, more than Lystra could count. Rhys did his routine perimeter sweep and finished at rock face, Indy still on his back.

'Who did all these?'

Lystra felt the hum in her blood that came with being back here. 'Every initiate who makes the climb leaves a mark.'

His gaze roamed the granite. 'I see wolves, ravens, goats, tapyrs...even weaver finches. I thought clans only came together on the border.'

She was surprised he understood even that much about Pyrien society. 'When Xanthe made peace between the clans, the old grudges were put aside.'

He scanned the rock face again. 'Which one is yours?'

She made no move to show him.

'I'm not going to touch it,' he said, as if reading her thoughts. 'That's what you're looking for, isn't it?' he asked Indy over his shoulder. The child nodded.

Lystra shot him a look that threatened violence and then walked to the wall. She found her mark easily: a badly drawn wolf with sharp angles and long teeth.

Rhys took Indy close enough to see it properly.

'How old were you when you came here?' he asked.

'I had seen eight winters.'

'And you got the egg?'

'Yes.'

His eyebrows rose but he said nothing.

Indy's stomach rumbled. They hadn't eaten all day, so Lystra opened the pouch they'd been given and took out a piece of dried goat. She handed it to Indy, who passed it along to Rhys and took the next piece for herself. He made a face but tore off a strip and started chewing. They sat under the rock, backs to the wall and facing the western horizon. With so much cloud cover, it would be dark early.

When Indy was finished eating, she disappeared behind a rock to relieve herself. Lystra tossed a red aprycot to Rhys that she'd snapped from a tree earlier in the day. He caught it on reflex and eyed her suspiciously.

'Eat it. Don't eat it.' She picked goat from her teeth, feigning disinterest. In her peripheral vision, she saw him sniff the stone fruit and open his mouth to take a bite.

Indy reappeared in a flash and slapped it out of his hand.

'Hey!' he said, watching the fruit bounce twice and disappear over the edge of the cliff.

The wolf-child mimed vomiting and then made more dramatic hand gestures to demonstrate what would have happened at the other end if he'd eaten it. The warrior surprised Lystra with a laugh that reached his eyes. 'You really want me shitting myself when we're going for stealth?'

Lystra shrugged. 'It would have been over quickly. Nasty, but quick.'

He nodded almost appreciatively. 'Cunning.'

Indy looked from Lystra to Rhys and back again, her mouth softening at the break in hostilities. Lystra dusted off her hands and stood up. 'Time to train.'

Indy was already on her feet, shaking out her bony arms.

'Now?' Rhys asked. 'What can you teach her in two days?'

'To hit a target.' Lystra took her axe from her belt, spinning and catching it without watching. She picked out the middle of three posts dug into the ground on the other side of the clearing, calculated the distance, and flung the axe. It had been weeks since she'd thrown her weapon, but the axe felt good as she released it. It flew end over end and struck the target cleanly, burying itself right where she'd intended. She walked over and wrenched it free.

She made a mark in the dirt with the heel of her boot and held the handle out to Indy.

The girl had a good grip and picked up the technique quickly. She struck the trunk on her fifth try. Lystra made her keep throwing until she hit it twice in a row with her right arm and at least once with her left.

'Can you kill a yapa with one of those?' The warrior stood by throughout the lesson, arms folded and biceps flexed.

'If you hit it between the eyes and split the skull. But easier to use a dagger here.' She pressed the tip of her finger into the soft skin under her chin.

He nodded that he understood and then his eyes snagged on the wolf inked inside her wrist. His expression hardened in a way it hadn't at her child-like carving.

'Of all the clans, you hate the wolf the most. Why?'

For a moment he could not speak. It was an odd thing to see this warrior turn so swiftly from curiosity to cold fury.

'Your clan chief butchered my father.' Rhys spoke between clenched teeth. 'Took his head.'

She shrugged. 'That is the price of invasion—'

His fist slammed into her jaw without warning. Her vision splintered into shards of white and Lystra staggered sideways, reeling. And then they were both on the ground, tumbling and swinging fists. It was a frenzy of punches, of grabbing and breaking holds. Her head pounded and the world was a blur but her body thrummed with the violence. She connected with the warrior's cheek. He landed a sharp jab to her kidneys—

A high-pitched howl filled the air.

Lystra and Rhys snapped out of their bloodlust, instantly disengaging and springing to their feet side by side to face the threat. But the only person with them on the side of the mountain was Indy. She had moved out of their way and now stood closer to the cliff's edge, her hands clenched into fists at her sides. Her chin was stuck out and her mouth was still open. Lystra and Rhys exchanged a startled look. The wolf-child had *bayed* at them.

Blood ran from a cut in Rhys's cheek into his beard and Lystra's lip had split again.

'She asked for it,' he grumbled. 'What do you expect me to do?'

Indy fumed at the pointlessness of the question. She was furious—at both of them. She closed her eyes, either to think or to block out the sight of them. When she opened them, her fingers unclenched a little—

The harpy came from below the cliff without warning, its great wings beating in a blur of brown and white. Indy spun around and stumbled away from the edge. Lystra and Rhys lunged for her at the same time but the bird stretched out its great feathered legs and hooked its talons around the wolf-child's waist.

With powerful beats of its wings, the largest airborne predator in Pyrie carried Indy away.

41

'What the fuck?' Rhys hissed at Lystra over his shoulder. He scrambled up the rock face, trying to keep the bird in sight. 'That's a harpy? You said they hunted at night!'

Lystra was right behind him, still reeling from the horrifying sight of Indy dangling from the harpy's talons.

'Did your dark magician see *this*?' the warrior accused as he sprang from rock to rock, all traces of exhaustion gone. 'Did he send us up here to watch her die?'

Lystra concentrated on keeping up and not losing her footing. They were climbing fast and Rhys had no idea where he was going. She doubled her efforts so she was within reach and grabbed him by his sword belt. She tugged hard enough to get his attention but not dislodge his grip.

'What?' he snapped over his shoulder.

She braced for him to strike out but he just glared at her, panting and eyes wide.

'We need to get to Lysa Qiqa—Slab Rock,' she translated, panting, 'and this is not the way.'

'What's there?'

'The rock overlooks where the harpies and yapa nest. It is not far.'

Rhys looked back to the sky but the harpy and Indy were gone, lost in the clouds. He met her gaze, measured her in a way he hadn't before. 'Lead the way.'

They clambered back down to the clearing to their packs. Lystra scooped up her spear and led the warrior to the track they would have taken when the light was almost gone. It was steep but it was the only way to the lookout.

Lystra's breathing settled into a steady rhythm as she climbed, but her heart was insistent against her ribs. She had been close enough to the harpy to see the curve of its hooked black beak, feel the beat of wind from its massive wings. She'd never realised the circle around its neck was golden brown, nor that the underside of its wings was a pattern of brown and white like a weaver's mat. And the size of it...It's body was bigger than the wolf-child's, it's wingspan greater than two spears placed end-to-end.

Rhys climbed without complaint, letting her keep the lead even when it was obvious there was only one way they could go. They were passing through a pocket of mist in the fading light, getting closer to the summit. A fallen tree was wedged over a stream and Lystra vaulted over the obstacle one-handed, careful to keep her spear out of the way. Rhys copied her technique. The sword at his hip should have impeded him, but he was aware of it as if it was another limb.

'We were going to do this at night?' he asked.

'I see better than you in the dark.' Lystra pointed to the ledge above. 'That is Slab Rock. We must be quiet from here. We don't want the yapa to wake until we are in position.'

The warrior fixed her with a penetrating gaze. 'Will Indy be alive?'

'Harpies do not hunt Pyriens. Yapa kill us only in defence. I do not know why the bird came for her but if she is in a nest, we can get to her. It will not be easy, but it can be done. When the hunt begins we should not have the chakwa to deal with.'

'The *what*?'

There was no Amadean word for it. 'Many yapa,' she

offered. She waited for him to climb up so they were shoulder to shoulder. Her jaw ached where he'd punched her and her split lip was bleeding again. The warrior's gaze fell to her bloodied mouth and then away. The cut on his cheek had dried, his beard was crusted with blood.

'We will look together,' she said. 'Slowly. Stay flat.'

They climbed onto Slab Rock and crawled on their bellies across the uneven surface toward the cover of grass trees at the edge. They were momentarily exposed without tree cover, but a patch of mist at least hid them from the sky. The summit was a series of wide granite peaks of varying heights, some bare rock and dirt, others with patches of beech and fir trees.

Rhys peered over the edge and let out his breath as if he'd been punched.

'Fuck. Me.'

His eyes were locked on the yapas on the next peak over. It was slightly lower than Slab Rock and almost within spitting distance. The birds were well back from the drop off, gathered in a clearing under the shelter of beech trees. The domi-hen was on the nest and Lystra counted nine more yapa clustered around her. All were sitting on their bellies with their necks held high, swaying gently with the breeze. Their eyes were open.

'Did we wake them?' Rhys whispered.

'That is how they sleep.'

The warrior hid his fear well. Even Lystra's scalp tightened at the sight of them.

The yapa were the ultimate predators. They had a cruel hooked beak, perfect for tearing at meat and sinew, and mottled green scales protected their long neck as they killed. Their legs were as long and strong as Lystra's and built for speed, and their claws sharp enough to pierce tanned goat hide. Even their stunted wings, useless for flight, were covered in long fine black feathers that hid them on the hunt.

All but one of the yapa had the head spur that grew from the back of the skull like a curved dagger.

'They are all male?'

She huffed at his assumption the males were the more dangerous. 'They are all hens except one.'

'Huh.' He scanned the other peaks. 'Where's the harpy's nest?'

Lystra pointed to the sandstone formations rising up beyond the cliff's edge. There were two, each once forming part of a seamless ridge line before being worn down by wind and rain. Now they resembled oversized stalagmites. The top of the closest formation was hidden in the mist.

'That one.'

'How—'

Lystra held up a hand to silence him. The breeze gusted, chilling her bare scalp. They did not have to wait long before the mist shifted and the pinnacle of the formation appeared.

Rhys swore again.

The nest was on the highest point. It was made from roughly woven sticks and feathers and large enough to fit a fully grown goat. One harpy was in the nest. It's mate was nowhere to be seen.

'Is it *sitting* on her?' he hissed.

Rhys picked up a pebble and tested its weight. Lystra clamped a hand on his wrist. 'No.'

'We need to know if she's alive in there,' he whispered. 'She's a clever girl. She'll give us a sign if she knows we're here.'

Lystra wasn't sure the warrior understood how terrifying it would be for a child to be in a harpy nest surrounded by nothing but air.

'Do *not* hit the harpy.'

He sat up and lobbed the pebble in a high arc, then ducked back under cover. The pebble landed on the edge of the nest.

The harpy's head whipped around, white feathers flaring around its face, making its head appear even bigger. Lystra lowered her eyes and hoped the warrior had the sense to do the same. When she risked another glance, the harpy was ruffling its feathers and settling again. There was a long, dreadful, beat in which nothing happened, and then the pebble was tossed out of the nest.

Rhys exhaled. 'Thank Verus.'

On that they could agree.

Below, the yapas began to stir in the dying light. Lystra measured her breath as one by one the birds rose to their full height. They ruffled their feathers and preened themselves, oblivious to their audience.

The warrior's eyes strayed back to the harpy. 'Will it go with them?'

'Yes. The hunt needs both harpies. It's mate has already left.'

They retreated back to the cover of the ravine.

Rhys dusted grit from his hands and Lystra saw the scar on his palm that sealed his oath to the half-breed siblings. It would be a sore point worth probing if they survived.

'What's the plan?' he asked.

'When the birds leave to hunt, you distract the domi-hen and I climb up and get Indy.'

She saw him run through the plan in his mind. 'Can you carry her down?' He glanced at her shoulders where the welts were again bleeding.

'You were not concerned about my wounds when you attacked me.'

He shrugged. 'Indy's life wasn't at stake.'

'Why do you care about this child?'

Rhys checked the position of his dagger in his belt. 'She's had a shitty start to life—'

'Because of Amadean greed—'

'And she deserves better.'

'She is wolf clan.'

'Not anymore.'

They eyeballed each other in the gloomy light.

'Are you afraid to face the yapa?' Lystra taunted. 'You think the climb is less dangerous?'

He gave her a flat look. 'Indy will be safer coming down with me.'

'You spend your life on a horse. You have no skill for this. She is safer with me.' Lystra selected a black stone from the path. 'I will prepare.'

She picked her way down the stream and found a rock flat enough for her purposes. She squatted, splashed water onto the surface and began grinding the tip of the black stone onto it. The warrior moved away to check his weapons and Lystra kept him in her peripheral vision.

When the paste was ready, she used two fingers to smear it over her face, neck and arms. It would have made Rhys's brown skin even harder to see but he did not ask for the camouflage and she did not offer it. The sight of her battle-ready had him on edge enough and they did not have time for another scuffle when he took offence.

She knelt and closed her eyes. It was a risk, but she had to complete the ritual. Lystra murmured a prayer to Ares for courage, Nyx to guide her through the night and to Verus for protection. Then she kissed the wolf inside her wrist and stood.

The warrior eyed her, both hands on the hilt of his sword. He'd slung the pack across one shoulder and their cloaks were tucked behind a tree root. They would only slow them down.

'Do you need to prepare?' she asked. He'd washed the blood from his nose and beard, but there had been nothing ritualistic about it.

'I'm ready.'

It was almost fully dark.
'Then we go.'

42

Tristan sat in the dark, considering his options.

He, Sabine and Axl had been relocated from the cell wagon to an empty hut guarded by a single askara. The only light was from the glow of the bonfire and it cast flickering patterns through the shutters onto the wooden floor. Tristan couldn't attempt a raid on the temple before Rhys returned, but he could plan. Ferugo had told him to trust Axl. He'd also told him to think for himself and it was well past time he followed those orders.

Alba had been allowed to visit and he was huddled with Axl under the window. Tristan couldn't see their faces and was only half listening to their hushed conversation.

Near him, Sabine was fiddling with one of her boots. He could make out the familiar shape of her silhouette. She'd been distant since their conversation at the lake and he wished he'd handled it with more tact. He would have done better if he'd had Dash to speak with first. She would have helped him explain himself without sounding so selfish. His sister always knew what to say in every situation—except, probably, the one she was in right now.

That unfamiliar sense of panic rose, squeezing his heart and stealing his breath. What if he never saw her again? He'd rather face the askari horde on the mountainside than the nameless fear that threatened to swallow his heart whenever he thought of Dash imprisoned in Augustmount. Ferugo would know how to play the game at the palace but Dash was too transparent, too open, to hide her true faith if she was dragged before the prophet.

What if Tristan couldn't save her? What if he couldn't save either of them and Iolia was handed to Pellus?

Warm fingers touched his wrist in the dark, tentative. 'Tristan?'

He realised his breath had shortened. He needed a moment or Sabine was going to hear the fear in his voice.

'What are you thinking about?'

He was too tangled up in his thoughts to lie. 'Dash.'

'Me too.'

He heard it in her voice, the burden he'd given her. She said nothing else but her fingers squeezed his wrist before falling away. That fleeting touch was calming, and his breath had almost returned to normal when three words from the traitor monk Alba snagged his attention.

'What did you say?' Tristan demanded.

'I...' Alba faltered. 'I wondered if the source of the sacred flame in the temple might be the stolen rib bone.'

Tristan's pulse stuttered. 'The Codex says the rib was extinguished the moment it was carried across the border.'

'The Codex *does* say that,' Axl agreed. 'But that record was written by the same high priest who declared the Tenth Prophet mad, took his place as the Eleventh Prophet, and then had the Tenth Prophecy destroyed.'

'You think the Eleventh Prophet lied?'

'Tristan, I don't believe the power of Verus can be snuffed out by crossing a line drawn on a map by a king a thousand years ago.'

Tristan wrestled with the idea. Questioning the Codex still did not come easily for him. But what if it *was* the rib bone of the First Prophet in that temple? That would make them the first warriors to be near the relic in two hundred years. And if they could reclaim it…The hope of it made his heart hurt.

'So, the Tenth Prophet made it all the way here on his own in search of the rib bone,' he said, thinking it through. 'Did he know it was being kept in the temple here, and if he did, what would make him return to Amadea without it?'

'The vision in the cave,' Axl said. 'Whatever he and the porpleza saw, it got them both killed. You heard it yourself: the wolf clan chief took Kyana's life with his own hands. The oracle says it's because she let the Tenth Prophet escape, but what if it was because of the prophecy she shared. Think about what happened to the Tenth Prophet when he returned to Amadea. Within weeks he was killed and replaced.'

'Because he was mad,' Tristan said.

'Or it was because he shared a prophecy nobody wanted to hear. The only reason we have any of it in Amadea is because a novice overheard parts of what he recited to the high priest, and *she* wrote down what she remembered. It was those fragments Anguston found two years ago.'

Giving rise to the heresy that had dragged Tristan across the border and made him a traitor. 'Maybe the vision was about the rib bone being here.'

Axl considered the idea. 'That would not have got the Tenth Prophet killed.'

'True,' Tristan conceded. 'King Tertullian would have scorched the earth to reclaim it if he'd been told where it was hidden.'

A horn blew in the forecourt and Alba rose to his feet. 'I have to go. Please, do not do anything rash.' He rapped on the door and the guard let him out.

When his footsteps faded Sabine turned to Tristan in the dark. 'What do you want to do?'

Tristan ran his tongue across his teeth, blew out his breath. 'If the rib bone is here, we have to steal it back and use it to bargain for Dash and Ferugo's release.'

Sabine and Axl whispered at the same time.

'How?'

'When?'

Axl's question was easiest.

'When Rhys returns.'

The monk exhaled softly. 'Good. If he and Lystra succeed, we'll have the Tenth Prophecy. It will guide our next steps.'

Tristan noticed he didn't mention the rib bone. 'And my plan?'

The monk's robes rustled and when he spoke again, he was so close Tristan could smell the lanolin in the fabric. 'You would need to get into the temple unseen, find your weapons, remove the relic without it burning you, carry it down the steps, and then find a way for all four of us to escape without being caught and killed by askari—knowing full well there is a trap set for us.'

All very good points.

'They're my problems,' Tristan said. 'If I can solve them, do you agree that we take the relic to Augustmount and exchange it for Ferugo and my sister?'

'I thought you wanted to use Lystra as leverage?'

'That only worked when she was our prisoner. The rib bone would be of far greater value. True?'

The monk did not answer.

'Axl?' Sabine prodded him.

A beat. 'I don't know.'

'What don't you know?' Tristan demanded.

'What if...' Axl hesitated as if afraid to say it. 'What if the prophet returns the rib bone to the sacred flames in Augustmount and it changes them? What if it allows the prophet to bend the flames to his will and he can finally *see* the usurper?'

'See *Sabine*, you mean?'

Tristan heard the monk's breath hitch. 'I figured it out, Axl. I'm not totally blind.'

'We've spoken,' Sabine said to her brother. 'Whether it's true or not, Tristan knows it all now.'

'Thank Verus.' Axl's voice dropped even lower. 'Then you understand that we can't put Sabine in any more danger until we understand what our god expects of her.'

'Do you trust Verus or not?' Tristan asked. It was a low blow, but he wasn't beneath challenging Axl's faith to get his way.

'I will better understand the will of our god and what's required of Sabine once we have the Tenth Prophecy in its entirety. To make a move as bold as to reclaim the relic, we need to be sure it's part of Verus's plans.'

Tristan could feel the blasphemous temple hulking in the dark less than a stone's throw away. The Tenth Prophecy may or may not hold truth; but the rib bone, if it was there, would be *real*. Its value wasn't tied to the usurper, it was tied to the birth of his kingdom. There was nothing the Thirteenth Prophet wouldn't agree to, to have it in his possession—even overlooking his suspicion of the overlords of Iolia.

'You best pray to Verus then that Rhys brings back answers,' Tristan said. 'Because if the relic is here, I'm going to get it back or die trying.'

43

They waited in the trees closest to the yapa nest. The other yapas and the nesting harpy had left, but Lystra needed the predators fully distracted with the hunt by the time the domi-hen raised the alarm.

'I could rush in and kill it,' Rhys had said when they went over the plan again before hiking here.

'You have never fought a yapa. You will die.'

'I didn't know you cared.'

'I cannot get to the harpy nest without a distraction. You dying quickly will not be enough.'

He'd offered a dark laugh. 'You should write poetry.'

All traces of mockery were gone now they had returned to the nesting grounds. The moon came and went as low clouds passed over the summit. Each time the clouds cleared, the harpy nest was cast in sharp relief against the starry sky. A light breeze came from the direction of the hunting ground, so at least that was in their favour.

Indy would be chilled to the bone in the nest. The wolf-child knew they'd found her and Lystra hoped it was enough to deter her from attempting to climb down on her own. One mistake and she would plummet to her death.

At last, the gods-awful sounds of the hunt rose from the mountainside: the screams of panicked and injured prey. It was as bone-chilling as Lystra remembered. Rhys swore under his breath but held his nerve, and Lystra tapped him twice on the shoulder to give him the signal. He melted off into the darkness, moving with unnerving stealth for an Amadean. He'd assured her he knew how to make a yapa call. She braced herself, ready to rush across the clearing as soon as the yapa responded. When it came, the high-pitched shriek sounded *nothing* like a yapa, but it served its purpose. The domi-hen jolted to her full height, head twitching from side to side, looking for the source. The plan was for Rhys to draw the yapa away long enough for Lystra to get to the harpy nest, grab Indy, and retreat to the initiate camp. Rhys would join them there.

If he survived.

The warrior waited a beat and then made the awful noise again, this time accompanied by a rustling branch. It was too much for the yapa. She stepped off the nest, more curious than spooked, and moved towards the forest. Her head spur caught the moonlight.

Keep going.

The cry came a third time deeper in the trees, and the yapa followed it.

Lystra waited another beat and then took off at a sprint. She'd brought her spear—just in case—and now cast it aside to make the leap to the rock face beyond the yawning gap. She reached the cliff's edge at full speed and jumped, arching her back to carry her further. The rock formation was at least three spear-lengths from the cliff. She made the distance easily but had to scramble for foot and hand holds when she landed. For a heart-stopping moment she thought she was going to keep sliding down, but then her boots reached a ledge and her grazed fingers found traction.

Lystra pressed her face against the sandstone, her heart smashing against her ribcage. She checked the clearing—the yapa was still in the forest tracking Rhys—and began the painstaking climb to the nest. It hadn't seemed that far up from the lookout, but now that she was over here, it was taking longer than she'd expected.

'Indy,' she whispered loudly when she was close to the top. There was no response, so she awkwardly half-climbed into the nest, branches and sticks scratching her arms. Indy sat on the far side, her knees to her chest and her eyes wide. There were no eggs in the nest but in the moonlight, Lystra saw a carpet of tiny skulls and bones and the carcass of a half-eaten hare, its eyes and organs freshly picked out.

'Come.'

The child crawled over the bones and flung her arms tight around Lystra's neck. She was silently crying. 'Climb on my back.'

Lystra knew she was asking a lot of the trembling child, but Indy inched her way over the lip of the nest, almost choking Lystra until her skinny legs clamped around Lystra's waist. Only then did the girl loosen her death grip. She didn't need to tell Indy to hold on.

The plan was to descend the formation to where it met the mountain further down. They were eye-level with the nesting ground cliff when the domi-hen let out a bone-chilling cry in the forest. It was louder and deeper than the screech Rhys had made and would carry far, even upwind.

Rhys burst out of the trees, his sword drawn. He skidded to a stop and spun around to face the charging domi-hen. Lystra instantly saw his mistake.

Blood-soaked Ares, he's only focused on her head.

'Look out for the—'

Too late, the yapa leapt at Rhys feet first, huge left claw swiping at his chest. He didn't expect it and the domi-hen took him to the ground before he could counter. The yapa stomped at him in a frenzy, whipping her head down to impale him with the spur. Rhys managed to roll away, arms up protectively as she kept stomping. Indy fretted, her grip again tight. There was nothing they could do. Even without the child on her back, Lystra could not cover the distance back to the cliff without a run-up.

Rhys managed to get out from under the yapa and scoop up his blade. His vest was torn and his chest shone with sweat or blood or both, but whatever wounds he had weren't slowing him down. Lystra needed to keep moving but she was held in place by the sight of the warrior rushing at the predator.

A lone askara would fight a yapa by defending and retreating. Rhys was doing neither.

He attacked with a series of fast strikes to the bird's neck, but even Amadean steel could not cut through yapa scales. The domi-hen backed away, whipping her neck from side to side and using the spur to block each blow. Rhys was forcing the yapa to defend, working her into tighter and tighter circles until she stumbled and—

Lystra blinked. Squinted. Blinked again.

The warrior had tossed aside his sword and leapt onto the bird's back. He was *riding* her. The yapa wasn't strong enough to keep her feet with the unexpected weight and threw her head back blindly as she staggered forward. Rhys ducked, gripping with his legs, and drew his dagger. On the yapa's next wild swing, he caught the spur with one hand, pulled back her head to expose the throat and stabbed deep into the soft flesh beneath her beak.

Once was enough. The great bird collapsed and pitched forward, throwing Rhys as she fell. He landed hard, rolled over and staggered back to his feet. The yapa was dead.

'Move!' Lystra warned, taking her own advice and resuming her awkward climb down the rock face. The chakwa would want blood for this.

Rhys was re-sheathing his sword when a new screech filled the air, followed by another. These came from above and Lystra knew what it was even before she saw the wingspans outlined against the stars.

The harpy was back. And it had brought its mate.

44

'Go!' Rhys shouted.

Lystra was already moving so fast she was half sliding over the rough surface, great chunks of rock breaking off under her fingers and boots. She had an axe tucked into her belt but there was no way she could fight off one harpy let alone two *and* hang on.

Rhys sprinted towards the cliff edge and Lystra realised with a jolt he was going to jump. He left the ground earlier than he should have—

'Ugh.' He hit the rock face hard above her, sending a spray of dirt and stones onto her and Indy. 'Shit,' he panted. 'Sorry. Keep going.'

The first of the harpies was almost on them. By sheer luck, Lystra's downward path provided plenty of hand and footholds and she gained confidence and speed, but the harpies would easily pick them off if they got close enough. Indy clung to her, trembling and panicking.

Lystra risked a look up.

The harpy was pulling out of its dive, beating back its wings and coming in fast, claws first—

The bird suddenly shrieked and plummeted sideways, flapping its wings frantically to slow its fall.

'Eat *that*!' Rhys shouted. He was hanging off the side of the rock face, gripping one-handed to keep his position while he worked loose another rock. His eyes shone in the moonlight as he grinned down at Lystra.

'Watch out,' she called as the second harpy swooped down. This one was coming for him.

He drew his arm back and flung the missile with speed and accuracy. Lystra watched long enough to see the rock find its mark—knocking the second harpy off its trajectory—and returned to scrambling down as fast as she dared. A heartbeat later and Rhys was sliding down the side of the rock face, this time off to the right so as not to rain down dirt on her and Indy. As soon as he found solid footing he searched for another rock and took aim at the regrouping pair of harpies. He was unlikely to make a kill shot, but his efforts might be enough of a distraction to give Lystra time to get Indy to solid ground.

When she next risked a look, Rhys was right above her, holding his sword one-handed and waiting for the circling harpies to make their next attack. He'd obviously run out of missiles.

'Tell me when to jump,' Lystra panted at Indy over her shoulder.

There was a nervous pause while she scrambled lower and then Indy frantically tapped Lystra on the head. Lystra didn't hesitate. She pushed off from the rock face and had a moment of panic when the drop was a beat longer than she was expecting, but then her boots struck hard ground. Her knees buckled on impact and she staggered sideways to keep her feet. 'Find cover.' She shoved Indy away from the edge and drew her axe, looked up to see Rhys now fending off the harpy with his sword one-handed. The bird beat its wings rapidly, attacking with beak and claws, close enough to knock the warrior from the ledge if he didn't watch his feet—

Godsstrike.

The other harpy was on its descent again.

Rhys saw it, knew he had to deal with the bird right in front of him or he was dead. He let go of the rock face to grip his sword with both hands and swung at the first harpy's leg with all his strength. The bird screamed as the Amadean steel cleanly lopped off a clawed foot. The limb fell like a stone, and the harpy dropped from sight in a spiralling free fall. Rhys managed to grab an outcrop of sandstone, mere fingertips away from tumbling after it. He sheathed his sword and resumed scrambling down.

Lystra held her breath. Only a little further and he could leap to safety. The descending harpy had tucked its wings and was diving. *Fast*. It was almost on him.

'Jump!' she shouted in Amadean. *'Now, scourge!'*

Rhys leapt with his arms out for balance as the diving harpy beat its wings backwards to slow, extending its talons—

His feet barely hit the ground before those talons hooked around his biceps and snatched him up. Lystra dropped her weapons and jumped, wrapping her arms around his hips to keep him from being carried away. It was all instinct, and by the time she'd realised what she'd done, she was fully committed.

The harpy fought her, its great wings whipping at her arms, sharp beak snapping. Lystra turned her face away and leaned back, using her full weight to hold Rhys, and still her boots were sliding towards the edge. And then she felt Indy's arms lock around her hips, helping. Lystra could have just let go. Instead, she jerked down with her remaining strength...and the three of them went tumbling backwards, all resistance gone. Lystra twisted violently so as not to fall on Indy, which meant Rhys hit the ground first and she landed on him instead. They both grunted.

The wolf-cub was scrambling to her feet and tugging on Lystra's vest to get her moving. Was that a cave entrance? Rhys took Lystra by the elbow and dragged her after Indy. The opening in the cliff-face was high and narrow, and there was enough moonlight that even the warrior could see they would have to squeeze in one at a time. He stood back so Indy could go first, urged Lystra past him, and then shuffled in behind backwards so he could see any threat that followed.

Lystra felt her way along the walls either side, relieved when they started to widen. It was dark and she couldn't see where the cave led. Right now all that mattered was the harpies couldn't get to them. Her legs gave out and she slid to the ground, her heart thundering and her ragged breath loud in her ears.

Rhys dropped down beside her, so close she could feel him trembling. Or maybe it was she who was shaking—she couldn't tell. The child crawled over Lystra's lap and onto his, hooking an arm around each of their necks and pressing her face between theirs. The warrior wrapped an arm around Indy, and Lystra did the same, all three of them touching. Lystra rested her head on Indy's shoulder, spent adrenaline washing over her in hot and cold waves. Outside, the harpies screamed their frustration.

Rhys found his voice first. 'Are you hurt?'

Lystra knew the question wasn't for her.

Indy shook her head.

'Same,' he said, though Lystra could smell the fresh blood on him.

As their breathing settled, she heard running water and gently prised Indy's arm from her neck. 'I will find the stream,' she said.

Before she could move away, Rhys's fingers slid around her wrist. 'Thank you.' He said it quietly and squeezed once before letting go.

If an askara had risked themselves for her the way Rhys had, and if *she* had rescued anyone else but him in return, they would be bonded for life. Not physically, necessarily, but they would exchange tokens and take oaths to have the other's back in any fight. But Rhys was the enemy, so she ignored the warmth in her chest and simply said, 'We are even.'

*

Much later, Lystra woke stiff and sore. She could feel every bruise and stiff joint, every fresh graze on her palms and shins.

She was also aware there were other bodies touching hers.

She remembered curling around Indy to keep them both warm, but sometime during the night Rhys had rolled over and thrown his arm across both of them. He wasn't pressed hard against Lystra, but he was close enough she could feel the warmth of his breath on her ear.

Muted morning light streamed through the entrance, illuminating the rock pool they'd drunk from last night. Lystra peeled her tongue from the roof her mouth, thirsty. She lifted Rhys's wrist and returned his arm to him. He reached for her again, this time running his hand down the length of her thigh, his touch light over her woollen leggings. He murmured something into her neck.

'Do you want to lose a limb?' she said, but her voice was low and there was no real threat to it.

His hand stilled on her hip but he didn't remove it. 'What's this made from?' He plucked at the wool, still sounded half asleep.

Lystra turned over to face him, careful not to wake Indy. Rhys gave her room. He lifted his hand as she moved and then casually rested it on the opposite thigh. She took her weight on one elbow so they wouldn't be nose to nose. He lay with his head in the crook of his elbow, as if he were anywhere but in a Pyrien cave on the side of a mountain with murderous birds somewhere outside. It was strange to make eye contact while he touched her without intent to hurt.

'Alpaca,' she said, answering his question.

'It's soft.'

'Better than your sheep's wool?'

He moved his palm in a pleasant circle on the outside of her thigh. 'I'd have to feel more of it to know.' The warrior genuinely seemed fascinated by the wool, but his touch brought a flush of heat that surprised and appalled her. She pushed his hand away and sat up stiffly. 'You need to rinse your wounds.'

He winced as he sat up alongside her. He blinked away the last of sleep and inspected his arms. They were raw from the grip of the harpy but, remarkably, his skin was not broken. His vest though was scarred with three deep scratches. Rhys ran his fingertip over each. Only one of the claws had torn through and sliced flesh.

'The buckskin wore the worst of it,' he said. Indy lay curled with her back to them, still breathing slowly and steady.

'Show me your chest.'

He narrowed his eyes. 'How close is your weapon?'

She nodded to the axe within reach. She'd retrieved it—and his sword—from the ledge last night when clouds hid the moon. Her spear was gone though, abandoned on the nesting ground, and his dagger was still buried in the dead domi-hen. 'If I wanted you dead, I would have given you to the harpy.'

His eyebrows lifted. 'Why didn't you?'

She shrugged one shoulder.

'And they say askari have no honour.' He said it in a way that made it clear *he* had said it. Many times.

She pointed to his chest. 'Show me.'

Rhys unlaced his vest and shrugged out of it. His chest was covered in soft blond hair. The skin beneath was mottled and bruised—not all caused by the yapa—and punctuated by a wound that ran in a straight line from the base of his throat to halfway down his sternum. The cut was not deep, but it had bled heavily when the warrior had kept fighting while injured. Without the vest, the yapa would have ripped him open.

'You should have cleaned that last night,' she said. 'Yapa claws are filthy.'

He made his way to the rock pool without argument, cupping his hands to take a drink and then to splash water over his chest. He sucked in his breath. 'Shit, that's cold.'

Indy stirred at the sound of his voice, louder with the shock of the water.

'You should check her over.' He glanced at Lystra. 'And you're banged up too.'

Lystra helped Indy sit up and they joined Rhys in the shaft of light by the stream.

'Here she is,' he said, grinning 'My hero.'

Indy gave him a shy smile and walked behind him to look at the tattoo across his shoulders. Lystra couldn't help it; she was curious to see it too. She knew there were designs for each of the five Amadean provinces but had never seen one in full.

Indy frowned. She pointed at the bird on his back and then outside where they'd last seen the harpies.

'No,' Lystra said. 'The wings and head feathers are wrong.' Without thinking, she traced her finger along the outlines of the wings and head as she said it and Rhys's skin goose-prickled at her touch.

'It's an eagle,' he said and his voice sounded different. 'Smaller than a harpy. Definitely doesn't snatch up children.'

The detail of the tattoo was impressive. The bird had its wings open and talons outstretched. Lystra knew from her own experience how much time, blood and pain were required for a work of that size. Her back tattoo was much smaller and it had taken days to recover from.

Indy sat down beside Rhys. The only sound for the moment was the gentle burble of the stream as it passed through the cave. She pointed to the eagle again and then to her bandaged wrist.

'She wants to know if it's your clan.'

His smile was sad and his mind went elsewhere for a moment. 'You could say that.'

Lystra caught Indy's eye. 'His clan chief is marching into Pyrie with an invading army.' She said it without malice. It was a fact.

Rhys shook his head. 'My *clan chiefs* are in Augustmount, as *guests* of the king.' He did not hide his bitterness.

'Why?'

'The prophet suspects they are heretics.'

Was that true? Lystra weighed the confession. Rhys was reckless and insulting and quick to violence, but she did not believe he was a liar.

'Ferugo and Dashelle would appreciate the irony of my situation. This,' he gestured to the three of them, 'is why they sent us over the border. To find out what the Tenth Prophecy says.' Rhys seemed about to say more and then became intent on cleaning the dried blood from his dagger instead. 'Your tattoo,' he said, not looking at Lystra. 'The oracle said it changes.'

Lystra nodded and beckoned Indy away from the warrior. She would tend to the child's scratches as best she could without herbs and honey.

'How often?

'There is no pattern. Sometimes I will go many moons without feeling it,' she said, and then realised something. 'It changed the day you and the others arrived.'

'Huh.' Rhys looked up from cleaning his dagger. 'What's it feel like?'

'Like I have a whip-snake beneath my skin. Afterwards I am hot and itchy.'

Rhys frowned as he thought about it and Lystra took a moment to study him. In some ways, he was like an askara. He was tall and strong, and his hair, although the colour of honeycomb, was long and wild. But his beard was long too, his eyes were brown—not blue—and she'd never before seen a man who had eyelashes as long as a woman's.

Those eyes went wide as a new thought struck. 'We didn't get an egg. What does that mean for Indy?'

The child looked at Lystra over her shoulder.

'Our initiate was captured by a harpy and escaped. That should count for more than snatching an egg while a domi-hen is distracted. If it does not, she will get another chance next yapa breeding season.'

'Who will care for her until then?'

Lystra didn't understand the question. 'She is a child. Wherever she goes she will be cared for.'

The answer didn't seem to satisfy him but he let it go.

Lystra washed her own face and neck and wiped her hands on her vest. 'We have to move. Harpies will not hunt in daylight but the yapas will if they know we are close.'

They'd all heard the moment the yapas returned to the nesting ground and found their domi-hen dead. The outrage had been loud and terrible.

Rhys got dressed and gathered his weapons. When he knelt down again, Indy climbed on his back as if it was the most natural thing in the world. He hitched her up so her legs were around his waist and his sword hilt easily accessible, and she slung her arms loosely around his neck, full of trust.

The warrior walked to the mouth of the cave, checked the way was clear and glanced back at her.

'Let's go find out if this was worth it.'

45

A horn blast carried to the forecourt mid-afternoon.

It had been raining off and on most of the day, and Tristan was pacing the hut deck while Sabine picked burrs out of her cloak and muttered about smelling like a warrior. The sound of the horn stilled them both. Axl emerged from inside as Alba hurried across the forecourt to them.

'The canoe has been sighted,' Alba said, slightly breathless. 'The oracle has ordered us to the cave.'

Tristan's pulse quickened at the news. 'Are all three of them in the boat?' he asked.

'I haven't heard otherwise.'

Tristan ran a hand over his jaw—he'd grown in a full beard again since leaving Iolia—and wrinkled his nose at the lingering traces of lunch. Pyriens ate with their hands, which meant the Amadeans had to as well. At least it had been fish—a flaky offering full of bones—instead the revolting fleshy lumps they had to suck from shells and that tasted like stagnant lake water.

Rhys's return meant that *something* had to happen now—good, bad or otherwise. Tristan had wasted enough time alone with his thoughts. It was like being attacked by ants: slap one away and another one found the same exposed skin. Since their capture, he'd been plagued with dark and difficult questions. He wasn't used to constant troubled thoughts; they tightened his chest in ways he didn't understand.

It was this god-forsaken place.

He didn't belong here. Everything felt different, even his own body. He was uncomfortably aware of the way he moved through the village, the length of his stride, how he held himself. He was conscious of every breath, as if he might stop breathing if his concentration lapsed.

Sabine stood beside him now on the deck, so close he almost slipped his arm around her out of habit. He honestly didn't know how things stood between them. She hadn't reached for him again last night, yet she'd lain close enough he could hear her murmuring in her sleep.

'Ready?' he asked, knowing his voice sounded wrong.

'No.' She gave a tight smile. 'But I will be when I need to be.'

He touched the small of her back, so light she would barely feel it through her cloak. 'Axl?'

The monk rubbed his scalp. Both sides—inked and bare—were as bald as the day Tristan had met him, no sign of fuzz or bristle. If Axl was an abomination, nobody had told his scalp.

'Yes.'

Xanthe, the oracle and the bone witch appeared from a long building beside the temple. The group then began to retread the path along the base of the cliffs. The expectation was palpable. Tristan scanned the lake, saw a speck in the distance that might have been a canoe...or another trick of the light. Whoever had spotted the returning craft clearly had a higher vantage point, and was less likely to make the false sightings Tristan had made all morning. Drizzle set in again, feather-light on his cheeks and nose and limiting the view. It was only when the group was almost at the cave that Tristan could properly make out the boat and its occupants.

He blew out his breath through puffed cheeks. *Thank Verus*.

Rhys was up front, his blond hair and beard easily recognisable even dampened by rain. He and Lystra were paddling hard as if being chased, maintaining powerful strokes in tight unison. Indy sat in the middle of the canoe facing the mountain, and the askara occasionally checked over her own shoulder as she paddled.

The oracle's group reached the cave first and Pyriens and Amadeans watched together as the trio drew closer. On instinct, Tristan moved forward to meet the canoe.

'No,' the oracle said. 'They must complete the journey without help.'

A flurry of lowered spears blocked Tristan's path and he waited, impatient, as the canoe kept coming until it ran aground. Rhys leapt out and dragged the boat further up the beach, ignoring the armed askari as he returned and knelt in the shallows. Tristan felt his jaw drop with surprise as Indy climbed onto his back.

'You good?' Rhys panted as he sloshed out of the water, shoulder to shoulder with Lystra.

Tristan nodded. 'You?' He took in the state of Rhys's busted face, slashed vest and red-raw arms. Fresh blood seeped from a wound on his chest. Indy was scratched and bleeding, and the askara had fresh scrapes too, but Tristan's cousin was by far the worse for wear.

'Yep,' Rhys managed. 'Killed a yapa.' He flashed a breathless grin as he passed.

The askara was breathing hard, eyes only for her sister. Whatever she wanted from Xanthe, the Pyrien ruler didn't give it. Instead, Xanthe signalled for the three of them to stop before entering the cave and gave a second command to Lystra alone. Lystra hesitated a beat before removing Rhys's sword belt from his hips. Rhys didn't glare at her as she did it and the askara didn't gloat. That was new.

The oracle gestured to Indy and spoke to Rhys in Amadean. 'Let her go.'

Rhys held out his arms to show the child was free to climb down whenever she wanted. The oracle spoke to Indy in Pyrien. The child wrapped her arms tighter around Rhys's neck. Lystra watched on, impassive, and made no move to prise Indy from him. The oracle continued speaking to the child until Xanthe growled and strode off into the cave. Tristan looked to Sabine for a translation.

'The oracle asked for the egg but all Xanthe cares about is the ritual.' She gave him a look. 'What's going on with Rhys?'

He shook his head. Something had changed for sure because his cousin's shoulders were no longer tight with rage.

Tristan put himself between Sabine and Axl and the spears at their backs, and followed Rhys, Lystra and the impatient Pyrien ruler into the cave of teeth. The fire was lit and as the flickering light pushed back the shadows, Tristan realised the marks from yesterday were gone. He watched, dry-mouthed, as the oracle again heated his blade.

Indy finally climbed down from Rhys so he could be bled, but she didn't leave his side. Rhys eyeballed the oracle as the porpleza cut him but there were no insults. Lystra too was silent as she offered her arm, and Tristan thought he saw something pass between the askara and his cousin.

Again the oracle mixed the blood with two fingers and offered the bowl to the flames. This time when the fire caressed the clay and the orb formed, its heart was neither blood-red nor vivid blue; instead it swirled a dozen shades of purple. The oracle dipped his forefinger into the warmed blood and tasted it. The hairs on Tristan's arms rose and the oracle let out a soft, satisfied sigh.

Lystra again stripped down to the waist and the oracle used her tattoo as his reference to paint them once more. As far as Tristan could tell they hadn't changed since yesterday. The orb hovered without the stave and the oracle's movements were measured, every step ceremonial. Tristan caught the moment Rhys met the askara's gaze, and this time his cousin didn't look away.

Sabine stood close enough to Tristan that he saw her pulse jump in her throat. His own skittered in response. The entire cave held its breath as the glyphs took shape on the cave wall. The air was charged, as if they were caught in a lightning storm. For a beat nothing happened. And then the orb left the glyphs and moved across the face of the wall.

The oracle gasped as its light revealed new markings.

At first they appeared random, but as more of the wall became visible, it was evident the marks were a mix of Amadean words and Pyrien glyphs, one above the other in haphazard rows. When the orb reached the farthest corner of the cave it flared orange and blinked out, and the stone-ringed fire immediately blazed brighter to replace its light. The markings remained.

Xanthe grunted her surprise.

Tristan's heart thudded at the dark magic but his eyes were drawn to a cluster of Amadean words painted immediately beside the original glyph. They were written in a steadier hand than the other markings; almost an afterthought. The oracle ordered Alba to read them aloud in Amadean.

'The truth as revealed to Kyana of raven clan, porpleza to the gods, and the Prophet of Verus, the tenth in her name.'

Fear forked through Tristan. What would these markings mean for Sabine? For Dash and Ferugo?

Steeling himself, he stepped closer and read the words that had been hidden from both kingdoms for two hundred years.

46

*Amadea and Pyrie must never meet in war.
If we do we will draw to us an enemy with the strength
to destroy both kingdoms.
The fiends who drove the ancestors to the seas.
They devour all before them. They have destroyed
kingdoms. Worlds.
Verus sank the ships that pursued the ancestors.
She has hidden all of us from them for a thousand years.
If we do not live in peace they will find us and come
across the ocean.
A usurper will rise with the power of a god to defend us.
The mantle of the prophets will pass away.
And the rivers of our lands will run with blood and fire.*

47

Sabine read and re-read the words scrawled in Amadean.

No wonder the Tenth Prophet was declared insane, because only a madman would forbid war between the kingdoms, especially at the time it was written. The porplezi had just desecrated the remains of the First Prophet and the blood spilt in the Harvest Day massacre still stained the streets of Augustmount.

And threats of an ancient enemy? Of rivers running with blood and fire? He really had lost his mind, which meant that nothing in these words painted in blood and ochre had any connection with her. She trembled at them, regardless.

'Goat shit!' Xanthe spat. '*This* is what we've waited two hundred years for, a command to *live in peace* with Amadea?'

'Kyana gives the same warning.' The oracle also spoke in Pyrien. He'd wiped clean his fingers and was squatting to study the porpleza's markings. 'Consider the context. Our kingdoms were on the brink of war after the cleansing in the Amadean capital.'

'The scourge king attacked the mines, enslaved our people and stole our gold!'

'But it was not a *war,* not like the one we are about to wage.'

'There is no enemy but Amadea.'

The oracle stood to his full height. He was terrifying in this cave, blurring with the shadows. 'The ward has been broken by a guardian and a warrior who were able to set aside their hatred for a common purpose. It has meaning.'

'It is the work of *Verus*,' Xanthe hissed. 'She favours Amadea over us. She always has. This is not the will of the other gods. Ares will curse the ground we walk on if we fail to meet our enemy in battle now they have brought their full army to the mountains. *Live in peace* with Amadea?' She spat the words. 'Over my burning body.'

Sabine could see Axl's mind working, willed him to look at her.

'It doesn't sound like anything in the Codex,' Rhys said to her brother, getting to his feet alongside Lystra. 'It's not exactly what you've been spouting, either.'

'No,' Axl admitted. 'But the Tenth Prophet had only blood and ochre to use here. He perhaps went into more detail when he repeated it in Augustmount.'

'Or the priest who overheard him embellished it.'

'That of course is possible. But this...' he gestured to the wall. 'There's no denying this is what he wrote immediately after the vision.'

Sabine broke out in a sweat. Did her brother *believe* these ramblings?

A usurper will rise with the power of a god.

The jagged teeth of the cave closed in and the fire blurred into a muddy smudge. The musty cave air stank of smoke and blood, making her queasy—

'*Sabine.*'

She realised Tristan was asking her to translate the continued argument between Xanthe and the oracle.

'I can't *breathe*,' she whispered.

He saw something in her face then, something he recognised. 'She needs air.'

He met a wall of spears.

'Let them go.'

Sabine was vaguely aware it was Lystra who'd spoken as she stumbled out of the cave and into the drizzly afternoon. Tristan had hold of her arm, his grip tight as if he expected her to fling herself into the lake. She bent over and gulped in the damp air, focused on her breathing.

'What are they arguing about?' Tristan pressed.

The prophecy is not about me.

So why did Sabine feel like she was being unstitched, that if she did not steady herself, all the pieces of her would be whipped away in the breeze?

'My sister rejects the prophecy,' Lystra said when Sabine didn't answer.

'She's not alone.' Rhys had followed them from the cave, shadowed by half a dozen askari with spears at the ready. Sabine forced herself to straighten despite an overwhelming need to dig her fingers into the sand and ground herself. The child on Rhys's back smacked him across the top of his head.

'What?' Rhys turned his head to speak to Indy. 'I stopped fighting with her to save *you*. When I meet Lystra in combat, we'll face each other as enemies.'

The child looked from one to the other, her small grubby face stricken.

'You wish to make peace with the scourge who enslaved you?' Lystra asked her.

Indy shook her head and drew her thumb across her neck.

'Yes, *they* are dead. Do you think others will not do the same to you if you are recaptured?'

The oracle's guards were unsettled by the exchange, not sure what to make of the askara being so close to the Amadeans without violence following. Tristan kept his eyes on the guards as he leaned in and said quietly to Rhys, 'That may not be such an issue if there *is* a usurper.'

Rhys grunted. 'You seriously think Axl's going to overthrow the prophet?'

But Sabine knew Tristan wasn't talking about her brother.

The oracle and Xanthe emerged from the cave, still arguing. Nyomi positioned herself in front of them. 'The prisoners,' she said. 'May I kill them *now*?'

Tristan and Rhys didn't need to understand her words to know what she was asking. They shifted their weight. Sabine did the same, saw Indy resist Rhys's attempts to prise her from his back. Xanthe's gaze was like granite as it flicked over the Amadeans.

'Do not make the same mistake as your ancestor,' the oracle warned her. 'Let them live long enough for me to understand their significance, to know if the monk is the usurper. If he is, he will bring us victory.'

'Pah!' Xanthe said. 'I have seen wet flax stronger than him.'

'He is the child of a porpleza—Sabyl, no less. He carries power, I feel it in the fire. His sister does too, I taste it in their blood. The gods have a plan here, Xanthe.'

'If either of them had power they would not be your prisoners.'

Nyomi's eyes shone. 'Then there is no reason to keep them alive.'

'You will *not* kill them!' the oracle snapped, and even Xanthe blinked at the force of his objection.

'Xanthe—'

The Pyrien ruler held up a hand to silence further protests from Sabine's bloodthirsty grandmother. Xanthe had heard enough. 'The oracle has spoken. The scourge are no longer my concern. If they are a threat to Pyrie and the oracle fails to protect my kingdom, he will burn for it.' She planted her feet, raised her spear above her head, and howled at the sky. The askari on the beach joined her, their voices carrying on the breeze. The cry seeped into Sabine's bones, made her shiver.

When Xanthe fell silent, she lowered her weapon and bared her teeth at the oracle.

'I am done here. I leave you with the gods and their games. I go to war.'

48

'And what of me?' Lystra asked, daring to keep her eyes lifted. She'd howled with her sister but it had not filled her with the fire it once had.

Xanthe's gaze raked over her, snagged on the bandage at her elbow.

'The ward is broken. The porplezi have no further claim on you.'

She waited, heart thudding.

'Gather your weapons.'

Lystra held her sister's stare. If she faltered now, if she scurried away in gratitude, she would never lead another pack.

Xanthe understood and taunted her with silence.

Could Lystra lower her head to another wolf? What if Xanthe deepened her shame and made her submit to an askari leader of another clan? The thought stuck in her throat. What if she had to submit to a *weaver finch*?

Xanthe watched all this play out across Lystra's face. Her sister was savouring the moment, even in her impatience to mobilise her army.

'Your pack was slaughtered. You were a slave in all but marking. You had to be *rescued*,' that part was the most insulting to Xanthe, 'and you bonded with the enemy'.

'I did not *bond* with the warrior. I kept him alive to fulfil the task *you* gave me.' Lystra felt Rhys watching her. She failed to mention that he'd also kept her alive, but he couldn't understand what was being said so it didn't matter. 'I did all that was asked of me.'

Xanthe turned to the askara closest to her. 'Go to the clan chiefs. Tell them to gather on the path.'

Lystra's nostrils flared. Was the moment done? Was this cruelty to stretch on?

Her sister folded her arms and flexed her biceps, then narrowed her eyes as if still deciding what to do with her.

'Your honour is restored,' Xanthe said. Lystra's breath rushed out of her until her ruler held up a single finger. 'But you shall remain a lone wolf.'

Lystra blinked, confused. 'How can I be both?'

'You are free to run and fight with any pack that accepts you. But you will never again lead.' Xanthe thumped her chest with her fist twice to seal the declaration. 'As the oracle is my witness.'

The oracle bent his head in acknowledgement.

Lystra swallowed, numb.

It was a fate worse than submitting to a weaver finch. At least then she would have had status, however lowly. Now, though, she would have to lie on her belly and hope a pack would accept her, knowing no wolf was under obligation to share food or cover her back in a fight.

It was a shocking humiliation for a sister of the ruler. More than that, it was without precedent among wolf clan. Her only recourse was to challenge Xanthe for the right to lead the clan chiefs and that had never been her ambition. Even if her shame demanded it, Lystra was in no state to best her sister. And Xanthe knew it.

Lystra bent a neck in submission and Xanthe grunted her satisfaction.

'Gather your weapons,' the ruler of the five clans repeated.

'Find a pack on the path and ready yourself to fight.' She stalked off without waiting for Lystra to obey.

The oracle gave her a beat to compose herself.

'Your ties to this place remain, guardian,' he said quietly. 'You are always welcome here.'

The kindness was salt in her wounds. Lystra gave a curt nod and turned away to obey the order she'd been given. Rhys caught her eye.

'See you on the battlefield.'

'How?' she scoffed. 'You are a captive.'

'You *still* underestimate me?'

The warrior's arrogance knew no bounds but the thought of facing him in war lifted her spirits.

'Nyomi has plans for you,' she reminded him.

'I reckon I could take her in a fight.' He said it deadpan and it surprised a laugh from her. Indy was on his back still, her arms wrapped around his neck and her eyes sad. The thought of leaving the child brought an entirely unexpected pang.

'Oracle.'

'Yes, guardian.'

She winced at his continued use of the title. She had hoped it had disappeared along with the ward.

'The place you offer me here. Give it to the child.'

The oracle considered the request, seemed amused that she asked it in Amadean. He gave a single nod.

Lystra touched Indy's arm slung across the warrior's chest. 'If I survive, I will come for you.'

Indy's chin wobbled and she gave a stoic nod.

'You better survive,' Rhys called as Lystra walked away. 'We have unfinished business, you and I.'

49

'Stop looking at me like that, all of you.'

Axl frowned. 'How are we looking at you?'

'Like I'm about to burst into flames.'

It was dusk and Sabine was locked in the hut with three sets of wary eyes. The Amadeans' so-called 'freedom' had been completely revoked when Xanthe and her askari swarmed back over the ridge late afternoon, leaving only the oracle's guards in the village.

'*Are* you about to burst into flames?' Rhys asked. The warrior was still coming to terms with the possibility she was the usurper.

'No, because the prophecy is not about me.'

'Tristan says the oracle thinks it is.'

'Then why haven't I been dragged before him?'

Rhys shrugged. 'Maybe he's shitting himself.'

Sabine huffed a humourless laugh. She had no idea why the most powerful porpleza in Pyrie had left them alone since the cave, but it certainly wasn't out of fear. *She*, on the other hand, had enough for the both of them.

Tristan was at the window, keeping an eye out for movement in the dying light. He'd been giving Sabine space but his attention was rarely far from her. Axl joined him to watch over the forecourt.

'Bryn won't come,' her brother said. 'Not now. Nyomi's

plan relies on an army hurling spears at us as soon as we're on the lake.'

Rhys fiddled with the poultice strapped to his injured chest, lost in thought. Something had happened across the lake and it was more than surviving a fight with a yapa. 'If your slave shows, it means the witch has set a trap for us in the temple,' he said. 'We get caught in there and she'll have all the excuse she needs to execute us, no matter what old black-eyes says.'

Sabine knew Rhys was right, and yet it changed nothing. They had to get away from this wretched place. They all agreed on that much, even if it was for different reasons. All Sabine wanted was to be gone, and if she could end Nyomi first, that much the better.

'The plan is to get our weapons and fight our way out?' she asked.

'Yes,' Tristan and Rhys said together.

'And then?'

In the forecourt, the bonfire had been stoked and the glow of the flames brightened Tristan's features. 'We rejoin the army.'

Axl's eyes lit up. 'To tell the king about the Tenth Prophecy?'

'To prove we're not traitors. *You* can be the one who tells him Torvus died for a prophecy that condemns the invasion he's leading.'

Sabine's brother drew his cloak tighter. 'And if the rib bone still burns?'

Rhys scoffed. 'It can't be sacred if it burns here so we snuff it out.'

'No,' Tristan said. 'We take it as is.'

Sabine no longer knew he if meant as leverage or as a weapon he thought *she* would somehow wield. She fizzed with nerves, thinking about all that could go wrong. What if their weapons were no longer in the temple? What if Bryn lied and they'd never been there? What if Axl was killed while they were fighting their way out? What if—

'Your slave is coming,' Tristan said. He moved to the entry and the three of them fell in line behind him. The outside bolts slid back and the door swung open to reveal Bryn alone on the deck. There were no guards or porplezi in sight. The forecourt was completely empty and the only sound was the roar of the bonfire—its guttering flames the only movement in the breathless dusk.

Oh, it was a trap all right.

Sabine steeled herself. Her grandmother wanted them dead and they were making it easy for her by going in blind. Bryn stepped past Tristan to check on her and Axl.

'Where is everyone?' she asked him.

'The porplezi are in the gathering house. Nyomi has called a meeting to discuss your fate.'

'And the rest of the village? The askari guards?'

The old Pyrien shook his head. He didn't know.

'What about Indy?' Rhys asked.

'She is with the libertini.' Bryn glanced over his shoulder in the direction of the gathering house. 'You should go. Now.'

Tristan didn't need to be told twice. He moved for the door.

'Wait,' Sabine said, her pulse already racing. There was so much she wanted to say to Bryn and no time to say it. 'I hope I live to see you again,' was the best she could do. She squeezed his shoulder, trying to convey the true depths of her gratitude to him for so much more than this moment.

'The gods protect you,' he said, placing his hand over hers and his pale blue eyes moist.

And then Sabine was crouch-running behind Tristan out the door and down the stairs. It was almost dark now. She glanced back only once, saw the hut door was again bolted and Bryn gone.

Her heart was in her throat as she and Axl dashed across the forecourt and scrambled up the temple stairs behind the warriors.

The climb was so steep that Sabine had to use her hands for balance. A rope would have been handy. She'd counted twenty steps so far and they weren't even a third of the way up. There was enough grey light left that they would be exposed to anyone who entered the forecourt and looked up. It didn't help that Axl lagged behind, nowhere near as fit as Sabine and the warriors.

Another thirty steps and they were about halfway. The bonfire already looked small below and Sabine was suddenly aware of how high she was and how much further she had to go. For a heartbeat she couldn't feel her legs. She sat down and caught her breath, knowing she didn't have time to wait for the feeling to return but having to wait just the same.

Don't look down.

No wonder Nyomi was so spry if she did this every day.

Axl was only a few steps away when Sabine set off again on trembling muscles. She'd lost count of the steps when Tristan stopped near the top to wait. Rhys, then Sabine, and finally Axl reached him, all four of them sucking in deep breaths. They had slightly better cover in the gathering dark, but they had to be sure the temple was empty. They were five steps from the top and Sabine could now see flickering shadows through the narrow doorway ahead. Sacred or not, there were flames up here.

She dared a glance over her shoulder and the sight was dizzying. They were so high she was eye level with the first stars in the east and when she looked down, she could have blotted out the bonfire with her thumb. One wrong step and she would tumble to a terrible death. And still it was less frightening than what awaited inside. She'd been so preoccupied with the climb she hadn't allowed herself to think about what was beyond the entry.

Tristan signalled his intention and set off first.

Four steps to go.

All Sabine could see from this angle was a bare stone floor writhing with shadows, and part of a wall painted with images she couldn't quite make out.

Three steps.

Two steps.

Verus, give me strength.

One.

Sabine stepped into the temple.

The space was larger than she'd expected, extending into the mountain and lit by blazing braziers on all four walls that guttered in the breeze. Her gaze locked on what was waiting in the centre of the room. Even before her eyes adjusted she understood what she was seeing.

A chair made of bones. Nyomi had not lied.

Sabine stumbled forward. Everything else in the room receded. She dropped to the floor before her grandmother's seat, aware only of the cold hard stone beneath her knees. The chair was partially draped with a wolf pelt. Sabine dragged it free to reveal the full horror of what lay beneath.

Bones of similar lengths had been used for the legs, seat and uprights; a spine and ribs interlaced to form the back support. The structure had been strengthened with mortar and the whole thing was held together with leather straps. But the worst...the *worst*...was the skull impaled on the chair's right arm as a grotesque hand rest.

'Don't...' Axl whispered, beside her on his shins.

She reached for it anyway.

The crown of the skull had been worn smooth from her grandmother's frequent touch. Sabine traced her fingers over the joints between the bone plates; lines on a map that told the story of her father. She found a crack at the base of the skull, the kill blow; felt the gaps where teeth had been knocked out. It was a strange mercy, but Sabine struggled to make the connection between these bones and the living, breathing Darius of her memories. The father with soft eyes who had carried her on his shoulders when she was small enough; who taught her to split wood and knead bread; who indulged her terrible needle work and wore badly patched tunics without complaint. Who always told her how much she was like her mother.

It was love, not bones, that drew her tears. And then regret for the choices he'd made.

Why did her father come here? If he had stayed at home he would still be alive.

'There are too many bones here for one person,' Tristan said, his touch light on her shoulder. 'They could belong to anyone.'

Sabine nodded, unable to speak.

'Come away.'

She shook violently as he helped her to her feet. He gave her a moment to wipe her cheeks and gather herself. Only then did she register the rest of the temple. One wall was a fresco of simplistic figures painted in black, grey and red. It depicted men, women and children being killed by spear and axe, with the Augustmount temple clearly recognisable above it all. The artwork was nothing like the detailed tapestries and mosaics in Amadea, yet there was something more chilling about this rudimentary re-creation, where the only colour was the sea of red beneath the bodies. And this version celebrated the slaughter of *Amadeans*.

Her gaze travelled to the altar. *Sweet Verus.*

It was a tall slab of granite stained brown with the blood of countless sacrifices, not unlike those in Amadea. But behind it the temple wall was lined from floor to ceiling with human skulls large and small; sun-bleached white and mottled brown. Too many to count.

Sabine knew she and the others should be acting with more haste, yet they each moved as if wading through molasses, stunned by the horror of it all. Even Rhys had strayed from keeping watch on the steps to come further inside.

'Over there,' Tristan said, breaking the spell. He strode across the temple to a mat piled with folded blankets and cushions—Nyomi's bed, Sabine guessed—and a long wooden chest. It wasn't locked. Tristan opened it and lifted out his sword and belt, then handed Sabine and Rhys theirs. The weapons were sitting atop a collection of Amadean and Pyrien trophies: swords, axes, spears, and daggers from both kingdoms. Sabine found her own dagger, unique among the Pyrien-crafted blades without a clan insignia. Hers had been forged from iron by Bryn under her uncle's nose; the one she used on Olidus the day she escaped the manor house. The familiar weight of it helped her slip back into her own skin.

Sabine had barely tucked it into her boot when she heard Axl gasp. Her brother stood between the altar and the wall of skulls, both hands pressed over his mouth. She and the warriors went to him—and all three stopped dead when they saw what he'd discovered.

Axl stood at a second altar, hidden behind the first. On it was a small, open receptacle made from beaten gold, about the size of an optimati jewellery box. Something flickered inside it. Her brother's eyes shone. 'Come and see.'

She edged closer with Tristan and Rhys, her neck craned, and they saw it at the same time: a solitary rib bone burning in the middle of the box. Except the flames did not consume the bone or give off smoke, and the bone appeared to float without support.

Sabine's skin prickled and her scalp tightened.

A now familiar voice filled the temple: 'What does it reveal about Verus that a bone from her first servant burns here?'

The oracle stood in the entrance, orb and stave in hand. Tristan and Rhys drew their swords and took up flanking positions either side of the altar. The oracle was only slightly breathless, which meant he'd had time to climb at his own pace while they'd been wandering about in a daze. Outside, his askari guards waited on the steps, fidgeting and looking warily into the temple. There was no sign of Alba.

'I'd say it shows our god has less sense than we thought,' Rhys muttered. He was acting as if unfazed that their only way out was blocked by at least twice their number, but his grip was tight on his sword. Sabine drew her own blade, only half-focused on the threat. A strange sensation had stirred to life and was building beneath her ribs.

'What do you think, monk?' the oracle asked.

Axl had not moved from the altar. 'Verus once considered the people of Pyrie to be her children. Perhaps this is a sign she hopes to see you return to her.' He held the porpleza's dreadful gaze, his features dancing in the bone-light. 'What does it mean to you?'

The oracle tilted his head, birdlike. He showed his bloodstained teeth and his irises shone black in the torchlight. He seemed taller, as menacing in here as in the cave.

'Your world is so small,' he said. 'I will never understand why Verus is so fond of you.'

Sabine didn't know if he meant Axl or Amadeans in general and she didn't get the chance to find out because there was a disturbance on the steps and Nyomi stormed into the temple, face flushed and eyes wild. The bone witch took in the scene and screamed at the askari in Pyrien: 'Get in here and kill them!'

They made no move to obey her, and the oracle's black eyes blazed. 'You would have armed askari set foot in this place?'

'*They* are armed,' she snarled, pointing at the warriors.

'Because you had their weapons brought here against my wishes.'

'This defilement cannot go unpunished!' Nyomi stared down the askari on the steps. 'You serve *me* in this temple!'

'Silence!' The oracle's voice bounced off the walls. 'The lake and all those who live here serve me, even up here.'

Sabine translated for the warriors, not taking her eyes from her cursed grandmother. The storm in her chest built.

'Did you not understand the will of the gods revealed to us in the cave?' the oracle asked the bone witch.

Nyomi sneered. 'My *daughter* was the will of the gods, and they now mock me with these half breeds. *Verus* mocks me.'

The oracle shifted his focus to Axl, still standing protectively over the rib bone. 'Son of Sabyl,' he said in Amadean. 'If you can touch the reliquary, you can take it.'

There was a stunned beat. The flame on the rib bone fluttered rapidly as if bellows had been set to it. Sabine's heart stuttered with it.

'Do it,' Tristan murmured. '*Now*, Axl.'

Axl hesitated and then tapped the sides lightly with his index fingers. He hissed as the beaten gold burned his flesh. 'I can't.' He gave Sabine a meaningful look and her heart offered a hard, painful thump.

'Pah!' Nyomi spat. 'Of course he can't touch it.'

'Can you?' Sabine asked her.

'I am the beloved of Ares, the keeper of the flame. I am the only one—'

'She cannot,' the oracle said. 'Not since your mother left us.'

Nyomi turned on the oracle, incredulous. 'Have you have lost your mind? Xanthe will toss you to the flames for this and I will praise the gods as you burn alive. Ares will not forgive this betrayal.'

'Sabine,' Tristan urged. Her mouth was dry, her pulse racing. She swallowed and handed her sword to him with jittery fingers. She took Axl's place at the altar, avoiding his gaze. If she couldn't touch the gold box either, then her brother was wrong and she had no connection to the fire of the First Prophet. There would be nothing more to her than flesh and blood and shame.

But she had to know, either way.

Sabine took a breath and rested her hands either side of the reliquary just as Axl had, not yet touching it. The flame danced along the rib bone, insistent. The temple air was chilly and the heat radiating from the box warmed her skin. She let her breath out slowly, readying herself. She didn't mean to exhale on the relic, but as her breath washed over the rib bone, the flickering flame settled to a languid dance.

Oh.

Sabine gripped the edge of the altar to steady herself, fixated on the flame. She felt the horrors of the temple fading away: the oracle and the askari; Nyomi; even the wall of skulls and the chair of bones receded. Her awareness narrowed to the warmth of the rib bone. A new tingling began in the scar on her palm. She shouldn't be dropping her guard in this place but the flame had her entire attention. It was different from the hunger of the fire in Axl's hearth and the wild fury of the bonfire far below. It was calm and gentle, and it fuelled something in her other than fear and worry. Something new.

Sabine realised with a start that she *wanted* to touch the box. And not just to spite her grandmother. She checked that her trembling legs would hold her and then tapped her fingers lightly against the reliquary.

The beaten gold was warm, not scorching hot. She sensed the stillness in the room, the breathless anticipation.

Sabine tapped her fingertips a second time, a beat longer,

and then pressed her palms against the metal. It was no warmer than holding a cup of mulled wine.

On impulse, she picked it up with both hands.

For a shocked beat, nobody moved or spoke.

'Sweet Verus,' Tristan finally breathed.

'Here...' Axl's eyes shone with fervour as he reverently handed her the lid. She fitted it into the grooves and sealed off the flame, and then panicked she'd snuffed it out. She slid the lid back enough to see the flame calmly rolling along the rib bone. Relieved, she closed it again.

The oracle watched it all with naked fascination. Nyomi's eyes were hard, her lips thin with rage. Sabine saw how much this moment had cost her grandmother. It wasn't nearly enough.

'We're leaving,' Tristan said to the oracle. 'Tell your guards to let us pass.'

The oracle signalled to the askari. 'Let them go.' The orb flared bright at his words and the askari stepped aside.

Sabine gave the reliquary the gentlest of shakes but nothing moved inside it. It seemed the rules of the world worked differently within its walls. Trusting the relic was safe, she tucked it under arm, took back her sword and followed Tristan toward the doorway.

'Remember this moment, children of Sabyl,' the oracle said as Sabine passed him on still-shaking legs. 'Without it, nothing that follows could have come to pass.'

By the time they'd finished the long climb to the ground, Sabine still had no idea if his words were a benediction or curse.

WAR

50

'The Pyrien army is massing in the northern valley. There must be two thousand of them. Maybe more.'

'Xanthe has arrived, then,' Felix said, his pulse quickening despite himself.

The breathless scout nodded. 'I got close enough to see askari kneeling before her.'

The king leaned from his saddle and clapped the scout on the shoulder. 'Good work.' He dismissed the boy and turned to Pellus. They had ridden together to a ridge that offered oversight of the entire army. 'She will come to us at first light.'

'Then we will be ready.'

Felix had to concede that Pellus kept cool under pressure. There was none of Gregori's second guessing or Alicia's snarky nerves. Or even Carmine's warmongering. Pellus was focused and purposeful, his emotions held well in check. It was tempting to think it was one of the gifts of being the prophet's warrior, but Felix had known Pellus since he was an ambitious provincial squire and he'd always lacked the passion that drove Torvus.

It made the next conversation less complicated.

'Xanthe may have Amadean hostages,' Felix said, his face turned north.

'From our forces?'

'From Mine Five. Askari attacked and killed the veterans there on the last half-moon. Burned the place to the ground.'

Pellus immediately understood the implications. 'Tristan and Rhys.'

'They were not among the dead left out to rot.'

'Escaped?'

'Do you honestly believe warriors of Iolia would flee while veterans were being slaughtered?'

'No,' Pellus conceded. 'They would have died fighting.' He was thinking harder now. 'Could they have left with the prisoner before the attack?'

'Askari would not have risked exposure on the border for anything less than one of their own. The raid was to free her.'

'So they were taken...alive?'

Felix gave him a moment, dared him to voice what even the prophet would not. But if Pellus suspected a connection with the Angustonians or the usurper, he hid it well. And wisely. Accusing Iolian warriors of treason was a dangerous move, even for the prophet's warrior. Ferugo might not be on campaign, but there had been no open accusation of treason yet and Felix hoped to keep it that way.

'Did you receive this news today?' Pellus asked.

'No.'

Felix caught the moment Pellus understood the prophet and his king had kept this from him. The warrior hid the injury so swiftly and so completely Felix almost missed it.

'There may be another warrior with them, a woman. And a Stonebridge monk.'

Recognition sparked in Pellus. *That* was a surprise.

'You know them?'

Pellus seemed genuinely confused. 'I met a Stonebridge monk on pilgrimage at Iolia during the tournament...after my contest in the lists with Tristan. But he was not travelling with the Iolian army, and there was no woman among Adward's cohort.'

'Can you be sure?'

The warrior frowned. 'Why would a monk on campaign hide from me—' He cut himself off before he could finish voicing that thought and refocused. 'Xanthe may not bring hostages to battle, but she will have them close by. The monk is the priority?'

It was a testament to Pellus's piety that he did not question why a lone monk warranted rescuing. Felix knew the warrior revered Stonebridge monks above even the priests at Augustmount.

'Yes,' Felix said. 'The warriors can look after themselves.' His gaze skimmed over the Iolian cohort, currently running drills on horseback below them in the valley. He'd sent Ty to Adward for the morning, not wanting him to overhear this conversation. It was a necessary cruelty to keep the boy grieving. The squire knew more than he was sharing, and he'd gathered his wits enough to remember that the reputation and lives of his overlords remained at stake. That might change, though, in the face of the looming battle.

Felix brought his mind back to the task at hand.

Until now, planning the scale of conflict like the one ahead had been in theory only. Instruction on the art of war was brought across the ocean by the ancestors. Their tactics had been thought lost until the Eleventh Prophet handed them to King Tertullian, along with the prophecy that Amadea would not have peace until Pyrie was destroyed. It sparked the rise of tournaments and the long march to war. Every broken lance in the lists, every arrow loosed in contest, every mud and blood-soaked melee...all of it had been to prepare the kingdom for this moment.

Felix's forces were spread out before him on the wide valley floor, a sea of tents and wagons; warriors, archers and peasants; horses and oxen. Even depleted, his army was awe-inspiring.

'Your father would be proud.' Pellus said it quietly, as if unsure how it would be received.

Felix huffed a laugh. 'He would be *surprised*.' In truth, he avoided thoughts of King Tertius. His memories of his father came weighted with bitterness. 'Any pride he might have in this moment would be about him, not me.'

'Hmph,' Pellus said. 'I know a little something about that.'

The king had forgotten for a moment he was speaking with Pellus. This was not a topic he'd discussed with anyone but Torvus. He glanced at the warrior. Of course he understood. He was Amadea's most famous bastard.

'What of your father?'

'Is he proud of me?' Pellus asked as if the question amused him. Here was the weakness Torvus had so easily exploited. 'I wouldn't know. Nor, in truth, do I care.'

Felix was tempted to suggest that attitude was a luxury of being the warrior's prophet, but he understood better than any that status did not replace a father's love.

'If that's true, Pellus, you are a better man than me.'

'No, sire,' the warrior said. 'I am the lesser for it.'

Felix searched for signs of flattery or false humility and found none. It was not what he'd expected from the recently appointed general of the Iolian army.

Pellus sensed his surprise and cleared his throat. 'So we face our enemy tomorrow. I'll send for the war council.'

'No,' Felix said and straightened in his saddle. 'No more talk. We've done nothing but go over this plan since we arrived. Tell the overlords to assemble their forces for the morning.'

'As you command.' Pellus gathered his reins and Felix did the same.

'Tomorrow, Pellus, we fight a war a thousand years in the making. Our fathers can make of that what they will.'

51

Tristan needed more than hard riding to burn off the frustration pent up under his skin.

He'd been primed for violence in the temple and was almost disappointed their escape had been without resistance. Aside from a handful of short-lived scuffles, he'd not used a weapon since they'd crossed the border. Even the initiative's death had been at Sabine's hands, not his. The need to *do* something was building like a forest fire.

They'd kept a steady pace since reclaiming their horses and fleeing the village. Tracking Xanthe was the quickest way to find the Amadean army and they stopped long enough to refresh themselves and the horses and then kept moving. It was the third day and they had to be getting close. Tristan was a knot of anticipation at what lay ahead. Would they reach the armies before the two sides clashed? Would they get to the king before Pellus intercepted them? What would the prophet's warrior do if he laid eyes on the relic first?

'I hope Ty is holding it together,' Tristan said when they stopped by a stream mid-morning under a dark and rumbling sky. It was only now they were getting closer to the squire that he allowed thoughts of the boy to creep in.

'Adward will be keeping an eye on him,' Rhys said, loosening Lager's girth while the gelding drank.

'Adward doesn't know what's at stake.'

'You wish we'd told him? That would have made it even tougher for him to be Pellus's right-hand man.'

Tristan sat on his haunches to splash cold water on his face and then took a long drink from cupped hands. The ground here was disturbed from Xanthe's army, so they were still heading in the right direction. Not far downstream, Sabine was stretching her spine and her brother fluttered around her like a moth.

'Is the relic all right?' the monk asked.

'It has been every time I've checked, Axl.'

'Can we look again?'

Rhys had found a shawl on a drying line as they fled the lake and Sabine had wrapped the reliquary in it and tied it across her chest like a newborn. Now, she blew out her breath and undid the knot at her shoulder. It didn't take a lot of convincing and, truth be told, Tristan wouldn't mind another look either. He dried his hands on his trousers and walked over to them. Sabine unwrapped the bundle and gently slid off the lid. And there it was: the stolen rib bone of the First Prophet, *floating*, and the sacred flame moving calmly along its length.

'No change,' Sabine said, breathless as always at the sight of it.

Rhys joined their huddle. 'You sure you don't want to touch it?'

'*Yes*,' she said, emphatic. 'I'm sure.'

'You have to try at some point.'

Tristan was glad it was Rhys who'd said it and not him.

'Not here.'

'Where then? It would be really handy to return to the king with the usurper.'

Sabine raised her eyebrows at him. 'My sword not enough for you now?'

'Yeah, but the *usurper—*'

'Is meant to do what? Scorch the earth with a flaming rib bone?'

'Could you do that?'

She gave Rhys a flat look and slid the lid back in place. 'I very much doubt it.'

He picked at the scab inside his elbow. 'I wonder if Lystra's tattoo will stop changing now.'

Tristan and Sabine exchanged a look. 'You think about her a lot, do you?' Sabine asked him, gently teasing.

'Hey,' Rhys protested. 'I think about a lot of things.'

Rhys had told them the story—more than once—of Indy being snatched by a giant bird and how he killed a yapa while Lystra rescued the child. What he hadn't fully explained were the claw marks on his arms, or how he and Lystra had made their truce. It tended to be Rhys's charm and sexual prowess that won him over with women, but Tristan doubted either had played a part on this occasion.

'Come on Axl,' Rhys said. 'Let's get these horses under cover.'

Sabine gave Tristan a half-smile at his cousin's evasion. It was an echo of their intimacy and brought a wave of longing for her. He watched as she positioned the reliquary in the sling, heat climbing her neck. Their eyes met again and his heart did a quick side-step. There was so much he wanted to say and no idea how to say it, even though the shape of it was on his tongue.

'Take a walk with me?' he said. 'Not far.'

They were in enemy territory, and a threat could come from any direction, but Tristan needed to make amends with Sabine. Who knew when the next chance might come?

She glanced up at the sky. 'It's about to rain.'

Rhys and Axl were already under the canopy of one of the wide-leafed trees unique to this side of the border. It offered plenty of shelter—and no privacy.

'There are other trees.'

Thunder rolled through the threatening clouds overhead as she nodded. 'Lead on.'

He set off back the way they'd come. As they walked, Tristan's mind leapt from one thought to the next, of what he wanted to say to her and how to say it. It didn't take much for his mind to land on the last time they'd been alone together, before the Iolian army reached the high plains. They'd ridden far from camp under the waxing moon and lain down their cloaks on the floor of the forest, took their time with each other. Tristan remembered the taste of her, the feel of her lips on him.

A fat raindrop splattered on his forehead, a reminder to cool his thoughts. Frustration wasn't the only thing he'd pent up.

He glanced at Sabine sideways, wondered what she was thinking. He was opening his mouth to ask when lightning forked overhead, followed by a deafening crack. They exchanged a startled look, just as the wind whipped up out of nowhere and brought a gust of cold rain.

'Might be time to find that cover,' Tristan said instead.

*

'Over there.' Sabine ran for a tree with a hollowed out trunk. Her heart was skittish, either from the sudden onset of the storm or the way Tristan was looking at her.

They made it to shelter right as squalls of rain blotted out the forest. The space inside the tree was dry and large enough for five times their number. Sabine's hair was wet now, and water dripped down her neck and formed rivulets under her vest. She took off her cloak and shook it out, and Tristan did the same. He found knotty growths inside the tree to hang them and then stuck his head back out into the rain to let out a sharp triple-whistle. Rhys's answering whistles cut through the wind.

'They're okay,' he said.

He slicked back the damp hair from his face and watched as she squeezed water from her plait. He took a step towards her. 'Sabine...'

She fell still. The air was so charged it was if they'd brought the lightning inside with them. 'Wait.' She untied the reliquary and placed it gently on the ground behind her. Whatever this was, she didn't want the relic between them. 'Before you start, let me say what I should have said long before now. I'll do whatever it takes to free Dashelle and Ferugo, by sword or anything else I can wield. I can't promise anything beyond that.'

His eyelashes dripped with rain and she saw how much that meant to him. 'That's all I can ask,' he said.

'Is it? Is that all you want from me?'

Tristan held her gaze. 'No,' he admitted. 'It's not.'

Sabine straightened her spine and kept the distance between them, her heart thudding. 'What if I'm not the usurper? What if I can't save Dashelle and Ferugo?'

The devastation of that possibility was written across his face, but he nodded anyway.

'Then I will be a raging mess. And I will still want to be by your side.'

A lump rose in her throat. She wanted to believe him. She *needed* to believe him because more than anything she wanted to close this distance between them. But need and want did not change reality.

'I am half Pyrien, Tristan.'

'You're also half Amadean.'

'Which do you think matters most in Amadea?'

'*You're* all that matters to me.'

Sabine's chest rose and fell, and when she didn't respond, he nodded as if agreeing with something unsaid in her silence.

'Yeah, I know, I have to earn your trust.' He gave a small huff of frustration. 'And I know I don't always react the way I should. I've given you plenty of reasons to doubt me. I understand why you didn't trust me with the truth.'

'It wouldn't have mattered what you did, Tristan. I wouldn't have trusted you with that.'

He blinked, stricken, and she realised he'd misunderstood her.

'Knowing what I've done…what's been done to me…and then to find out who I am…I wouldn't trust *anyone* to stand by me.'

The truth of that confession washed over her, and with it the deep sense of worthlessness she'd tried so hard to bury since her uncle first struck her. She hung her head so Tristan couldn't see her shame, but he lifted her chin with gentle fingers. The storm in her chest was as wild as the one outside.

'I know what you've done, Sabine.' He said it loud enough to be heard over the wind. 'And I know who you are. You are fierce and loyal and strong, and you have more courage than any woman I've met.' He brushed a thumb over her cheek, wiping away rain or tears or both. 'You have, and will *always* have, the loyalty of my dagger and my sword.' He swallowed. 'And you have my stubborn and useless heart…if you want it.'

Sabine searched his eyes, saw that he meant it. It was another moment before her body caught up and the churn under her ribs began to settle, even as the rain and wind raged on outside.

'You have the loyalty of *my* sword, Tristan,' she managed, her voice quavering. 'And my messy, furious heart has always been yours.'

He gave a soft laugh, surprised and pleased. 'A pledge as warriors and lovers.'

'Because we are both.'

'That we are.' The smile lingered on his lips as they closed the distance between them and Sabine lifted her mouth to his. The kiss was tender and sweet, and said all the things they did not yet have the words for. Tristan's hands moved to her hips and drew her closer, and the conversation changed to something more familiar. She looped her arms around his neck and arched into him as the kiss deepened. They barely broke apart as they removed each other's sword belts, and then Tristan lifted her so she could wrap her legs around him. He positioned her against the tree wall and she could *feel* what it was he wanted to say next.

She had never wanted him more.

They unlaced each other's vests with expert fingers and Tristan's mouth went to her breasts. She ran her fingers through his wet hair and over the wings of the eagle on his shoulders. The rain was still gusting sideways outside and it felt like they had all the time in the world in this space that was theirs alone.

'You won't be cold?' Tristan asked when she unhooked her legs and unfastened her trousers and then his.

'Not for long.'

The bark of the tree was rough and the air *was* chilly, even with their skin blazing, but it was like being with Tristan for the first time. There were no secrets between them now, and that new intimacy heightened every touch, deepened every sensation. They moved together, out of sight from the world, lost in each other until Sabine finally bit down on Tristan's shoulder to muffle her cry of pleasure and he did the same before slumping against her.

Afterwards, when they'd wrestled their damp bodies back into their clothes, Tristan sat down and stretched out his legs and Sabine sat between them, the reliquary within reach. She was still flushed and tingling, not yet ready to end the moment. The wind had stopped but the downpour continued. The lightning also lingered, but each rumble of thunder sounded further away. They wouldn't have much longer before they'd have to return to Axl and Rhys.

She leaned back against his chest and he slipped his arms around her, brushed his lips to her temple. They sat together, contented at least for the moment, watching the rain fall.

'At least I'll have one good memory of this place,' she said.

He rested his head against hers. 'I'm sorry about your father.'

The reminder of the lake stole some of her warmth. She didn't want to think about what had been done to Darius there. 'I wish I knew how my parents met and came to be together. There's so much I don't know about either of them.'

'The bone witch acts as if your mother was meant to single-handedly destroy Amadea.'

'I know…it makes no sense. Truly, Tristan, she didn't look or sound Pyrien.' Sabine watched as a hare darted out from a bramble, blinked in the rain, and ducked back under cover. 'And why in the name of Verus did my father go looking for that godawful woman after so many years? The abbot said something to him at last year's planting day and I've been assuming it was about Axl. Maybe it was more than that.'

Tristan tucked her hair behind her ear. 'There was no justice in leaving that bone hag alive. When Dash and Ferugo are free, I'll ask permission for us to take the Iolian cohort back there to finish the job.'

Sabine shivered at the thought of returning to the lake. 'Once we cross that border, Tristan, I never want to set foot here again.'

52

Pellus sat deep in his saddle, King Felix on his left and Adward of Iolia on his right; the might of Amadea behind them. His entire being hummed with purpose. This was it, the moment his life had been leading to: the chance to fight beside his king as Amadea conquered Pyrie and shook free their kingdom from the grip of heresy. Bits and bridles jingled as four hundred mounted warriors held leather-clad warhorses in check, waiting for the signal under a storm-washed sky. Behind them were close to three thousand foot soldiers. On their flanks were a thousand archers.

Xanthe and her army were pouring through the northern pass and spilling out onto the valley floor, coming quicker than Pellus had expected for forces on foot.

'Hold!' the king shouted.

Pellus felt the nervous energy rippling up and down the ranks. Every last man had to wait until the entirety of Xanthe's army was in the valley. This is what the king had come all this distance for: to make a stand on ground that suited the Amadeans and drew the Pyriens into a fight they could not win. Felix had chosen the wide valley floor in the belief the sight of an enemy force this deep into Pyrie would be too much for Xanthe; that she would attack even without the advantage of ambush. It had been Pellus's suggestion to send an advanced contingent of Iolian forces under the cover of darkness to flank the northern pass and be in place to block off retreat. The divided Amadean army would have the numbers to surround the Pyriens and crush them in a single frenetic battle. There were to be no prisoners. No slaves taken. The only trophy would be the head of the Pyrien ruler and whatever the Amadean troops could plunder and carry.

'Sweet Verus,' Adward breathed as the enemy kept coming.

Pellus's mount snorted and danced sideways. Even the seasoned warhorse was not immune to the charge in the air. Pellus took his lance and reins in one hand and patted the mare, murmured soothing words. She stamped a hoof and settled at the sound of his voice.

Pellus wondered whether the Pyriens were equally awed by what they faced: a wall of warhorses protected by hardened leather on their chests, necks and rumps, ridden by warriors wearing breastplates and shoulder armour—no helmets because unobstructed vision trumped safety—each carrying a steel-tipped lance and wooden shield, and a sword on their hip. Xanthe must know the mounted cohort put her at a severe disadvantage.

'Hold!' the king repeated, his eyes on the approaching horde.

The Pyriens were now close enough that Pellus could make out the five clan leaders by their headdress. The woman leading them front and centre could only be Xanthe. Her face was smeared with river mud, even without the need for camouflage.

A horn sounded from the ridge to signal the tail of the Pyrien army had cleared the valley. The trap was set.

Felix raised his lance, steel tip pointed to the sky. 'Now!'

Pellus loosed his reins and barely shifted his weight to send his warhorse leaping forward. Four hundred horses thundered at full gallop towards the Pyriens. Xanthe and her fighters did not waste breath with a war cry. They didn't falter or change course, even when the Amadeans on the flanks loosed a storm of arrows overhead. Pellus gave a brief thought to Tristan's squire somewhere among the archers and then lowered his lance, ready for impact. A frustrating number of arrows thudded into the muddy ground ahead of the charging warriors, but enough found flesh among the unprotected askari to serve their purpose. Pyriens stumbled and fell as they were struck, tripping those behind them who weren't quick enough to react. The rest kept coming, spears held above their heads in a manner Pellus hadn't seen before.

The distance between the armies narrowed. Pellus sat forward in his saddle, lance tucked under his arm. When there were barely fifty paces between the armies, the Pyrien ruler let out a shout. The askari slowed their pace and turned side on, running strangely—

A hail of spears came at the Amadeans low and fast.

Pellus wasn't expecting it, none of them were. This wasn't how Pyriens attacked.

His reflexes were quick enough to knock away the first missile with his shield, but the spear immediately following it struck him in the shoulder. It clattered off his armour and spun him sideways in his saddle, right as the two armies surged together. The askari who'd thrown their spears had now drawn axes and were using them to hack at the legs of horses thundering past. Pellus's mare kept charging. She shouldered aside an askara as Pellus righted himself, and he reset his lance in time to impale a wild-eyed Pyrien about to hurl an axe at him. The lance carried the snarling askara a few yards before barrelling into another Pyrien, and Pellus had to let it go or risk being dragged from his saddle. He drew his sword and felled two more of the enemy before he had a chance to orient himself. In all the confusion, he had lost track of Xanthe. A quick check over his shoulder reassured him the king and Adward were still in their saddles. He needed to get back to them.

The Pyriens had taken them by surprise. And now, instead of staying pressed together to create a barrier and slow the horses, the enemy had spread out to give themselves room to swing axes and thrust spears. It meant that as the Amadean infantry rushed into the fray, the battle was turning into a sprawling melee rather than a crush. It benefitted the Pyriens—it was getting harder for the Amadeans to surround them.

Pellus began to carve a path back to his king, taking down by blade or hooves any Pyrien in the way. It was slow going. Already, the dead and injured littered the ground, and Pellus feared he would trample his own men in the chaos. His shoulder throbbed where the spear struck, but he could still use his arm. The joint would have shattered if not for his armour.

Ahead, the king was now on foot, his horse nowhere in sight. Where was Adward? Pellus searched from his higher vantage point and instead found Xanthe a stone's throw away. The Pyrien ruler was short, muscled and barely out of adolescence— and ruthlessly efficient with long axe and dagger. She was in perpetual motion, thrusting, slashing and chopping; maiming and killing with frightening accuracy. Pellus had time to see her leap on the back of a warrior, plunge her knife into his neck and ride him to the ground...before Pellus's own mare stumbled sideways.

He'd been so fixated on Xanthe he hadn't seen the spear coming. It was now buried deep in his mare's eye. The warhorse was dead before she hit the ground, taking Pellus with her.

No, no, no.

The mare landed on him and pinned his leg with her full weight, but he had to get up because the askara who threw the spear was coming. Panicked, Pellus struggled with increasing urgency, but his leg wouldn't budge—

The askara leapt.

Pellus lifted his shield against the descending axe and thrust up his sword where he expected the attacker to be. He absorbed the impact of the axe and the Pyrien. The blade must have found its target because now he bore the weight of the impaled askara along with the smell of freshly opened intestines. He grunted as he pushed the dying Pyrien aside and awkwardly withdrew his blade from the man's belly. It was an untidy kill. Necessary, but untidy.

Another askara was charging, this one with a spear.

'Shit.'

Pellus bucked and squirmed and shoved at his saddle but his leg wasn't coming free without help. The askara left the ground, spear in two hands, and Pellus had less than a heartbeat to cast aside his sword and use both arms to block the strike with his shield. He felt the timber crack when the spear found its mark. The impact drove his arms against his chest and the askara dropped a knee on to the wood, crushing the broken shield against him. Now Pellus's arms were pinned, too, and the spear tip was wedged between them. He could barely breathe. For the first time since he'd been marked as the prophet's warrior, he felt a spike of panic. What use were strength and speed and wits when you were trapped under a horse and your own shield? The askara panted hard, her pale blue eyes lit with bloodlust. She wrenched the spear from the shield and raised it above his head—Pellus twisted violently, knowing the next strike would be to his skull—before an arrow struck the askara in the throat and toppled her backwards.

'Never heard you swear before.'

Adward was there, dragging away the two dead Pyriens to get the weight off the horse. The Iolian warrior's face and arms were covered in blood, his hair wild. He'd lost or discarded his shield but still had his sword.

'Behind you,' Pellus warned, and Adward spun around to face two new attackers. He dealt with them quickly—they weren't askari—and then grabbed Pellus under his arms and pulled.

'You're a heavy bastard.'

Pellus slid off his broken shield and tried to help, but it was Adward's strength that got him free and hauled him to his feet. 'Thank you.' Pellus was relieved when his legs took his weight.

'Thank Ty.'

Pellus followed Adward's head gesture to see the squire running through the fray, barely pausing to unleash arrows. Adward scanned the chaos around them and found what he was looking for.

'The king has reached Xanthe.'

Pellus picked up his sword and they fought their way to where Felix was holding his own against the Pyrien ruler. The king's brute strength had forced Xanthe to change tactics. She'd swapped her dagger for an Amadean shield and was using it surprisingly well—not to defend, but to attack, holding back with her long axe until she had a clear opening to swing.

Without exchanging a word or a glance, Pellus and Adward covered the king's flanks, and it was Pellus who saw the goat clan chief rushing to Xanthe's aid.

'Mine,' Pellus panted and stepped over a dead foot soldier to block the chief's path.

The clan chief charged, thrusting his spear at Pellus's head. Pellus twisted and parried, tightening his grip on his sword and wishing he'd picked up a shield. The clan chief came again and this time Pellus dodged sideways to counter, but the Pyrien followed with another strike, denting Pellus's armour so that it poked uncomfortably into his ribs.

Sweet Verus, the flea was fast.

Pellus quickly understood that sword against spear was a vastly different fight on foot than on horseback. He needed to adjust.

The length of the spear kept his opponent beyond striking distance, so Pellus had to get him closer. He feigned a cut and when the chief thrust at his ribs, Pellus caught the spear shaft and jerked it out of the Pyrien's hands. As the chief stumbled forward, Pellus angled his blade and thrust with enough force to pierce the Pyrien's toughened goat-hide tunic and stop his heart.

Felix and Xanthe were circling each other, dragging their feet and waiting for an opening. The Pyrien ruler was so much smaller than the king and Pellus had to remind himself this was the girl who had united the clans and led a reign of terror against the borderlands for the past five years.

He could step in and end this now, as could Adward, but both knew their king would not thank them for it. Instead, Pellus grabbed the dead clan chief by his head dress and dragged him into Xanthe's line of sight, dumping the limp body in the dirt. Before he could see if the distraction worked, his own attention snagged on an askara prowling closer. He'd never seen her before but he recognised her in a heartbeat.

And he needed her alive.

53

Lystra burned with frustration as she cut her way through the scourge. She'd picked up another long axe and both were dark with Amadean blood; her spear abandoned after finding its target in the charge.

All this killing should be enough. She should feel vindicated. Whole.

There was satisfaction in felling these slave mongers and butchers of children, but there was no triumph. No sense she was earning back what the Amadeans had taken from her. Her place in a pack. Her pride. Dex. No matter how many of the enemy she slew, she could not shake off the shame. There was not enough blood on this battlefield to wash away her failures. Even the ink across her shoulders had betrayed her, tied her to the scourge.

All that was left was to fight for Pyrie and its unforgiving ruler.

Lystra had been behind Xanthe in the charge and they'd been separated when the armies met, but she'd caught a glimpse of her sister snatching up a shield and leaping on the back of a warrior to pound it into his skull. How long ago was that?

She was heading in that direction and saw the moment the goat clan chief met his end. Beyond him, she saw Xanthe fighting a broad-chested Pyrien with hair and beard the colour of fire.

Her eyes fell to his hands to be sure.

Blood-soaked Ares. The rings.

Xanthe was fighting the scourge king.

Lystra faltered in her charge. Would her sister thank her or punish her for involving herself?

Movement caught her eye: the blond chief-slayer was stalking her. His hair was pulled back in a long plait, his hairless face flushed and eyes bright. It wasn't Rhys, but he would do. Lystra spun her axes and crouched, ready for him.

She would have her sister's back. That would count for something.

'Don't kill this one,' Not-Rhys said as he advanced. A dark-haired warrior fighting near him glanced over his shoulder.

'Mine Five?'

'Has to be.'

Goat-rutters.

Lystra understood. It was her cropped hair and neck welts. Her status as a captive could not have been more obvious. Had the Amadeans been searching for Rhys and the others? Was he even still alive?

The blond warrior came at her so fast and strong she had to use both of her weapons to parry the thrust. The force of it sent her stumbling sideways. She recovered as he swung the blade down again and she managed to block it with the top of one axe and strike out with the other. The Amadean rounded his back to avoid it cleaving into his side. He swung his arms down to free his sword and block the backswing aimed for his knee. Lystra was unprotected for barely a heartbeat, but he kicked her hard enough in the chest to drive her backwards.

She kept her feet, fleetingly aware of the clash continuing between Xanthe and Felix. Lystra circled the blond warrior and he waited, reassessing her, the tip of his sword angled towards the ground. He was methodical and calculating, nothing like

Rhys. Every movement spoke of self-control. Lystra could see he favoured his left leg and that his breast plate was dented in more than one place—so he was not invincible. And keeping her alive would be harder than trying to kill her. It was her only advantage.

She let one axe slide through her hands until she gripped it beneath the iron head, holding the handle against her forearm for protection. Hurting and breathless, she threw out her protected arm to block a cut aimed at her side and swung at his legs with the other axe—

The warrior *caught* it by the handle and wrenched it out of her grip. The force of it spun her around and she felt his boot slam into her back. She sprawled forward and hit the ground so hard it knocked the air out of her. And then the goat-rutter dropped a knee between her shoulder blades and she was pinned in the mud.

It was hard to draw breath but she dragged in enough air to stay conscious. It meant she saw when Xanthe stumbled over the dead clan chief and the scourge king sprang forward and swung his blade down with murderous intent. Lystra's sister reacted fast enough to duck beneath her shield but the blow drove her to her knees. The scourge king struck again and again, beating Xanthe to the ground under a barrage of rapid two-handed sword blows, giving her no time to recover. Lystra cried out as the shield splintered, but Xanthe managed to launch herself to her feet, axe drawn back—

And the scourge king thrust his blade through the soft flesh of her exposed throat.

Xanthe dropped her arms and collapsed to her knees, eyes wide with surprise. The scourge king pulled his sword free and she toppled forwards, landing only a few feet from where Lystra lay.

Lystra stared into the eyes of her sister as her life left her.

Xanthe, ruler of Pyrie, uniter of the five clans and daughter of the Great Wolf, was dead.

54

The prophet felt the call through the flames.

Felix and Pellus were with Gwinny, the men bleeding and filthy and the morning sky vivid blue behind them.

'Xanthe is dead,' Felix said, not waiting for a greeting.

The prophet's heart swelled in his chest. 'Verus has rewarded our faithfulness.'

'We have sustained high casualties.'

'That is the price of war, Felix. What of the enemy?'

The king's lips pressed together before he answered. 'Their rear guard prevailed over our troops positioned to block their retreat. I've sent scouts to see if they are fleeing or regrouping.'

'What is their strength?'

'Less than half the number that met us on the field. The goat clan leader is also among the dead.'

The prophet felt a plan coming together.

'They will be in chaos until a new ruler is appointed, assuming the clans can even remain united. We must crush them while their numbers are low. Leave enough troops to finish what we have started and bring the rest of the army home. The Day of Atonement draws near.'

'It will take half a moon to march to Augustmount, maybe longer with our wounded.'

The prophet could not wait that long.

'The overlords and their generals can oversee the withdrawal.

They can make their sacrifices of atonement on the march. You will ride ahead. You must be here by the full moon.'

Felix thought on this and nodded. 'We will come east once I have a full scout report. I'll need a day at least.' The king glanced at Pellus. 'We have recaptured the escaped askara from Mine Five.'

The prophet hid his surprise. 'Are you certain?'

'Her hair is shorn, she's scarred from whip and chains, and she bears ink across her shoulders.'

'Have you interrogated her?'

'Not yet.'

The askara was an unexpected gift and he would need to make good use of it. The prophet considered his next words carefully, delivered them devoid of emotion.

'Pellus, you will bring me Xanthe's head. And this prisoner.'

Pellus had been listening intently to the exchange between king and prophet. He looked to Felix for a reaction. The king gave none. The prophet took a moment, careful not to put too much urgency on the request.

'You will leave in the morning. If the king can spare you.'

Felix could have denied the request—Pellus was general of the Iolian cohort and his campaign was not over until the king deigned it so—but instead Felix dipped his head in acquiescence. 'As you wish.'

The prophet withdrew from the flames, his head light. He could already *feel* the power that would soon be his.

His greatest challenge now was to wait.

55

Sabine clung to the memory of being with Tristan in the storm the day before. It warmed her, even riding at a canter with the cool wind whipping at her face and her hands, a welcome distraction from the other thoughts swirling for attention. The closer they got to the army, the sharper reality became. Would the king believe what they had to tell him? Would he force her to relinquish the relic? The idea of it set her teeth on edge and she tried not to think too hard about it.

Ahead, Rhys held up a hand to signal for them to stop.

'Thank Verus,' Axl puffed from behind Sabine. He was coping better with being on horseback these days, but prolonged riding still taxed him.

'Rider approaching,' Rhys said as they reached him. 'Scout.'

The young Amadean wore a dappled cowhide vest—a warrior from the Southlands. He reined in a good stone's throw away.

'Announce yourselves!' he called out.

'We are warriors of Iolia returning to the king's army,' Rhys responded. 'How far away are we?'

The scout brought his horse nearer. 'Where have you been?'

'We don't answer to you, Southlander.'

The scout was barely older than Ty and already inked. Even at a distance Sabine could see the hooves of one of the rearing horses tattooed across his shoulders. He straightened in his saddle.

'What's left of the Pyrien army fled this way—'

'The battle is over?' Tristan asked.

The scout came closer, frowning. 'It was yesterday.'

Tristan and Sabine exchanged a look. The churned up mud they'd been following since dawn was from the Pyriens retreating not advancing.

They were too late.

'Xanthe is dead, killed by the king himself.'

Tristan's eyes dropped to the box slung across Sabine's chest. She saw his mind working.

'Take us to the king,' he ordered.

Sabine's unease intensified as they rode through a ravine and into a wide valley. They'd been upwind, so the stench didn't hit until they arrived and then it was inescapable. There were bodies *everywhere*. Hundreds...no, thousands of dead men and women; Pyrien and Amadean. The rain-damp ground was soaked with blood and gore. Amadean foot soldiers, each with cloth wrapped around the lower half of their face, hauled wagons by hand through the muddy field, loading up weapons and picking over the dead.

Behind Sabine, Axl wept openly. Tristan and Rhys were silent as the scout led them to the army camp at the far end of the valley. It was smaller than Sabine remembered.

Amadea and Pyrie must never meet in war.

She could not shake the warning; couldn't un-see the words on the cave wall. She reminded herself the Tenth Prophet had been mad. But what if he hadn't been? Sabine had an overwhelming urge to open the box and see the flame again. Maybe Rhys had been right. Maybe she *should* have tried to touch it before now. But the time to do that had passed because she could see the king's banner flying over his pavilion and they were headed straight for it.

Fear leached through the horror as they cantered beside

the field of death, stealing the last of the warmth from Sabine. Her mouth went dry as they rode into the mounting yard. Ty was sitting on a stump, preoccupied with re-stringing a bow. He glanced up at the sound of horses and then went back to what he was doing—

His head whipped up and his mouth fell open, staring wide-eyed from Tristan to Sabine to Axl to Rhys and back to Tristan again. And then he let out a sob and stood on legs that almost went out from under him.

Sabine felt a stab of anxiety.

'What's happened?' Tristan dismounted and strode to the squire. Ty met him halfway and threw his arms around Tristan, pressing his face into his shoulder. Tristan looked up at Rhys, alarmed.

'Come on, Ty,' Tristan said, patting his back awkwardly. 'I can see the battle was tough but you can't let it break you—'

'The king...' The rest of the sentence was muffled into Tristan's vest. Tristan grabbed the boy by the shoulders and held him at arm's length.

'The king what?'

Ty sniffled. 'He told me you were dead.'

Tristan blinked, absorbed the news. 'Clearly we are not.'

The boy took in Tristan's face with a mixture of wonder and disbelief. And then his eyes went wide in alarm.

'What?'

Sabine and Rhys had joined them and understanding hit her like a slap. 'What did you tell the king?'

His face was stricken. 'I thought you were dead...all of you.'

'What did you *tell* him?' Tristan pressed.

Ty grabbed a fistful of his own hair in despair. 'That Sabine and Axl had gone with you to the mine...' He glanced at Sabine's brother. 'And that Torvus believed Axl was the usurper...' He was pleading now. 'I thought you were all *dead*.'

Tristan stared at him. 'How in the name of Verus did you find yourself in *any* conversation with the king, let alone one that brands us as heretics?'

Ty took a shaky step backwards so he was free of Tristan's grip. It had barely been half a moon but the squire looked a year older. Even the wispy hair on his jaw and neck had been replaced by stubble. Maybe the change had started before now and Sabine hadn't noticed. He'd already carried the weight of Torvus's execution. Being in the company of the king must have been agony for him, and then to fight and survive the horror of that valley...

'After you left,' Ty said, 'King Felix took me from Pellus as his own squire. Whenever we spoke of you...it was just the two of us.'

'Cosy,' Rhys muttered. 'Did you confess anything of your own?'

The squire dropped his gaze, well aware of what Rhys meant. 'No.'

'So, just our secrets then.'

Tristan rubbed his eyes. 'Shit.'

'It won't matter,' Rhys said. 'Once he sees what's in that box of Sabine's, he won't care about anything else.'

The warriors exchanged a calculating look.

Axl understood it before Sabine. 'We still have to tell the king about the Tenth Prophecy,' he said quietly.

'Why?' Tristan asked. 'We didn't stop the battle.'

'That was only part of the prophecy. The king needs to know the rest.'

'You're alive!'

Adward was striding out of the king's pavilion, his face lit with relief. He pulled Tristan into a back-slapping hug and then grabbed Rhys, taking them both by surprise.

Sabine braced for his reaction to her desertion, but the king appeared from his pavilion before Adward had disentangled from Rhys.

'In here. All of you.' He disappeared back inside.

Adward nodded a greeting to Sabine without comment and seemed unsurprised to see Axl there.

'Is Pellus inside?' Tristan asked as they followed Adward.

'No, he's riding to Augustmount with Xanthe's head. He has the askara with him. The one with the inked shoulders you were meant to collect.'

Rhys stuck out his arm to stop Adward before he entered the tent. 'Alive or dead?'

'Alive.'

'What did she tell him?'

'Nothing. The prophet ordered him to take her to Augustmount where he'd interrogate her himself.'

Sabine flashed hot and then cold. Lystra had seen with her own eyes that she and Axl were descendants of porplezi. The askara was just as likely to give up that information purely to spite the prophet.

Adward pushed Rhys's arm aside and entered the pavilion. Sabine followed Tristan, cradling the box protectively. The king's quarters were twice as large as the Iolian tent, with plush rugs covering every blade of grass except for the ground beneath the brazier at the centre. A table was set with ornate iron chairs. It must have taken two wagons alone to cart the setting over the mountains. A man and a woman were seated at it, parchment spread out before them. Sabine could see enough to understand a map maker had been busy charting their route across Pyrie. The king stood waiting at the head of the table, his arms folded and mottled with bruises. There were still traces of blood and gore in his hair.

The woman took them in with a cursory glance. She was fine-featured and tall, with a thick ponytail cascading over one shoulder and disappearing below the table. Sabine recognised her as Alicia, overlord of the Southlands. Alicia had been her overlord before Sabine joined the Iolian household—not that they had ever met. Sabine had only ever seen her at a distance on feast days.

Alicia's companion at the table was darker skinned again and greying at his temples. By the ring on his index finger, he too was an overlord.

But where was the other one?

'Tristan and Rhys of Iolia have returned from the dead,' the king said as they reached him. He did not sit down. 'I have not yet met the other two.'

Adward took the hint and stepped forward. 'This is Sabine of Iolia, a warrior among our cohort who is yet to be inked, and the monk is...' He looked to Tristan for help.

'This is Axl, a faithful servant of Verus' Tristan offered. 'He is also Sabine's brother and came east with us as our spiritual guide.'

Sabine dared a glance at the king. Whatever Felix did or didn't know, he was allowing the introductions to stand unchallenged. The king looked each of them over, his eyes lingering on the sling across Sabine's chest before settling on Tristan.

'You were taken alive by askari and survived. How?'

Tristan stood perfectly still, feet planted and hands clasped in front of him. His expression gave nothing away but Sabine saw the pulse jump in his throat. If they handled this badly they would all be executed and Ferugo and Dashelle's fate would be sealed.

'The king may wish to hear this news alone,' Tristan said.

'*I* am not going anywhere,' Alicia snapped. 'And neither is Gregori. We've sacrificed enough this side of the border to be privy to anything you have to say.'

Gregori. Sabine recognised the name. The overlord of Bloodstone.

The king's nostrils flared. 'Answer my question, Tristan,' he said finally. 'How are you alive?'

Slowly and carefully, Tristan gave a version of what had befallen them since they'd left with Caius half a moon ago. He told the king they had *all* been poisoned and captured by askari and taken by the oracle to the lake and its temple, where Xanthe and her army arrived soon after.

'And then...' Tristan faltered. Sabine could see his hesitation. So could the king.

'And then what?'

It was Axl who answered. 'We were taken to the Tenth Prophesy.'

Alicia hissed, but the king remained impassive. 'Go on.'

Tristan grimaced and gestured for Axl to continue, and Sabine's brother described the blood ritual that broke a two-hundred-year-old ward woven by a prophet and a porpleza. He made no mention of Sabine's and his bloodline or of what had been required of Rhys for his part.

'What did the prophecy say?' the king demanded.

'Felix,' Alicia warned. 'Don't let this poison into our ears.'

'What did it say?'

Axl closed his eyes and recited the prophecy in full.

Amadea and Pyrie must never meet in war.

If we do we will draw to us an enemy with the strength to destroy both kingdoms.

The fiends who drove the ancestors to the seas.

They devour all before them. They have destroyed kingdoms. Worlds.

Verus sank the ships that pursued the ancestors.

She has hidden all of us from them for a thousand years.

If we do not live in peace they will find us and come across the ocean.
A usurper will rise with the power of a god to defend us.
The mantle of the prophets will pass away.
And the rivers of our lands will run with blood and fire.

The king's chest rose and fell.

'Again.'

Axl repeated it, slower this time, and when he finished, the pavilion fell into a stony silence. Adward ran a hand through his beard and stared off in the direction of the battlefield, his expression unreadable.

It was Alicia who spoke first, choosing attack as the best defence.

'You were at the mine when it was burned to the ground and yet you were not killed. You were a prisoner of Xanthe *and* this so-called oracle and you escaped. And now you say we should not have gone to war against our one and only enemy because a worse threat will somehow find us...based on a prophecy of a mad man *and a porpleza* that was hidden with dark magic two hundred years ago?' Alicia's eyes flared. 'The most reasonable explanation is that you are all traitors and heretics, seduced by dark magic and sent back to us to do the oracle's bidding.'

'Careful, Alicia,' Adward growled. 'These are warriors of Iolia you accuse.'

Axl took a long, deep breath. 'What if we are none of those things you say we are? What then?'

All attention shifted back to Sabine's brother. His mendicant's robe remained torn where Lystra had slashed it, his face streaked with tears. And he was *angry*.

'What if Verus has guided us every step of the way? What if the Tenth Prophet was declared mad *because* he dared to share such a warning? What if the cost of that blood-soaked field out there is a new enemy we cannot defeat without a new power rising to defend us?'

Alicia narrowed her eyes. 'You say the Tenth Prophecy foretold there would be "a usurper to defend *us*". Who is "us"? Amadea or Pyrie?'

Axl did not flinch. He glanced at the reliquary and straightened his shoulders as if remembering he was not a border monk but a servant of Verus who had walked the fire at Stonebridge *and* wore the mark of the porplezi. Sabine saw the fierceness of his conviction.

'It took the blood of a willing warrior and askara to break the ward. I would say it is all of us.'

Gregori cleared his throat. 'You certainly sound like heretics.' He held up a hand to stop Adward interjecting. 'How do you expect us to believe you? You've been in enemy territory. How do we know you've not been corrupted?'

The box against Sabine's breast seemed to expand and contract. Her heart gave a hard thump against it. She gestured to the sling across her chest. 'May I?' she asked the king.

Even with the claim of heresy in the air, Felix was curious. He gave a wary nod.

Sabine unwrapped the box of beaten gold and set it down on the table. Almost immediately the timber beneath it began to smoulder.

'Porplezi magic!' Alicia hissed.

'Hush,' the king said, his gaze not leaving Sabine.

Sabine lifted the reliquary and Tristan hunted around until he found a metal chest. He hefted it onto the table and Sabine placed the reliquary on it, her heart racing. She took a moment and then slid open the lid.

The king stepped forward so he could see.

'Great thunder and lightning...'

The rib bone floated as it had since Sabine first laid eyes

on it, the flame rolling lazily along its curved length. A sense of calm settled on her as she watched it move back and forth. Like the king, she could not look away. Adward, then Alicia and finally Gregori came closer to see.

'Impossible...' Alicia breathed. 'How...?'

'We took it from the temple at the lake,' Tristan said, steadying Sabine with a hand in the small of her back. 'It's been burning there since it was stolen.'

'Impossible,' Alicia repeated, but she was fast losing her conviction. 'And the oracle just let you walk out with it?'

Tristan grunted at the thinly veiled accusation. 'Xanthe and her army had left and the oracle, it seems, has his own agenda.'

'Which is what?' Gregori asked.

'We don't know, but the fact Sabine is the only person alive who can touch that box no doubt helped his decision.'

'Not even the oracle or the bone witch guarding it could do that,' Axl added, careful how he referenced Nyomi.

The king locked eyes with Axl with unnerving intensity. 'What about you? Can you touch the box?'

'No.' Axl said purposefully. 'I cannot.'

The king understood what that meant in the context of Ty's confession.

Felix flexed his fingers and Sabine saw it as clear as sunshine: the king believed *he* could touch it. And he did not need her permission, even though for a fleeting moment she felt as if he should ask her for it. She turned side-on to give him space. It was as far as she was prepared to move away from the relic.

As Axl had done in the Pyrien temple, the king held his hands either side of the reliquary. He tapped his index fingers to test the heat radiating from its sides and instantly snatched them back. He looked at Sabine with a mixture of accusation and awe. The king tried again, using different fingers. The result was the same.

'Let me try.' Alicia moved in and hissed when her own fingers burned as instantly as the king's. She tried twice more before giving up. 'Gregori?'

He shook his head. 'Two of us with singed fingertips is enough, don't you think?'

The king cupped the back of his neck as he thought. 'Send Ty to get the priestess.'

Rhys left to deliver the order and they waited in strained silence for the prophet's servant to appear. Sabine had heard there was a sacred flame carrier with the king's party but had not seen her on the march. She was surprised at how young the priestess was when she stepped into the pavilion. The girl was dark skinned and delicate, bird-bone thin with golden glyphs covering half her scalp. She looked no more than fifteen or sixteen, barely older than Ty. The squire slipped in behind her and took up a post by the entrance. His reddened eyes went straight to Tristan, ignoring the king entirely.

Felix tapped the table. 'Close it up,' he ordered Sabine. She did as she was told before the priestess reached them. The girl gave Sabine a curious glance before she bowed her head before the king.

'Gwinny,' he greeted. 'Take this box into your tent.'

Sabine's chest tightened. *No.*

The priestess, Gwinny, did not hesitate. She reached out with open hands—and yelped as her skin came into contact with the beaten gold. The girl's eyes went wide. 'My king, I cannot touch it.' She turned her hands over where her skin was red.

Sabine's relief was swift and surprisingly sweet.

'Tend to your wounds and prepare to travel,' the king said. 'Ty will help you.' The priestess left confused, cradling her hand.

Alicia stared at Sabine as she dipped her own burned fingertips into her wine to soothe them. 'What is special about you?'

It was a completely valid question and Sabine hesitated before attempting to answer. Did they tell the king and these overlords that she and Axl were from a line of porplezi? Did they show them the tattoo on Axl's chest barely covered by his tattered robe?

'Who knows the will of Verus?' Axl said, before she could decide. 'We should be grateful that it is one born in Amadea who can carry it.'

Sabine marvelled at her brother's skill to hide the truth without lying. The king eyed the closed reliquary and absently turned the rings on his fingers.

'My king, we need to return the relic to Augustmount,' Sabine said. Because only there could she use it to bargain for Dashelle and Ferugo.

'*We?*'

'We go where Sabine goes,' Tristan said.

Felix raised his eyebrows. 'Are you making demands of your king?'

'We are honouring the will of the abbot of Stonebridge. He bonded us to Sabine and her brother.'

Sabine caught a flicker of...*something* in the king's expression. She didn't know him well enough to understand it.

'So be it,' Felix said. 'We will ride to the border and then take the river. We leave as soon as I brief the generals.'

56

Pellus was furious.

'You should not have abandoned the king.'

Carmine was unapologetic as he rode alongside him. 'Felix does not need me to clean up the scraps.'

'The *king* is obeying the will of the prophet.'

'And why do you think the prophet tasked *you* with bringing him Xanthe's head and not Felix?'

Pellus did not dignify the question with an answer.

'Because you are the one the prophet favours above all. You will be highly rewarded on your return.'

And you want to bask in that glory at the cost of your king and your own army.

The overlord of Paramore had caught up with Pellus mere moments ago and finally had enough breath to speak. Pellus would have been out of reach had he not had to ride to match the pace of the wagon carting his prisoner. He'd taken the best heavy horses from Iolia's wagon train, but they were no match for a warhorse when it came to speed.

The askara was tied by her wrists and ankles to the front of the empty food wagon. There had been no cells taken on campaign because there were to be no prisoners. This one was the exception. He'd spoken to her last night when he'd sent his squires to gather wood. It wasn't an interrogation, simply a few questions. She'd snarled at him and acted as if she didn't understand, even when he used her own language. Her refusal to speak had not troubled him. He'd thought he would have more opportunities before they reached Augustmount.

And now Carmine was here and those chances were gone. So, instead of coaxing information from the enemy, Pellus had to listen to Carmine prattle on because the overlord loved the sound of his own voice.

'Anyway, you have only squires for back-up. I know you're invincible, but surely another blade will be useful?'

Pellus swallowed his laughter. Yesterday, he'd seen peasants with more courage and skill than this preening overlord. Carmine had let his warriors lead the charge, preferring to watch from the ridge to provide a 'tactical advantage'.

'Another blade is always welcome, yes, but I am not anticipating trouble retracing ground we have taken.'

'Better safe than sorry.'

Carmine lasted barely a quarter mile before he started up again.

'That head is going to stink in a few more days.'

Pellus grit his teeth and pushed his new mount until he was alongside the wagon driver. 'You need to pick up the pace.'

57

Felix felt the weight of the relic even though he didn't carry it. *Couldn't* carry it. That fact shouldn't have chafed as much as it did—he was king, not prophet—and yet this optimati woman from the Southlands who dressed and moved like an Iolian warrior could, when a servant of Verus could not, so why not the king of Amadea, too?

He kept close to Sabine as they rode at a full canter toward the river. They were making good time thanks to the wide tract carved by the army during the invasion. Travelling by riverboat for the final leg meant they would reach Augustmount in far less time than the slow trek in had taken.

The sky was clear and the air fresh and crisp, a world away from the carnage of the valley. The battle had been both a nightmare and a destiny fulfilled. After all these years of the prophet talking about killing Xanthe, Felix had been the one to do it. She'd been almost half his size and yet was one of the fiercest opponents he'd ever faced. It was no wonder the clan chiefs had fallen in line behind her.

And now, within a day of that victory, the Tenth Prophecy and the stolen rib bone had come to him.

Memories of illicit teachings crept in, of sitting with Torvus in darkened rooms listening to Anguston whisper about lost prophecy and a usurper. But even Anguston hadn't known the entirety of what the Tenth Prophecy said or *why* a usurper would be needed. Was Felix truly now in possession of the warning the high priest and Torvus had long searched for? He felt Torvus's presence, especially now they'd stopped to make camp for the night. He could almost hear the warrior gloating.

Felix had spoken with the prophet through the flames before leaving the army. He had not mentioned the relic and the prophet *had not known about it*. The old abbot on the Stonebridge pinnacle knew something, though. Why else had he bonded two Iolian warriors to an optimati woman and her monk brother?

Fear pricked at the back of Felix's mind. What if the relic was born of dark magic and he was about to deliver it into the heart of Amadea? He needed to test Sabine and the rib bone before they crossed the border, and this last night on the road was the time to do it.

They made camp at dusk and the king watched Gwinny totter about on unsteady legs, not yet accustomed to travelling by means other than wagon. Felix had ordered Ty to take her on his mount and the squire of course obeyed, even if he still wouldn't look his king in the eye. That was an issue he'd deal with another day.

While Gwinny stretched her legs out, Ty took down her bedroll from the pack horse, along with the bowl carrying the sacred flame. The squire had fashioned a lid to hide the flames while they travelled in Pyrie with only the king's personal garrison, and he carried it awkwardly to the priestess. The priestess gestured for him to put it on the ground, which he did with a sense of ceremony, leaving the lid on.

The king waited until the campfire was lit and they had all eaten, and then sent his garrison to their watch posts. When Sabine was wiping the remnants of dried venison from her fingers he said to her, 'Show Gwinny what you're carrying.'

Sabine paused, her hands in the air as if about to catch a tossed ball. 'Now?'

'Now.'

One hand went to the box, nestled between her breasts in its sling, and the other strayed to the hilt of her sword. It had been reflex, pure and simple, and—in the moment at least—Felix found it more amusing than treasonous.

'Are you planning to use that against me?'

Sabine's eyes dropped to the sword as if unaware she'd reached for it, and she quickly drew back her hand. She kept her eyes lowered. Felix felt Tristan's gaze on him and understood with cold clarity where the Iolian warrior's loyalty lay.

'I gave you an order, Sabine.'

The priestess had sat forward, her eyes bright. She'd known of course that Sabine was carrying the golden box but a priestess did not ask questions. She was the prophet's vessel—no more and no less—and answered only to him and the flame.

Until now.

Sabine unwrapped the reliquary in the flickering campfire light and gently slid off the lid. Gwinny's lips parted in surprise as she watched Sabine handle the box and then she saw what was inside. The priestess stared at the rib bone and the flame. It flickered once before falling still again. Her expression, usually so unreadable, transformed into shining joy. A single tear slipped down her cheek.

'Is that what it looks like?' Felix asked her.

She nodded mutely, a smile tugging at her lips.

'How do you know?' He saw her hesitate, knew the reticence to speak was ingrained in her training. 'I am your king. You will answer me.'

Gwinny met his gaze, and he was surprised by the unguarded love he found there. 'I can feel it. The same way I feel the sacred flame.'

And over the mountains the Thirteenth Prophet most likely could feel *her* emotions. Had her reaction called to him through the flames? Was he watching this moment right now?

'Can you touch it?'

Her eyes widened. 'It would be blasphemous to try. Only the prophet may touch the sacred flames.'

'It is also treasonous to disobey your king.'

Gwinny seemed to consider where she was and what was being asked of her. She moved to sit beside Sabine, who watched her warily. The priestess bowed her head. 'May I try?'

Sabine's face softened in surprise. 'Yes, of course.'

Gwinny's hands were wrapped in bandaging from the earlier burns, and she unwound one. Her palm glistened with honey. Sensibly, she offered the back of her hand this time and barely reached the flame before she lifted it again.

'The flame is hot, my king. I cannot touch it.'

Felix could see it was the truth.

'What about you?' he asked Sabine.

'I haven't tried.'

'Why not?'

'What if I'm only meant to carry it?'

'There's only one way to find out. Or am I still to believe the monk is the one Torvus spoke of?'

Axl shook his head. 'I assure you, my king, it is not me.'

Felix glanced at Ty, saw the boy's confusion, and was quietly pleased the squire had not intentionally fed him misinformation.

Sabine looked to Tristan.

'I'm right here,' the warrior said.

The monk laid a hand on his sister's arm. 'We need to know. *You* need to know.'

She nodded, inhaled, and held her palm over the flame. As if sensing her, it grew taller and wrapped around her hand like a glove, still anchored to the rib bone. Felix held his breath, mesmerised.

'Does it hurt?'

'It's cool,' she said, wide-eyed. 'Like flowing water.'

The only sound in the campsite was the pop and crackle of the campfire.

'Touch the relic.'

Felix expected resistance but this time she didn't hesitate. She curled her flame-wrapped fingers around the stolen rib bone of the First Prophet.

'Oh,' she gasped, right before her entire body stiffened and her eyes rolled back in her head.

'What's happening?' Tristan demanded, gripping Sabine by the shoulders.

'It's a vision,' Gwinny said, breathless. 'Is she a priestess?'

Felix felt light-headed. Was someone other than the prophet receiving a message from Verus? Was this Pyrien magic...or was this girl truly the usurper Torvus was expecting?

'Bring her back,' Tristan said, agitated.

'The flame has her,' Gwinny said. 'Verus will release her when she's ready.'

'No!' Sabine sobbed and opened her eyes. She jerked her hand from the box, leaving the bone and flame behind. She looked to Tristan and then Rhys, stricken.

'What did you see?' Tristan asked, still gripping her arms.

She shook her head, her lips caught between her teeth and hands pressed over her heart.

'Is it Dash?'

Icy fingers slid around Felix's heart. 'Speak, woman.'

Sabine locked eyes with the king, devastated and accusing.

'Ferugo is dead.'

58

Dashelle wept in the dark.

Verus had abandoned her.

She had trusted her god and her god had looked away in her hour of greatest need. Had it all been for nothing? The hope, the signs, the risks she and Ferugo had taken? Grief snatched away her breath again, twisted her into an unfamiliar shape. She was puffy with tears, her heart a tightening knot in her chest. How did it keep beating?

She had lost all sense of time. How long had she been back in this room? Days? A quarter moon?

She was moaning again. It came from a place so deep she barely recognised her own voice. The smell of Ferugo was everywhere: lye and thyme and leather oil. Dashelle crushed his pillow to her face and breathed in his scent. She was on the bed they had shared, huddled and trembling, her spine pressed to the backboard. It took the last of her strength to stay upright. There was an ember of awareness that if she lay her head down, she might never lift it again. She'd drifted in and out of a feverish sleep, propped up by cushions. A tumbler of wine and a bowl of pottage sat untouched on the bedside table.

The man she loved had blinked out like a candle.

Whatever the prophet had done to Ferugo, it burst the vessels that carried his blood and stopped his heart. Dashelle had checked for signs of life over and over again—Verus forgive her, she'd *slapped* her husband—and when she had lain her head on his chest she heard the stillness beneath his breast. The prophet was long gone from the temple when Gael scooped her from the floor and carried her away screaming for her husband, her hands sticky with his blood.

'You must eat.'

The monk was back. She came and went, always silent except for this request.

Dashelle lifted her face from the pillow she clutched, found Gael standing in a pool of light cast by a freshly lit candle. The monk stood rigid, fidgeting with the belt on her Stonebridge robe.

'Where is he?' Dashelle asked. Her voice was hoarse and her lips swollen from crying.

'Please, my lady...You are wasting away.'

'Has he had the death rites?'

Gael evaded eye contact and Dashelle sobbed in understanding. The prophet was going to declare them heretics. It was the only way he could justify killing an overlord of Amadea and then denying Ferugo the rites that would deliver him to Verus in the next world.

Fear finally spiked through her grief.

'Am I too to die?'

There was a pause and then Gael blurted. 'Do you follow the teachings of Anguston?'

Dashelle's heart gave a panicked thump and then, for the first time since he'd left her, she heard Ferugo's voice.

Iolia needs you. Stay alive.

It was in her mind, she understood that, and it was exactly what her husband would say. If she too died, what would become of their province and their people?

Dashelle sniffed and wiped her face on the pillow. 'I follow the teachings of *Verus*,' she said carefully.

Gael's shoulders relaxed. She either missed or ignored the fact Dashelle did not answer the question. 'Then you have nothing to fear.'

It was untrue and Dashelle, now sole overlord of Iolia, needed to find a way to keep living.

Because she knew that if Tristan and Rhys had survived in Pyrie, they would find a way to come for her.

59

'No.'

Tristan paced at the edges of the firelight. He couldn't see straight, couldn't think.

'*No.*'

It was the only word he could form as Sabine answered the king's questions by the fire.

'How did he die?'

'There was blood from his mouth and nose...and his eyes and ears.'

'You saw him laid out on a slab?'

'Yes.' A sob. 'And Dashelle is in utter despair.'

'In a cell?'

'No...in a bed covered in pillows and cushions.'

The pang for his sister stole Tristan's breath. He felt Sabine watching, aching for him, wrestling with her own despair. He kept his eyes focused on the dark trees beyond the firelight because whenever he looked at her the rawness of her grief undid him.

'No,' he said again.

It wasn't that he didn't believe Sabine had seen those things. It was that they could not be true. Even Axl was uncertain.

'Perhaps it hasn't happened?' the monk ventured.

The priestess tutted at him. 'Only the prophet sees what is yet to come.'

'Only the prophet can touch the sacred flame, too, yet you know what you just saw.'

'Did you see the prophet?' the king asked Sabine.

'A glimpse. He was alone with the sacred flame. He's not grieving, he's impatient. He's waiting for something.'

'That prick,' Rhys said. Tristan's cousin snatched up a branch from the pile of wood near the fire and hurled it into the night. He'd moved straight past denial into full-blown rage. 'He's waiting for Xanthe's head.' Rhys sidestepped as Tristan changed direction and came back around. They locked eyes and shared a moment of complicit murderous thoughts towards the Thirteenth Prophet of Verus.

'Are you going to let him get away with killing an overlord without your consent?' Rhys demanded. 'Without a trial? Will you punish him for *this* crime or will you sit back like you did with Torvus?'

The king sprang up and Rhys charged—

'Rhys, it's the king!' Sabine shouted, scrambling to get between them. It snapped Tristan out of his misery. He lunged and grabbed the king in a bear hug and Sabine shoved Rhys away to increase the distance between them. Felix strained to get at Rhys but Tristan had him in a vice-like grip.

'Do not speak his name,' Felix hissed between clenched teeth. 'And get your hands *off* me!' Tristan immediately loosed his grip and the king shouldered his way free as four of his garrison charged into the clearing with swords drawn.

'Stand down,' the king said. He glared at each of the Iolians, not sparing Sabine from his fury, and then stalked into the shadows. His men went to follow. 'Give me a moment!' he snapped over his shoulder..

Only Ty and the priestess remained cross-legged by the fire. The squire—the *king's* squire now—had pulled his knees up to his chest and was staring into the flames. The priestess sat beside him, her attention again focused on the rib bone. Sabine glanced once at the reliquary and reached for Tristan. Before he could protest, she put her arms around him and held him tightly. The truth was in her trembling and the full force of the horror hit him.

'The last words I said to Ferugo were in anger...'

All the strength flowed out of him and he leaned into Sabine. He was taller and heavier than her, but she bore his weight, her hand on the back of his neck, holding him to her. He shook as he sobbed. Nobody spoke. She held him until he was spent, helped him sit on the ground and then moved onto his lap so she could keep holding him. The pain in his heart was unbearable.

Finally, he pulled back enough so he could see Sabine and asked the only question that mattered now.

'Is Dash in danger?'

Sabine met his gaze, her own eyes red-rimmed. 'Yes.'

60

The wine barrel stank of dank wood and her own sweat and blood. Lystra's knees and spine ached from being stuffed in the cramped space for the past few miles. It was like the mine all over again, but worse because she was all but blind, and *this* cage bounced and slid every time the wagon beneath her struck a dip or rut. The barrel's bung hole was too low for her to see out, but at least she could get her nose and mouth close enough to breathe in fresh air, and splinters of daylight penetrated the gaps between the staves.

The panic came in waves.

'We should ride through Augustmount as heroes, not creep in under the cover of dusk.'

It was the first thing the one called Carmine had said for some time, and as much as Lystra despised the sound of his voice, his chattering was useful. She learned nothing about their destination or her fate when he stayed silent.

The blond warrior's patience was thin when he answered. 'What do you imagine would happen if we rode in proclaiming that we have Xanthe's head?'

'Crowds will follow us to the temple mountain, cheering and celebrating.'

'No, they will work themselves into a frenzy, desperate to tear the hair and flesh from her skull for themselves. Is that what the prophet wants, do you think?'

Lystra clenched her jaw. The goat-rutters didn't care if she understood every word they uttered. They spoke openly of their trophy and their destination. It was a bitter seed to suck. But at least she knew her sister's head was with them, which gave her the slimmest of chances to reclaim it.

Every part of Xanthe had to be burned—or her token in place of her body—otherwise she would never reunite with their father and dwell with the gods. There was no affection lost between Lystra and Xanthe, but her sister did not deserve to be denied the reward she had earned many times over. Lystra didn't know who carried her sister's token or if it had survived the battle, or even if any of the surviving clan leaders would go back to retrieve her body. But the gods would show Lystra favour if she denied the Amadeans the glory of displaying Xanthe's head in the scourge capital.

Thanks to Carmine's constant chatter, Lystra had learned that the Amadean who'd bested her in battle was the so-called prophet's warrior. Rhys had spoken of him with the same expression he wore when he ate mussels. On her first night as Pellus's captive, the warrior had questioned her about the mine attack in his own tongue and then in hers. He'd mentioned Rhys and the others by name, wanted to know their fate, but it was the monk he was most interested in. There had been no more questions after Carmine's arrival.

They passed through increasingly populated areas and Lystra's skin crawled at the thought of how many stinking Amadeans were in this gods-forsaken kingdom. All of them living off the blood and sweat of Pyrien slaves. She frequently flexed her fingers and toes and rolled her wrists. She was in enemy territory, entering a *city*, and she needed to be ready. She'd heard about such places. She knew by heart the story of the oracle who'd plucked the bone from the fire of Verus while her people punished the Amadeans for their greed in the streets below. Lystra understood the danger of her situation. This was not a mine camp guarded by broken down warriors. She was entering *Augustmount*. Home to the Temple of Lies and the Great Pretender.

The wagon came to a halt and Lystra braced as her barrel rocked against the one next to it.

'Greetings Pellus.' A new voice, nervous. 'The prophet is expecting you.'

The warrior did not speak and they were soon moving again.

The city was noisy: men jabbering and shouting; hooves clattering on stone; fowls squawking. She heard something squeal and could only guess it was a pig or boar. She'd never seen either. New smells wafted into the barrel—a fishy tang she didn't recognise and then one she did: human waste. Her stomach roiled. This place was a shit pit.

The wagon began to climb and Lystra had the sense they were frequently turning, working their way through the labyrinth of the city. All Lystra knew of Augustmount's layout was from the oracle's stories: a maze of streets and a temple on the side of the mountain with a floor of blood-stained Pyrien gold.

The higher they went, the more the rabble of the city fell away until it was gone completely. The wagon pulled to a stop and Lystra's heart climbed into her throat. She wanted to be fearless, she needed to be.

'Where do you want these?' More new voices.

'Those go to the lower temple,' Pellus said. 'This one though,' knuckles rapped on the lid above Lystra, 'is for the first open cell you pass. Carry it upright. Do *not* drop it.'

There was muttering and grunting as the barrel was dragged to the back of the wagon. An eye appeared in the bung hole. 'What the—ow! Fuck!' One side of the barrel smacked back down onto the cart. 'They poked me in the eye.'

'Then don't look inside.' Pellus was close now. 'Step aside. I'll do it.'

'That's grunt work, Pellus,' Carmine said. 'Get another guard.'

Pellus ignored him, because it was his voice who guided the lift. And then he said, most likely to Carmine, 'You bring the head.'

Lystra reminded herself she was wolf clan: strong, skilled and afraid of no Amadean.

But then the daylight squeezing through the cracks disappeared and the barrel became as dark as the inside of a cave, and Lystra knew she was in deep, deep trouble.

61

Dashelle had fallen into a restless sleep when the knock came at the door.

She jerked awake and reached for Ferugo—

And remembered he was gone.

It stole her breath. Every single time.

Gael waited a respectful time before entering without invitation. The monk had learned that if she waited to be invited, she would never set foot inside. She came with a fresh jug of mead. It was late afternoon and the columns on the balcony cast long shadows into the room.

'I have news.'

Dashelle wiped her face and steeled herself.

'Pellus has returned. The overlord of Paramore is with him.'

Her heart gave a tiny desperate skip. 'And the king?'

'Not yet.'

Dashelle eased back into her pillows, caught a hint of Ferugo in the air that puffed out of them. 'The war continues, then.'

'No, Amadea has prevailed. The prophet is most pleased.'

She couldn't bear to think of how much blood must have been spilt to please the one whose greatest desire was to wipe Pyrie from the world. What did it mean that Pellus had returned without the king? Dashelle wondered what the prophet's warrior would make of Ferugo's fate.

Gael poured a fresh tumbler of mead. She was trembling.

'What else have you come to tell me?' Dashelle asked, her throat raw from crying.

The monk straightened. 'You are to be tried during The Day of Atonement for heresy. The prophet has brought forward the festival. It starts tomorrow.'

Dashelle felt the blood drain from her face. She was almost out of time. The first three days would be for the people's sacrifices. The prophet would make his sacrifice on the fourth and then the kingdom would feast on the fifth.

'Am I the prophet's sacrifice?'

'Of course not! The Codex demands a trial for anyone accused of treason or heresy.'

'Torvus didn't get a trial and the prophet murdered Ferugo without ever laying a charge. You saw both crimes with your own eyes, Gael.'

The Stonebridge monk flinched. She'd been on the dais when Amadea's most revered warrior was led out to his execution.

'The only way the prophet can justify killing Ferugo is if I am guilty of a crime. Will you hold me down while he slits my throat on the altar and my blood flows down the steps?'

Gael blanched.

Dashelle understood the prophet would know of this conversation, either because Gael would tell him or he would relive it through the monk's memories. She no longer cared. The prophet had taken her husband and he was going to kill her now, too. He would get no more of her fear.

'Will you say no when your prophet demands that of you?' Dashelle pressed. 'Because if you do, you too will be labelled a traitor and share my fate.'

The monk sat heavily on the chair by the bed and leaned forward to rest her elbows on her knees. 'I did not lay down my sword for this.'

Dashelle and Ferugo had long suspected Gael had been a

warrior, and here was the admission, wrapped in melancholy and...was that regret? Would Gael help her if she asked?

'Why *did* you become a servant of Verus?' she asked the monk.

Gael traced the scars on her palms and held up her hands for Dashelle to see.

'These were made for violence,' she said, matter of fact. 'Violence to protect our people, not to snatch up children so slave mongers can grow fat on the wharves.' She spoke freely, perhaps forgetting for a moment her thoughts were not private. 'I trekked to Stonebridge for planting day two years ago. The abbot found me in the grove sitting before the sacred flame, weeping. He told me Verus had called me to walk the fire, so I did. And when I passed the trial, I felt such *purpose*.'

Dashelle considered how much trust the abbot had put in Gael in sending her rather than a more seasoned monk to Augustmount with Axl.

'What do you feel now?'

The monk touched the glyphs on her scalp. 'I was humbled when the prophet singled me out to stay on and serve in the temples here for a year as part of my pilgrimage.'

Dashelle gave her a moment, and when the silence stretched out she gently pressed, 'Do you still believe Verus has a purpose for you?'

Gael closed her eyes for a long moment. Whatever she was imagining or remembering, it took some of the weight from her shoulders. When she opened them, her gaze was clearer. 'Yes.'

'Here or at Stonebridge?'

'I don't know,' the monk admitted and a tear slid down her cheek. She ran those big hands over her face and scalp, clasped them behind her head in a very un-monk way. 'What about you?'

Dashelle let out a laugh so bitter she barely recognised it.

'My husband is dead and I'm about to be charged publicly with treason. I feel abandoned by Verus, Gael, and powerless to protect my people.'

Gael frowned. 'I don't believe Verus abandons those who love her. You must trust there is a purpose to this suffering.'

Trust.

Dashelle almost laughed again at the irony. That was what she and Ferugo had told Tristan repeatedly since he'd discovered they were trafficking illicit Codex transcripts. Was it hypocrisy that she could not take that advice herself now that the worst had happened? Now that she was to be tried for a crime she was, in fact, guilty of? She searched her heart, probing to see if there was a flicker of trust left for the god for whom she had risked—and lost—so much.

'Where is Axl?'

The question stopped Dashelle's self-pitying spiral mid-spin.

'He never made it to Augustmount,' Gael added.

Axl.

Sabine.

Dusty hope sparked beneath her ribs. *That* was why she and Ferugo had put them all at risk: to buy time for the usurper to come to power. Did it still matter?

Dashelle was choking on grief and anger...and none of that helped Sabine.

Yes, it still mattered.

Amadea needed to be freed from the clutches of the power-hungry Thirteenth Prophet. But just as importantly, Sabine was her friend and she was out there somewhere, coming to grips with a destiny she hadn't sought and wasn't ready for. Dashelle wished she'd had more time with her.

'My lady...?' Gael prompted. The monk held out the tumbler of mead again and Dashelle finally accepted it.

'I don't know where Axl is,' Dashelle said honestly. 'But

wherever he is, he will be honouring the will of Verus.' She took a sip and the honey wine soothed her raw throat. 'Just as you must, Gael.'

The monk frowned, sensing there was a challenge beneath her words. It was a risk, but Dashelle needed this unease to stay with Gael in the days to come.

'All I ask, Gael, is to remember who it is your heart serves.'

FIRE

62

'What's the plan?' Rhys asked.

Sabine's pulse skipped. She only had eyes for Tristan when she answered, flexing her fingers to hide her nerves. 'We use the rib bone to bargain for Dashelle.'

The blood-bonded four stood together waiting to board the king's riverboat at Slaveton. The village was on the Pyrien side of the border, a river port built to bring captives into Amadea.

'And then we kill the prophet,' Rhys said quietly.

Axl murmured his disapproval. His eyes were bloodshot from crying, the confidence he'd found in the king's pavilion tempered by Sabine's vision. 'We must let the king mete out justice.'

Tristan grunted. 'If Torvus was here, he would storm the mountain and snap the prophet's neck.'

It wasn't true, but it bolstered the warriors to imagine it. They needed something to picture other than what Sabine had described to the king. She, however, saw those images again and again: Ferugo rigid and sightless on that great stone slab; Dashelle gaunt-faced and wailing into a pillow; the prophet smiling into the flames. Sabine had always been afraid of the prophet—long before she knew Axl was a heretic—but now she also *loathed* him. Not only for the lies he told or the power he craved, but for what he had done to Ferugo and those who loved him.

The Iolian overlord had always been fair and just and a seeker of truth. He was a powerful man who'd cared deeply for his family, his people and his kingdom. Tristan loved and admired him above all other men and Sabine honestly didn't know if she could stop the warrior's fury boiling over when they reached Augustmount. If she even wanted to.

The king's riverboat was low and flat, large enough for horses and supplies. Travelling by boat from Slaveton meant the journey to the capital would take half a day rather than the two-day ride via the Blood Pass. Sabine had never been to Slaveton, never imagined she'd have need to visit. She'd kept her eyes between Trout's ears as they rode through the village down to the docks, sensing the human misery without needing to see it.

The slave pens, thankfully, had been mostly empty but Sabine hadn't missed a cry of pain that could only have come from a child. Her gaze had slid to Rhys, wondering if he was thinking of Indy. His nostrils had flared as if he too was seeing Pyrie through new eyes.

The king whistled from the gangplank for them to board.

Sabine slid her fingers through Tristan's, not caring what the king or anyone else thought. She needed to touch him, for them to keep each other grounded as the boat rocked beneath them. Ty helped the priestess aboard and reluctantly took up his station with the king's garrison, his bloodshot eyes constantly tracking to Tristan and Sabine.

Dockhands pushed the boat out into the wide river. When the vessel was clear of the dock, a dozen oars slid out of holes in the hull and splashed into the water. The drum began its slow beat, setting the pace for the oar-slaves below deck. The king eyeballed Axl for a long moment and then came across to where the Iolians sat together.

'Do you not think it's justice that we return the First

Prophet's rib bone under the power of Pyrien slaves?' he asked Sabine's brother.

Axl did not respond, keeping his gaze down. The oars swung and dipped and within two strokes the boat had picked up speed, travelling downstream.

'Pyriens slaughtered our people in the streets when they stole the relic, monk, and Tertullion did what he had to in order to secure our borders.'

Sabine's brother raised his face to the king. 'King Tertullion did not know what was in the Tenth Prophecy. You do, and yet you sent troops to continue the slaughter.'

The king's eyes flashed. It was a testament to his reliance on Sabine to carry the relic that he did not punish Axl for his insolence.

'If the prophecy in that cave is the word of Verus, we'll have a new enemy to deal with. I don't need foes coming at me from two sides.'

Sabine watched Axl carefully consider his next words, aware the priestess was listening to the exchange from where she sat.

'I believe we're meant to face that threat together,' he said.

The king gave a tight smile. 'Let us see what our god instructs when the rib bone returns to the sacred flames and the First Prophet is entire once more.'

Sabine's agitation grew as the current and the oar-slaves carried them towards the capital. The landscape grew more familiar the deeper into Augustmount they travelled, and the riverbank changing from twisted vines and towering trees to watermills and weeping willows. The mills reminded her of the fuller's cottage, which reminded her of Torvus and his fiery end in the very city to which they were headed.

The riverboat captain had barely pointed out the three-mile marker to the city when Sabine felt the change. The dull ache of grief in her chest sharpened and swelled until it pressed against her heart, making it beat harder. Then her bones began to *hum*, a strange, silent sensation that set her teeth on edge and brought an itch beneath her skin. She was at once terrified of setting foot in the city *and* impatient to get there. Tristan sensed her energy and took her hands in both of his to settle her.

They reached Augustmount in the afternoon as the sun began its descent to the border mountains. The docks in Augustmount were all but empty. Two slave boys met them when the riverboat bumped into the wharf and the slave master was quick on their heels, a hand shading his eyes to see the new arrivals.

'There is no trade today—' He faltered, recognising the red hair and beard of the king. 'Your majesty.' He dropped to one knee before Felix.

'Why aren't you trading?' Rhys demanded.

'The festival,' the slave trader said, as if they should know such things.

'When did it start?'

The slave master frowned at his ignorance. 'Three days ago.'

The itch under Sabine's skin intensified and the faint, familiar buzzing returned to her ears. That meant today was the Day of Atonement. The day of the prophet's sacrifice. It was not news to the king, which meant two things.

The king had been in contact with the prophet since they'd left the army.

And any deal they would make for Dashelle's release would have to be made before a pious crowd, on a day where the prophet's power and influence were at their height.

63

The Thirteenth Prophet stood on the dais as the people of Augustmount poured into the lower temple. The men and women of the capital had not been expecting to see their prophet before dark. Over the past three days they had made their blood sacrifices. Today, it was their gold. As they saw him, they fell to their knees in waves and crawled across the floor, clutching the coins they would offer to atone for the great sin of losing the rib bone. Shoulder to shoulder, optimati and peasant grovelled before their prophet.

The air was heavy with the magnitude of the day. It had been an agony, but the prophet had resisted the urge to have Xanthe's head brought to him before now. This would be the most important moment in Amadea's history and it demanded an audience. The prophet needed his people to see him come into power, to witness that Verus had chosen *him*, her thirteenth in the line of prophets, to usher in a new era for the kingdom.

Pellus was waiting in an alcove close by, the prophet's trophy washed, perfumed and sealed in an iron box to contain whatever power it held. Carmine hovered close by, the overlord insistent on being with Pellus for the delivery.

The prophet felt the sacred flames of Verus flickering behind him, agitated under a bright blue sky. They were *his*, the flames that burned on the bones of the First Prophet. He'd had the entire chalice brought down from the high temple. It was the first time the bones had been moved since the Harvest Day massacre two centuries ago. Still they held their shape, the remains of the First Prophet curled up as if asleep, her bony hand tucked beneath her skull.

The sacred flames had fallen quiet since the arrival of Xanthe's head. They did not call to him, nor show him anything he demanded to see. For the first time in his long life as the prophet of Verus he was truly blind, and he understood it was the dark before the dawn. The mantle was about to be swept aside.

His priests had assembled. His prisoners were in place. The king was coming.

All was ready.

64

Tristan fought the urge to draw his sword as they followed the king and his garrison into the heart of the city. He was on home soil in his kingdom's capital, and it felt like entering enemy territory. His sister was somewhere ahead of them, bereft and in danger, and he was so mad with worry for her he could barely keep his thoughts straight.

It was the Day of Atonement, the fourth day of the festival, which meant the prophet would make his sacrifice. Was it to be Dash? He broke into a fresh sweat at the thought.

'Dear Verus,' Axl breathed as they turned into the temple quarter.

The cobblestone street was stained dark with blood, and the unmistakable smell of death filled the air. Sabine reached for her sword hilt and Tristan put out a hand to stop her. He'd forgotten she and Axl had never been to Augustmount for the festival.

'The people have been sacrificing animals for three days. The blood has to go somewhere.'

'This has flowed down from the temple?' she asked, horrified.

'No,' Tristan said, his eyes on the king ahead, watching for any sign they were being led into an ambush. 'The temple priests set up altars here at the base of the mountain to cope with the volume of sacrifices. What do they do in the Southlands?'

'The sacrifices are in the temple and the priests collect the blood before it hits the floor.'

Rhys grunted. 'That's because Quintus doesn't want to get his robes dirty.' The jibe at the Nominatian high priest was a reflex response and barely half-hearted. Tristan's cousin was as on edge as the rest of them.

They fell silent as they passed a long line of blood-stained stone altars in the now-empty street and began the steep and winding path up to the lower temple. The babble of a thousand voices carried from further up the mountain. Tristan's heart was insistent against his ribs and his legs shook as he climbed. A hundred paces from the temple, the babble hushed.

Verus, let Dash be alive. I'll do whatever you want, just spare my sister.

Felix stopped a few paces from the temple entrance. 'Keep your hoods up until I tell you otherwise,' he said to the Iolians. 'You too, monk.' The king stared long and hard at the reliquary strapped to Sabine's chest before she covered it with her cloak. 'You will all do as I order. There will be *no* mention of the Tenth Prophecy, and I will decide when and how the relic is returned to the sacred fire.'

Tristan felt himself resist. 'My sister—'

'Is my concern,' the king said, and signalled for his men to surround them.

Rhys bristled beside Tristan.

'Trust me,' the king said, and Tristan realised with a jolt that he didn't. It undid another tether that had anchored him to his kingdom.

A temple guard stepped out to meet them. 'No weapons inside—' He recognised the king and dropped to one knee. 'Majesty. Welcome home.'

Felix moved past him and the others were granted entry without question, even with their faces hidden.

Despite the fact that half of the kingdom was across the border in Pyrie, the temple was packed. Women, children and old men sat cross-legged on the tiles, faces upturned to the colonnaded dais. The steps were lined with monks from all four orders and below the dais were dozens of empty barrels ready for the city's gold offering. At least twenty of the prophet's beardless temple guards lined the wall at the rear of the dais.

In the centre of the raised platform, the prophet stood with the sacred flame. It burned in a golden chalice Tristan had never seen before. Where was Dash?

The prophet saw Felix and his face lit up.

'Behold, the king of Amadea and conqueror of Pyrie!'

A ripple of surprise went through the crowd and all heads turned.

'Hail King Felix!' someone shouted and it quickly grew to a chant as the seated crowd scooted sideways to make space for Felix and his garrison to pass through.

'Hail King Felix!'

'Hail King Felix!'

Tristan kept his head down, felt the energy of the chant like a two-palmed strike to the chest. Was it a bad sign that Dash was not yet onstage?

The king signalled for his garrison to wait at the foot of the steps and Tristan and the others halted with them. Felix took Gwinny with him when he climbed to the dais. She found her place with the other priests and priestesses at the top of the steps and placed the fire bowl at her feet. Tristan watched from under his hood, careful to keep his face hidden. Sabine stood beside him, that strange, frayed tension still radiating from her. On the dais, the king was absorbing the adulation. Was he playing a part, or was he as power hungry as the prophet?

The prophet held up his hand and the crowd fell silent. Felix moved to an ornate chair positioned beside the sacred flames, the customary position for the king during the final atonement ceremony.

'Today, we atone for the sins of our forebears,' the prophet began. 'That generation whose worship so displeased Verus that she looked away while the enemy crept into our city, butchered our people, and stole the rib bone of the First Prophet. That enemy carried the sacred relic into their kingdom where it was snuffed out by the dark magic that festers there.' The prophet let the weight of that condemnation settle before telling them what they came every year to hear: 'But our god is merciful and your sacrifices of blood have pleased her.'

There was a collective exhalation of relief.

'Your gold will seal the offering. As will my own sacrifice. This year, I will offer not one, but three sacrifices to our mighty god Verus. My first—' He signalled and three figures came onto the dais from the side entrance: two temple guards and an askari prisoner with shorn hair.

Rhys swore under his breath.

Lystra's hands were tied behind her back and her ankles were bound, forcing her to shuffle forward. A solid iron clamp was around her neck, attached to two long poles that enabled her guards to handle her from a safe distance. They jostled her to the western colonnade. Not front and centre as Torvus had been, but off to one side as if she was there for entertainment, not the main offering. A third guard kicked out her knees to force her to the floor.

The askara's eyes were wide and un-drugged. The prophet wanted her fear and she was trying not to give it to him.

'My second...' the prophet declared.

Pellus and the overlord of Paramore appeared.

'The lapdog made it home,' Rhys muttered behind Tristan.

The prophet's warrior carried an iron box that he placed at the prophet's feet. The prophet's eyes shone with fervour and he stared down at it longingly. It seemed an effort for him to tear his gaze away.

'And,' he said grimly, 'my third.'

Tristan saw who walked out of the side entrance and his legs almost gave way.

65

Felix tasted the bitter tang of resentment as the euphoria from his reception faded.

Dashelle of Iolia was going to be the prophet's third sacrifice?

He had spoken with the prophet through the flames twice on the journey here and there had been no mention of Ferugo or Dashelle. Felix had clung to a thread of hope that the relic carrier's vision had been false.

'It is generous of you, my prophet, to invite my guest to a place of honour on this day.' Felix kept Tristan in his peripheral vision, watching for any sign of disobedience. 'Where is Ferugo?'

The prophet did not answer. Dashelle came forward flanked by two temple guards, and a broad-shouldered monk in Stonebridge robes followed close behind. The overlord's steps were shaky but her spine was straight and her chin up. When Felix dared meet her gaze, he found grief and accusation there.

The thread frayed and snapped.

'Get a chair for the overlord of Iolia,' Felix commanded, and two temple priests quickly brought out a seat not quite as ornate as his but befitting an overlord. Dashelle sat down and gripped its arms so tight her knuckles turned white. The king was aware the crowd had fallen into a confused silence. His question about Ferugo had gone unanswered, but it was the Day of Atonement and this was the prophet's domain.

Felix had been on edge since they'd entered the borderlands, expecting the prophet to sense the rib bone. But whatever darkness had hidden the relic in Pyrie for two hundred years continued to cloak it from the prophet, because he surely would have demanded it by now if he knew the king had it in his possession.

Felix's gaze fell involuntarily to the tiles at the front of the dais, still scorched from the fire that had consumed Torvus. The knot in his gut was all too familiar.

The prophet held his hands together over his white robes. His *executioner's* robes.

'Today, children of Verus, we will learn if the debt to our god is finally paid. Before you are two women who will offer me the truth or they will forfeit their lives.'

There was a collective intake of breath. The people of Augustmount had witnessed the last time the prophet had sought *truth* in this temple. Pellus, that great study in stillness and discipline, shifted his weight. He briefly met the king's gaze and looked away.

'The askara will confess the identity of a traitor scheming to overthrow me and destroy our kingdom. The overlord of Iolia will confess why her husband was taken by dark magic under questioning about his ties to Torvus.'

Dashelle stiffened beside Felix, her nostrils flaring.

Felix bristled at the audacity of the Thirteenth Prophet. He, like all prophets, was forbidden from interrogating an overlord without the king present and yet here he was announcing he had done just that in front of a thousand of the king's subjects.

Dashelle's breath was quickening, readying for whatever it was she planned to say.

Felix placed a hand on her trembling wrist. 'Wait,' he mouthed, and then, louder, 'Before you begin, my prophet, I have something for you. It is, perhaps, the true gift of Verus you have been waiting for.'

66

Pellus watched two hooded figures climb the long flight of steps to the dais, his pulse unsettled in a way completely foreign to him. He was uncertain at a time when he should not be. This was a moment of triumph for Amadea. The Pyrien horde had been routed. The prophet had its leader's head as a trophy. The king had returned for the Day of Atonement, and Pellus had acquitted himself well on the battlefield at Felix's side.

But Ferugo was dead and his widow, the beloved Dashelle of Iolia, was about to be publicly questioned under the threat of death.

The prophet said Ferugo had been a heretic and the prophet did not lie. Pellus had known of his suspicions—he himself had been sent to the Iolian tournament as a thinly veiled warning—but an Amadean overlord was *dead*. Not on border patrol, not in a battle, not from disease or choking at a banquet or dysentery. Ferugo was killed by dark magic under interrogation to prevent him giving up the secrets he harboured.

One of the approaching figures had something under their cloak.

Pellus's hand strayed to his sword, even as his mind urged him to trust that the king would not put the prophet in danger.

'Show your faces,' the prophet ordered them.

The pair pushed back their hoods and Pellus felt a jolt of recognition. It was the monk Axl, but he was in mendicant robes, not Stonebridge. The warrior beside him was familiar but he could not yet place her.

Dashelle gasped.

The prophet's sharp gaze flitted from Pellus to Dashelle and then Gael, who had also recognised Axl, and back to the monk. His eyes hardened.

'My prophet,' the king continued. 'I bring you—'

'Traitor!' the prophet bellowed. He flung his hand forward and a ball of fire leapt from the chalice. Pellus watched, open-mouthed, as it arced over his head on a clear trajectory to Axl.

'STOP!' The king leapt up so fast his chair fell backwards. At the same moment, the warrior shoved Axl aside, and instead of striking the monk, the fire dove into her like a heron into a lake. *No*, Pellus realised, it dove into whatever was strapped across her chest, and that thing swallowed the fire whole.

'Sabine—!' The cry came from within the king's garrison but Pellus couldn't look away from the warrior because she had not caught on fire. Not her clothes, not the woman herself. For a frantic beat, there was silence in the temple, and then the prophet roared, 'The witch wields dark magic! Kill them both!'

'Stand fast!' the king commanded before either his garrison or the temple guards could react. 'These two are *not* your enemy. We bring you the stolen relic!'

'Lies!' the prophet spat and the temple crowd recoiled. 'The king has been corrupted by his time in Pyrie!'

Pellus's heart thundered at the accusation because it put him squarely between the prophet of Verus and the king of Amadea. Two of the king's men broke ranks and were bounding up the stairs, their hoods falling back—

It was Tristan and Rhys.

Even with his heightened awareness Pellus could not stitch these pieces together, but he needed to, he needed to do *something,* because the temple guards were moving forward from the back of the dais and the king's garrison were drawing their swords—

'Place Xanthe's head at my feet!' The prophet screamed at Pellus even though he was right next to him. 'And arrest the king!'

67

Chaos erupted around Sabine.

She repositioned the reliquary with one hand and drew her sword with the other. She took quick stock of friends and foe.

The king's garrison, surging up the steps as the temple garrison rushed forward from their positions at the rear of the dais.

Tristan and Rhys, fighting their way towards Dashelle, both of them a blur of fury and violence.

Pellus, opening the iron box for the prophet.

The king, drawing his sword.

'Protect the relic!' Axl cried. Sabine saw a flash of dark grey robes and understood her brother had ducked for cover behind the nearest column.

The shock of the prophet's attack still reverberated through her. He had tried to burn Axl alive.

Her back was warm where she'd positioned the reliquary. She could only assume the rib bone had somehow absorbed the fire the prophet had aimed at her brother. It had been pure instinct to push Axl aside, and somehow, *somehow*, the relic had saved her.

A temple guard found a gap in the fighting and came at Sabine. He was young and wiry, his mouth set in a grim line. Sabine blocked and parried the strike, felt the hesitancy in his attack. It was madness, Amadeans turning on each other.

Tristan's words came to her then, the answer he'd given Ty not so many days ago when the squire had asked who his enemy was. *Anyone who attacks you...if they're trying to maim or kill you, they are your enemy.*

It was good advice then, as it was now.

When the guard came again with a descending cut, Sabine blocked, sidestepped and used his momentum and a well-placed kick to send him barrelling into the temple guard beside him.

'Stand *down!*' the king shouted and then took out a temple guard with a pommel strike to the head. He was trying not to kill these men, even as they turned on him.

'Verus will punish us all!' the prophet bellowed, making his voice terrifyingly loud in the open air temple court. 'KILL THE TRAITORS AND ARREST THE KING!'

Sabine caught a glimpse of the prophet at the chalice and the humming in her bones intensified. She understood with sickening clarity what she had to do. An arrow hissed past her and bounced off the tiles. She looked up to see where it had come from. *Oh shit.*

The prophet had archers in position on the top of the temple walls.

*

Lystra's guards hesitated barely a heartbeat before joining the fray. She dropped to the ground and scooted herself through her arms so that her bound hands were in front of her and she could deal with the neck clamp. It came free and clattered to the marble floor, and she went to work on the rope around her ankles. An Amadean fell to the tiles next to her, bleeding out. They were killing each other. Good. She would add to the numbers on her way out of this gods-forsaken place. With her ankles free, she crawled to the dying temple guard and jerked a dagger from his chest. She ducked back behind a column and frantically worked the blade against her wrist ropes. The binds fell away and she sprang up in a crouch, dagger in hand, and saw—

Rhys

How in the name of blood-soaked Ares had he escaped?

The warrior cut down one of her guards with a single, brutal strike. His eyes locked on hers and then went wide as she hurled the dagger in her hand. He spun around as it flew past him end over end and buried itself in the shoulder of a charging temple guard.

'Archers!' someone shouted.

Lystra looked up to see an arrow loosed from the top of the temple wall—right as Rhys charged and bumped her behind a column. The missile thudded into his back and spun him around, and the next one took him above the collarbone.

'Pricks,' he grunted as he fell sideways.

Lystra leaned out and dragged him by the armpits to safety. He grunted again as she propped him between her legs. The arrow in his back had hit on an angle with enough force to puncture his buckskin vest but not hard enough to lodge too deeply in his shoulder muscle. She yanked it out without warning.

'Faark,' he said between gritted teeth. The wound was bleeding, but not enough to kill him.

Lystra slid him closer so she could see over his shoulder to check the rest of the damage. The second arrow had lodged above his collarbone. The sight of an Amadean arrow jutting out so close to the jugular took her back to the forest, to Dex drowning in his own blood. It almost unravelled her.

'Are you weepy for me, wolf?' Rhys managed and then he saw something in her face that took the next taunt from his lips. 'Can you get it out?'

'Not here. You will bleed too much.'

'Not much choice.'

'Put your hand here.' She pressed his fingers around the arrow head. While it stayed in he wouldn't bleed out.

'You going somewhere?' he panted.

Her escape route was on the other side of the temple. She could steal a cloak and join the crush of Amadeans pouring out of the temple into the streets. Or she could help the sister-murdering, scourge-king nullify the Great Pretender's guards and reclaim her sister's head in the chaos.

If she fled, Rhys would be an easy target. If she stayed, she might die or be captured.

She was still undecided about what to do when she took his sword and joined the fighting.

*

Tristan was maiming and killing Amadeans. He didn't care.

He had to get to Dash.

He had to save her. He'd failed Ferugo but he would not fail his sister, even if it meant killing temple guards. The chair she'd been in had been toppled and kicked aside but Tristan was sure he'd caught a glimpse of her blue dress among the columns at the back of the dais.

There—Dash was pinned to the rear wall and Gael was prowling the space in front of her, eyeballing the two temple guards who had come for the prophet's prisoner. The hulking Stonebridge monk was unarmed, but her robes or her size made them hesitate.

Tristan scooped up a discarded dagger as he approached.

Dash saw him. 'Tristan!'

One of the guards turned and swung on instinct and his eyes went wide when he saw who he was facing. Tristan had a heartbeat to quell his rage. Instead of running the idiot through, he trapped the blade with his sword and dagger, and levered it hard and fast, snapping the guard's wrist. The other guard wavered and Gael lunged forward. She knocked his sword aside with her palm and grabbed the guard by the throat, then lifted his feet from the tiles. Dash darted in and snatched up the dropped sword while the guard dangled in the monk's strong grip. Gael choked him a moment longer before dumping him on the floor with his mate. Both men made a show of laying on their bellies in surrender.

Dash handed the sword to Gael and threw herself at Tristan. He moved his weapons to one hand so he could hug her, turning them both slightly to keep an eye on the fighting.

'The prophet lies,' his sister panted. 'He *killed* Ferugo.'

'I know. Sabine saw it. Dash,' he rushed on, 'we found the stolen rib bone and the prophecy.'

Her bloodshot eyes widened. She twisted around. 'Where is she?'

They saw Sabine at the same time, fighting her way to the chalice. 'Sweet Verus,' Tristan said. 'She's going to the flames.'

'Go,' Dash said. 'Help her.'

Tristan hesitated, torn.

'I will keep my lady safe,' Gael said, standing over the prostrate guards.

'Even from the prophet?' Tristan knew he needed to move but he didn't want to risk Dash again so soon.

Gael's face crumpled at the reality of what she was promising. 'If that is what it takes to protect her, then yes. Even from him.'

*

Sabine approached the chalice. Her entire body was tingling

and her bones hummed. It was the flames in the reliquary doing it. It had to be.

'Kill her!' the prophet commanded, positioning himself behind his warrior.

Pellus made no move to obey. He stood with his sword in one hand and the prophet's grotesque trophy in the other, studying Sabine like she was a puzzle to be solved.

The sacred flames tugged at her, irresistible now. She risked a glance into the chalice and her heart stuttered. There were bones in there. Not just any bones, but an entire skeleton curled up as if asleep, the sacred flames dancing on every inch of the remains. Not even Axl had expected the prophet to be so reckless as to bring the entire relic down from the high temple.

'You,' Pellus said, his eyes widening in recognition. 'We met at Augustmount.'

The prophet sensed he was losing control of the situation. 'Put the head at my feet!'

'Who are you to the monk?' Pellus pressed.

'She is his sister.' It was the king who answered and Pellus lowered his blade.

'OBEY ME WARRIOR! PUT DOWN THE HEAD!' the prophet roared.

Pellus tore his eyes from the king and bent on one knee to place the head of the Pyrien ruler at the prophet's feet. The prophet's eyes flared and he used both arms to summon the flames. Sabine stepped back, aware the fighting was all but over behind them now—

A tongue of fire leapt from the chalice to the prophet. It formed a halo around his head, covering his face without touching him. 'Mighty Verus,' he cried out, triumphant. 'Behold your most faithful servant!'

'Sabine,' Axl called out from somewhere on her left. 'Return the relic!'

Her gaze dropped to the chalice as the prophet kept shouting. For a beat, the rest of the world faded as Sabine understood a long-forgotten truth. All the stories, all the artwork, depicted the First Prophet as a giant, the only one worthy to be chosen by the god who had stormed across the ocean cloaked in fire and storm. But the figure curled in the flames was tiny...smaller even than Sabine. Petite. Yet it was to her Verus gave the living fire. This tiny woman had been the one to wield the power of a god.

'Do it,' the king commanded and Sabine's focus snapped back to the temple.

'First free the overlord of Iolia.'

The king was furious. 'Do not *dare* defy me—'

'Dash is safe, Sabine.' It was Tristan who said it. Only now did she realise he'd been covering her back while she was distracted. 'She's over there.'

Sabine twisted to see where he was pointing and saw Dashelle watching her with her hands clasped over her heart. 'Do it,' Dashelle mouthed, urging Sabine to finish what she'd come to do. What Sabine had known in her heart she must do the moment she saw those bones.

'Burn the witch!' the prophet cried. The flames around his face were spinning, building up speed.

Sabine opened the reliquary one-handed and the flame inside was flickering as if caught in a wild wind. Her heart galloped. What if the bone paralysed her with another vision when she touched it?

It was too late to worry about that now.

Sabine lifted the relic out of the box and thrust it into the sacred flames. She let go and stepped back, astonished she hadn't been burned. Her mouth went dry as the flames rose and curled around themselves, like water sluicing upwards.

The lick of fire circling the prophet returned to its source as if caught in a vortex.

And then those swirling flames left the chalice and leapt at Sabine.

*

The prophet opened his eyes to see the sacred flames, *his* flames, writhing around the traitor, consuming her. She was reeling, slapping at the fire on her arms and face and body.

The prophet willed it and the flames had obeyed. The power was his! He had conquered the dark magic this woman had brought into his temple and when the flames were done with her he would cast them onto his traitorous king. He glanced at the chalice and then back to the traitor, who was screaming now—

His attention snapped back to the golden vessel. The prophet blinked, confused, until understanding gripped and tore at him. The sacred flames were gone from the chalice. All that was left were the shining white bones of the First Prophet, intact again at last.

The entire original fire of Verus was on the woman.

68

Sabine was on fire.

And it *hurt*.

The flames scorched and stung and roared in her ears as they caught her in their vortex.

Her clothes were blazing, she could smell the buckskin vest as it burned. The fire was so fierce she felt as if she was being lifted from the ground. She was all fear and fire and thundering heart.

People were screaming. *She* was screaming.

Tristan was shouting—

And then the fire swallowed Sabine whole, and the world blinked out.

*

Tristan watched on horrified as Sabine hung in the air, burning. Whatever power of Verus had kept the rib bone suspended in the reliquary now held Sabine ten feet above the temple floor.

The ferocity of the heat had burned away every stitch of clothing and all that covered her nakedness were the flames themselves. Her skin was intact, but she'd been in agony before her body went limp. At least when she was screaming and writhing he'd known she was alive. Had he got Dash back only to lose Sabine? The possibility almost ripped his heart from his chest.

Tristan sensed the king beside him, needed somewhere to channel his fear.

'If she dies, I will kill you.'

*

'Get me to safety.'

Everyone on the dais was transfixed by the flaming figure, utterly distracted. Still Pellus hesitated.

'You are my warrior,' the prophet hissed. 'You are bound to me by your oaths and the flame.'

Pellus felt the pull between the king and the prophet. He had made oaths to both, never imagining they would be in conflict. The prophet was behind him, using him as a shield and prodding him to move. 'It seems the overlord of Paramore has proven useful.'

Pellus saw Carmine had forced Gwinny into the alcove at the western end of the dais. She was clutching her fire bowl and the tiny-boned priestess was wide-eyed with fear.

It made the decision for him.

69

The silence was deafening. There was no screaming, no shouting. No pain. There was no *anything*. Just silent, inky blackness. Sabine couldn't feel her body, couldn't tell if she was even in the temple anymore.

Was she dead? Or was this what it felt like to be in the grip of the fire of Verus? If so, she didn't want it. This terrifying sensation of being untethered, tied to no-one and nothing. As if she had no substance at all—

Sabine.

Her heart gave a hard thump. Her *heart*. She could feel it again now, punching against her ribs. Who'd said that? The voice was neither young nor old, wrapped in smoke and ash. It was everywhere and nowhere.

Sabine. Look.

Was that Verus speaking to her? Was this how their god spoke to the prophets? Her heart lurched and thrashed. Was she about to be punished for touching the most sacred of relics? Was she—

The darkness shifted to murky grey, and Sabine almost sobbed with relief at the changing light. She still couldn't see who had spoken, but she wasn't trapped in blackness anymore. The grey began to shift and ripple. Briny air filled her nostrils. What was that coming into focus?

Oh...

Sabine understood with a jolt that she was looking down on the world, and the rippling expanse beneath her was the sea. She was rushing over an ocean, flying with the speed of the wind.

Sweet Verus. Was this a dream? A vision? Or had the flames made her mad?

She had no sense of her body except for her heart, the smell of the ocean and the sudden feel of icy air against her skin. Even in the strangeness of the moment, the cold sensation was a welcome balm after the flames. She lifted her gaze—she could do that now—and saw the horizon.

Sabine. See.

That voice again, still unseen. Still everywhere and nowhere.

Something was taking shape in the distance. *Land.* Was that Amadea?

Sabine raced towards the horizon, although it took no effort on her part. She began to slow as she drew closer and realised the shape wasn't land at all. It wasn't even a single mass. It was something else altogether, something vast and…moving. Dread vined around Sabine as she was taken lower and she understood what she was seeing.

The ocean was black with ships.

Ships as tall as manor houses, great sails carrying them across the white-capped ocean. There were more than Sabine could count, row after row after row. Understanding came to her in a rush, thrust upon her whether she wanted it or not.

These ships were coming for Amadea and Pyrie.

They were coming for gold.

She could see figures on the decks and they made her skin crawl. She couldn't make them out clearly, but she instinctively knew that the men who sailed this fleet were not men at all.

Sabine. Prepare.

She jolted back into her body.

Her throat was sore from the smoke and her hair stank of burnt buckskin. She was lying on the cool tiles. And she was naked. Tristan rushed in and threw his cloak around her. He was shaking and his breath hitched as he drew her close. 'I thought you were dying,' he whispered into her hair.

She squeezed his arm, not yet able to speak.

'The flames are gone from the bones of First Prophet and you were...*on fire*...'

Sabine remembered. Only then did she become aware of a new sensation in her body. It was like a thousand butterflies beating their wings beneath her skin. She brought a trembling hand out from under the cloak and Tristan sucked in his breath.

Flames moved slowly beneath her skin like a living tattoo. Licks of oranges, blues, and reds, swaying as calmly as they had on the rib bone.

'Is it...anywhere else?' Tristan asked, barely above a whisper. Sabine opened the cloak enough for him to peer down and see her breasts and belly. 'Sweet Verus.' He locked eyes with her, startled.

'Is it on my face?'

He shook his head and pointed to her collarbone without touching. 'It stops here.' He was trying to mask his horror and was failing badly. Sabine closed her eyes to concentrate on the sensation. She could feel the flames anchored in the marrow of her bones.

It wasn't painful.

It was terrifying.

'Are you okay?'

Sabine's heart was thumping so loudly she could barely hear Tristan. It was hard to concentrate between the foreign sensations in her body and the panic coursing through her. She was vaguely aware that Axl and Dashelle were there, gingerly helping Tristan get her to her feet. She caught snatches of conversation between the three of them.

'The prophet is gone...'

'...Pellus and Carmine aren't here.'

'...took Gwinny.'

'...will find them before they leave the city, surely?'

Sabine took her own weight and forced herself to focus on what was happening around her. The surviving temple guards had surrendered to the king's garrison and the priests were huddled together, gaping at her. Rhys was propped against a column, an arrow poking out of his shoulder but alive, and Ty was on his knees weeping, his bow and arrow discarded beside him. He'd had to kill more Amadeans today.

The king was barely three paces away. His eyes shone with awe and wonder.

'They are coming,' she croaked. 'The enemy we were warned about. Hundreds of ships, on their way to us.'

Felix took a slow breath as he absorbed this news. His nostrils flared and a muscle twitched in his jaw. And then the king of Amadea knelt before her.

There was a confused beat, followed by movement across the temple as warriors, priests, optimati and peasants joined him on their knees. Even Dashelle. Even Tristan. Axl lowed his head gravely and then he too bowed before her.

Sabine squeezed her eyes shut, tried to calm her thundering heart. The living fire was in her body and she had no more idea how to control it—or what she was supposed to do with it if she *could*—than she had before she entered the temple.

Surely Verus would speak to her again?

She waited, every part of her prickling and tingling. But her god had nothing to say in this moment and it was as if Sabine was on the Stonebridge pinnacle again, only this time she had made it all the way to the cliff and was teetering on its edge. One more step and she would topple over.

Sabine opened her eyes to find the king was still on his knees, his face now lifted to her. What she saw there frightened her even more than the ships.

'Tell me what I must do to save our kingdom.'

***

ACKNOWLEDGEMENTS

Writing may be a solo pursuit, but producing a book certainly isn't – a truth that's especially evident when you're the publisher as well as the writer.

I'm fortunate to have an ever-growing 'team' of technical and creative experts, beta, ARC and proof readers, and enthusiastic cheerleaders. Many of you are more than one of these.

So, a massive thank you to: Michelle Reid, Dan Hanks, Tiffany Munro, Rebecca Cram (AKA Place), Annemarie Lloyd, Tony Minerds, Carly Willats, E.C Glynne (AKA Elyse), Winnie Seuala, Renae Burkhalter, the Eagle Vanguard Street Team (special shout out to Holly Pirie), Suzy Baines and Greg Hunting (The Emporium), Heather Scott, Nicola Weston and Pam Hall.

I couldn't do any of this without you guys.

To the Bookstagrammers, BookTokkers, book sellers, librarians, reviewers and readers who have embraced this series, I don't have the words to express my gratitude – but know that you have it in abundance!

Thanks as always to my friends and family, who make the

right sounds of encouragement and seem to not mind too much that I'm frequently more preoccupied with the people I've made up than I am with them. (Sorry.)

To the person holding this book in your hands/on a device: thank you for reading this series. As with all the stories I write, I hope my worlds can help you take a break from yours for a while.

And last, but most certainly not least, thank you to Murray. For everything, as always.

(Note: Everything in this book was created by humans, including the cover art.)

THE REPHAIM

Paula Weston's fast-paced urban fantasy favourite

It's almost a year since Gaby Winters watched her twin brother die.
In the sunshine of a new town her body has healed, but her grief is raw and constant.
It doesn't help that every night in her dreams she fights and kills hell-beasts.
And then Rafa comes to town and tells her things about her brother and her life that cannot be true, things that are dangerous.

Who is Rafa?
Who are the Rephaim?
And who is Gaby?
The truth lies in the shadows of her nightmares.

COMPLETED SERIES

A stand-alone near-future thriller set in Australia

'The characters are endearing and believable, the romance meaningful without being saccharine and the plot races along with impeccable timing.'

-Books + Publishing

Find me online

 @PaulaWestonBooks

 @PaulaWestonAuthor

 @PaulaWestonAuthor

 paula-weston.com

Join my mailing list:

paula-weston.com/subscribe

www.ingramcontent.com/pod-product-compliance
Lightning Source LLC
LaVergne TN
LVHW031535060526
838200LV00056B/4509